D1737071

THE LEGACY OF KATHLEEN ANGEL

Cover and interior design by Krista Nelson
knelsonauthor@gmail.com - www.justgetitdonenow.com

ISBN-13: 978-1985069640
ISBN-10: 1985069644

THE LEGACY OF KATHLEEN ANGEL

Alice Gelston Migliore

A CLASSIC CASE OF SYNCHRONICITY

The Vice President of Sales of the Kraft Paper Mills came from a family with a history of heart disease. Despite long hours at the Fitness Factory and a low fat diet, at age 47, he was found slumped over his steering wheel in the parking lot, stone dead.

The following week, Tom Harris, Sales Rep for the Eastern Division, was offered the newly vacated position. Tom deliberated; he prioritized; he brainstormed; he networked; he filled waste baskets with endless crumpled lists of pros and cons; and he discussed his dilemma with everyone he ran into in his daily travels across Pennsylvania, New Jersey, and Delaware. Life on the road suited Tom, and he hated the thought of being cooped up in an office all day long. But the consensus was that he could not afford to let this opportunity pass him by, particularly at his age. In the end, he accepted the offer, and soon thereafter, he and his wife Susan moved to Port Williams, Pennsylvania, where the corporate offices were located. They rented the main house on the Angel Estate, a quaint old place dating back to the turn of the Century. Hardly a month had passed, and they were still in the process of settling in, when Tom, on his way home from work one day, stopped for a drink at the Bullfrog Valley Inn and met a waitress named Mya.

Now Mya believed that all of the above occurred – that a young man died 20 years before his time was up; a wife was widowed with a skimpy supply of life insurance, a huge mortgage, and no marketable skills; three small children were left fatherless; and the Harris family was forced to relocate – all so that Tom could come into her life and father her child. She had no doubts about it. It was a classic case of synchronicity. Right people appear at the right time if you are in the right place. Tom Harris was the right person; 1980 was the right time; and Port Williams, believe it or not, was the right place.

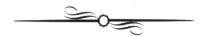

THE RIVER

Only an unrealistic dreamer like Mya, wandering aimlessly about in the labyrinths of the esoteric, could think of Port Williams as the right place for anything. Port Williams was nothing but a small stagnant Pennsylvania town that had known better days. The better days, as well as the present state of decline, were due to the fact that the poor city's fate was inextricably bound to an unpredictable and destructive river, a river that was not content to lie quietly and watch life go by, as a river is supposed to do, but a river that felt compelled to interact, even when her unsolicited help might cause more harm than good. No one in his right mind ever trusted the river, no matter how breathtaking she sometimes appeared to be.

On a map, it looked as though someone had dropped a wide, blue, silk ribbon from the sky on a windy day, and, as it settled onto the landscape, it twisted and curved and folded back over itself. Then someone else came along and picked up the end and tried to straighten it out and point it toward the south, in hopes that it would flow away and leave the town in peace.

Although nowadays the river is taken for granted, there was a time when she was the very lifeblood of Port Williams. In the latter half of the Nineteenth Century, the shipbuilding industries of Baltimore needed the white pine and hemlock that grew in the Pennsylvania forests. The river and her little tributaries created a perfect system to transport the lumber, and Port Williams, which at the time consisted of a few scattered farmsteads, turned out to be an ideal location for booms and cribs, where logs could be sorted before they headed south. Soon the town prospered and grew.

By the turn of the Century, Port Williams had become a charming, bustling, little city. There were several hotels, an opera house, wide streets lined with mansions, and lush green parks with formal gardens and elaborate stone fountains. Huge rafts, log jams, and boats of every size and shape cluttered the river from bank to bank. Newly wealthy families went on afternoon excursions up the river on paddle wheelers, and in the evenings, lovers walked hand-in-hand on the bridges, enjoying the sights, smells, sounds, and each other. The river was a woman in her prime. She worked hard all day to try to please everyone, and when evening came, she was thoroughly exhausted, yet satisfied, and she slept well.

Nowadays, she is more like a middle-aged woman whose children have grown up and moved away and whose husband is losing interest. In order to get the attention she deserves, she has to threaten to behave badly and make a scene. When times are dull, she's been known to snatch an unwary swimmer from under the Lark Street Bridge, and for a day or two, she is featured on the front page of the Port Williams Chronicle. Every few years she feels the need for a good flood. When large amounts of snow accumulate in the mountains during a bad winter and the warm spring rains arrive before the snow has had a chance to melt, the creeks overflow their banks and rush to the river with more water than she can handle. She accepts the challenge, of course, and promptly takes on a terrifying new personality. She swells and churns and foams until she is dark brown and gritty. She sticks branches and tree trunks in her hair like a wild woman. She licks angrily at the cars hurrying across the bridges and terrifies the people who live in houses near the banks. Of course she is featured on all the local news programs. Flood levels and flood watches are announced, old floods discussed and analyzed, and the casual greeting on the street is a prediction of how high the river's gonna go this time round.

The river loves to hear her name wafting through the air. She slurps and splashes the undersides of the green bridges until they sparkle. Then she turns her attention to the houses along the banks and gives the porches a good, thorough rinsing. She is like a woman with PMS, cleaning her house in a fit of unexplained energy when her period is a day or two late.

When the radio announcer mentions twenty feet and still rising, old people call their grown children to come home to help them get ready for the flood. Good things that they don't want ruined are dragged up out of the basement and the porch furniture tied down and cars moved and parked a few streets away. In the meantime, women bake beans, make potato salad, and put extra soda and beer in the fridge. Everyone crowds into the front room to watch television, while, in the kitchen, a radio is tuned to the local station. The vigil begins. They take turns checking to hear what the radio's saying, glancing out the window at the river, using the bathroom, grabbing another beer, and returning to the front room to report. It's an exciting time when everyone has a purpose.

But, as likely as not, despite all the preparation and anticipation, the flood peters out. A feeling of disappointment replaces the apprehension, but, of course, no one admits to this. They all say they're glad it's over so things can get back to normal.

The river is an undiagnosed manic depressive. No one can count on her. While the entire town waits for the disaster to hit, she suddenly changes her mind, for no particular reason, just like that. She settles down, wraps herself in her favorite old dark blue terry cloth robe and goes to sleep for a few days. Once the people have untied the porch furniture and carried everything back down to the basement and brought their cars home, the river yawns, stretches her arms, and comes to life again. She slaps playfully at the broken trees hanging down her banks as though she had nothing to do with their pitiful state. She cleans off a porch or two and sweeps away debris from the yards. And when everyone has stopped talking about her, she turns herself into a dark gray slug and lies in a deep depression, barely able to move. Her mood is contagious and brings out nostalgia and despair in all who pass by. They don't know why, but they just don't feel like themselves.

When the river is not in the flood mode, she is a lovely creature. Her wardrobe is phenomenal. She has more outfits than the infamous Kathleen Angel owned during her entire reign as Queen of the Lumber Society. On a May afternoon, the river reflects a pale blue sky with fluffy white clouds and looks as pretty and bright as a young girl in springtime. In October she dons silks and satins in swirling patterns of golds, oranges, and reds, and shimmers slowly down her course, going someplace special, no doubt, like Harrisburg or Baltimore. Some like her best in her autumn splendor, yet it is in January, when she is dressed as a member of the Russian nobility, that she is truly her most magnificent. She arranges layers of snow and ice on her shoulders like winter white furs, and then she sprinkles herself generously with diamond chips, which glitter like silver in the winter afternoon sun, and then gleam like gold under the first full moon of the New Year.

She may seem to be a fascinating and frivolous lady, but she is not to be trusted under any circumstance. There are few in Port Williams who have not lost a family member, or a friend, or even a pet, to the river.

Although Mya lost her mother to the river, she harbored no bad feelings and always gave the river the benefit of the doubt. She thought the river was just another victim. When the lumber industry was at its peak and thousands of trees were being cut each day, there were no groups of activists willing to throw themselves in front of an ax. No one had a SAVE THE PLANET bumper sticker on his wagon. The lumber men cut down every tree, replaced none, and, as a consequence, disrupted the drainage pattern of the entire area. As a result, the friendly spring floods became natural disasters. The river was not at fault.

But, instead of acting like a victim, the river was always very comfortable with her powers. Her first strategy was to target the enemy. She washed away booms, freeing millions of logs with loud explosive chaos; she swirled through the saw mills with such force and speed that they were smashed to bits; she attacked everything remotely connected with the lumber industry, including workers, their wives and children, and sometimes their family pets. In three successive annual floods, she destroyed the industry beyond recovery. In the third flood, it seemed as though she was trying to destroy the entire city, but, fortunately, she changed her mind and took only three bridges and an impressive number of citizens and distributed them haphazardly in an area nearly a hundred miles to the south.

Regardless of who was ultimately responsible, there is no doubt that spring flooding completely destroyed the lumber industry and put an end to prosperity in Port Williams. Decades later, when Tom and Susan Harris appeared on the scene, all that remained of the glorious days was a row of enormous mansions in great disrepair, rented out room by room, to people struggling to make a living where there wasn't much living to be made.

HOPE FOR SALE

Hope was in very short supply in Port Williams, and people were forced to purchase it in the same way they might buy a loaf of bread or a six pack of beer or a scratch ticket. Because hope was not to be found on the shelves of any of the local stores, a small cottage industry had developed around the rare commodity. Hope was sold in parlors by a handful of women with names like The Countess Lara Shevelaski, Madame Celestina, Olga-the-Seer, Sister Dory, and Mya. Most of the sellers of hope were gray-haired, rotund, post-menopausal women with spurious Eastern European accents. Their warm parlors were permeated with the odor of simmering cabbage soup. Each had a bag of tricks which contained a few handsome, dark strangers; a scattering of possible inheritances; seven hairy cancers; three dead children; and, since the institution of the State Lottery, a handful of lucky numbers. In general, these ladies were notoriously stingy with hope and preferred to hand out an ill-fated romance, or a spell of bad health, rather than a springtime love or a slot in a rich aunt's will. The client left, feeling the weight of one more worry to bear, and she was sorry she had decided to come in the first place. Often the only benefit was an amusing story that made her feel interesting and popular for a few days, and, for some, that was worth the price.

Sister Dory was of a different ilk from the others. She marched among the avant-garde of the profession, and her goal was to change the image of psychic as old Gypsy woman or misplaced Romanian immigrant. Sister Dory was a slight 53 year old with short black hair, and she wore bright colored sweat suits with matching socks and headbands. She lived in a three bedroom ranch house, drove a Camaro, and took aerobics classes at the Fitness Factory four times a week. She had a car phone (533 FATE), vanity plates (STARS), and a personal computer with software custom designed for the occult professional. At tax time, she filled out the small business Schedule C, listing her occupation as counselor, and including candles, incense, and her car phone as itemized deductions. She was Secretary-Treasurer of the Port Williams Women's Business Association, was known for her astuteness, and was often sought out for advice by fledgling entrepreneurs. Some suggested she would make an excellent Mayor, if the present one would only be nice enough to die off.

Unlike the other psychics, who were not a sociable lot, Sister Dory had taken under her wing a gifted protégé whom fate had led into her parlor. The young woman first came to Sister Dory in the guise of an awkward twenty-year old who claimed to have some sort of psychic abilities and wanted to see if they were worth developing. But Sister Dory was not fooled by appearances. She had been experiencing recurring dreams about a tall, blonde, bejeweled young woman, and when such a woman showed up at her door, Sister Dory recognized her at once. The jewels were a pair of large, sparkling, aquamarine eyes.

Over the years, Sister Dory helped transform this ordinary woman with special powers into a special person with extraordinary powers. Sister Dory felt blessed to have been chosen to be the mentor of such an incredibly gifted psychic, and she began to live her own dreams through her charge. The first thing she did was to encourage her to change her name. When fate deposited her in Sister Dory's parlor, she was called Marie, a name which had credibility only in a church. After much deliberation, they chose "Mya," a variation of a Sanskrit word meaning illusion.

It was a perfect fit, for Mya was truly an illusion. It was difficult for anyone to believe she was a gifted psychic, bearing the dreams of others, as she floated from table to table at the Bullfrog Valley Inn, carrying sweating brown bottles to a crowd of rowdy young men and pausing to laugh at the latest dirty joke. But Mya bore her dreams as deftly as she carried the tray. Dreams are very light, and there is no limit to the number that can be carried at any single moment by a person willing and able to do so.

THE KING OF HEARTS

Mya and Sister Dory were not responsible for setting into motion the chain of events that brought Tom Harris to Port Williams; they had merely intuited the fact that he was coming. Although they had no idea of the circumstances that would surround his arrival, they had been expecting him for three years. First he had appeared to Mya in a dream as a sleek gray wolf, loping across the Lark Street Bridge. Sister Dory spent an entire morning sitting at her computer, punching key words into her Dream Catcher program. She tried wolf, wild animal, river, water, bridge, and various combinations thereof, but she could pull up no appropriate matches. Nonetheless, the wolf continued to frequent Mya's dreams, following her at a safe distance as she walked along the river, and eventually gaining her trust. One night she turned to the wolf and he allowed her to pet his soft gray muzzle, while he gentle licked her fingers with his warm rough tongue. Sister Dory punched in tongue, wolf tongue, muzzle, girl, bridge, night, moon, and river, but she came up with nothing that made any sense. It was very frustrating. She knew something important was happening, but she just couldn't get a hold on it.

The wolf returned night after night. He encouraged Mya to hold onto his fluffy gray tail and fly behind him as he ran through the forests. She was so exhausted from her dream adventures that she began to take naps during the day. Sometimes she wished the wolf would stay away for just one night so she could catch up on her sleep. But he was a persistent fellow, and Mya became very fond of him, and she began to fear for his safety. The forests were filled with hunters, following a long tradition of shooting first and looking second. But even more dangerous than the hunters was the river. She would drown anything she could get her hands on. A common sight from the Lark Street Bridge was the bloated corpse of a deer, or a bear, artfully arranged on an improvised raft of branches and debris, making its way down the river to Harrisburg. Mya had a nightmare in which the river tried to drown her wolf and she could do nothing but sit on the bank and watch him go under, again and again, struggling to keep his head above the water. She awakened as he crawled up the bank, wet and dripping, and she couldn't get back to sleep. Sister Dory punched in wolf, dead wolf, near dead wolf, drowning wolf, river bank, and survival. No match.

The next night, as the wolf carried Mya across the river, safe and dry, Mya's mother came up out of the water and waved at them from under the bridge. She was wearing a large blue hat, and she had arranged a picnic on a blanket spread out on the opposite bank. At last Sister Dory got a match: mother's ghost, blue hat, picnic, wolf, river, and beautiful maiden. The dream portended happiness, approval, romance, and sensual pleasures. Something wonderful was surely about to happen.

As the big, warm wolf continued to pad along behind Mya wherever her dreams carried her in the night, the King of Hearts suddenly appeared in her cards. He was to come to her in a three in a three in a three. Sister Dory was pleased. She was much more comfortable with the cards than with the computer. She encouraged Mya to light a lavender candle in a west window each night at sundown to show the mysterious stranger the way to her heart.

Over the months, from the Tarot, from the crystals, from the charts, and the cards, they cautiously drew a profile of the King of Hearts. They knew that an older man, someone more than ten years older than

Mya, a man who usually wore a suit and tie, was going to come into her life and father her child. They knew he had been to Port Williams, although he had never spent a night there. They also knew there was a woman in his life, and although she had once been the Queen of Hearts, she no longer had any power over him. They determined that she must be an estranged wife. Perhaps the King of Hearts was divorced.

For three years they awaited his arrival. Sometimes Mya became impatient and asked a presence above her in the heavens: "When is he ever going to come?" And Sister Dory, acting as a ventriloquist for Fate, replied: "In a three in a three in a three," and shrugged her shoulders. Whether it would be three days, three months, or three years was anybody's guess. Theirs was not an exact science.

Once the King of Hearts arrived, however, Mya sat with her charts and worked out the figures. She was 33 years old, and Tom Harris came into her life three years, three months, three weeks, and three days after her first dream of the gray wolf. An ordinary person would not have noticed such a coincidence.

In the meantime, in a comfortable three-bedroom home in Laurel Hills, 200 miles to the south, Tom Harris, a handsome 45 year old man in a suit and tie, told his wife, Susan, that he had just received an offer he could not refuse. The big cheeses wanted him to become Vice President of Sales in the corporate offices in Port Williams. Susan rubbed her lips on the smooth, warm rim of her coffee mug and stared at the familiar, animated face, telling her news she had wanted to hear 15 years ago, 10 years ago, even five years ago, but now it was too late. Her life had changed and nothing could make a difference. Her only daughter and best friend, Heather, had joined the Air Force and was in basic training some place in Texas, 2000 miles away. That, coupled with growing suspicions of infidelities on the part of the person in whom her entire adult life had been invested, resulted in Susan's not caring much about anything these days.

"That's wonderful, Tom," she said. She was good at thinking one thing and saying another. She'd had years of practice.

SYNCHRONICITY

As Tom Harris told his teary-eyed wife about the job offer, and as Sister Dory and Mya stood around the cauldron, stirring a thickening brew, Mr. Edwards, owner of the Angel Estate, scrubbed graffiti from the basement walls in the main house.

The trisodium phosphate solution burned holes in his rubber gloves, and he was beginning to feel frustrated, but he couldn't stop scrubbing. The task master who stood over him was the spirit of Kathleen Angel, the woman responsible for creating the estate some eighty years before. Mr. Edwards had a strong feeling she would not want "Ludes," and "For a good suck, call Marcie," painted on the walls of her beloved home. He couldn't imagine, or maybe he could imagine, the repercussions of this latest insult to her property, so he scrubbed on, despite painful burning on the tips of his index fingers, and on the tip of his tongue, which he used to try to alleviate the burning on his fingers.

Mr. Edwards had a reputation for mumbling to himself in public. When he was alone, however, he didn't mumble; he talked aloud, and not only to himself, but to his dead father, and, at this moment, to the spirit of Kathleen Angel, or, as she was better known, Mrs. Angel's Ghost. He was bemoaning the fact that he could never find decent tenants for her lovely old house. Surely, somewhere there must be someone who would like to live in the beautiful mansion and help keep the place up, instead of trying to destroy it. He apologized profusely for the foolish writing that he couldn't scrub off the walls, and he begged her to be patient with him. He promised this time he would try harder to find some decent tenants for a change.

There had never been a decent tenant on the property. Perhaps this was because Mr. Edwards never advertised, nor checked references, nor required a security deposit. The moment he discovered the place was empty, for the tenants often left in the middle of the night, owing back rent, he mentioned it to everyone he saw in his daily travels about town, and someone always knew someone who was looking for a big cheap place away from everybody. When a prospective tenant came around, if he had an honest face, and if he knew someone that Mr. Edwards knew, or had heard of, the place was his. No questions asked.

The nice thing about synchronicity is that when good things are happening in one person's life, others get dragged into the happy circle. One of the first to get lucky in this case was Mr. Edwards' old gray dog, Rags. Fortunately, Rags happened to get a terrible case of ticks the week the Agway was having a free dog-dip afternoon, and due to the ticks, Rags got a ride in the old truck. The destination was of no importance to Rags; it was the ride itself he loved, and when Mr. Edwards snapped his fingers, Rags jumped up into the front seat and made himself comfortable. Once they got to the Agway, however, Rags changed his mind about the importance of the destination, and Mr. Edwards had to drag him down from the truck, and then pull and push him across the parking lot to where the line had formed for the dip.

As Mr. Edwards took his place at the end of the line, he noticed his old friend, Eleanor Flynn, just a collie and two beagles ahead of him. Eleanor was married to Mike Flynn, who owned the Kraft Paper Mills. Mr. Edwards had known both Mike and Eleanor since grade school. He dragged Rags past the nervous dogs and settled in beside Eleanor for a nostalgic chat as they waited, their trembling dogs pressed tightly against their legs.

Eleanor seemed pleased to see her old friend. "Well, hello there, Paul. I'm glad to see Rags made it through another winter."

"He's almost 16, and he's slowing down," Mr. Edwards said.

"Aren't we all?" Eleanor said. "How are things going with you?"

As was his habit, Mr. Edwards began talking about what was foremost on his mind. "The big house's vacant again, and I don't know where I'm goin' a find a decent tenant."

The words had barely left his lips and had not yet reached Eleanor's ear when an idea popped into his head, and he knew it was a good one.

"Mike ever bring new people from out of town into the plant?" he asked.

"Not very often," Eleanor replied. "Fortunately for us, we bury most of our employees."

"That's a wise policy," Mr. Edwards said, "But if he should ever decide to change that policy, tell him to keep the Angel Estate in mind. It'd be nice to have some decent working folks living on the property for a change."

Eleanor told Mike that evening that she had run into Paul Edwards, and he was getting weirder by the year.

"Getting weirder?" Mike asked. "Not possible, Eleanor. You're telling fibs again."

"He gave me a message to pass on to you," she said. "He wants to upgrade the quality of tenants in the big house, and he told me to ask you to keep an eye out for new people coming to work at the plant."

"Well, actually, this is a remarkable coincidence," Mike Flynn said. "I have that new VP coming up in a month or so with his wife. I think he intends to rent until they get to know the area. He just might want to live way out there. It would be a beautiful place if it were fixed up."

It was that simple. Mr. Flynn mentioned the Angel Estate to Tom Harris. Tom told Susan there was a big, old lumber baron's mansion for rent, but that it was a couple of miles out of town and maybe not in very good condition.

Susan replied, "Whatever," and Tom accused her of sounding like Heather, and Susan began to cry. It was settled.

"Okay," Tom said. "Let's go up this Saturday for a look-see. We have nothing to lose."

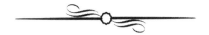

A LOOK-SEE

From a distance, Susan Harris appeared to be a teenager, but on closer inspection, she was an attractive 42 year old woman with a stylish short fifty dollar haircut. Although she was dressed in a bright pink cotton sweat suit with matching pink crystal earrings, she looked like she should be wearing black. She moved slowly and silently, like a person in mourning. She crawled into the front seat of the blue sedan, clicked her seat belt across her lap, and leaned back and closed her eyes. Her husband Tom, a handsome devil, was already in the driver's seat with the engine running and his fingers on the radio dial.

"Blast off," he announced as he backed carefully down the driveway, pausing for a car to go past before he moved onto the street. Two women walking up ahead waved and blew kisses as the car passed them. They were Susan's neighbors, Sally and Ann, out for their morning walk. Susan would have been walking with them if it weren't for the trip to Port Williams to check on the rental house. They were no doubt talking about how sad it would be to lose their dear friend who had been in the neighborhood for nearly 17 years.

From Laurel Hills to Port Williams was a long, warm four hour drive north, up and down low hills and mountains, around gentle curves, and through small towns that all looked alike. The road never once strayed from the side of the wide blue river that gleamed and sparkled as she hurried south to better places. Susan napped and daydreamed, as nostalgia and fatigue swirled slowly through her. There was a time when she would have held Tom's hand between them on the seat, or even rubbed at his crotch to tease him as he drove, but today she stayed in her capsule, thinking about the condoms she had found in his toilet kit and the receipt for an aqua teddy that had somehow fallen beneath his desk.

At the top of the mountain, before the final descent into Port Williams, Tom turned into a scenic outlook and pulled the car over to a gray rock wall.

"Let's take a look-see," he said to Susan as he opened his door, stepped out, and stretched his arms high above him. "Thar she blows," he announced as he leaned over the wall and looked down at the town below.

Susan joined him at the wall and the two looked down on a miniature town set in an oval depression, surrounded on all sides by low, green mountains. A blue river snaked from one end of the town to the other, and tiny green bridges and tall church spires were tastefully placed here and there among the buildings.

"Doesn't it look like a charming little place?" Tom asked. "Sort of quaint and isolated."

Susan shivered, although the temperature was in the 80s.

As they drove down into the center of town, charming and quaint were no longer fitting. Store fronts were boarded up and windows covered with newspapers and rags. On the side streets were rows of dilapidated houses with "No Trespassing" and "Beware of the Dog" signs tacked to the porches. Tiny yards were cluttered with bicycle parts and plastic toys; here and there a skinny cousin to a German Shepherd was tied with a chain and provided with a bundle of old towels for comfort.

"Interesting, and wow," Tom said, as he turned from one sad street to another. Susan said nothing.

"This is more like it," Tom said, as he turned onto Queen Street, which was lined with enormous mansions, still impressive, although they had seen better days. Tom drove very slowly down the wide, quiet street, pointing now and then at a grand house that caught his eye. "Will you look at that mother! It must have 40 rooms." For a few moments, the elaborate old houses pulled Susan out of her pit, but as she was trying to imagine the glorious lives of these long-gone people, a big, black motorcycle parked on a Victorian porch, a batik sheet tacked across a window, and an old car up on blocks in a driveway shocked her back to reality. People no longer knew how to live beautiful lives.

At the end of Queen Street, Tom pulled a neatly folded piece of paper out of his shirt pocket and read it aloud as he drove. "Left on Lark and across the bridge."

They were soon driving slowly across one of the miniature green bridges. At this point, the river was very wide, and a little turbulent for a warm summer day. As Susan looked down from the car window, she saw flashes of light bouncing off the water. The river was trying to get her attention by tossing glass figurines into the air, where they smashed against each other and threw glittering chips in all directions. Susan was unable to look away.

"What a magnificent river," she said, and as the words passed through her lips, several soft drops of water blew in the window and kissed her on the cheek. "I love this river," she whispered, and she looked to see if Tom had heard her foolish words. He hadn't. He was trying to read the directions and drive at the same time.

"One half mile," Tom read. "Look for Bullfrog Valley Road. We can't miss it. It's the only road back this way."

"Is that it on the left?" Susan asked. "There's a road, but I don't see a sign."

"Must be it," Tom said as he took the turn.

The road was very narrow, and on either side was a dense forest where no sunlight penetrated. Some of the taller trees intertwined their fingers to form a long, green tunnel, while others arranged and rearranged their branches to create slow moving lacy shadow plays on the surface. It was beautiful, and it was creepy.

"The place is up ahead here somewhere," Tom reported. "Look for a bunch of mailboxes on the left."

And just as the words came out of his mouth, three gray mail boxes sitting atop thick wooden posts appeared among the bushes along the road. Tom made a smooth, quick turn to the left and stopped the car a few feet from the gray stone bridge.

"Voila," he said, and Susan sat up straight and looked.

ENCHANTMENT

How few times in life does reality surpass expectation. Susan saw before her an idyllic Nineteenth Century landscape painting. She put her hand gently on Tom's leg. "Don't go yet," she said. She wanted to sit and absorb the view. The bridge itself was an indication of what the rest of the estate might be like. It was made of large, irregular gray stones, held crudely together with generous ribbons of mortar. At each end of the bridge were short, squat pillars. The pillars, as well as the sides of the bridge, were covered with vines and moss, and patches of short grass struggled to grow between the tire tracks on the road bed. Whoever built the bridge had something in mind other than a means to get from one side of the creek to the other. It was heavy on the aesthetic and light on the functional, and it blended in with the rest of the scenery as though it was a natural formation. Susan was enchanted.

"Now drive very slowly," she said to Tom. "I don't want to miss a single thing."

As the car crept over the smooth ruts and mounds to the other side of the bridge, the rest of the painting came into view. On the left was a pond and what appeared to be the remains of a gray stone dam, and beyond the pond sat a small green cottage, nearly hidden by large, wild rhododendron bushes and evergreens. To the right, on top of a smooth round green hill, sat the main house. The rambling structure was built of brown sandstone with a roof of gray slate. White wooden shutters framed every window, and a large circular patio, surrounded by a low, stone wall, spread out from the carved white front door. What were once small decorative shrubs grew wild, ragged, and unchecked over the stone wall and up the sides of the house in all directions. Several large pine trees towered over the house, brushing the roof gently with long soft green arms, obviously whispering secrets to her. Only the white shutters belied the fact that the house had not grown right up out of the earth. She was as much a part of the landscape as the big hovering pines, the looming green mountains, and the soft white cotton clouds that someone had pasted here and there on the azure sky.

It was the most beautiful painting Susan had ever seen. She allowed her doubts to float out of the car window and ride away on the soft warm breezes. At last she was coming home, coming to a place where she belonged. On the hill in front of the house sat a heavy brown stone bench, nearly hidden by a chorus of wild orange and yellow lilies. She pictured a woman seated on the stone bench, overlooking the estate. The woman was wearing a lovely old fashioned white satin dress and a bonnet with ribbons hanging down the back. For a moment, Susan fancied that the woman looked down at her and waved. She thought about waving back, but not while Tom was watching. He had a very low tolerance for what he called kooky behavior.

No sooner had Tom parked the car behind the house when Mr. Edwards' big, green, rusty truck chugged up behind them, smoking and coughing like a tubercular, and clanked to a stop. When Mr. Flynn told Tom about the house, he mentioned that the owner was quite the character, but Tom had no idea what to expect. Mr. Edwards was at his best. Here was a fresh audience who had never heard any of his tales, and since they were from out of town, he wouldn't have to be careful about the facts. These were decent people who were sincerely interested in the history of the place and who asked intelligent questions. Mr. Edwards was in his glory, and he hoped Mrs. Angel's Ghost was hovering around. She was going to be so pleased with them, and with him, as well. Life was so much easier when she was on his side.

As they walked up and down stairs, and in and out of rooms, and opened closet doors and compared views from different windows, Mr. Edwards talked about projects he was going to take care of when he got some time, problems he had with tenants in the past, and told amusing tales of the courtship of Mike and Eleanor Flynn, interspersed with historic facts and rumors about the town and about the estate. The past, the present, and the future were so interwoven in Mr. Edwards' tales that Susan and Tom were unable to follow most of his stories and gave each other bemused looks behind his back. Kathleen Angel's name came into the conversation so often that Susan began to think maybe there was another Kathleen Angel, maybe a grandniece or a distant cousin, someone who was still alive.

"Mrs. Angel was furious when them last tenants tried to raise goats in the vineyard," Mr. Edwards snorted.

"She's alive?" Susan asked.

"No, she's not alive," Mr. Edwards corrected her. "But she still don't like smelly goats around the property, eatin all the bark and ruinin the shrubbery."

Tom shrugged his shoulders and winked at Susan.

Mr. Edwards never finished a story. He interrupted himself in mid-sentence with "Now this window here just needs a little loosening up," and "I've got an old rug over at my place that you can use in this room if you can get the smell out of it," or "This old fireplace is a bugger to light, but boy does it give off the heat once you get it goin'."

He led them down the dark, narrow stairs to the basement, pausing to point out a little niche where a previous tenant's woman used to hide her vodka bottle.

"If you'd a met the fella she was livin with, you'd know why she needed that vodka," he chuckled.

In the basement, he showed them the "do hickey" that could be connected to the furnace if they wanted to heat the house with oil instead of wood, and the cold room where Mrs. Angel stored all the venison, rabbits, and quail for her lavish parties.

By the time they had thoroughly toured the house and were standing on the driveway, all of Susan's trepidations about the move had subsided. She had a feeling everything was going to be okay from now on. Perhaps she had fallen under the spell of the old house. The Angel Estate exuded happy endings. Only the most morbid person could imagine anything bad ever happening in such an enchanting setting.

"What do you think, Hon?" Tom asked. Tom had not called her "Hon" in years.

"I guess we'd like to live here," Susan said to Mr. Edwards. The pronoun "we" felt strange, yet nice, on her tongue.

"Then it's yours," Mr. Edwards said, "It's empty, and it's all ready to rock and roll."

"What about a security deposit?" Tom asked. "I can give you a check right now, if you'd like."

Mr. Edwards shook his head. "You have an honest face," he said.

"Would a one-year lease be okay with you?" Tom asked.

"I don't bother with none of that stuff," Mr. Edwards said. "When folks want to leave, I can't stop 'em, and as far as security deposits go, it's been my experience you can't get hair off a toad."

Without thinking, he added: "Them boys over in the summer house ain't paid the rent for four months now. As I said, you can't get hair off a toad, and you get even less hair off two toads."

When he realized what he had said, he was horrified. He had been trying not to say anything that might discourage these nice folks.

"We have neighbors?" Tom asked. "In the summer house? Is that the little place beside the pond?"

"They'll be gone in a week or so," Mr. Edwards reassured him. "They'll be moving back in with their folks. That's what young people do around here. They move in and out and in and out til their parents get smart and change the locks."

Just in case he wasn't convincing enough, he added, "When they go, I'm going to get a nice, quiet, little, old lady in there, someone that won't cause any trouble at all."

EVERYTHING IS GOING TO BE OKAY

The return trip to Laurel Hills was much more pleasant than the trip up had been. Tom and Susan could not stop chuckling about Mr. Edwards and his tales.

"What are we getting ourselves in for?" Tom asked.

"God alone knows," Susan replied, "but I'm ready to rock and roll. How about you?"

"Always," Tom laughed, as he reached over and gave her thigh a gentle little squeeze.

Susan took Tom's hand in hers and held it between them on the seat. She dreamed about starting their married life all over again. Tom would be home every night and away from temptation. They would be living in that splendid big house, and she would finally get a chance to try all the gourmet recipes she had been clipping and saving for years. She would sew lace curtains for the windows and refinish antique furniture, which she would find for a song at the local antique stores. Surely Heather would want to come back to live with them in the big house once she was finished with her two-year stint in the service. Susan designed and decorated in her imagination the little suite of rooms on the second floor for Heather. She daydreamed the whole way home.

She couldn't wait to tell her friends about the estate. They had been as miserable as she about the move, but now she would be able to reassure them that it wasn't going to be all that bad. From now on, everything was going to be okay. She could just sense it.

For many years, things had not been okay with Susan Harris, but she had kept herself so busy that there was little time to regret that life had not turned out the way she had hoped it would. In fact, she lived as though her every dream had come true, and she pretended she was content and happy with her lovely home, perfect daughter, and weekend husband.

Over the years, Susan went to Bible study, joined the tennis league, was president of the PTA four different times, and took Suzuki piano lessons with Heather. There were quilting classes, the Great Books Club, and a volunteer job at the local public radio station. Susan learned picture framing and furniture refinishing, and she belonged to the neighborhood progressive foreign gourmet dinner club.

During the week, when she had no husband, she concentrated on Heather, and, on weekends, she had Tom. They never had time to get bored with each other. On Friday evening, she put on a special outfit, prepared a big dinner with one of Tom's favorite desserts, and had a date with her husband. On Saturday afternoons, while Heather played at a friend's house, Susan and Tom made love on the sofa under a big warm blanket. On Sundays, they caught up on chores around the house and yard, and on early Monday mornings, they hugged in the doorway and said goodbye for the week. This was the pattern of their marriage for over seventeen years. Having an absentee husband and one well-behaved little girl made Susan unique and popular. She was the one invited to run along over to the mall to pick up a last minute gift. She and Heather were the first to be asked out for pizza when a friend's husband was out of town, or to dinner when in-laws were visiting.

Yes, life was very pleasant in Laurel Hills, but Susan had no idea that her world was also very fragile until everything began to fall apart. At fourteen, Heather changed overnight from a friendly, sweet child, into a silent, depressed, rebellious adolescent.

She stopped talking with Susan and would address her only to argue and criticize. Susan waited patiently for Heather to grow out of this stage, to mature, to become her friend again, but by the time this happened, Heather had graduated high school, and Susan was hugging her goodbye at the Harrisburg Airport, as she flew off to basic training in Texas.

Without her best friend, Susan became very lonely and sad. And one day, in this lonely and sad state, she came upon a crinkled receipt under Tom's desk for an aqua teddy, size small, purchased at The Soft and Lovely Shoppe in Rochester, New York. Tom was able to glibly explain that he had charged the teddy on his card to protect a colleague who was buying it for his girlfriend and didn't want his wife to know. Susan sarcastically asked if this was the kind of activity he and his colleagues engaged in while they were on the road, and Tom said it was a one-time thing, very unique, and had never happened to him before or since. That colleague was a slime ball, but his company placed huge orders, so Tom had to be nice to the guy. What else could he do? What other choice did he have? What would she have done different in the same situation?

Tom's voice was a little too loud; his tone, a little too persuasive. He sounded like he was trying to sell her a bill of goods. After all, that's exactly what he did for a living, and he was very good at it. A little trust seeped out of the marriage. She felt she was losing, or had already lost, both Heather and Tom. Over the next few months, she would experience a sudden onslaught of sadness and despair so intense that she would lie on the couch for hours, unable to get up and do a thing. She was too tired and angry to love, wait for, and placate Tom, as she had always done, and she felt she had lost Heather, who had become a distant voice on an infrequent phone call.

The week Susan finally decided to do something about her depression and had written the number of a counselor on the pad beside her phone, Tom came home with the news about the promotion and the move to Port Williams, and Susan put her own problems on hold and began to make lists. Maybe a change would do them all good.

While Susan was clearing out the attic and having a goodbye lunch every day with the different old friend, Mya dreamed that she made love with the wolf on the river bank under a perfect sickle moon. By this time, Sister Dory had lost all patience with the Dream Catcher program and reverted to a more traditional technique. She put Mya in a trance, and under hypnosis, Mya said the wolf was so close that she could smell his warm meaty breath on her neck, under her chin. That was a clear sign that The King of Hearts was very near. Perhaps he had already arrived in Port Williams. As Mya walked down the familiar streets, she looked for new faces and was naturally disappointed. Seldom did new faces appear in Port Williams.

Sister Dory twice saw a faint blue aura around Mya's head when she walked through her door, and she read that as an indication that Mya should be wearing her special blue hair clasp every day now, just in case.

While Susan packed up boxes of pots and pans and took endless bags of old clothing and books to the thrift stores, Mya cleaned and shined her magic blue hair clip and waited for the coming of the King of Hearts. Both Mya and Susan, each in her own way, knew, that, from now on, everything was going to be okay.

IT WILL BE AN ADJUSTMENT

Hocus pocus played no part in the modus operandi of Tom Harris. Under ordinary circumstances, Tom and Mya's paths would never cross. The Vice President of a large company was not likely in his daily activities to run into a psychic. But Tom Harris was not your typical Vice President. Tom Harris was an alley cat. He had the habits of a man who had spent twenty years on the road, setting his own schedule and doing whatever he damned well pleased whenever he damned well pleased to do it. Although the traveling had been fatiguing at times, it enabled him to eat when and where he felt like it, to fall into bed at seven o'clock and sleep all night if he was tired, or, on the other hand, to rest for an hour and get up and go off and find a friendly bar and a lonely woman and spend the night with her. Or, he could sit in his room with a book, go over accounts, or watch television. What he did was not important as long as it was what he himself chose to do and not what someone else thought he should be doing.

Everyone had predicted, even Mr. Flynn, that the new position would be an adjustment for Tom, and Tom reached into his bag of clichés and replied: "Not to worry. That's what life is all about, adjustments. I've made quite a few in my time." But this adjustment turned out to be a bit more challenging than any Tom had heretofore encountered, and it was Tom's effort to adjust that finally brought him into contact with Mya, or so it seemed.

What Tom found to be the most difficult chore of the day was to steer his car each morning towards the Kraft Paper Mills and not up the ramp to 15 north to New York State. The challenge was to head down Sawmill Drive and turn into the parking lot, and then to walk into the building and make his way to the office. He felt like a caged animal. The cage was comfortable, no question about it. Mr. Flynn had gone all out. He promised Tom it would be first class, and it was. They had broken through the thick walls and made a large window that overlooked the river. This window saved Tom's sanity. When he was feeling cooped up, he stood and watched the river. She was always dressed up and heading off to some place special, even if he wasn't.

Tom escaped from the plush cage as often as he could. He found any excuse to meet the reps anywhere but in his office. He went to lunch with someone different every day and lingered over coffee and pie. He was the exciting new guy from out of town and everything he said and did was interesting. By 4:30 each afternoon, the building cleared of everyone except a few stragglers. That's when Mr. Flynn buzzed Tom and asked him to wander over to his office so he could pick his brain. Tom enjoyed this opportunity for a little shop talk with the big boss. He had been selling for the company for over seventeen years and knew every customer and every competitor up and down the line. And Mr. Flynn always let him know how much he appreciated his extensive knowledge and expertise.

However, Mr. Flynn ate dinner faithfully each night at six, so Tom could predict that no matter how interesting the conversation, at 5:40, Mr. Flynn would look at his watch, announce that he didn't want to keep Eleanor waiting, collect the papers from his desk and stuff them into his worn leather briefcase, and head for the door.

"I still have a few things to tie up," Tom said, whether or not he did. "Have a good evening."

"Don't work too late," Mr. Flynn called, pleased to have one person in his employ who needed to be warned about excess working.

As soon as Mr. Flynn's car was gone from the lot, Tom was on his way out of the cage. He felt like a school boy when the recess bell at last rang. His briefcase flapping at his side, he fairly ran to his car and drove out of the parking lot and down Sawmill Drive so recklessly that it brought his heart up into his throat.

When he reached the bottom of Sawmill Drive, Tom made his second important decision of the day. Should he drive directly home, or kill some time driving around? Susan had fallen effortlessly into the routine of having a husband home each evening. She waited for the sound of his car on the driveway, and as he walked through the doorway, she magically produced a dinner that looked as though it should be photographed for a gourmet magazine. As she sat across the table from him, she got up and down a dozen times to get an extra napkin, bring more butter from the kitchen, fill the pepper grinder, and make fresh coffee. As Tom ate, he had the feeling that she was waiting for him to share his day with her, and he didn't know why, but he hated to give her the satisfaction of knowing anything about his work, no matter how trivial the topic. He found a perverse satisfaction in thwarting her efforts at conversation. If the evening paper was handy, he spread it out on the table and read as he ate. If Susan asked, as she sometimes did, "How was your day?" he replied, "Pretty good," or "So, so."

When her questions became more specific, Tom dug for an appropriately vague answer. He had a supply of phrases like "Hard to tell," and "It's out of my hands." When he inadvertently slipped and allowed Susan to learn the name of an account, her question, "Did anything develop with the Cleveland deal?" called for painful creative avoidance on his part.

"Still on hold."

"Why is that? Is there some sort of problem?"

Tom reached into his bag of clichés. "That's just the way the cookie crumbles," or, better, "It's still sitting on the back burner." Tom's back burner was always overloaded.

When Susan had something to tell Tom, it   was easier to take, for all he had to do was grunt, or put in a periodic "Hmmmmmm," or a "Really?" Once in a while, Tom felt guilty for the way he treated Susan, but when a man has become accustomed to a week-end wife, it is very hard to adjust to a full-time wife. Susan got on his nerves, and the problem was that he had no diversions in Port Williams. Tom was not the sort of man who could live without diversions.

As he paused at the bottom of Sawmill Drive, the scene at the dinner table flashed before his eyes, and his mind and body rebelled. At 6:20 he found himself driving along 44 north, thirty miles from home, enjoying the way the trees filtered out the sunset. Susan's quiet voice came into his thoughts: "What about firewood? Are we going to order some, or do you think we should try to cut it ourselves? Maybe I should ask Mr. Edwards about it?" Tom drove ten miles farther. Then came her voice again: "Do you think we should try to put the storm-windows in before it gets too cold? How about this weekend?" Tom drove another five miles.

As Susan grated, sliced, and chopped, Tom drove around the outskirts of Port Williams, following little roads for short distances just to see where they went, circling back to where he started, and heading off in another direction. As Susan freshened her makeup, changed her blouse, and put on a different pair of earrings, Tom parked along the bank and watched the river create lovely impressionistic water color pictures. She took a few white clouds, some green trees, and a hunk of the orange setting sun, and, like a child with finger paints, smeared them around on her palette. The moment she finished one perfect picture, she washed it away and began another. Eventually, dusk descended and the river got bored with her painting, and Tom began to feel a little hungry, so he turned and headed towards home, where he knew Susan would have something delicious waiting for him.

"It'll be an adjustment," they warned him, and he replied: "Adjustments are like loose women. They keep a man young and flexible."

That new guy, Harris, had the best sense of humor. There were some people at the Kraft Paper Mills who hadn't cracked a smile in years, and Tom Harris had them laughing out loud. Everyone agreed that he sure livened the place up, and that was a good thing.

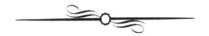

THE FROG

What turned out to be fortunate for some and yet unfortunate for others was that there existed in Port Williams a place where a person experiencing adjustment problems could go for an alignment. The troubled of Port Williams did not seek psychological counselors, nor pastors; they sought solace and comfort from life's troubles at the Bullfrog Valley Inn.

Every time Tom happened to mention that he lived out on the old Angel Estate, someone, anyone, everyone proclaimed how lucky he was to live so near the Frog. Naturally, Tom became a little curious about the infamous old hang-out, and it was just a matter of time until he checked himself in to seek help with his particular adjustment problem.

The Frog was a legend. The Inn was built at the turn of the Century on the west side of town in hopes of attracting travelers before they reached the more expensive hotels in the city center. It was built by a dreamer who thought the town would grow. Nearly eighty years later, time had left the Bullfrog isolated in a quiet glen without a house nor a road in sight. One narrow, unmarked dirt driveway snaked its way from Bullfrog Valley Road to the parking lot. The Frog was not so far out as to be inconvenient, yet it was far enough out to be private. It was the sort of place where a man could take his girlfriend and not have to worry that it would get back to his wife. Everyone went there after work, after the ball games, and late at night when there was nothing good on TV. On weekends, the parking lot overflowed, and pickups, motorcycles, and four-wheelers lined the little road down through the forest. Older folks pretended to be ashamed of the Frog and clicked their tongues and shook their heads when it was mentioned, but the younger crowd joked about it like it was a silly, eccentric, reliable old friend. Any special event – a new baby, a new car, a raise, a divorce, a pregnant girlfriend—called for a quick trip to the Frog to celebrate, or to mourn, depending. The fact that over a month had passed before Tom ventured up to the Frog showed how hard he had been trying to work out his adjustment problems on his own.

One particularly harrowing day, three different co-workers mentioned the Frog to Tom, and he decided maybe it was time to check the place out. On his way home, without giving it too much thought, he turned up the dirt road and found himself in the parking lot. Because no one had ever bothered to describe the place, he had no idea what to expect at the end of the winding dirt road. From its name, he thought it might be quaint, perhaps a wooden shingled building with shutters and vines and stone steps. Instead, before him sat a large, gray, rectangular building without a single window. It looked like a storage facility, a warehouse of some sort. But on one side was a door with a bright blue neon sign hanging above it: Bullfrog Valley Inn, Eats and Drinks. An enormous parking lot stretched out on all sides of the building and was bordered by a thick green forest. A few cars and trucks were scattered here and there on the lot. Tom drove to the opposite side of the parking lot, hoping to see a main entrance, but there he found only a small porch, covered with overflowing trash cans, cardboard boxes, and cases of beer bottles. He pulled around to the front once more and sat in his car with the engine running, trying to decide if he wanted to bother to go inside. This was just another example of the cultural shock he was experiencing daily in Port Williams. This dreary old building, this gigantic barn, was the hot place to go. In no way did the Frog resemble the sort of place where Tom used to enjoy an afternoon pick-me-up when he was on the road. He was accustomed to dark, cozy lounges with brass fixtures, leather seats, and soft music.

"What do I have to lose?" he thought, foolishly, as he opened the car door and walked briskly towards the building. He smiled at the sign and shook his head. As he pushed open the door and stepped inside, he was greeted by twangy, thumping country music, and another smile lit up his face. The room was incredibly large and so dark that it took several seconds for Tom to distinguish shadows and forms milling about in the overall gloom. Straight ahead of him was a circular bar, around which sat ten or twelve lumps, and in the middle of the bar was a large, dimly lit, green aquarium that cast an eerie glow on the dismal faces around the bar. Tom saw a myriad of small tables pushed closely together, encircling a bare area, which he assumed must be a dance floor. At the far end of this area was a small platform with a microphone on a stand and several large amplifiers sitting nearby. The place was huge. Near the far wall was a pool table with two figures circling around it, crouched and armed with pool cues.

If there had been someone with him, anyone who would understand, Tom's smile would have turned into one of his favorite clichés: "I don't believe this place!" Until that moment, he might have escaped, but two young men appeared behind him in the doorway, and a rough, "Scuse me, comin through," was the impetus for Tom to move up to the bar and slide onto an empty stool.

Tom was the only man in the bar wearing a suit and tie. He drew a few nonchalant glances from the others, but was then left alone to study the creatures gliding around among the plastic greenery and neon-colored bridges and caves in the aquarium. He was soon engrossed in trying to figure out just how many weirdo things lived in that tank. He counted ten small goldfish, three sleek gray and white fish, and a brown thing that looked like a short, fat, snake. All the creatures seemed to be moving slowly around in an effort to avoid one lumpy, fat, giant fish that looked as though a child had molded him from pinkish-blue play dough. Small green and white tendrils waved at Tom. He thought they might be plants, or maybe worms. He couldn't see if they were connected to anything at the bottom. He squinted and leaned forward on the bar to get a better look.

"With you in a jif." A tall lady whisked from a door behind the bar, carrying a heavy tray. As Tom looked up, she disappeared into a dark area filled with tables. Tom glanced after her, and now that his eyes had grown accustomed to the dark, he noticed there were several people sitting at the tables.

The cultural shock had subsided enough for isolated observations to flit through Tom's mind. There was no television in this bar. How long had it been since he had been in a bar without a television? There were only a few women in the place, and they were with men. None were unescorted. How unlike his favorite bars on the road, peopled with hungry men on the make and just enough attractive females to keep the competition stiff. He wondered where white collar workers went for their early evening cocktails, and a grim reality struck him. He recalled Mr. Flynn's nightly comment: "Don't want to keep Eleanor waiting." Men in suits went home to their wives and children. And the feisty, liberated females, where were they? Another grim reality surfaced. There may not be any. He had moved back into a time warp. Girls in Port Williams still married young; the ones who didn't moved away.

Tom was not the sort of person who often felt depressed. He was a man of action. If something didn't feel right, he did something about it. Susan, on the other hand, was the one who fussed about every little thing. Tom thought if Susan were sitting with him in the Frog, she would be saying something about these pathetic people who have no purpose in their lives. She would even be pitying the fish in that tiny tank without enough room to swim around.

Tom's ruminations were interrupted when the tall waitress slipped her body between him and the aquarium, and he looked up from the soft glowing green water into a pair of large, glowing green eyes. Time stood still. Mya saw a strange man in a suit and tie, a handsome man, graying at the sideburns, probably in his late forties, a man she had never seen before in her life, a very unlikely man to be sitting at the bar in the Bullfrog Valley Inn. A slow smile crept over her large mouth. She knew why she had taken an extra ten minutes to do her hair that morning, why she had struggled to braid tiny blue satin ribbons into long skinny braids around her face, and then clip them all together with the special blue sapphire hair clip; why she had chosen the white gauze peasant blouse that garnered so many compliments from the customers; and why she had felt the need to douse herself with jasmine water before she headed out the door that afternoon. She stood quietly for a moment longer. She liked what she was seeing. She sent a silent message to Sister Dory: "He's here," and received back a motherly warning, "Take it slow."

"They say you'll live longer if you sit and stare at the fish each day," she said. "I'm Mya. What can I get for you?"

Tom was suddenly confused. Instead of giving her his order, he asked: "But do fish live longer when they are being watched?"

"These fish definitely live longer," Mya said. "They're in a controlled environment with lots of food and no predators."

Tom fell back in step. He assumed a very serious demeanor. "Are you telling me there are no predators in this place?" he asked.

For a long moment, Mya stared directly into his dark, teasing brown eyes. A smile played on the corners of her mouth, and she casually wiped the bar in front of him with a neatly folded damp cloth. "We never had a problem with predators," she said quietly, "until a few minutes ago when one managed to get through the door."

Tom breathed in a deep whiff of jasmine, and he shook his head and smiled. "Chalk one up for Mya," he said.

"You look like a martini man," she said. "Am I right?"

"What are you, a mind reader?" Tom asked.

"Yep," Mya said. "One olive. No," she corrected herself. "You don't like olives. In fact, what am I thinking? You hate olives."

"Right," Tom said. "Chalk two up for Mya."

The drink magically appeared on the bar in front of Tom, and it was perfect. And just as he finished the first and was about to order another, a second drink appeared before him.

"You're good," he whispered.

"You don't even know," she whispered back.

Once again the odor of jasmine knocked him for such a loop that he couldn't think of a seductive reply that would encourage the conversation to continue in the direction he hoped it was heading. As he was trying to clear his thoughts, Mya turned and pointed at the big lumpy creature in the aquarium. "By the way," she said, "Since you're going to become a regular here, I'd like you to meet Hugo. He's the brains of the joint."

Tom wondered what made her think he was going to become a regular, but he didn't ask. Instead, he turned his attention to the aquarium. "Pleased to meet you, Hugo," he said, and then to Mya, he said, "He seems to have thin skin. Will he be insulted if I don't shake his hand?"

"What hand?" Mya laughed, as she hurried off to respond to a young man who was whistling loudly for her in the distance.

Tom carefully folded a ten dollar bill into the shape of a crane, and slipped it under his empty glass and left the bar.

The moment Mya noticed his place at the bar was empty, she hurried to the phone and called Sister Dory.

"Did you get my message? He's here," Mya said.

"I know," Sister Dory replied. "What do you think of him? Will he do?"

"He's quite a change," Mya said.

In a very serious voice, like the family doctor giving advice to a sick patient who calls in the middle of the night, Sister Dory said: "Continue to light the lavender candle for a few more days until we are absolutely sure he's the right one."

"No problem," Mya said. "Listen, I've got to go now. I'll call you later when I get off."

"Wait, one more thing," Sister Dory added. "I hope you were wearing the blue hair clip."

"Absolutely," Mya said. "I've worn it every day since you suggested it."

"Drop it off with me tomorrow," Sister Dory said. "I'll see if I can get a sense of how fast this thing is going to go."

Mya carefully unclasped the silver filigree hair clip from her long golden braids and wrapped it gently in a clean dish towel. Then she tied a scarf around her hair and went back to work, singing along with the loud twangy music.

"Off-the-wall," Tom said aloud as he got into his car. "An off-the-wall waitress at the Bullfrog Valley Inn." He laughed out loud at himself, at life, at fate, at what a crazy world it was. He sensed that his adjustment problems were coming to an end.

He was in an excellent mood when he got home. He fixed a drink for himself, made one for Susan, and then regaled her with tales about Port Williams. He told her about a bar called "The Frog," which was the in-place to go. Everyone at work talked about it. He said some night they were going to have to go there and check it out.

"I've already heard more than I care to hear about the Bullfrog Valley Inn," Susan said. "Mr. Edwards claims Kathleen Angel tried to burn it down any number of times because she didn't want that kind of establishment near her home."

"Now there's one smart ghost," Tom said. "Even from her grave, she's thinking about property devaluation."

"Seriously, Tom," Susan said. "Going to the Frog for a simple little drink might turn out to be a very expensive proposition for us."

"How so?" Tom asked.

"For starters, I'm sure we don't have the appropriate wardrobe," she said. "If we don't want to stick out like sore thumbs, we'll have to invest in some flannel shirts, and I bet you don't have a single pair of denims."

"Nor shit stompers for that matter," Tom laughed.

"What about a four-wheeler?" Susan asked. "Would they let an ordinary sedan into the parking lot?"

"You're absolutely right," Tom said. "That one drink could cost us thousands. We're going to have to rock and roll right here at home."

He hugged Susan and they chuckled together for a few moments. She felt he was beginning to relax at last, and she knew by the way he hugged her that they were going to make love that night. She made a point of wearing a pink silk nightie instead of her old flannel pajamas, and before she came to bed, she grabbed a cologne bottle and splashed herself under her arms, behind her ears, and on the insides of her thighs. It was just something Heather had left and Susan hadn't been able to throw out. She glanced at the label: "Jasmine Memories."

Tom and Susan had not made love in weeks, and it was such a good feeling to crawl into bed and have Tom waiting there for her, warm and welcoming, instead of sound asleep on the far side.

As she slipped into his arms, Tom took a deep breath and buried his face in her neck, inhaling deeply the arousing sweet scent. He closed his eyes and pretended she was tall and blonde and had blue satin ribbons in her hair. He couldn't get enough of the jasmine and he couldn't get enough of her. As Susan was falling asleep, she thought of how funny marriage is. It goes through highs and lows and a person never knows what's coming next. She almost wanted to ask Tom: "What brought this on?" But, instead, she lay quietly, reminding herself to write to Heather the next day and ask her where she had bought that fabulous perfume.

As Sister Dory had advised, Mya took her time with Tom Harris. Without too much difficulty, he developed the habit of stopping in at the Bullfrog nearly every day after work, and Mya managed to take a few minutes to sit and talk with him, and to flirt, very cautiously. Tom flirted back, even more cautiously. His plan of attack was to take it slow until they were comfortable with each other, and then let nature take its course. Mya had no plan; she knew fate would do whatever it was that fate intended to do, and all she had to do was be in attendance. They talked about the Frog, the town, the weather, and about the Angel Estate. Mya was fascinated to the point of obsession with Kathleen Angel. She knew every rumor, every legend, every theory about not only Kathleen Angel, but her husband, Lloyd Angel, and about the enchanting Angel Estate. She had combed the Historical Room at the Library for articles and photographs of the Angel family. She had created pet theories of her own about them, and one of her favorite and most shocking was that Lloyd Angel had murdered his wife, but had never been found out. She called herself a Kathleen Angel advocate.

"You're really into this stuff," Tom commented.

"Well, it's a shame you're not," Mya said. "In fact, it's absolutely unfair that you are the one who has the privilege of living on the Angel Estate, when I am the one who cares so much about it."

"It's not such a bad place to live," Tom said, "if you like old things that only work when they're in the mood."

"I would like to live on the Angel Estate more than anything in the world," Mya announced, "and not only because it's haunted."

Tom assured her she was better off where she was. "Better to live in a place that's not haunted and where things work," he said. "Trust me on this one."

TOO CLOSE FOR COMFORT

It was a short time after Mya's pronouncement that she had always wanted to live on the Angel Estate that the party boys left in the middle of the night, owing Mr. Edwards three months' rent. With one run-on sentence and a rambling tale about all the trouble those boys had caused, Mr. Edwards conveyed the news to Susan at the mailboxes one morning, and Susan repeated the meat of the story to Tom at dinner. It was no big deal. It seemed no one stayed in the summer house for more than a few months.

But it became a big deal when Tom mentioned it to Mya at the Bullfrog the next afternoon. In the semi-darkness, with loud, twangy music echoing from the walls, Tom casually said that he was going to be able to get a good night's sleep at last since the noisy party-hardy guys had moved out of the summer house. Then he corrected himself. "Maybe, he said. "Maybe I'll get a good night's sleep, depends on who crazy old Edwards moves in there next. One thing for sure, it can't possibly be anyone louder." He smiled at Mya and sighed: "He promised to find a nice quiet old lady."

When Mya heard Tom's words, it was as though Fate had spoken. She wrinkled up her face, squinted her eyes, rounded her shoulders, and bent over near Tom. "I'm a nice quiet old lady," she whispered in a quivering high frail voice. "Can I be your neighbor?"

Tom laughed nervously. He could think of nothing to say.

"What's the trouble?" the frail voice continued. "Would the clicking of my knitting needles keep you awake at night?"

Tom found his voice. "Are you looking for a new place?" he asked. "I thought you loved it down on Queen Street."

For the past two years, Mya had been living on Queen Street in the maid's quarter on the fourth floor of a huge Tudor, which had been divided up into nine small apartments. Tom had driven past it and had crept slowly down the alley behind it. He liked the idea that a black wrought iron fire escape twisted its way from the ground to the fourth floor in the back of the house, where it could not be seen from the street.

Mya had taken advantage of her home on Queen Street to join the weekly house tours run by the Port Williams Historic Society. She was on intimate terms with all the lovely mansions and knew every detail of the artifacts they contained. She had placed her hands on ivory powder boxes and felt vibrations of the pains and sorrows, as well as the joys, of long dead occupants. By sitting quietly on a Queen Anne sofa in the parlor of a 23 room Victorian painted lady, she was able to connect with the historic life force that runs through all human beings and has since the beginning of time. She could take the tour only infrequently because the experience was so emotional that it exhausted her for days afterwards.

She had talked endlessly about these experiences with Tom, so he was quite surprised that she would want to move away from there. But typically, Mya had introduced a new wrinkle that Tom had not anticipated. He had introduced the topic of the summer house merely to make conversation to entice Mya to sit with him a little longer. Now she had thrown him a curve ball. He thought of Mya in the summer house, not 100 yards from his front door. He took a long sip from his glass, held it up to the light, and pretended to be studying it. He needed time. In those few seconds, he prioritized, analyzed, and came to a decision. But, as he began to say, "I think it's probably not such a good idea for you to be living so close to my home," Mya got called across the room, where four young men in an intense pool competition desperately needed immediate liquid reinforcement. Then a group of six came in the door and noisily began to pull two tables together to make room for the entire party. Mya hurried over to help them get settled and to take their orders. Tom waited for a few moments until he saw that she apparently was not going to have any more free time, and then he walked out to his car, feeling uneasy, as though something had been left up in the air, something that should have been settled.

As Mya filled six big heavy glasses with draft beer from the tap, she smiled at her reflection on the smeary silver surface. "You're the luckiest person in the entire world," she whispered. "The Angel Estate is the perfect place for me and my little one to be living for the next few years."

Early next morning, Mya wasted no time in heading out to the estate. She hoped to find Mr. Edwards working somewhere around the property. She just didn't hope to find him; she knew she would find him, and she did. He was trying to fish a beer can out of the dam with an old broken rake. Mya wasted no time with idle chat. She told him exactly why she was there. "I would like to rent the summer house," she announced, and Mr. Edwards looked up into her face and broke out with a big, happy smile.

And he couldn't stop smiling, no matter how hard he tried. The idea that a woman would want to live in the summer house pleased him to no end. He had it up to his eye teeth with reckless young men who wanted to live away from town so they could hunt, drink, do drugs, trash up the gray stone bridge, and worse. And after a few typical questions about which of the Clarks Mya was related to, Mr. Edwards was able to place this young woman in his genealogical scheme of Port Williams, and that pleased him even more, and his smile grew wider.

Mr. Edwards' mind was a lot like the houses and buildings sitting here and there on his properties, filled with old stuff, some worthless, some valuable, much useless, and some too old and strange for anyone to figure out what its use once was if it had ever had a use. Everything was mixed up together, and, like a busy, town dump, things surfaced now and then, like an old Victrola worth five hundred dollars, and a snuff box that belonged to Napoleon himself. As Mya stood before him, towering over him by four or five inches, a friendly, open, beautiful, young lady, with long, golden brown hair, and big green eyes, a memory that had been buried for decades worked its way to the surface. She was the spitting image of a woman named Pauline Clark, but the river had taken Pauline Clark years and years ago. But, if it wasn't Pauline Clark standing here before him, then who could it be? Mr. Edwards' cluttered brain began to grind old memories and voices and stories, just like the wooden coffee grinder he used each morning to reduce little hard beans to fine aromatic brown grounds. The grinder came to a sudden halt, and what remained was an image of a little girl.

Mr. Edwards found himself in a very unusual state. He was speechless. Mya reached out and placed her fingers gently on his grimy, scarred, much abused hand.

A confused, yet gentle, smile once again crept across his face, and his eyes teared up.

Mya shook her head. "Yes," she said to the unspoken question that dangled in the air between them. "It's me."

Mr. Edwards' voice returned. "You're her?"

Standing before him was the pathetic little child once known as Pauline Clark's mistake. Mya suddenly became a relic of Port

Williams, and Mr. Edwards felt he should treat her with the same respect he held for Herbert Hoover's belt buckle or the antique cider mill he kept on his front porch. He was tickled to death to have her there, and she was of course tickled to death to be there.

"How'd you know this place was vacant?" Mr. Edwards asked.

"I sensed it," Mya replied. "I'm good at sensing things."

Mr. Edwards nodded his head. He understood.

"Speaking of sensing things," she said. "I do have one little problem I need to ask you about. I sometimes read cards for people. It's not a big business with a lot of traffic or anything, just a lady dropping by now and then for an hour. Would that be a problem? Do you think you'd mind?"

Mr. Edwards had two standard reactions to whatever life had to offer. He was either curious, or he was amazed. This time he was amazed. He shook his head back and forth and said: "Mind? Last boys in here had beer parties every Saturday night. Cars and trucks and motorcycles up and down the road, all over the bridge, blocking the driveway." He shook his head in disbelief. "A little old lady dropping by to have her tea leaves read, no problem at all. She probably won't smash the pillars off the bridge." He shook his head and chuckled. "Then again, she just might, if she drives like all the little old ladies I know."

He guffawed for a moment at his joke and wiped his nose on his sleeve. Then he paused for a few seconds as though he was trying to think of something to say. He leaned closer to Mya and his voice became very quiet. "You know, she used to hold séances in the summer house. It's what they say." He looked up into Mya's big green eyes and saw not a glint of skepticism. She knew, and she believed. "She'll be tickled to death that you've come at last," he added.

So, everyone was tickled to death: Mr. Edwards, Mya, and She. But, what about Tom? When Mya greeted him that afternoon with a wide smile and a loud "Howdy, Neighbor," he wondered to himself. "What in God's world am I in for now?" Ever since he moved to Port Williams, he had the feeling that he didn't make things happen anymore; things happened to him, and he asked the question "What am I in for now?" much too frequently for his own comfort.

Mr. Edwards was not familiar with the term synchrony. He preferred "great guns." Everything was going great guns for him. A vice president of Kraft Paper Mills, a classy fellow, always in a suit and tie, was living in the big house. His wife was a quiet, hard-working little soul, and, in less than a month, she had the place looking better than it had in decades. Living in the summer house was a fortune teller, not an ordinary fortune teller, but the infamous Pauline Clark's Mistake. Mr. Edwards could not get over this remarkable coincidence. He repeated the story to every crony he met in his daily travels, and with a little coaching, most were able to recall the mother, the child, and some of the circumstances surrounding them, even though they hadn't thought about the tragedy in twenty or thirty years.

PAULINE CLARK'S MISTAKE

Pauline Clark and the child, Marie, lived with so many different families and moved so often that all that remained in the Port Williams memory bank was a vague image of a beautiful young woman and a quiet little girl who would curl up on any knee that welcomed her.

"Biggest mistake I ever made. Only mistake I ever made," Pauline said often enough that some referred openly to the child as "Pauline Clark's Mistake." Port Williams accepted both Pauline and her mistake in the same way they accepted the old maid elementary teacher, the shell-shocked World War I veteran, and the crazy preacher who sold plastic glow-in-the-dark crosses from a wagon in front of the Post Office. All of the small town stereotypes found comfortable niches in the bosom of Port Williams.

Pauline was difficult to label. She wasn't a whore. Someone else was the town whore. She wasn't one of the bags who hung around saloons and went home with anyone who bought her a drink. Others filled that niche. Pauline was a gentle woman, full of life, and very gracious. She worked now and then, sometimes living with an older man or woman who needed help around the house, or with a new mother who had given birth and was having difficulty recovering. For such jobs, she collected a small salary plus room and board. The jobs didn't last for more than a few weeks or months, but she never had trouble finding another one. She was a permanent fixture in Port Williams.

She knew everyone, and everyone knew of her. Pauline was today's hospice worker and home care aide, all wrapped up in one small, energetic woman.

Pauline Clark was flashy, and she was a flirt. She flirted with men, with old ladies, and with little children. The old people she cared for adored her, and they gave her rings, trinkets, and old furs and hats, much to the chagrin of their daughters and nieces who were often pitching in to pay for Pauline's services.

Pauline was not a married lady; she was not a slut, nor a whore; she was not even a nurse, nor a housekeeper; and she was certainly not an old maid. Pauline was Pauline, long before a woman was allowed to be herself. And Pauline wore bright colors decades before bright colors became fashionable. In the drab neighborhoods she frequented, a patch of royal blue stood out. A bright red cape could be seen for blocks against the background of dingy gray buildings. An emerald green sweater brightened up a chilly autumn morning. Pauline Clark was a flower. She had a head of thick, dark brown hair, and light blue eyes. But hers was not an untouchable beauty. She talked with everyone she met. She told animated stories, and she burst into frequent peals of musical laughter. In an earlier century, she might have graced the court of some French king, but, having been born three centuries too late for that, she moved through the working classes of a small Pennsylvania town, dispensing light and gaiety into a few somber lives.

Little Marie trailed along behind. She quietly adored her mother and waited patiently hour upon hour for her attention. Her patience was rewarded with quick hugs and kisses which left painted red lip marks on her white cheeks. Her mother was either going or coming and somehow never sat still long enough for Marie to be able to attach her warm, insecure little self to her and hold on for dear life, as she so desperately wanted to do.

Instead, the child spent endless quiet hours confined to warm rooms with very old people who tried to amuse her with trinkets that she had to be careful with and give back once she was finished playing. All the old people looked alike and smelled alike, and no matter how kindly they treated her, she was always a little afraid of them. She feared they might lash out at her for some small transgression the way they often lashed out at each other. Marie tread very lightly and was ever so careful all the time with everything and everyone. Some called her an angel child.

It was during these years of sitting in dark, warm, quiet rooms, playing with an antique thimble collection, that Marie Clark first discovered a world into which she could escape and which became more real for her than the world in which she lived. Trying to enter this special world became an obsession with the little girl.

During the months they lived with Charlie and Rose Shell, Pauline was in the midst of a brief relationship with the Shell's youngest son, Mike, who lived with his wife and three children in a large home near the center of town. Mike's interest in Pauline had come first, and, as a result, he arranged for her to care for his parents, the elder Shells. In fact, Mike had to convince them to allow Pauline to move into their home. They felt they were not really in need of help yet and didn't look forward to having a stranger living with them. But Mike convinced them to give it try, just for a month or two.

"It would be good to have someone in the house," Mike said, "just in case anything happens."

Like most of the men with whom Pauline became involved, Mike Shell desperately wanted to confine her, to put her in a cage so she would be accessible to him, and only him, and dependent on him for support. It was no trouble for the Shells to house Pauline and Marie in two large rooms on the second floor of their old Victorian house. The fact that their son had hired her and was paying her pleased them. It wasn't everyone who had a son so generous and thoughtful.

After years of experience, Pauline knew how to blend in, be helpful, size up what needed to be done, and always consult lest she transgress on someone's eccentricity, and most of these old people had eccentricities to spare. So, without a lot of noise and fuss, the house was soon a little cleaner, a little brighter, a bit more orderly, and nobody's nose was out of joint. The beds were changed more frequently; the laundry was never given a chance to pile up; and pleasing odors wafted from the kitchen and uplifted the spirits of those resting on the day bed in the living room. "We don't really need any help." soon changed to "I don't know how we'd get along without Pauline."

By the time they moved in with the Shells, Marie was four years old. Their lives soon fell into a predictable schedule. During the mornings, Pauline worked around the house, and at noon, she left to do errands, without Marie. At first Pauline left her for two hours, but soon the afternoons extended to four hours. Pauline took the bus at noon and returned on the four o'clock, bringing with her some special treat from the bakery. Mrs. Shell napped all afternoon, and Mr. Shell worked around the house and yard, and little Marie followed him from chore to chore, watching and listening as he explained what he was doing and why. He was glad to have an ear, even a little four year old ear, and Marie was glad to have company, even that of an eighty year old man.

As Marie followed him around from the garage to the cellar to the back yard to the mail box on the corner, she missed her mother. She was scared and she was lonely, and she turned inward to try to find a way to ease her anxiety. Each time she passed the dining room, she touched the glass door knob, not once, but three times in a row. She arranged the perfume bottles and jewelry boxes on the bureau in a pattern and straightened them each time her mother dabbed perfume behind her ear or selected a different ring from the silver box. These rituals made Marie feel better.

The day Mrs. Shell asked Mr. Shell to put the thimbles down where Marie could reach them was the beginning of the real magic.

"Dear, maybe little Marie would like to look at the thimbles. She'll be real careful, won't you, Dearie?"

Marie was almost asleep on the big couch when she heard Mrs. Shell's voice. She sat up quickly and shook her head. She slid down onto the spot on the wooden floor where she often played. Mr. Shell carefully set the glass display case in front of her. It was a clear glass dome which contained four glass shelves, and on each shelf were seven little thimbles, each a different color and shape. Mr. Shell lifted the dome off the wooden base. Heretofore, Marie had seen only glimpses of the thimbles from a distance, but now that they were sitting in front of her, she could see that each contained a beautiful enchanting world right within her reach. But she was afraid to touch them. Marie stared at the thimbles for so long that Mrs. Shell called down gently from her day bed: "Go ahead, Dearie, you can pick them up and look at them. They won't break if you're careful and don't drop them."

And slowly, one by one, Marie carefully picked each thimble up and studied it. A miniature pewter Dutch windmill had tiny sails that spun around. When the transparent cobalt blue thimble was held up to the light, magic rays flitted around the room like soft blue kisses. A white porcelain thimble had a small delicate green hummingbird painted on the side; the hummingbird was drinking from a tiny red tulip. Each thimble contained a magic world that Marie could enter and leave at will. From that day on, as soon as her mother left the house, Marie asked if she could play with the thimbles, and Mr. and Mrs. Shell exchanged amused glances. They'd never in all their lives seen anything like the dear child's fascination with those thimbles. They were becoming very fond of the quiet, gentle presence.

If the afternoon grew late, Marie tried to line up the thimbles in a pattern that would cause her mother to come home.

She placed similar colors in a single row. She set the thimbles with the small blue crystals between the blue ceramic and blue cobalt. On either side of these she placed a thimble with a bird on it. She made a row of the silver thimbles, and in the middle, placed the clear glass one which had no color at all. In front of all the rows, she put her very favorite, a pink lace metal thimble with a cameo on it. The lady on the cameo looked exactly like her mother.

The little girl sat and stared critically at the pattern she had created. If she wasn't completely satisfied, she carefully moved a blue from the back row to the front and put the white ceramic with the tiny painted sailing vessel in the center of a row of flowered thimbles. Then she sat and stared at the new pattern until she was no longer aware of anything but the beautiful little worlds sitting in front of her on the wooden floor. Often her mother's footsteps, or the touch of her mother's hand on her shoulder, awakened Marie from the trance. She turned and hugged her mother's legs.

"I knew you'd be missing me, so I hurried home," Pauline whispered into Marie's hair. And then she called loudly to the old couple, "Did you all have a nice afternoon? Anyone ready for a cup of tea? Anyone hungry for a nice, warm scone with raisins?"

Pauline opened the drapes at the front window and switched on a lamp. Everything brightened up. The Shells shifted in their chairs and took a deep breath of the fresh air that Pauline had brought into the room. They looked forward to hearing the tales she brought back from town. She told them the old factory building at Sixth and Maple was going to be turned into a mall with a dozen little shops. Pauline described the plans for the mall in great detail. Mr. Shell talked about the old factory, and Mrs. Shell said when she was young, she had always wanted to own a shop, but women didn't do things like that in those days.

As Marie sat beside her mother at the table, she felt warm and happy. Marie's magic had brought her mother home, and her mother brought her own kind of magic wherever she went.

It was just in the nick of time that Marie discovered her magic world, for one day soon thereafter, Pauline went off on the twelve o'clock bus and never returned.

It happened on an afternoon in early November. A light snow was beginning to fall and every few minutes, Mr. Shell sent Marie to the front windows to look out and see how much snow had fallen on the street. It became a game which so engrossed Marie's attention that she couldn't concentrate on the thimbles, which were scattered all around on the floor where she was playing. Because she was having such a good time helping Mr. Shell check on the snow, she had mixed the cameo thimble in among the rest. She wasn't ready for her mother to come home yet.

"Little Marie, go see if the sidewalk's covered yet," Mr. Shell called.

The little girl hurried as quickly as she could without running.

"It's not covered," she said in the quiet voice she always had to use around the old people. "The grass is all white, but the sidewalk is wet."

"Good girl," Mr. Shell said, patting gently on the top of her head. "Just a few more minutes and it'll start sticking."

As Marie sat down to play for those few minutes, she heard Mrs. Shell say softly to Mr. Shell: "I hope Pauline doesn't have any trouble getting back in this."

Marie looked down at the cameo, lying on its side among the others and felt a frantic need to get the special thimble in its proper place.

Mr. Shell got up from his chair, folded his newspaper, and walked over and turned the lamp on beside Mrs. Shell. As the room became lighter, the world grew suddenly darker, and Marie shivered. She tried to propel herself into the world she usually entered when she was concentrating on the thimbles, but she was too distracted. She began to arrange the thimbles so quickly that some toppled over. She heard Mr. Shell leave the room, and she heard the front door open. From always having to be considerate of the old people, Marie did not move, jump about, nor talk like a normal child of four. Her purpose was to fade into the old drapes and furniture and not be any trouble. But on this late November afternoon, darkness descended in such an unusual way that Marie was confused. The snow diverted her attention from the thimbles, and the concern in the Shells' voices built up a feeling of insecurity to the point where, when Marie heard the front door open, she leapt up, knocking the thimbles all over the floor, and fairly ran down the hall to the door. Her mother was not there. Mr. Shell had opened the door to check on the snow. When Marie arrived suddenly at his side, her heart beating in her throat, and her whole body aware that something terrible was happening, Mr. Shell said, in his usual calm, deep voice, "Well, Child, I guess I'd better get a broom and sweep off this porch so your mother can get up these steps without breaking a leg."

Marie slipped one arm around Mr. Shell's corduroy pant leg and leaned against him, staring out into the white and gray world. Mr. Shell pushed the door closed and took her little hand in his.

"You go pick your things up," he said, "and then get your coat, and you can come out and help me sweep the porch. Now, hurry," he said, as she clung to his big, warm hand.

Mrs. Shell's voice calling out from the living room caused another shiver to pass through Marie's little body. "Is it too bad for the busses to get through yet, Charles?"

Marie sat down among the thimbles. She knew there was no use in trying to create a pattern. She gently placed them one by one back on the glass shelves, and she wasn't surprised nor upset when she realized that the cameo was not among them. It had rolled under the bookcase, and when she reached under and fished it out, the pretty pink thimble was covered with dust and hair. She cleaned it off on the hem of her dress before she kissed it gently and put it on the shelf with the rest of the collection.

Marie got her coat out of the hall closet and slipped her arms into the cold, silk lining. She stood and watched while Mr. Shell swept the front porch and all six steps leading down to the sidewalk. The street lights had come on and tiny diamonds fell from the bulbs onto the ground, where they sparkled amidst the snow. When Marie looked up at the sky, she saw nothing but a thick dark gray blanket, and it was obvious to the little child that all the stars had fallen onto the street and broken into tiny sparkling fragments of glass.

When Mr. Shell finished sweeping, she followed him into the hall where he took off his coat and hat. As he stomped the snow from his big black boots, he announced, "Girls, it's time for tea." He made the two of them come out and sit at the kitchen table. He got out a jar of jam, a loaf of bread, and the butter dish.

"No treats from town today," he said. "We're going to have to eat emergency rations."

"As Marie put an extra spoonful of sugar in her tea, she looked up to see if anyone was going to caution her, and when no one did, she stirred it round and round, and it was the best cup of tea she had ever drunk in her short little life.

The three sat quietly sipping, putting the tea cup back in the saucer, spreading butter and jam on a slice of bread, folding it over, taking a small bite, taking another sip of tea, waiting. The clock ticked loudly in the adjoining room. Waiting was a mode to which the Shells were accustomed. They spent every day waiting. They lay awake and waited for the dawn. After breakfast, they waited for the mailman, and then they waited for the thud of the newspaper landing on the porch. They waited for lunch, and, after a brief nap, came the most important wait of the day, the wait for tea.

"Almost time for tea," Mrs. Shell would say, but she would mean, "Almost time for Pauline to get back from her errands, almost time for the house to come alive."

Mr. and Mrs. Shell were not of an analytical bent, so they were perhaps able to recognize, but were unable to put into words, the change Pauline and the child had brought into their lives. It was true, as they had told Mike, that they did not need help. Mr. Shell was perfectly capable of taking care of all of Mrs. Shell's needs. He was a little slow, but he had all the time in the world. The two had not looked forward to the arrival of the woman Mike had hired, a woman with a young child, to boot.

"It'll be more trouble than worth," Mr. Shell repeated to Mrs. Shell before Pauline and Marie arrived, but once they were there for a week or so, neither Mr. Shell nor Mrs. Shell could imagine life without them in the house. The waiting was easier now. They were waiting for Pauline, and they had an angel child to keep them company while they waited.

If tea time was bad, supper was worse. Mr. Shell put it off for as long as he could, looking out the front door again and again. Once time had passed for the four o'clock bus, then the five, and then the six, they listened for cars going by slowly in case someone might have given Pauline a lift, but few cars were passing by.

"I guess I'd better be heating something up," Mr. Shell finally announced after one last glance out the front window. As he unwrapped a fat circle of sausage and adjusted the heat under the frying pan, he said to no one in particular, "She'll probably get here by the time this is done, and I bet she'll be starving."

No one had much of an appetite. Some of the sausage was eaten; the rest was put in the refrigerator to wait. Eventually, it was bedtime. Mr. Shell tried to reassure Marie. "Your mother had to stay in town because of the storm," he said. "She'll be home first thing in the morning."

Marie slid deep down under the covers and closed her eyes. Maybe she slept; maybe she didn't. Throughout the night, when she pushed her leg back to feel if her mother's body was on the bed next to her, she felt only the smooth, cold sheet against her skin. And every time she felt the warm tears welling up under her eyelids, she heard her mother's quiet voice whispering from the other side of the bed. "Now remember, Marie, nobody likes to see a little girl cry."

MARIE BECOMES MYA

It is only in recent years that the Port Williams Chronicle runs classified ads for free children. Between an offer to pick your own raspberries, and an ad for cute mixed breed puppies, loving couples are sought to provide care for children in need. They are promised training, support, and reimbursement in exchange for making a difference in a child's life. A little farther down the page, a cookie-baking mother in a cozy Tudor house wants to hear the laughter of a child and is willing to pay, a lot, for such a privilege. These ads did not exist when Pauline Clark disappeared and left Marie in the hands of two old people past eighty.

Marie stayed with the Shells for a few days until their minister found a family whose eldest son had moved out and who were willing to take care of the poor little girl until a more permanent home could be found. Marie, accompanied by a small box of souvenirs and the treasured thimble collection, was passed on from family to family until one enterprising lady petitioned the Methodist Church to provide some support from its social and missionary fund. After that, Marie moved less often. She lived in a total of eleven homes, but that didn't seem unusual to her. After all, she and her mother had moved surely as many as eleven times in the first four years of her life.

In each of the homes was a father, a mother, and often a grand-parent, if not two. Most homes had other children, and there were aunts, uncles and neighbors who befriended the little girl who had no one. These kind people provided Marie with clothing and shoes and saw that she got enough to eat, but her best friend and companion throughout these years was her mother, the beautiful Pauline Clark, frozen at the age of 32, with her dark full head of hair and with a voice so soft and gentle that only Marie could hear it. And only Marie was able to see her mother, wearing any number of bright, fancy dresses, and sometimes sporting an antique garnet ring or a blue sapphire necklace that had remained in Marie's memory. Marie not only talked with her mother, but when she learned to write, she wrote notes to her mother and stuffed them under rocks along the road, and into holes and crannies in trees and buildings around the neighborhood. In spring, she picked small bouquets of wild flowers, arranged them in glass jars, and placed them on a sunny rock or a flat tree stump where her mother could find them. Marie always slept on the far side of the bed so there would be room for her mother to join her in the night.

No one trespassed on Marie's strange little world, and as she grew older, she pulled this strange little world around her like a security blanket and went nowhere without it.

Of course the security blanket was invisible, but not so the armful of books that she carried around with her. From the time she learned to read, Marie had a book in her hand, and she wasn't more than ten years old when she began to comb the library in search of books on magic, and, later, dreams, and then astrology. At first she looked at pictures, but soon she read the books from cover to cover. As she grew older, she found biographies and memoirs of famous and infamous seers and clairvoyants, who then became Marie's best friends and mentors. She took notes and made lists of any books these authors claimed had influenced them. Her reading led her down strange, seldom-trod paths, which sometimes led to nowhere, and sometimes led to new depths of understanding and enlightenment.

Marie was encouraged by everyone except the old librarian, who periodically asked Marie when she was going to start reading something that might improve her mind, and one foster mother who expressed concern that all that reading was going to ruin Marie's eyes. She told Marie she should put her beautiful big eyes to better use. It was time she started noticing the boys. But Marie did not heed such advice.

While other girls her age went to the movies or flirted with boys at the roller skating rink, Marie scanned the 133 section of the public library for books about the occult. While her classmates pierced each other's ears with a sewing needle and a bloody string, Marie read the Rites and Mysteries of the Rosicrucians. While they shopped for prom dresses, Marie plowed through the I Ching and Nostradamus. On Saturday afternoons, when other girls talked on the phone and made plans for the evening, Marie frequented used book stores and flea markets and found esoteric books for a quarter; sometimes she bought an entire armload for two dollars. She collected palmistry books with fine black illustrations, and Tarot books with beautiful colored pictures of fools and knights and queens and swords. On her shelf were books on astrology, hypnotism, and dreams, as well as manuals on how to make ESP work for you, and an easy guide to astrotraveling. She read, reread, took notes, and copied random thoughts into her journals.

She did not at first read with a critical mind, but skimmed superficially, allowing the ideas to play on her subconscious. And while other adolescents were picking and choosing from values of parents and siblings and supplementing these with the latest fads of their peers, Marie was creating a philosophical system all her own. Had she ever tried to write it down, it would have sounded like a flight of ideas. She believed in astrotraveling, ESP, psychokinesis, ghosts, astrology, dreams, hypnotism, the Tarot, and, most of all, she believed in destiny. Fate had given her a map which showed where she was heading. Although the destination could not be changed, the choice of roads and paths she took was her own. The journey itself was important, yet she must always keep the destination in mind. Others her age had no map and would not have looked at one if it had been given to them. They meandered, and at crossroads, made impulsive decisions which were often devastating. Not only did they not end up where they were supposed to, but their trip was filled with worry and confusion and unpleasant experiences.

Marie seemed to sail through life. When she was an adolescent, her air of maturity was attributed to the suffering and deprivation she had endured in her status as an orphan and a foster child. Parents saw their own rebellious and confused teenagers as normal and healthy, and this polite young woman with her strange ideas as an aberration.

Because Marie had grown up without close family ties, she did not have to spend years shedding all the uncomfortable and ill-fitting skins that parents and siblings stitch onto each other. She was free to choose her own spot from which to view the world. She did not have to stand on a spot preselected for her by a caring family. Because her thoughts were not bound down with traditional and conventional notions and beliefs, she was open to anything she could fit into the framework she had created, and that framework was so loose and flexible that it could bend in all directions, and could support a multitude of different ideas. Her philosophy was an eclectic mishmash that she had absorbed from the crackling brown pages of old esoteric books that fate had chosen to place in her hands.

The fact that Marie had no blood relatives was the strangest notion to people who complained endlessly about their demanding old parents, their thoughtless children, and their shiftless brothers. Marie did not miss what she had never had. When she felt lonely, she was able to summon the warm and secure presence of her perfect, undemanding mother.

From the night Pauline disappeared, November 12, 1956, Marie had no idea where her mother actually was, physically. Naturally, she had been told that her mother was in Heaven, watching down on her. Once Pauline Clark was no longer on the scene, people gave her more thought and attention than they had when she was a presence in their daily lives. They began to look a little more deeply at the lovely creature they had so taken for granted, and they found they really didn't know anything about her at all. They speculated on whether she had run off with someone, whether she had perished in the storm, had been a victim of foul play, or had chosen to drown herself in the river, as troubled people sometimes did. Quiet little Marie had overheard some of the speculations and sensed that the river had something to do with her mother's disappearance. As she grew older and was given the freedom to walk about town, she began to spend more and more time sitting beside the river, trying to contact her mother. In time, she selected one particular area just south of the Lark Street Bridge, where a large tree had grown up from the bank and bent itself over the river, forming a comfortable seat. When Marie perched herself on that tree and cleared her mind, she always sensed that her mother was somewhere nearby.

At the time of Pauline's disappearance, Mike Shell was the only person overly concerned with finding Pauline, dead or alive. The storm, which dropped twelve inches of snow on Port Williams in one afternoon, obstructed all efforts of a rescue for several days, and young Mr. Shell was beside himself with worry. The Police understood his concern about the whereabouts of this woman who worked for and lived with his parents and who had left a small child that certainly couldn't remain in the house with two old people who could barely take care of themselves. The Police did the best they could with no clues whatsoever except that Pauline had left the Shells' house on the noon bus that day as usual. The driver remembered dropping her off in front of the Post Office.

He was the last person to see her alive, and he noticed nothing unusual about her behavior.

One officer who questioned the Shells in great detail seemed to be searching for some indication that Pauline Clark was in a mood to do harm to herself. Mr. Shell found that notion preposterous. He couldn't praise Pauline Clark enough. She was a gentle, caring, happy person. She was like a saint, always doing nice things for everyone. She enjoyed life to the fullest, and she adored the child, no question about that.

The Officer was thinking about the river, who seemed to have a taste for beautiful women. During his 23 years on the Force, every unexplained disappearance eventually floated to the surface of the river, decomposed and bloated, and ruined the day of some innocent person fishing along the bank. But he didn't mention these thoughts to this nice old couple who were so concerned about Pauline.

Other than pushing to continue the search for the sake of the child, Mike Shell had nothing to say to the Police about Pauline Clark. He hardly knew her. He had hired her to take care of his parents and he had seen her only now and then when he stopped by to visit with them. She seemed like a nice enough person, and his parents adored her.

The file of Pauline Ann Clark was marked "Missing, November 12, 1956, 12 noon. Last seen in area of Post Office, City. Last known address: 1213 Ridge Avenue, City." Twice the file was taken out when unidentified female bodies were pulled from the river, but neither turned out to be Pauline Clark. The file was put to rest in a crumbling folder in the storage area of the basement of the old court house.

Of course, a dead mother could not take an interest in Marie's long-term future, nor worry about how she would be able to support herself once she finished school. No one told Marie to learn to type or to apply for a nursing scholarship. She didn't seem to be interested in anything like that. But it was commonly known among the high school kids and some of the teachers that Marie Clark did have a particular talent. She had a knack for sensing things. She often knew which team was going to win the football game, and the amazing thing about that was that she knew nothing about football and didn't even go to the games.

"The other team is going to win, but only by a couple of points, two or three, I think." This brought friendly laughter at Marie's naiveté, and when the Bears beat the Eagles, 21-18, a moment of quiet reflection. How in the world did she know that when she doesn't even know how the game is played?

During her junior year, Marie knew she wouldn't have to finish a research paper for Miss Collins on the causes of the Civil War because she sensed that there would be a different history teacher before the end of the term. She mentioned this in passing to a fellow student who was complaining about all the work she had to finish before the break. It became an amusing story that was passed around among the students.

"You're not wasting your time on the Civil War paper, are you? According to Marie's secret source, we're not going to have to turn them in at all, none of us." But didn't they laugh out of the other side of their mouths when Miss Collins was bit by a friendly cat and ended up in the hospital with a super virus. The substitute didn't feel the inclination to collect, read, and correct a few dozen papers on the causes of the Civil War.

"How did you know?" everyone asked Marie.

"I sensed it," was Marie's totally unsatisfactory reply.

To the other students and teachers, Marie's gifts were merely a part of the mosaic of high school life. Joann had a beautiful voice; Chris had musical talent; Michael was a math whiz; Lisa could twirl a baton better than anyone; and Marie had a knack for sensing things. Joann would go on to sing solos at weddings. Chris would start his own band. Michael would go to Penn State on a scholarship. And Lisa would teach baton twirling at a dance studio. What would Marie do with her gift? She would wander around, filled with the knowledge that she had extraordinary powers and that she had the ability to divert people from catastrophes and make their lives better, if only they would listen to her. No school counselor said: "Get yourself a little parlor; hang a fringed curtain in the window; and gaze into your crystal ball." Instead, they handed Marie a very small packet of very small dreams: "Become a check-out clerk at a convenience store. You're good in math." "Take tickets at a movie theater. You'll get to see all the pictures for free." "Be an animal caretaker at the SPCA. You're a compassionate person."

As Marie acted on the package of small dreams she was given, she carried her big dreams tucked inside her in a safe place. The little dreams enabled Marie to support herself while the big dreams expanded, but there were days when she felt she was going to burst at the seams from trying to hold them inside.

By the time Marie Clark was 20, she began to feel she was just marking time. Her dreams had been on hold for much too long, and she decided to do something about it. She began to search for a mentor among the psychics in Port Williams, someone who could guide her and tell her where to go next. There were five such psychics practicing in Port Williams at the time, and Marie gave her choice much deliberation. She eliminated most of them for what appeared to be trivial reasons. "Madame Rita, Licensed Professional Psychic," had a sterile off-putting sign. "Celestina holds the key to your happiness," written with a ballpoint pen on a 3 by 5 card and stuck in a downtown store window, was hokey. A half-page newspaper ad for "The Countess Lara Shevelaski, Professional Palmist," was pretentious. Eventually, Marie chose "Sister Dory, Spiritual Advice," a no-nonsense wooden sign, stuck in the front yard of a small, neat ranch house. Or, perhaps, as she was to learn later, Sister Dory had been chosen for her.

Sister Dory was very different from the rest of the group. She believed that every person has psychic abilities, and she was always on the look-out for people with these special abilities who didn't even know they had them. She thought peace would come to the world only when every living being was in touch with her spiritual dimension and acted accordingly.

As Marie walked up the steps and tapped lightly on the door, she was still trying to decide whether to appear as an ordinary person dropping by for a reading, or whether to be up-front with Sister Dory about her gifts and dreams. It was a decision she never had to make. Sister Dory answered the door after the first tap and looked as though she had been expecting Marie. As they stood for a moment, sizing each other up, Marie could already sense there would be no secrets between them.

"Come right in," Sister Dory said. "I'm more anxious than you are to see what is in those stars."

Sister Dory was a slim lady in her forties with shiny black hair tied on top of her head in a neat, smooth knot. She wore black slacks and a white blouse with a soft royal blue scarf tied loosely around her neck. She was not tall, but she walked like a dancer as she led Marie into a tiny octagonal room off the kitchen and motioned her into one of two chairs that sat on either side of a small round table. In a slow, methodical way, Sister Dory seemed to be rushing. As she closed the door behind them, she pulled a cigarette lighter from her pocket and lit the candle that was sitting in the middle of the table. As the light spread about the little room, she sat down in the chair across from Marie, folded her hands together under chin, and said: "I'm Sister Dory, and you are…"

"Marie Clark."

"You have aquarian eyes, Marie," Sister Dory said, and Marie smiled.

"And you have aquarian hair, my dear," Sister Dory said, running her eyes over Marie's braided, twisted, beaded hair.

She reached across the table and took hold of Marie's hand, which she squeezed and then patted gently. "Now tell me why you think you're here today."

In reply, Marie gave a very matter-of-fact description of her interests and abilities. "I'm pretty thorough with the charts. I'm so-so with the cards. I love the Tarot. I've never done any palmistry. That doesn't interest me at all. What I think I am best at is psychokinesis, and I seem to have a special ability to sense things. I can't explain it."

"That's very impressive," Sister Dory said. "You have no idea how glad I am that you finally arrived. I've been expecting you for a long time. Did you sense that?"

Marie shook her head.

"I didn't know what form you would take," Sister Dory said, "but I've had a recurring dream about you."

She described the dream to Marie in great detail. The time in the dream was always late afternoon, that period when the day has already departed, but the night has not yet arrived. Sister Dory would be alone in the house and not expecting anyone when there would be a soft knock on the door. As she tried to make her way to the door, lamps and coffee tables and waste baskets got in her way. Sometimes her shoe came off; other times, she wouldn't be able to find her glasses. In every dream, by the time she reached the door, the caller was no longer there.

"This afternoon, when I heard you knock, it was just like in the dream, but nothing got in the way, and I was able to get to the door in time to meet you at last," Sister Dory said.

"I wondered why you acted like you knew me," Marie said. "It seemed like you were expecting me."

"I was," Sister Dory said. "Now we have a lot of work to do, Marie. Are you ready for a lot of hard work?"

"Always," Marie said. Until this moment, she had been a strange creature, alone in the world, but now she had at last come upon another creature just like herself. She was ecstatic. They were both ecstatic.

In Marie's world, nothing happened by chance, and her silly efforts to select a mentor were a ruse. The choice had already been made at a higher level. Sister Dory was the best teacher to whom she could have been assigned. Sister Dory was eclectic in her practices, and she knew a great deal about any method or technique available to a professional open to new ideas. And she was ever so pleased to learn of Marie's years of extensive, almost haphazard, excursions into every facet of the occult.

Marie's unofficial apprenticeship with Sister Dory was like a love affair. During her twenty years, Marie had talked intimately with only her dead mother. With Sister Dory, she could not only talk about everything in and out of this world, but she could also talk about the same dead mother whose presence and absence in Marie's life had been so upsetting to most people who knew about it. Sister Dory too had a dead relative that she visited at the river, her loving husband, Charles, who had drowned in a boating accident and whose body had never been recovered. She assured Marie that there was nothing unusual about visiting with her mother in the river. After all, weren't the cemeteries filled on Sunday afternoons with people visiting the dead.

Sister Dory came to love Marie as a friend, as a daughter, and as a gifted colleague, and she was willing to help her in any way she could, but she also got a great deal of satisfaction from vicariously living Marie's dreams. Sister Dory had been in her mid-thirties, married, with no children, when the river one day, for no good reason, decided to take Charles. She had no time to dream and plan. As long as Charles was supporting her, she could limit her readings to a few regulars, but once Charles was gone, she tried to attract more clients. Because she needed money, she was frantic, and, naturally, no new clients came into such a tainted atmosphere. To make matters worse, before this dilemma resolved itself, she spent several years working at a bank, which so sapped her energies that she nearly lost touch with her true calling.

It was only after her mother died and left her the house and a little money that she was able to start up her business in the right way, and ever after, she thrived. She had learned many invaluable lessons which she was more than anxious to share with Marie. How she envied Marie, young and energetic, with no husband, nor children, nor family, to distract and discourage her, and with gifts that amazed even Sister Dory.

Over the next few years, Sister Dory helped her eager enthusiastic student learn to take control of her gifts. She taught her how to center herself, focus her energies, and harmonize her emotions with both the inside and the outside world. She encouraged her to move into one of the mansions on Queen Street, where she could enmesh herself in the historic psychic milieu of the area.

Although Marie willingly followed Sister Dory's advice and counsel, one suggestion caused her a great deal of consternation. Sister Dory told Marie she should choose a different name, something less Christian, something more exotic. Marie's name was the only thing she owned which her mother had given her. She was and always had been Marie Elizabeth Clark. From the depths of her memory, she could conjure up her mother's voice calling her, sometimes sweetly, and sometimes impatiently, "Marie Elizabeth Clark."

Sister Dory could see in Marie's large aquarian eyes the tumult her suggestion had caused. "Do you want to know what my name used to be?" she asked.

Marie shook her head.

"My mother, bless her soul, named me after my two grand-mothers, Bernice and Josephine." Sister Dory smiled. "Could you ever imagine that a person with a name like Bernice Josephine would have special abilities of any sort?"

"I guess not," Marie said.

"I was known all my life as Bernie," Sister Dory said. "When I first decided to try to do some readings, I did just what you did. I visited all the local psychics to pick up tips and see how it was done. And, of course I couldn't help but notice that every one of them had an exotic name. Some went to great lengths to dress in eccentric clothing and look as wild and foreign as they could. Naturally, this bothered me at first. I thought people with names like the Princess Such and Such were obvious fakes. But then I slowly began to realize that it wasn't necessarily so. They were merely doing something which today we would call smart marketing."

The tumult in Marie's eyes subsided, as she sat back in her chair and settled in for one of Sister Dory's long, yet educational, and often interesting, monologs.

"As you'll discover when you get out there, the public doesn't know that you're a person just like them and the difference is that you've allowed yourself to tap into the universal consciousness. They still call us fortune tellers, and when they come for a reading, at least for the first visit, they expect to see an old Gypsy woman with a wart on her nose and a crystal ball sitting on the table."

"And a big simmering pot of toads and bats," Marie added.

"Whatever works," Sister Dory said. "Not to you nor me, but to them, the atmosphere is very important, and your name helps to create that atmosphere."

After the particularly long monolog, Marie walked home and sat in the window with an old ivory hand mirror and tried on new names the same way she might have tried on new hats. She held each out in front of her and admired it. She slipped it on and patted her hair up under it. She adjusted the brim, and then she stood and walked around the room to see if it felt comfortable.

Marie wrapped a maroon voile scarf around her head and whispered: "Countess Helena." She laughed quietly to herself. "The Countess Helena of Port Williams." It was all wrong. How about "Madame Shablatski?" No, she was too young to be Madame. Crystal held her attention for a moment. Crystal—pure, clear, beautiful. But young girls were being named Crystal. If it became a popular name, it would no longer be exotic. While Marie was trying on new names, she became more comfortable with the idea of giving up her old name. By the end of the week, she had settled on Maija, which looked like an exotic form of Marie.

"No one will be able to pronounce it," the practical Sister Dory said, "let alone spell it.:

"The j is silent," Marie said. "It's pronounced Myayah."

"Then let's spell it the way it sounds," Sister Dory said. "M, Y, A. It's simple; it sounds nice; and it has three letters. Everyone can spell it, and everyone will remember it. It's absolutely perfect. How did you come up with it?"

"I found it in one of my old books," Marie said. "In Sanskrit, it means illusion."

"How lovely," Sister Dory said.

Thus, at age 22, an awkward, ordinary Marie Clark became an exotic, mysterious illusion named Mya, but the change was not much in evidence as she continued working at lunch counters and in convenience stores in Port Williams.

As years went by, a less optimistic person would have given up hope of ever finding her niche and would have settled, as most girls did. Working for minimum wage, Mya could never do more than cover her room and board, and even in order to do that, she had to work long hours and give up valuable time that could have been spent in more productive ways. Sister Dory encouraged her to be patient. The money card and the three cards came up again and again. Mya and Sister Dory were both disappointed when Mya's thirtieth birthday came and went with no change in her life, but they did not give up hope, and, in time, their persistence was rewarded, as they knew it would be. It was shortly after Mya's 30th birthday that things began to change. She was offered a job at the Frog with excellent tips and flexible hours; shortly thereafter, the wolf appeared in her dreams; and, somehow, the train of events that led to Tom Harris' move to Port Williams was set into motion.

A stranger looking in on the diorama of Mya's life at this point would have difficulty accepting it as the realization of anyone's dreams. She was a 33 year old, unmarried woman, without a relative in the world, working as a waitress, and living in a shabby old summer house in the middle of nowhere. She didn't even have a car.

But dreams are always customized to suit the dreamer. Thirty-three was a wonderful age. Mya was not old, and she was not young. She was ageless. Unmarried was a state of having to answer to no one. Working as a waitress gave Mya a lot of free time and yet brought in enough money to meet her basic needs. Her earnings were under her control. The size of the tips she received depended on her efficiency, attentiveness, and her ability to give as well as take in the suggestive banter that passed as conversation at the Frog. Most important, the job did not use up valuable emotional energy. The little summer house wasn't in the middle of nowhere; it was on the Angel Estate, a location famous, as well as infamous, for psychic phenomena. What better home for a person who wanted to tap into the historic and cosmic energies of the area. Tom Harris, whom fate had sent to her, was ideal. He was in no position to make any demands on her, and yet he was solidly entrenched in her life and would be accessible to her when her need for him arose. Mya was on top of the world and happier and more productive than she had ever been in her life. All the sparkling bubbles that had been floating around above her head were now descending and about to envelop her in a beautiful blanket of wonderful promises and dreams come true.

LIFE ON THE ENCHANTED ESTATE

As Susan bound lace curtains with tiny strips of pink satin and polished the silver chandelier with cotton balls and q-tips, life in Port Williams dragged along at the same old pace. The new Center for Mankind began serving the hungry daily hot, nutritious meals in the basement of the St. Francis Church. A black bear was hit by a truck on Route 15 north and the driver died in the intensive care unit at the Port Williams Hospital. The County Fair had a record-setting five day high of over 200,000 people, and a home style ham and bean supper, with hot lettuce, was so well attended that the First Baptist Church ran out of ham and had to bring in chicken dinners from the Colonel, which ate into their profits considerably.

Susan rubbed and shined and stitched until chirping birds and gentle shafts of sunlight called her out of doors. Like a tired, underpaid inspector, she toured the grounds. So many things cried out for attention. A lilac bush was slowly being choked to death by dozens of her own children, who stretched up around her on all sides. Because no one had taken the time to transplant the greedy children to homes of their own, they stayed so close to their mother that the sun could no longer reach her branches to give her the nourishment she needed to survive. Anorexic black eyed Susans had taken over the vineyard on the hill behind the house. Susan could seldom find enough pretty ones to put together a small bouquet for the dining table. Remnants of grape vines clung to the arbor, hoping for the return of better times. Susan gently examined the few small clusters of hard green grapes that were struggling to fatten themselves up. She knew nothing about grapevines, so she resolved to ask Mr. Edwards for advice. He knew all there was to know about everything in the world.

At the entrance to the forest sat a white carriage house with the windows boarded up. Someone long ago had created terraced rock gardens on either side of the little house, but, over the years, aggressive daylilies, which had grown to twice their normal height, had chased all the other plants away. Only creepers and moss had enough gumption to cling to their old home. In the yard behind the carriage house, a ragged shroud from an abandoned volley ball net danced in the wind like a long forgotten prayer flag.

Susan sat on the broken dam by the summer house, nursing a cold cup of coffee, and tried to plan the most productive way to get through the day ahead. But the pond drew her attention away from the planning. Green scum shared the water's surface with ailing lily pads, hunks of old bicycle tires, crushed paper milk cartons and soda cans. On either side of the dam, armies of cattails, flanked by skunk cabbage, maneuvered to gain more territory. At first glance, the pond appeared to be devoid of life, other than the wretched, struggling plants, but after she had sat quietly for a few moments, she heard strange little plopping sounds, as tiny frogs dove into the water.

At first it seemed to Susan that all she saw was ruin, but after a spell of sitting and reflecting, with the sun gently warming her shoulders, a cool breeze carrying the scent of pine and hemlock down from the mountains, with background music provided by insects playing string quartets, Susan came to the realization that the ruin was only superficial. In reality, everything was trying to be the best that it could under the circumstances, but it was a difficult task, and help was definitely needed. Everything was pleading for her assistance. In response, she bounded up from the cold cement wall, wiped off the back of her pants, and hurried up to the house to find a hoe, a rake, some clippers, a bushel basket, and a pair of gardening gloves. She forgot all about the need to plan her day.

Mr. Edwards arrived each morning with the back of his truck filled with rakes with broken handles, rusty shovels, boards, dented buckets full of sand and gravel, and wooden tool boxes that had been in his family since his father was a child. His newest acquisition was a chain saw, bought second hand at the Quickie Cash Pawn Shop. Even though Mr. Edwards called it new fangled, the saw was already dented and rusted enough to fit in nicely with the rest of his collection.

Sometimes Susan worked alongside Mr. Edwards, but more often than not, she worked alone. She attacked the unruly shrubs and cleared out the abandoned little flower gardens that had been taken over by iron weed and skunk cabbage and dandelions. She pulled out the grass that was invading the cracks between the flagstones on the patio; she picked up pine cones from beneath the huge friendly trees; and she spent endless time clipping the grapevines and the bushes that grew among the arbors. She walked deep into the forest and collected walnuts, which she stored in the basement. She moved about in a capsule which contained her body, her tangled thoughts, and a little bit of dry September air, warmed with golden sunlight. She was merely a part of the landscape with no more sensations than a clump of moss or a big gray stone. She liked the way she felt.

One afternoon, as she dragged a heavy basket of weeds and clippings across the driveway, she noticed some of the leaves on the small bushes were changing color. When she sat on the stone bench for a few moments' rest, she became aware that the birds were no longer whistling cheerful mating calls and nesting tunes, but were anxiously chirping about plans for their autumn departure. Susan wasn't going anywhere, but instinctively she dug through the trunks and made certain that heavy sweaters and coats were hanging in the hall closet.

All through September and into October, Susan weeded, clipped, raked, walked, and stored. The only sounds that broke the silence of her world were the rhythmic pounding of Mr. Edwards' hammer and the periodic growl of his chain saw. Crows flew overhead; squirrels chattered as they ran up and down fat tree trunks; and insects practiced violins and sometimes flutes in the hot afternoons. After a full day's work, in the evenings, Susan allowed herself to be consumed by satisfaction and fatigue. At dinner she stopped trying to make conversation with Tom. They were both so preoccupied that they ate in silence, each with a magazine beside his or her plate, like a happy, contented, old, married couple.

Susan soon became comfortable with the sounds of all the creatures that shared her new home, or, rather, shared their old home with her. She often paused to try to identify the sources of the cries, the calls, the chirps, the shuffling and the clicking. She was never alone on the estate, and even when it was silent, Susan was aware of a friendly presence hovering about her as she worked.

She first noticed the presence one day when she was balanced high on a ladder, scrubbing the windows on the second floor landing. These were three long vertical stained glass windows with elaborate borders, and in the center of each was a large intricate medallion in shades of pink, yellow, and green. With every swipe of the cloth, Susan watched transparent pastel rays magically break through what had been filthy, opaque glass. As Susan's wet cleaning rag swept across the first medallion, a spontaneous "aaahhh" escaped from her throat. Someone had opened a can of gem stones and tossed them about the room. Susan looked down and saw beams of yellow, pink, and green dancing about on her arms and hands, while others waltzed on the walls and the shiny hardwood floor. Susan moved her hands around to try to catch some of the gem stones, but with their first taste of freedom in decades, they were too swift and elusive to get caught.

Susan was unaware of the "oooohs" and "aaahs" that were escaping her like a small child in a burst of soap bubbles, until she heard "ooohs" and "aaahs" echoing hers, and she paused to listen. For a few magic moments, she was certain it was the voice of Kathleen Angel, expressing her approval. But the flapping sound of bird wings brought her back to reality. What she was hearing was a family of doves who lived under the eaves. She laughed at herself and went on cleaning while the doves continued to coo to her and to each other.

Often it was difficult to distinguish the voices of the doves from the cry of a tiny tree owl who called to Susan as she painted the black wrought iron chairs on the patio. He called to her in a soothing voice, reassuring, approving, and encouraging. The owl asked: "Whoooooo?" and answered his own question with a soft "Youuuuuu." And Susan asked in all sincerity, "Meeeee?" and the owl replied, "Youuuuuu, youuuuuu, youuuuuu," and she believed him.

Mr. Edwards was thrilled to have someone working on the property. He offered the loan of his rickety ladder, his rusty shovel, and other mysterious antique tools he thought she might need to complete her various tasks. When he saw her working near the driveway one afternoon, he called encouragement from the open truck window. "First thing you know them ladies from the Port Williams Garden Club'll be wantin' to come for a tour."

One afternoon, he parked the truck and walked over to offer her a stick of teaberry gum from a flat, warm pack he had been carrying around in his glove box for a few weeks, or months, or years.

"She'd be so pleased to know someone like you was here caring for her things," he said.

As Susan bit into the slightly sticky, very sweet pink gum, a rush of nostalgia for her childhood swept through her.

"She does know," Susan dared to reply, feeling nervous, even though she suspected it was all right to sound crazy in front of Mr. Edwards. He, of all people, wouldn't even notice.

"I'm sure she does," he answered, as he stuffed another pink stick into his mouth and offered the rest of the pack to her.

With a "Thank you ever so much for the nice treat," Susan put the pack into her jacket pocket. She would offer Tom an antique stick of stale gum after dinner tonight; she would warn him that it was not quite as good as the homemade ice cream Mr. Edwards had brought her earlier that week, but it was a bit cleaner and there was no cat hair in it. She would enclose a piece of the gum in a letter to Heather. "Just a little souvenir from Mommy's early childhood that surprisingly turned up here today in Mr. E's glove box. I can never guess what that man is going to come up with next. He is truly a marvel."

One early morning as Susan stepped out the back door to check the weather, Mr. Edwards drove up and stopped on the driveway. He reached into the back of the truck and pulled out a package wrapped in old newspapers.

"What do you have there?" Susan asked. She had grown accustomed to Mr. Edwards' show and tell sessions. He was forever bringing over unusual artifacts that he thought or hoped might interest her.

"Careful you don't get your nice sweater dirty," he said, as he handed the package to her. "Here's a surprise for you."

As she carefully removed the newspaper, she saw a beautiful heavy wooden oval frame, trimmed with tiny round pieces of mother of pearl. But the beautiful frame was not the surprise. An elegant, old fashioned sepia tinted woman looked out from the frame and smiled at Susan through the decades. She was wearing a bonnet with feathers that framed her forehead.

"She's lovely," Susan said, as she wiped her hand across the dusty glass.

"Nobody ever claimed she wasn't beautiful," Mr. Edwards said, and after a short chuckle and a snort, he added, "If I had that much money, I'd be beautiful too."

Susan put her hand on Mr. Edwards' coat sleeve. "You are beautiful," she said, and she meant it. Under the tattered, ragged, unkempt exterior was a gentle, sensitive, and, yes, beautiful soul.

"You're the first person ever claimed that," he snorted, "besides my mother."

Mr. Edwards was blushing, and Susan couldn't help but smile at the idea of Mr. Edwards having a mother.

"I thought maybe you'd like to put her some place in her house," he said. "I wouldn't trust just anybody with her, but I thought you two might become friends."

Susan made direct contact with the woman's eyes. She saw that they were pleading. No, Susan thought, not pleading, more like demanding.

"Are you sure?" Susan asked Mr. Edwards.

He shook his head. "She doesn't like everyone," Mr. Edwards said, "But I know she'll like you. Sure I'm sure."

"I like her," Susan replied, as she clutched the dusty picture frame to her chest. "Thank you ever so much, Mr. Edwards."

"She might need a good cleaning," he said as he crawled back into his truck.

Susan licked a finger and ran it across the glass. "I was thinking the same thing," she said.

As she stood and listened to the sounds of Mr. Edwards' truck heading down Bullfrog Valley Road, Susan held the picture out in front of her. "Welcome home," she whispered to the eyes. "I hope you're going to be pleased with what I've done."

As she carefully cleaned the glass with a soft white napkin, dampened with warm water and a touch of window cleaner, the practical Susan Harris, lately of Laurel Hills, wondered what a frame like this would go for in an antique store, and, for a moment, she entertained the familiar, but unlikely, question of why Mr. Edwards didn't sell a few of these old treasures and get himself a new truck. As she rubbed lemon oil into the dark, smooth wood, she pondered over the realization that it was becoming more and more difficult to think Twentieth Century thoughts while she was living on the Angel Estate.

Once the picture was dry and clean, she carried Kathleen Angel around the house, showing her the new lace curtains, the shiny hardwood floors, the gleaming silver chandeliers, the healthy green plants in the windows, and asked her advice on whether she should use gray, white, or pink for the accessories in their favorite bathroom.

"And now, where would you like to be?" she asked the now friendly eyes and smiling face. "Where is the best place for you?"

Susan closed her eyes and tried to sense if the picture was telling her something. She had a faint sensation that she was getting a message, but she wasn't certain if it was coming from the picture, or from her own subconscious. She listened to the message, nonetheless, and carried the picture up the stairs to her bedroom.

"Is this the place?" Susan asked. She held the picture up so Kathleen Angel could see the lovely room. The windows were covered with white lace curtains; on the floor lay two small antique hooked ivory rugs; from the ceiling hung a smoked glass lampshade with crystal pendants dangling from the bottom; and on the crocheted bedspread were a half dozen small ivory satin pillows in all shapes and sizes, each trimmed with satin ribbons and pearls. The only flaw in the perfect room was a totally bare wall that had been patiently waiting since the day Susan had finished the last curtain. The search for an old fashioned picture for the wall was far down on her list below other more pressing chores. As she stood before the bare wall, holding the oval frame, she smiled once again at the irony of how things worked out in her new life on the enchanted estate. A hook was already in place, waiting for Kathleen. As Susan hung the picture on the wall and adjusted the frame, she saw a faint flicker of a smile on the sepia lips and she knew that Kathleen Angel was pleased.

THE NEW NEIGHBOR

For weeks after the party boys moved out, Mr. Edwards spent his days trying to get the summer house ready for a new tenant. As the burning barrel sent ribbons and puffs of gray smoke high up into the clear blue sky, Mr. Edwards dragged bags of beer cans and whiskey bottles to his truck, which was parked along the driveway by the dam from dawn to sunset.

One bright crisp morning when Susan stepped out onto the patio, something seemed to be missing from the landscape. The dark little house was sleeping quietly in the forest. No trails of smoke were marking up the clear morning sky, and the truck was nowhere to be seen. So Susan decided to walk over and see for herself what kind of progress Mr. Edwards was making.

The summer house was separated from the driveway by a broken cement dam. A narrow walkway had been constructed with long boards placed across the broken sections and held there by faith. As Susan paused at the slippery wet walkway, planning her dangerous journey, she heard the plopping sounds of the little frogs, now a bit bigger, diving into the pond. Each frog left a circular ripple on the surface, but within seconds, the ripples faded out in all directions and the pond became smooth once more. She began to walk cautiously across the dam, pausing after each step. She didn't take a breath until she reached solid ground on the opposite side.

She had never been this close to the little summer house. She paused for a moment and looked around. Three cats lay entangled like snakes on the stone wall, and, like snakes, they slithered away and disappeared into the tall weeds when Susan took a step in their direction. She turned and looked back up at her house on the hill, and for a moment she recaptured the intense hopeful feeling she had the first time she saw the house some three months ago, or was it years, or was it in some other lifetime?

She turned her attention once again to the summer house. The front of the building, which faced the dam, was taken up by a large, dirty, nearly opaque, bay window. The rest of the low, damp structure was literally shoved into the forest with bushes and moss and vines forming a generous border along the ground. When Susan tried to peer through the bay window, she could see nothing but vague shadows in the dark interior. She walked around to the back of the house where a flimsy black wooden screen door hung at an angle. The wood had swollen so that it would not close. Susan pushed it open and reached for the knob on the inside door. It wasn't locked, and she wasn't surprised. She opened the door and walked into a tiny kitchen. Except for distant light coming in the big window in the front room, the place was very dark. All of the windows faced out onto tree trunks and underbrush, where no sunlight penetrated. She headed towards the light, down a long hall, past two small square empty rooms, through a central living area with a fireplace, and out into a large empty room with a built-in bamboo bar and the bay window.

Stepping carefully, Susan made her way closer to the window. The mid-morning sun filtered through the dirty glass, wide rays made up of floating particles of dust and hair. Where the light struck the dumpy, cracked linoleum, circles of dried beer and dirt formed a pattern of ragged gray flowers. Susan sat down on a clean spot where a traveling sun ray hit the floor and stretched her legs out in front of her, leaned her head back and closed her eyes. In her present wardrobe, designed for yard work, she had the freedom to plop down any place on earth when and where the urge struck her.

She wondered what kind of people would live in a dark, gloomy, dirty little house in the forest. She thought of the seven dwarfs, Hansel and Gretel, and even the three bears. People with real lives wouldn't live here. Then she wondered who might move in. For one irrational moment, she found herself hoping it would be a friend. What a silly idea. She smiled to herself. She thought about her friends in Laurel Hills. The incongruity of her old friends existing in the same world as this Grimm's fairy tale house was amusing.

"Nobody I would ever have for a friend would live in a hole like this," she thought. "Some crazy hunter will move in, someone I'll have to worry about and avoid." But she thought of how nice it would be if it were a friend, a stranger who knew nothing about her, a stranger to whom she could tell her story from beginning to end, and it would be a fresh story, and the friend would listen and understand, and maybe have a story of her own to share.

"How ironic," she thought, "to be wishing for a friend." For most of Susan's life, there were more people around than she wanted. But, right at this moment, she thought she needed a friend more than anything in the world. All of her old friends were somewhere else, and Heather had changed from her best friend into a few scribbled notes and a phone call once a week. Susan didn't want to talk on the phone, nor write letters. She wanted to sit across the table from a friend, a cup of coffee in front of each of them, and maybe a plate of cookies. Susan would talk and the friend would listen, and then the friend would get to tell her story, and Susan would listen. The dream made Susan feel a little better. She felt relaxed enough to drop off to sleep.

She had no idea how long she had been sleeping when she was awakened by a husky female voice. "Oh dear, I thought for a moment I'd come upon the Ghost."

Susan looked up and saw a very tall woman that she had never seen before in her life. She blinked her eyes and looked around and tried to remember where she was.

The woman smiled down at her. "The sun has such healing powers," she said. "How many times in my life when things were so bad I thought I couldn't go on, a little fling with a friendly sunburst picked me right up and kept me going."

Susan tried to clear her sleepy brain. She sat up straight and looked at the woman. She decided she wasn't dreaming. This woman was real.

"Who are you? Susan asked, but when she realized she sounded rude, she softened her voice. "Are you looking for someone?"

The woman had an honest, rather common, wide face, with light green eyes. "I'm supposed to meet Mr. Edwards here this morning. I'm thinking of renting this place." She reached down and gave Susan her hand. "I'm Mya," she said, "Mya Clark." She nodded at the wall behind Susan, and she opened her mouth and made a series of expressions that Susan read as totally perplexed, disgusted, and amused. "Do you think Mr. Edwards would mind if I paint over this monstrosity?" she asked.

Susan looked behind her to see what was causing the reaction. She couldn't believe that she herself had not noticed that her head had been resting against a grotesque mural that covered the entire wall. It looked like a copy of a record album cover with the head of a skeleton in the center and long, bloody tendrils reaching out from it in all directions. Susan stood up quickly and smacked the dust off the back of her pants. "Yuck," she said. "I didn't even notice that. No doubt it was the work of the party boys."

She turned to Mya, who was laughing at her reaction. "I'm Susan," she said. "I live up in the big house."

Mya took Susan's hand in hers, held it for a moment while she looked directly into Susan's face with her big, clear green eyes. They were light, gray-green, the color of marbles from Susan's childhood.

"Well then, we'll be neighbors," Mya said, "And friends. I'm Aquarius, and you?"

"Libra," Susan said.

"Libra and Aquarius," Mya said. "Then we'll be the best of friends."

"A friend, just like that, just by wishing," Susan thought. "This truly is a magical place."

The thought of having a close friend made Susan warm all over. Now there would be someone to have coffee with in the morning before she started her day, someone to walk back into the woods with in the late afternoons when there was a half-hour to kill before time to start dinner. And, most important, someone to talk with, someone who had not heard all of her stories, someone to tell about Heather. It was only when a friend appeared that Susan realized how much she had been missing one.

But this strange lady looked like no friend Susan would ever have. She was wearing a long, navy blue gauze skirt with gold flecks, a white peasant blouse, thick leather sandals, several necklaces, bangle bracelets, and one long crystal earring that hung down to her right shoulder, and in her left ear, a small gold hoop. Her light brown hair was piled atop her head in a complicated arrangement of tiny braids, curls and twists, with gold ribbons intertwined and a large gold clip placed at an angle across the back of her head. She seemed to be incredibly tall. As if to show herself off, Mya made a deliberate circle around the room, running her hand along the smooth bamboo railing on the bar, pulling at a chain that turned the overhead light on, and then slipping behind the semi-circular bar, she cupped her chin in her hands and stared across at Susan.

"I feel right at home," she laughed. "What'll you have, Missy?"

Susan smiled. This strange lady wanted to play pretend. "Let me think," Susan replied. "You know, I don't usually drink this early in the day."

Mya looked up at an imaginary clock on the wall. "It's six p.m. here in the bar," she said. "Now let me guess what you'll have." Looking behind her at the empty shelves that contained imaginary liquor bottles, Mya pointed at each one in turn. "Not that. No, not that one." She paused at one bottle and pretended to pick it up in her hand and read the label. She looked at Susan and she looked down at the imaginary bottle and shook her head. "You're a tricky one to figure," Mya said.

Susan assumed a smug, secretive aspect. She wasn't going to give out any hints.

Once more Mya looked from the imaginary bottle in her hand to Susan. Her face took on a very serious demeanor, as though she was deep in thought. With her mouth closed, her eyelids partially covering her big eyes, she looked exotic and mysterious, rather than common, as Susan had at first thought.

With a flat affect, Mya said. "You don't drink it straight. Of course not. " And the serious Mya disappeared and the friendly one was back, reaching for an imaginary glass, slicing an imaginary lemon, and opening an imaginary bottle of soda that foamed all over the bar. Mya wiped it up with an imaginary wet rag. "I'm such a slob," she said. With a broad smile, she placed the imaginary drink on the bar in front of Susan.

"Oooops, wait," she said, as she reached under the bar for an imaginary jar, had imaginary trouble opening the lid, pulled out one imaginary cherry by the stem and put it on top of the imaginary drink.

"You always have it with a cherry," she said, "and if you are out of cherries, you put an orange slice on the side of the glass. But, as you can see," she reached both arms out to the sides, "I am totally out of oranges, so lucky I found that jar of cherries. And, in a lower voice, "I can't promise they were purchased any time in this century, but I don't think they ever go bad."

Susan felt a little embarrassed that this totally uninhibited lady was putting on such a show for her, but when Mya opened the imaginary jar of cherries, Susan suddenly felt it was not a game at all. Susan didn't drink often, but when she went to fix herself a drink, the first thing she checked for was the jar of cherries. If there were no cherries left, she wouldn't bother to make the drink. When she was a little girl, her mother always gave her the cherry from her drink, and when Heather was a child, she would beg for the cherry from Susan's drink, and when Susan made a non-alcoholic big-people drink for Heather, a handful of cherries was always the main ingredient.

"Well, aren't you going to try it? Mya asked, holding the imaginary liquor bottle in her hand. "If it's not strong enough, I can add more."

Susan was hesitant to ask what the drink was because she was afraid that she already knew that it would be her one and only favorite drink, a Vodka Collins.

"It's a Vodka Collins," Mya announced, as though she was reading Susan's mind. "Three ice cubes, a dash of lemon juice, a tablespoon of sugar, a jigger of vodka, two jiggers of soda water, and a cherry."

"It's perfect," Susan said, taking a long, pretend sip from the glass and carefully setting it back on the bar. "How did you do it?"

"I waitress up at the Bullfrog and I often have to help out at the bar. Everyone says I make great drinks," Mya explained.

"No, I mean, how did you know what I always drink?" Susan asked. "I haven't drunk anything besides a Vodka Collins for at least 15 years. It's the only drink I've ever liked. How did you know that?"

"I sensed it," Mya said. "I'm good at sensing things."

Susan felt a chill go down her spine. She had never met anyone who was good at sensing things. Mya's imaginary drink was Susan's first direct experience with something that couldn't be explained away, and it was unnerving.

"Imagine how good it will be when I use the real stuff," Mya said, as she came out from behind the bar and pressed her face close to the window. "Nice view," she said. She stepped across the room, making flapping sounds on the floor, then lifted the corner of the linoleum near the wall and looked at the floor underneath. "Nice hardwood floor," she said. She then went back to the bar and leaned on her elbows once again.

"You know," she said. "This place is basically in pretty good shape. It has potential. It just needs some cosmetic changes."

"Don't we all?" Susan asked, and Mya replied, "Nope. Cosmetic won't do for humans. It's got to be much deeper than that."

She unlocked the front door and pushed it open and the room suddenly turned light and cheerful. She stood in the doorway, looking out at the world. "I'm going to take it," she said. "It's absolutely perfect for what I want."

Susan was afraid to ask what that might be. "I'm glad," she said. "I was afraid some old hunter was going to move in and I was going to have to fear for my life every time I walked out the door."

"And wear safety orange to the mail box," Mya laughed. "By the way," she added. "Once I'm in here, we'll have to work on Mr. Edwards to get rid of those hunters. You are aware, I am sure, that he leases a big hunk of this forest to a hunting club, aren't you?"

"No," Susan said. "I don't think he ever mentioned it, or at least I haven't picked up on it from any of his conversations. That's horrible."

"It's worse than horrible. The killing is a major cause of the bad karma around this place. Hunting those poor animals, and things like that disgusting mural, and all the other destructive stuff that goes on, well, once that ends, things could be beautiful around here again," Mya said. "Just wait and see."

As they stepped out into the sunlight, Mya stretched her arms up to the sky. "I am going to love it here," she announced in a voice so loud that it echoed from the dam, the creek, and the bridge, and made the little frogs jump into the pond, and Susan felt a shiver slide down her back.

Mya stood for several seconds in the sunlight with her head leaning back on her shoulders, her eyes closed, and her arms stretching out and reaching up to the clear, blue morning sky. Susan was amazed at how tall Mya was. She was probably even taller than Tom. As Susan studied this unusual woman, she felt an intense curiosity about her. At first glance, she looked like someone who had little money and had pulled together a bunch of old clothes and cheap jewelry from the local thrift store, maybe like a hippie from the Sixties. In the morning sunlight her hair was flecked with gold and copper, and there were even more blue crystal beads and ribbons intertwined among the braids and curls than Susan had noticed in the dark room. Although she prided herself on her ability to size people up, Mya was not an easy one to figure out. She looked poor, but she didn't act poor. She had a confident air about her. And her attire, although casual and worn, was not haphazard. The gold ribbons in the hair picked up the gold flecks in the skirt, and the white blouse had tiny gold threads running through the bodice. Susan looked down the driveway to see if she could see Mya's car parked anywhere. The kind of car she drove would help Susan figure her out, but there were no cars parked on either side of the bridge as far as she could see.

As Mya relaxed her posture and shook her head and seemed to come back down to earth, Susan asked, "Where'd you park your car?"

"I don't have a car," Mya said. "I don't drive."

"You don't drive?" Susan asked. "You don't know how to drive?"

"Nope, I walk," Mya said. "That's when I do my best thinking, recharge my batteries, commune with Mother Earth."

"I never met anyone who didn't drive," Susan said, unable to accept yet another unbelievable aspect of this enigmatic figure smiling down at her.

Mya shrugged. "Sometimes I cheat and ride the bus," she said.

She turned and extended her hand to Susan. "I don't know what happened to Mr. Edwards," she said. "I'll walk down in the direction of his house and see if I run into him. He's probably on his way."

"Maybe his truck broke down," Susan said. "There's always a good possibility of that happening."

Mya held Susan's hand gently in hers. She closed her eyes for a moment. Susan watched and waited, once again unable to even fathom what was going on. Then Mya opened her eyes and shook her head. "No, the truck's okay," she said. "I think he's helping his brother with something." With one last squeeze, she dropped Susan's hand and turned and walked down across the dam, where she paused, looked back, gave a casual wave, and called, "Later, Friend," before continuing down the driveway.

As Susan watched her walk across the slippery boards with her long, sure strides, and then down the driveway and across the bridge, she had a scary feeling that her wish had been granted, that she now had a friend, and that this friend was not like any friend she had ever known before, and that was both exciting and scary.

Her first problem was how to tell Tom about their new neighbor. Like many married couples, Susan and Tom conversed in a pattern that was as familiar as an old melody. When Susan heard the first note, she could hum the entire song, verses and chorus. She wanted to avoid the old song when she told Tom about the new neighbor. She wanted him to like Mya. She reminded herself to be careful not to mention the imaginary drink. Tom was intolerant of weirdos.

He was of course going to ask what Mya did for a living. What people did was very important to Tom. A waitress would never do. Susan decided to say she didn't know what Mya did for a living. Tom would ask if she was married, or divorced, and whether she had children. Susan had not thought to ask, but she felt certain Mya was not married, nor divorced. She seemed too self-contained.

As Susan planned her conversation with Tom, she analyzed Mya. Her first impression was that Mya was a happy human being. She was so positive about everything in the little house. Susan couldn't recall one complaint nor criticism. Mya looked at the filthy, cracked linoleum and saw the nice hardwood floor underneath. She looked through a dirty window that had not been cleaned for years, and said, "Nice view." The thought of Mya's optimistic, happy attitude made Susan feel the need to be positive. She didn't want to concentrate on the fact that Mya was a waitress, didn't own a car, and dressed like a Gypsy. She thought about Mya's pretty hair and the funny faces she made as she looked at the mural. She felt a need to make Tom like Mya.

As she chopped green peppers, onions, mushrooms, and broccoli for a stir-fry dinner, Susan missed Heather. Heather and she would have discussed and analyzed this strange new friend and fabricated an interesting past for her. They would have changed her from a waitress into an enchantress, weaving magic spells in a little cottage in the forest. They would have given her a funny name and giggled like teenagers. Heather would have tried to help Susan figure her out, but, for the moment, Heather was thousands of miles away, and Susan was stuck with only Tom, and he had no imagination at all.

"It looks like we're going to have a new neighbor," Susan said calmly, as she handed him a bottle of soy sauce.

"That's nice," Tom said, as he gently shook the bottle and sprinkled brown liquid generously over his rice.

Tom seemed interested, so Susan continued. "It's a woman," she said. "I met her this morning."

"What's she like?" Tom asked. "Old? Young? Fat? Ugly? Beautiful, I hope? All of the above?"

"None of the above," Susan said. "I hate to disappoint you." She began to describe Mya, and she tried to say nothing that would make her sound strange. She stuck to the physical.

"She's sort of pretty. I mean, some people might think she's pretty," Susan said. "She's incredibly tall. She's probably taller than you."

"Sounds like an Amazon," Tom said.

"Nope," Susan corrected him. "She's not masculine at all. She's kind of feminine, but in an unusual sort of way. I mean, she's aaah." Susan was at a loss for words.

"Did you talk to her at all?" Tom asked. He waited nervously for her reply.

"Not much," Susan said. "We just introduced ourselves. Her name is Mya Clark. Isn't that pretty? Mya. I don't think I've ever heard that name before."

Tom felt relief. So Mya hadn't mentioned that she knew him. Mya was discreet; Tom thought she would be.

As Tom and Susan made efforts not to communicate as they talked and ate, they were interrupted by an apparition outside the dining room window. It was Mr. Edwards, gesturing to them that he had something to say. Susan let him in the front door, and he stood in the hallway, looking into the dining room.

"Don't want to interrupt your nice meal," he said. "Just come by to tell you folks you'll be getting a new neighbor, nice young woman, a Clark, born and raised around here, hard-working young thing, up at the Frog with that crowd til' all hours and that ain't easy work I bet with all them drunks."

He smiled as though he was trying to contain within himself an amusing secret. "You're goin' a have to watch yourselves around her, though, cause she can read minds. She'll be a nice change from those last young fellas and all that commotion."

Susan had to laugh to herself. In one run-on sentence, Mr. Edwards had spilled all the information she had been so carefully keeping from Tom. He had turned her pretty, new neighbor into a mind-reading kook. But when she saw Tom smiling at her across the table, she knew that he had not understood, nor believed, half of what Mr. Edwards had said.

"Takes all kinds," Tom said. He was thinking of his first martini at the Frog.

"Is she really a clairvoyant?" Susan asked, thinking of her Vodka Collins.

Mr. Edwards shook his head and smiled. He was thinking of Pauline Clark's Mistake. "Her real name's Marie Clark," he said quietly, as though he was revealing a secret.

"Marie?" Tom and Susan both asked at once.

"She don't go by her real name," Mr. Edwards said. "She picked one of them fortune teller names, but I still think of her as little Marie Clark, Pauline Clark's Mistake."

As Susan and Tom waited for Mr. Edwards to elaborate, he moved onto another subject. "I'll let you folks finish your nice dinner," he said. "She'll be moving in next week sometime. I got a lot of work to do over at that place. Them party fellas left a mess. Worse than usual."

Tom and Susan both got up from the table and accompanied Mr. Edwards to the door, where he paused and stood with his hand on the knob. He looked pensive, and they waited patiently and nervously to hear what more he had to say.

"She was the first one I remember the river takin'. I'm sure there were lots of others, but she's the first one I can recall."

Tom looked bewildered, and Susan assumed an appropriately sympathetic look that one would have when hearing about a drowning. But neither had any idea who it was the river had taken.

"Do you mean Mrs. Angel?" Susan asked. Lots of people thought Mrs. Angel had died in the river.

"Oh, no, I don't think the river got her. If it did, it sure got a mouthful," he snorted. "I was talkin' about Marie Clark's mother, Pauline. Beautiful woman."

"How tragic," Susan said, but before she could ask for any details about the drowning, Mr. Edwards moved onto another topic.

"You can visit with that other one any time you like," he said, as he jerked his head over his right shoulder. "She's buried right up there in the little cemetery in the woods." He turned the knob, opened the door, and stepped out onto the patio. He looked back at Susan and Tom and grinned, not at them, but at some silly reflection that was forming in his busy mind. "She's buried up there when she's not floating around, poking her nose in everyone's business," he said.

With a "Night, folks," he snorted his way out to his truck.

"Nothing like a little touch of local color with your meal," Tom said, as he sat back down at the table and attacked his now cold pile of rice.

Later that evening, Susan sat down and wrote a long letter to Heather. She described the new neighbor, who was surely an enchantress; the magic house in the forest; and the infamous river that takes people anytime she feels the urge. "I'll send pictures," she promised. "If I'm lucky, and if I can find some very fast film, maybe I'll get one of the Ghost. Mr. E. claims she's very beautiful and that she resembles me. P.S.: Did I tell you he gets his eye glasses free from a box at the Salvation Army store?"

MRS. ANGEL'S GHOST

The infamous ghost who had assumed the impossible task of keeping the natives of Port Williams on their toes, was none other than Kathleen Hannigan Angel, wife of Lloyd Angel, the 19th Century lumber baron and philanthropist who was responsible for most of the churches and public buildings in Port Williams, and whose portrait still hangs in the main hall of the town library. Although parks, streets, and elementary schools were named for this illustrious and generous man, in truth, his fame was based on the charisma of his beautiful and influential wife. Kathleen Angel's power was such that her opinions and ideas were passed down for years like the Ten Commandments and the Gettysburg Address. To both believers and non-believers, even her ghost demanded respect. No one ever referred to her as "The Ghost," but always formally as "Mrs. Angel's Ghost." Although she had been dead for over seventy years, Kathleen Angel was one of Port Williams' most prominent citizens.

Like his father before him, Mr. Edwards was so accustomed to following Kathleen Angel's wishes that he did not find it at all strange to blame her, consult with her, and talk about her like she was a woman living next door and not someone who supposedly had departed this earth decades ago.

Few listened to what Mr. Edwards had to say. No one took the time nor effort to follow his long-winded tales, composed of clichés, connected to non sequiturs and run-on sentences, and accentuated with snorts, coughs and loud guffaws provoked by his own bad jokes. If Mr. Edwards was asked a simple question, he did not answer the simple question, but responded in great detail to a multitude of questions that no one had any intention of asking. The most anyone knew about Mr. Edwards' thoughts were a few choice themes that he played so frequently that bits of the melodies stuck in the mind of anyone who had spent time listening, which everyone tried not to do if he could help it.

From the time he was a child, he had heard his own father, who spoke a similar language, talk about what SHE would or would not like to have done around the place, what color SHE liked the dining room to be painted, and whether SHE would mind if he cut down the Japanese maple that was growing too close to the bathroom window. And when his father passed away and Mr. Edwards assumed ownership of the Estate, he continued to respect HER wishes. Mr. Edwards was not an analytical man, but he was wise enough to pay attention to cause and effect.

One summer, he decided to do what was for him extensive landscaping. He cut down a row of forsythia bushes that were past their prime. There was a time when they waved paper-thin yellow blossoms in profusion along the driveway between the house and the creek. They provided endless bouquets that welcomed spring into the house long before other flowers were ready to make their seasonal debut. But, from lack of attention and care, over the decades they had grown large and unruly. Instead of bright blossoms, they produced wayward vines and tendrils, which hung onto the driveway and tried to scratch passing cars with their long fingernails.

Mr. Edwards himself didn't know why he chose this project over dozens of more pressing ones, but he was soon sorry he had. Within days, the entire valley was blessed with spring squalls, the likes of which had never been recorded in Mr. Edwards' extensive mental history of the area's weather patterns. Throughout most of June and into July, thunder and lightning storms roared and flashed across the valley with gales so strong that trees were downed and family gardens destroyed for the season.

"SHE's got some temper," Mr. Edwards muttered as he replanted forsythia bushes all along the driveway. Within a few weeks, autumn arrived with the most beautiful Indian summer on record, and the following spring, yellow blossoms waved profusely in the air, gaily diverting the eye from the genteel shabbiness of the estate.

The main house was between tenants when Mr. Edwards made the unfortunate decision to paint the dining room a new color. Why did he choose the dining room when all seventeen rooms needed painting? Perhaps it was the fact that the dining room, because of the wainscoting, built-in French cupboards and elaborate French doors and windows, had very little wall surface. Mr. Edwards preferred projects that he could start and finish in one fell swoop, although he usually found the starting much easier than the finishing.

For the dining room, Kathleen Angel had chosen what today might be called charcoal blue, a gray-blue which appeared to pull the sky right in through the windows, and which accentuated the silver sconces on the walls, as well as the silver chandelier which hung from the center of the ceiling. After months of searching, Kathleen had found a lovely carpet to perfect the room, a large Bokharas, deep burgundy and gray with just a smattering of intricate blue floral patterns along the border. The carpet was large enough to accommodate a dining table for twelve, yet allowed for a border of oak floors to show on all sides. That carpet had of course been one of the first things to disappear after Lloyd's death in 1931. Tenants thereafter covered the floor with pieces of linoleum and old rag rugs, and later with remnants of bright green indoor-outdoor carpet.

Mr. Edwards first looked in the basement among the cans of paint that had been collecting there over the years. There were some twenty or thirty dented, rusted gallon cans, most marked with drips and patches of the color they once contained. Mr. Edwards was pleased to see a can covered with long drips of the special blue of the dining room, but when he picked it up, he found that it was nearly empty. He was forced to make a run to the paint store, bringing the blue can along with every intention of having some new paint mixed to match the old. That's how his father had always done it, and that's how Mr. Edwards had always done it heretofore. He had no intention of altering the way something had always been done. That was against his nature.

While the clerk was involved in a lengthy phone conversation about the disadvantages of dipping furniture to remove the varnish, Mr. Edwards checked through the paint cans on the "Reduced for Quick Sale" table, and, in this moment of carelessness, temptation led him astray. He got swept away by the idea of a bargain, and instead of having the paint custom-mixed at $13.99 per gallon, he picked up a can of Spring Green #1641 at $4.99. There was only one gallon can of Spring Green #1641 on the table, but Mr. Edwards was sure that one gallon would be more than enough to cover the entire dining room.

Later that morning, with the first track of the roller across the wall, Mr. Edwards realized that one coat of the light green was not going to completely cover the blue wall. He was forced to spend the next day putting on a second coat, which looked better, but, unfortunately, Mr. Edwards ran out of paint with several square feet of wall left. Of course the clerk said he could mix more of the Spring Green #1641, but store policy did not allow custom mixing of quantities less than a gallon, and special mixed paint could not be sold at the sale price.

With a second gallon of Spring Green #1641, at more than triple the price of the original can, Mr. Edwards finished painting the room. When he first stepped back to glance at his work, he had to admit aloud that it didn't look too bad. The green seemed to pull the trees and the lawn into the room. He went to bed tired and pleased, but on the following morning, he found that the paint had not yet dried. Despite the fact that he kept the windows open for days, the walls remained sticky to the touch. Weeks later, when they finally did dry, there were several spots where a little hint of blue peeked through the green, just enough to remind Mr. Edwards of his folly. It took longer to paint that one little room than it would have taken to paint the entire second floor, but Mr. Edwards never did get to that project, which had been moving steadily down his list for over a decade.

No spectacular means were used to keep Mr. Edwards on his toes, only minor unpleasant reactions, like those he experienced when he chose the wrong paint, or cut down the wrong plants, or did anything slightly different that might upset HER. Whether he believed or didn't believe wasn't the issue. He did what he had to do to keep from having to do more than he wanted to do.

Mr. Edwards was not the only one influenced by Mrs. Angel's Ghost. Generations of Port Williams natives claimed to have seen something, or heard something, or sensed something as they drove down Bullfrog Valley Road near the Angel Estate. A favorite pastime of the teenagers was to first spend an evening drinking beer, and then to pile eight or nine kids into a car and drive down Bullfrog Valley Road late at night with the car windows tightly closed and the doors locked, hoping to see something, and by "something," they meant Mrs. Angel's Ghost. Some had seen her near the gray stone bridge, where moonlight and water tended to create apparitions. Others had seen her near the Angel graveyard, some distance down the road from the bridge. At the first telling, the impressions were vague and out of focus. They saw something weird, like something really strange and scary, but the more the story was repeated, the clearer the image became, as though fingers were adjusting the focus knob on the projector as they talked.

With years of remembering and focusing, the indistinct blur eventually became a beautiful woman with dark hair in a billowy, white dress, like a wedding dress. For the fence-sitters, the wedding dress made it all the more believable. A wedding day must be the point at which a woman's dreams are at their most expansive, and the time in her life when a woman is most beautiful. There were others, of course, who thought that a woman was most beautiful when she was pregnant, but no one was ever drunk enough, nor imaginative enough, to have seen a pregnant ghost.

For decades, trying to catch sight of Mrs. Angel's Ghost was a rite of passage in Port Williams. Even though adults no longer drove by the graveyard, they recalled clearly when they had, and they also distinctly remembered what they had seen, or not seen, or thought they had seen. They were pleased that their offspring were sharing the same experience. Mrs. Angel's Ghost was just one of the many myths that provided Port Williams with a sense of community.

Mya had never driven around in cars with other teenagers, but she had listened with great interest and disgust to their tales. She could not understand why anyone would deliberately seek out and torment a soul already in such agony that it could not rest in death, even after seventy years.

No one knew for certain where Kathleen Angel lay buried. A tombstone in the Angel cemetery bore her name, but she was not buried there. The tombstone was erected five years after her death was made official. Like the parlor game of gossip, Kathleen's demise changed with the telling over the years, and there were any number of elaborate and apparently accurate versions: she was killed in a train wreck in Austria; she hanged herself from a beam in the carriage house with a long, blue, silk scarf; or she threw herself off the Lark Street Bridge in a fit of hysteria. Others believed that she ran off with an Italian opera tenor who was passing through town; that she died in childbirth; or that Lloyd Angel murdered her in a fit of rage, but, because of his wealth and influence, was never brought to trial.

Like most famous people, the Kathleen Angel who came down through history never existed. Even the Kathleen Angel who built the Estate and reigned over Port Williams society never existed anywhere but in other people's imaginations. A handful of rumors, a few wild speculations, and a couple of facts were mixed together to create a romantic tale of love, wealth, and happiness, or unhappiness, depending. When Kathleen was alive, the proof was right before their eyes. No one had more expensive horses, more beautiful dresses and jewelry, and no one had a wealthier, more handsome, nor more devoted husband. No one had a home as grand, nor gave parties as extravagant. Kathleen Angel had it all.

Long after Kathleen Angel disappeared bodily from Port Williams, she continued to be an influence. The Opera House gave an annual gala performance in her memory; a wing at the Port Williams Hospital was named for her; and stained glass windows in several churches were dedicated to her devotion and care for the downtrodden of Port Williams.

It would be difficult to explain how and when Kathleen changed from an idealized romantic historical figure into a vengeful ghost, who not only openly haunted the Angel Estate and its neighboring properties, but caused untold destruction in the town. The best explanation is that a number of coincidental disasters occurred at about the time Lloyd Angel himself was laid to rest in 1931.

The disasters could have happened anywhere at any time. For instance, someone decided to build a tavern on a piece of property adjoining the Angel Estate. Twice the structure burned while it was being built. It was late fall, and the woods were dry. Then, as now, some workmen were careless. Someone said in jest that no one would have dared to build a tavern so close to the Angel property when Kathleen was alive. After the second blaze, another person said, "Someone don't want us to build a tavern here," and everyone had an idea who that someone might be.

One of the first owners of the Angel Estate after Lloyd's death decided to lease a large parcel of the estate to a hunting club. For the first time since the estate was created, men stomped through the forest, smoking and swearing and carrying guns, and the sound of gunpowder blasts rang in the air on sunny autumn afternoons. Several bizarre hunting accidents occurred during the first season. One man shot his buddy's hand off when he waved at him. He thought the gray glove was a squirrel. Another hunter's best dog came yelping to him with his back leg dragging behind, connected only by a piece of bloody skin. As the dog looked up in agony, his owner had no choice but to put it out of its misery. To make matters worse, game was scarce that year, so all the bother wasn't worth a couple of wormy rabbits and a tough old deer with a broken rack not worth saving. Once again, people said: "Someone don't want no huntin' up there. Someone's lookin' out after them animals." And everyone knew exactly who that someone was.

Although the river had flooded every few years since anyone could remember, suddenly the floods were blamed on Mrs. Angel's Ghost. And the fires that had always been common in the dry season were now blamed on Mrs. Angel's Ghost. At first the blame seemed to be in jest, but over time, people began to think there must be some truth in rumors that persisted for decades.

Wouldn't Kathleen Angel have been surprised to hear somebody in the Twentieth Century accusing her of poisoning the family dog, causing a television to go on the blink, or kidnapping a little boy from the Third Street Car Wash. In truth, Kathleen was just an ordinary woman who made some very wise choices and, as a result, managed to do very well in life. And who can say why anyone manages to do well in life? Maybe she was born lucky; perhaps it was because she was beautiful, or wise, or driven. Or, perhaps it was just another classic case of synchronicity at work.

LET ME INTRODUCE YOU TO
KATHLEEN HANNIGAN

Kathleen was the third daughter of an Irish drunk named Frank Hannigan. Although she preceded the term by almost a century, clinically, she was the child of an alcoholic, a COA. Since alcoholism was so prevalent in the Irish families in Port Williams, there was an abundance of COAs in the community. In Kathleen's family alone, there were eight children: five daughters and three sons. Her father was a working drunk; her mother, Jennie, was the co-dependent, or enabler, who scrubbed, scrimped, and performed miracles to keep the family alive and intact. Her dream was to see that her daughters didn't end up like she had and that her sons not follow in their father's staggering footsteps.

Jennie herself had once had dreams and prospects, until she met a prospect with a dream and the two sailed off for America. From the beginning, Jennie had trouble adjusting to the ship that swayed and wallowed its way across the stormy Atlantic, but she thought the feeling would be only temporary. She blamed it on the rough seas. Little did she know that rough seas are not confined to water and that her entire life would be as tumultuous as the voyage. The passage was a mere taste of what was to come. She almost got her footing when the deck shifted, and as she grasped onto the railing, her foot slipped out from under her and she landed on the deck. When she got herself upright and began to brush her skirt down flat, a huge wave washed across the deck and left her drenched. She felt like a drunk might feel, trying to make it up an unlit narrow staircase to his bed at four o'clock in the morning after a night at the pub.

Jennie Hannigan soon learned a lot about drunks because it turned out she had married one. She hadn't actually married a drunk, but by six years and three children into the marriage, he was well on his way. By eight children and 15 years into the marriage, he was a certified drunk.

At first Jennie coddled, begged, and teased to no avail. By the time she accepted the reality that, like his father and several of his uncles and brothers, Frank was a hopeless drunk, Jennie Hannigan became a survivor. Once she accepted the fact that she was never going to be able to depend on Frank for anything, she felt better. By not expecting anything, she was never disappointed, and she stopped slipping all over the deck.

As the years went by, to help her brood find security in an insecure world became her obsession. From observing her own life and the lives of the hard working women who lived around her, Jennie saw their common mistake had been that each and every one of them, including herself, had not anticipated what was going to happen to them in years to come. She had in her naïve 17 year old mind thought that Frank and she would move to America, where Frank would miraculously earn a decent amount of money and they would have some children and live happily ever after. She could still bring tears to her heart when she thought about that dreary April morning on the dock in Dublin when she hugged her mother for the last time and promised her they would send money so she and dad could come for a visit.

For years there wasn't enough money to pay the rent on time nor to buy food for supper. When Jennie got to thinking, usually when she was leaning over a large basin on the back porch, scrubbing clothes, she wondered how she had ever had such lofty dreams. She wondered if there had been some way she could have foreseen how her life would turn out. And, straightening and stretching her tired back, she looked around at the neighboring houses, where gray paint was peeling off in big curly flakes, and dirt yards were cluttered with bits of coal and wood, and she wondered how all of her friends had ended up in this neighborhood. Almost without exception, the women were kind, hard-working, and generous, and they didn't complain all that much. But despite the fact that every single woman worked as long and hard as she could, there was no end in sight to their struggle to get even a tiny bit ahead. When back yard conversations took a turn towards this injustice, usually at Jennie's instigation, everyone hushed, or suddenly had to go inside.

"You think too much, Jennie," a once lovely young girl, now disguised as an aging, disheveled woman, told her, as she lifted a basket of neatly folded clothes and trudged up the dirt path to her back porch. "Too much thinking's going to get you in trouble."

The times were not yet ripe for Jennie's sort of wondering. Husbands like Frank who drank too much were excused if they held down a job and brought home a weekly paycheck. There would be no revolution, and Jennie had no intention of starting one. She taught her girls all the things a girl should know in order to be a good wife, and she resolved to do everything in her power to see that each daughter got a good husband. Jennie Hannigan resented her parents for allowing her to marry good-looking Frank Hannigan when she was only 17 and foolish. She did not intend to allow her daughters to follow in her path.

As each girl reached maturity and was ready to go out into the big world, Jennie encouraged them not to race into marriage like she had done. One moved on to be a nurse maid for a wealthy family on Queen Street; a second worked as a clerk in the dry goods department of Stone's Variety Store. The youngest daughter was to become the token gift to the Church. With each daughter placed, Jennie felt a little more confident, but she knew from the start that Kathleen was going to be the challenge.

Jennie Hannigan had a special word to describe each of her eight children: there was the wit, the slow poke, the mule, and the little nun. Kathleen was the complainer. Nothing ever pleased Kathleen. Life for the Hannigan family was not easy, and there were few pleasures, but the others seemed more willing to accept their lots. No one complained as much as Kathleen. She was not yet ten years old when she began to say that she wanted to get out of the West End. She did not intend to live like they did, ten people crammed into four small rooms. She was going to do whatever she had to do to get away. Her sisters and brothers called her "the snob," and accused her of thinking she was better than they were.

"I'm not better than you," Kathleen explained in her snobbiest voice. "I just refuse to live like this for the rest of my life. I shouldn't have to."

As Jennie wrung her hands over her discontented daughter, she heard her own young voice informing her mother that she wasn't going to spend her life in Ireland. She was going to America to get rich. Thirty years later, Jennie repeated the exact words her mother had said about her: "She has her own ideas about everything. There's nothing I can say or do to change her mind."

Fortunately, when Kathleen was nearly eighteen, there came a time when her ideas and her mother's ideas merged. Kathleen became interested in a young man who surpassed even her mother's wildest dreams. Because the classes in Port Williams were highly segregated, there was little hope that Kathleen would marry into one of the established families. Those families intermarried with each other and seldom did someone of the working classes have an opportunity to meet these people on a social level, let alone marry one of them. But Kathleen found someone who was not yet connected with any of the established families, but who was on his way up and beyond those families, and this was evident not only to Kathleen, but to anyone who chanced to meet him.

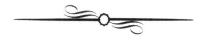

A RISING STAR

Lloyd Angel was a rising star. Like many ambitious young men in his day, he was attracted to the Port Williams area by the booming lumber business. According to the rumors that reached his home in Maine, it was impossible not to make money if you were working in the Pennsylvania lumber boom. There were endless tales of penniless young men with nothing but energy and grit who became millionaires almost overnight. For generations, Lloyd's family had worked in lumber in Maine, and when Lloyd showed an interest in going to Pennsylvania to seek his fortune, his father, who had been a millwright for thirty years, gave him encouragement, plus a few dollars to get him started.

The Port Williams that greeted Lloyd the morning after his 23rd birthday was a stimulating place. The population had doubled in the past ten years. From a town of 14,000 in 1878, it had grown to over 30,000, and the pace of the business life was indicative of growth that would never slow down. Strong, shiny horses pulled wagons piled high with construction materials for the buildings that were going up all over the area. Young men in rough work clothing shouted back and forth to each other in loud voices. The place was bustling.

Lloyd Angel was taken on by the Phillips Sawmill, and inside of three years, was running not only the original mill, but two others that had been built in the interim. He put in long days, and his life consisted of nothing but work, but his situation was hardly unique. Every ambitious young man with promise and an ability to work long hours was following the same path. If a man was in lumber, Port Williams was the place to be. By the time Lloyd Angel was 27, he was partial owner of a string of sawmills and had invested money in two big hotels that were going up in the center of town. It was at this point that fate placed Kathleen Hannigan in his pathway.

No one was surprised that Kathleen Hannigan married above her. She always thought she was better than anyone else; any neighbor would have verified that, or any of her sisters, too, for that matter. And it was only because she thought she was better than anyone else that she happened to be sitting at a charming little table in the window of the Market Street Hotel, eating a piece of cake and drinking a cup of tea when Lloyd Angel first laid eyes on her. It was Kathleen's 18th birthday, and she had decided to treat herself to something special for the occasion.

Weeks before the big day, she whispered an invitation to her favorite sister, Polly. "I'm 18, and I'm going to do something extravagant. Want to join me?"

It is astounding sometimes that a world so close physically can be so far away. The street where Kathleen had lived all of her life was only eight blocks from the Market Street Hotel, yet Kathleen had never been inside the luxurious building. The rich and the poor of the town were separated by an impermeable wall. While Kathleen's father plodded off to work each morning, still feeling the after-effects of the previous night's overindulgence, and brought home barely enough money to put food on the table, people on the other side of the wall owned horses that each cost as much as Kathleen's father earned in a year. They sent their children to private schools and ordered furniture custom designed in Italy.

If Kathleen had been content to stay on her side of the wall, she wouldn't have been sitting in the window of the Market Street Hotel that day, and Lloyd Angel would never have noticed her.

As Lloyd stepped through the doorway of the Hotel restaurant that afternoon and paused to glance around for a friend he was to meet, his eyes were drawn from the darkness of the area where he usually sat to a light green dress near the window. On the first pass of his eyes, the color caught his attention; next time around, quantities of shiny auburn hair, some tied up in large smooth curls with bits of green ribbon, and the rest hanging down over the shoulders, caused his eyes to pause in admiration. His friend forgotten for the moment, he moved a step to the right in hopes of getting a glimpse of the face that went with the wonderful hair, but Kathleen was looking at the young lady sitting across the table from her, and the most Lloyd could see was the angle of her cheek. He glanced once more around the room and then stepped out onto the street to look for his friend, and at the same time, to look into the window to try to see the girl's face.

Kathleen was glowing. It was exciting to be in the Market Street Hotel, sitting at a small, round table, covered with a cloth of such a smooth, fine weave that it felt like skin, and holding in her hand an elegant china tea cup with tiny pink roses around the border. In quiet voices, she and Polly discussed everything that was going on around them, as they tried to look as though they were comfortable in such surroundings.

"You should see the man standing in the doorway," Polly said quietly with a smile.

Kathleen replied, holding her cup to her bottom lip: "I can't very well turn around and look at him, and I don't have eyes in the back of my head. Describe him to me."

"He's very handsome," Polly said into her cup. "Very, very handsome." She lowered her voice even more. "And he's staring at you."

"Stop being silly," Kathleen said. "Why would he be staring at me?"

"Whoops, he's leaving," Polly said. "Look out on the street, quick."

Kathleen looked out the window directly into the eyes of the man. She was too surprised to turn away. She blushed lightly and hoped it didn't show through the glass.

"What a handsome man," she thought. "Wouldn't it be wonderful to marry a man like that?"

"She's beautiful," Lloyd Angel was thinking. "What I wouldn't give to spend my life with a woman like her."

Although it was Kathleen's beauty that first attracted Lloyd, as he began to court her, he found there were other things about her that he found intriguing. First there was her poor, struggling family: the father, a drunk; the mother, a drudge. Her sisters were plain, nice, and hard-working; the brothers were typical young workmen, strong and loud and full of energy. How had Kathleen ended up in such a family? Lloyd thought of himself as a prince whose mission was to rescue a princess who had accidentally been born into the wrong family.

And the princess was a devout Roman Catholic. Although her faith made little sense to Lloyd, her adherence to the rituals and the importance of its trappings in her life was mysterious and appealing. She looked beautiful with a string of crystal rosary beads in her hands. He didn't mind that he had to share Kathleen with God, although he did resent sharing her with God's representative in Port Williams, Father John, whom she consulted and worshipped, perhaps even more than God.

The first time Lloyd Angel told Kathleen he would like to marry her, she stared into his eyes for several minutes without replying. He could see doubts whirling around in her soft hazel eyes, and he waited patiently for them to stop. Her response, when it finally came, took him by surprise.

"Father John would be furious," she said with an enigmatic smile, "absolutely furious."

"Father John?" Lloyd asked. "Well, what about your parents? Would they be furious too?"

"No," Kathleen said. "My mother is very sensible and practical. I mean, as long as I don't leave the Church, and as long as our children are raised in the faith, I don't think she would mind."

When he heard her say "our children," Lloyd felt a warm surge creep through his body. He gave Kathleen one of his "I can handle anything" smiles. "Well, then, why should this Father John care so much?" Lloyd asked. "Maybe I should have a little talk with him."

It was Kathleen's turn to smile back at Lloyd's grand pretensions. She shook her head in amazement. Lloyd Angel was totally charming. "You think you can talk anyone into anything, don't you?" she teased.

"I do okay." Lloyd beamed at what he took as a compliment.

Months passed before Kathleen finally told Lloyd she would become his wife. Her sisters, her mother, and Lloyd all pushed, gently, of course, because Kathleen was not the sort of person to be pushed. What the wait and uncertainty did was plant an insecurity in Lloyd's otherwise confident self, and his patient treatment of Kathleen and his tolerance of her indifference after their marriage lasted much longer than it otherwise would have.

How long did Lloyd's enchantment last after the wedding trip? Weeks, possibly months. What Lloyd Angel came to understand was that Kathleen was an essentially unhappy person. It was only in public that she was gracious and charming. In the privacy of their home, she was anxious, sad, and discontented. It seemed that once she had it all, she was overwhelmed with the nothingness of it all.

And who could she talk with about nothingness? Kathleen was not surrounded by young college students speculating on the meaning of life. Her mother and sisters believed in hard work, suffering, and the Holy Catholic Church. Lloyd was also captivated by the idea of hard work, with success, money, and friends who shared the same values, coming in a close second.

Kathleen told her mother that perhaps the emptiness came because the children did not come.

"You're really so much better off," her aging, fading mother told her. "Children are wonderful, and I don't regret a single one of you, but they sure are a lot of hard work."

There was no way for her mother to comprehend Kathleen's ennui. In her long life of responding to the mechanical and emotional demands of eight children, there had been no room for emptiness. But Kathleen, on the other hand, had adequate time and space for the emptiness to grow and develop into a cancerous tumor. She had spent 18 years of her life in a crowded flat with nine other people, her mother in the midst, ordering, pleading, pacifying, and cajoling. In what seemed like overnight, Kathleen awakened alone in a seventeen room house with only the sounds of servants trying not to make noise. Lloyd was always up and out by 6 a.m. Kathleen slept until 8, or 9, or 10. She had no reason to get out of bed.

It was not that she would have been willing to exchange her life for one like that of her mother, or any of her sisters, or anyone she knew. She was disappointed with life in general. It hadn't turned out the way she had imagined it was going to be. Young girls got married, and that's when their lives began. Kathleen had been married for five years, and she was still waiting for something to begin, and no one seemed to understand why she was troubled, not even Father John, who had been the Hannigan family priest for thirty years. All Father John had to offer was a cure all for hopeless causes: patience and prayer.

Patience was so against Kathleen's nature that it hadn't a chance, and prayer, improvised, as well as multiple repetitions of the rosary, left her feeling that no one was listening. The only thing that gave her momentary pleasure and satisfaction was heavy forest green velvet trimmed with intricate white lace. Each piece of smooth cherry furniture, each vase, each crystal chandelier brought a moment of pleasure when it arrived, but none that lasted through the month. As Kathleen walked through the rooms, touching an inlaid marble table surface, moving a pewter candle holder from one shelf to another, and gazing at a large painting of a bouquet of wildflowers, she felt contentment and pleasure, but the sensation was fleeting. A book now and then transported her away from her discontented self, and an evening at the opera relaxed her spirits for several days, but the ennui would always manage to creep back in through an open window and wrap itself tightly around her soul.

THE ENVY OF PORT WILLIAMS

Sisters love, but sisters also talk. When Kathleen was married and settled into the big house, they remembered the discontented young Kathleen and marveled that she had got what she wanted out of life, and yet she was still unhappy. From ten people living in four small rooms, she was now one of two people living in 17 rooms, one of seven people if the maids, chore girl, cook and groom counted for anything.

"Discontented people are born, not made," their philosophical mother explained. "Nothing will ever make Kathleen happy. She's been fussing since the day she was born."

For the first five years of married life, while she adjusted to Lloyd and tried to start a family, she could sometimes put the discontentment on a cellar shelf alongside colored jars of jam and apple butter. For several busy years while she and Lloyd planned and built the estate, she was able to hide it in a heavy wooden cedar chest, along with her furs, or in an ivory jewelry box among her growing accumulation of sapphires and opals. By the time she turned 28, Kathleen was the envy of Port Williams. She was married to an ambitious, wealthy man, and lived in one of the most luxurious homes in town, and yet she was totally miserable.

Kathleen spent endless time patting her eyes with soft wet pieces of cotton, hoping no one could tell how much and how often she had been crying. As she added the finishing touches to the estate, she designed benches where a person might sit and cry in comfort. Two sandstone benches were set beside the creek along the path, a ten minute walk from the house, adequate time to think enough sorrowful thoughts to bring on a flood of tears. A bird bath of matching stone, thick and solid enough to last for centuries, was set a short distance from the benches, in hopes the birds would collect there and provide songs to uplift the spirits of the person sitting on the bench. A twenty minute walk down the wide path through the forest led to a small fish pond, which, in its day, sported a few lily pads, a collection of turtles, and several friendly oversized fish. Beside the pond was a wrought iron bench with a matching chair and a small table, and, if a person could not make the ten or twenty minute walk into the forest, closer to home, to the right of the patio on top of a small knoll, sat another stone crying bench, placed at an angle so a person sitting there could have a view of the dam, the summer house, and the tall pines behind. After a spell of weeping, when her eyes had cleared, Kathleen surveyed the beautiful world she had created and she felt proud. Even a sad and discontented young woman had to admit that the Angel Estate was a very enchanting place.

Enchanting is an old fashioned term used to describe things that no longer exist, things like unicorns and magic wands and fairy princesses; and, for some reason, it is the term that has always been used to describe the Angel Estate. On a May afternoon in 1901, a lady in a sky blue afternoon tea dress, descending from a pleasure carriage with a parasol in hand, called the place enchanting, said she herself was enchanted, and accused Kathleen Angel of being an enchantress. Seventy years later, a bleary-eyed young man, high on marijuana, looked at the big house up on the hill and stammered: "Like, it's like enchanting. Yeah, enchanting. That's it." Enchanting was the only word that came to his muddy mind, and he had never used the word before in his life. It sounded gay.

Enchanting was the very state Kathleen Angel had in mind as she directed workmen to lay the stone wall along the dam, plant the Japanese maple just to the right of the leaded-glass door, install pastel translucent stained glass windows on the second floor landing, and hang miniature Victorian bird houses in the trees.

Although enchanting seemed to be the appropriate word to describe the Angel Estate, few paid heed to the fact that enchantment isn't always a positive. Enchantment can cause unrealistic expectations, followed by disappointment and despair. Lloyd Angel was enchanted with Kathleen Hannigan, and his enchantment lasted well into the first five years of their marriage. He was amazed at her loveliness, and it was a thrill to have her by his side, immaculately dressed, coiffed, and tastefully bedecked with jewelry, which he generously provided her on any occasion. She was splendid, and he wished she were made of porcelain so he could put her on a shelf and gaze at her, take her down and fondle her whenever he wished, and not have to put up with the human being she became once they left the public eye.

Although Lloyd was becoming disillusioned with his wife, not so the other members of Port Williams society. Kathleen was the original triple threat woman. No one could keep up with her, although everyone tried. At every social event, ladies waited anxiously for Kathleen to make her appearance just so they could see what she had chosen to wear. The annual Victorian Ball was the highlight of the season, and that's when Kathleen outdid herself. Of course she arrived just a bit late, and when the Angels were announced, the room became silent. Kathleen stood for a few moments and looked over the crowd before she descended the stairs to the ballroom. Her dress was the latest sculpted fashion, dark teal, trimmed with navy velvet and lace. A peacock feather was fastened in her hair, and she wore short navy lace gloves without fingers. Suddenly, all the insecure women looked down at their own dresses, which, until this moment, had been splendid and fashionable. They saw Kathleen's long, delicate fingers, a simple diamond catching the light and flickering, the navy lace framing her wrist. In contrast, their own hands appeared clumsy in last season's gloves that covered their entire hand and fingers.

They waited for a glimpse of Kathleen's shoes, hidden beneath the long, full gown. When she finally began to descend the staircase, holding her skirt up just a little so she wouldn't trip, dark teal and navy blue silk shoes peeked out, and on the front of each was a navy lace ruffle, pinned in place with a silver bow. They were bought in New York, but imported from Milan. The ladies couldn't wait until morning to pressure the local shoemaker to duplicate the shoes.

"That damned Kathleen Angel," he swore. "She causes me endless work. But, on the other hand," he added, "I make money every time she decides to change her shoes. I guess I shouldn't be complaining."

Kathleen not only kept the shoemaker on his toes and earning money, but she kept every fashion-conscious woman in Port Williams on her toes and spending money. Kathleen introduced the latest fashions from New York to Port Williams. She set the style for horses, carriages, paintings, and grand parties with themes, decorations, music and food fit for the gods. There wasn't a woman in Port Williams who wouldn't have given all she had to change places with Kathleen Angel.

An evening of laughter, dancing and dining, with Kathleen so charming and elegant that she would be discussed and imitated for weeks afterwards, ended the moment she and Lloyd were ensconced in the carriage. As soon as they made the turn onto Lark Street, where the horses realized they were on their way home and picked up their pace, Kathleen suddenly changed. She unpeeled her gloves and rolled them into tight little lace balls that would be found on the floor of the carriage in the morning by the groom, Andrew, who would hand them to the maids with explicit instructions to give them a thorough cleaning and to be very gentle with them. Kathleen removed the clips from her hair and shook it loose. She drew her cape around her neck and leaned her head back against the carriage seat and sighed. If Lloyd's arm happened to be resting there, she wiggled her head until he moved it.

"Tired?" Lloyd asked.

"Ummmmmmmm," Kathleen replied, already on her way to a world where Lloyd was not welcome.

Lloyd tried to reach Kathleen. When they were first married, he was very affectionate and held her and kissed her as often as he could. She accepted his attentions with indifference and never initiated any herself. He then began to buy her gifts. He brought her flowers and jewelry, a special vase, or a painting he thought she would like for the house. She enjoyed these gifts for a moment or two. The jewelry was appreciated more by those who admired it when Kathleen was wearing it than by Kathleen herself. As she placed another bauble in her jewelry box, Lloyd placed his young wife on the shelf and resolved to deal with her later. Then, as now, an up and coming millionaire had no time to dwell on someone else's personal problems.

Lloyd had problems of his own. Disastrous changes were taking place in the lumber industry, and Lloyd, as well as the other young entrepreneurs of Port Williams, was being forced to make daily decisions to keep afloat and hold onto his wealth.

Because of massive deforestation, which caused several major floods that nearly swept Port Williams off the map, the lumber industry was beginning to fail. Lloyd wisely switched many of his interests to utilities, hotels, and a furniture business. He invested cautiously in the new railroad and joined a number of other men in an ambitious plan to build row houses near the center of town.

Each day was filled with meetings, plans, and decisions. He had once thought of taking Kathleen abroad for a few months. He thought if he got her away from her mother and Father John, she might relax and maybe children would come. Children might be the answer to Kathleen's problems. He resolved that once he got his finances stabilized, he would take care of Kathleen. In the meantime, Lloyd's holdings changed daily, and as he supervised and made wise decisions, his wealth, as well as his responsibilities, increased, and Kathleen was left to fend for herself.

While Lloyd diversified, Kathleen focused on putting even more finishing touches on the house and grounds. Today she would have joined a health club, had a brief fling with the tennis instructor, scheduled lunch dates with friends to talk about the fling and compare it with their own flings, and rent videos to watch at night. Instead, she met with her seamstress, had her portrait painted, rode her mare back through the trails on the property, visited with her mother weekly, and spent an inordinate amount of time wondering and weeping.

SOMEONE NEW TO MEET HIS NEEDS

While Lloyd was too busy to focus on Kathleen, fate placed someone in his path who required no focusing. Lloyd was in the right place at the right time, or the wrong place at the right time, and afterwards, he no longer thought about changing his old wife. He met someone new to meet his needs.

Years later, when everything had come and everything had gone, Lloyd still thought Kathleen was the most beautiful creature he had ever seen. In contrast, Ellen, the other woman who came into Lloyd's life, was not a beauty by anyone's standards, but she was kind and affectionate, and she bore him three children and loved him faithfully for years without making a single demand on him. The longer he knew her, the more he appreciated and loved her, and when he compared her with his untouchable crystal wife, he was sorry he had ever been smitten by a young girl in the window of the Market Street Hotel.

Lloyd was not actively searching for a replacement for Kathleen when Ellen came his way. He had gone to the East End to check on his latest project, the construction of thirty row houses. The ground had been broken in early August, and there was pressure to get the buildings under roof before the first snow fall. Lloyd had hired thirty workmen to complete the job.

It was on an early October afternoon, as Lloyd was standing on Walnut Street, gazing with great pride and satisfaction at the nearly finished project, when a young woman, no more than a girl, came running up the street, her blonde hair loose, her dress mussed, and tears streaming down her face. Before she could catch her breath to speak, Lloyd asked: "Is something wrong? Do you need help?"

She stopped and looked up at Lloyd with eyes pink and wet from crying. "I'm looking for my dad," she said, pointing with her hand at the row houses. "He's working in there somewhere."

"Is something wrong?" Lloyd asked again.

She looked up at his face. Her eyes once again filled with tears and her top lip trembled as she tried to speak. Lloyd reached over and lay a gentle hand on her shoulder.

"Who is your father?" he asked.

"Patrick Yerges," she replied.

"Patrick Yerges," Lloyd repeated. "Stay right here and I'll get him for you."

Lloyd soon learned that the girl's small brother had died of a fever. He had been sick not more than a day. Lloyd drove the girl and her father home in his trap.

"He seemed to be better this morning when I left for work," Patrick said in a quiet voice. "Poor little guy."

Lloyd dropped them off in front of a dilapidated gray wooden building. As Patrick hurried into the house, the girl paused for a moment and looked back at Lloyd. "Thank you very much, Mr. Angel," she said. "You were very kind."

"Is there anything more I can do?" Lloyd asked.

And the girl looked at him for a moment and then made the strangest request. "Pray for us," she said, as she turned and ran into the house.

Lloyd felt drained. He had been dragged into the center of someone else's emotional maelstrom. As he drove home, he couldn't stop thinking about the tragedy he had just witnessed. His own life had been so devoid of emotion for so many years that he felt like an outsider to the human race. This experience reminded him that other people were living, suffering, and feeling all around him, and he was missing out, missing out on the bad, but also missing out on the good. He suddenly realized that he was very lonely.

He began to fantasize about the girl. She was very plain. She could never be a painted porcelain doll to set on his mantle, but when she was standing beside him, shaking with sobs, he could have held her and loved her, and he knew she would have been warm and wet and soft against him.

In the next few days, he relived the scene again and again, and he closed his eyes and pictured himself taking the blonde girl into his arms to comfort her and to comfort himself as well. When he lay in bed beside his cold and brittle wife, he thought about the girl, and he felt happier than he had in a long time.

After two days, Patrick came back to work. Lloyd sought him out to ask how he was doing.

"I'm all right," Patrick answered. "These things take time."

Lloyd tried to think of a way to introduce the girl into the conversation, but he had not even learned her name, so, instead, he asked, "How about your wife? Is she doing okay?"

Patrick gave Lloyd a look of surprise. "I don't have a wife anymore," he said. "I lost my wife right after Timmy was born. It's a good thing," he added. "It would have broke her heart to have to live through this."

"I'm so sorry," Lloyd said.

"It's going to be hard on my daughter Ellen," Patrick said, shaking his head back and forth. "My Ellen's been taking care of Timmy since he was born. My Ellen takes care of us all."

Lloyd had a dozen questions, but he felt it would be inappropriate to stand there and interrogate Patrick about his family at a time like this.

"If there's anything I can do," he said. "Just let me know."

"Thank you, Sir," Patrick said. "That's very kind of you."

Lloyd made no plan to see Ellen again, but she was often on his mind. He hoped he would accidentally run into her on the street as he drove past her house on his way to and from the site each day. Children played on the sidewalk; women sat talking on wooden porches; but there was not a glimpse of life behind the peeling gray façade of the building where he had deposited her that sad afternoon.

An October afternoon in Pennsylvania can still today make a rational person do foolish things. The warm, dry air, the gold and red leaves, and the stillness of a distant sun make a person glad to be a part of it all. The river was at her finest in October, dressed in swirling oranges and reds, accessorized with silk scarves of gold and yellow and brown. Lloyd pulled his carriage to the side of the road and sat looking at the lovely river. He was in no hurry to get home, and as he watched the shimmering palette flowing past, he felt an overwhelming loneliness. He was all alone in a magnificent world. He began to think of Ellen. Maybe she was alone too. The memory of her face, streaming with tears, flashed before him, and he felt an irresistible urge to see her again.

"There's nothing wrong with stopping by to see how she's doing," he told himself.

Suddenly a churning swell rushed down the river, washing the colors off the palette and splashing red and gold paint all over the bank. Just as suddenly, the river settled back and arranged her skirts about her like a lady.

Lloyd laughed aloud. "The old river certainly approves of my plan," he thought, as he clucked his nodding horse into action and headed back towards town. Once the decision was made,

Lloyd did not hesitate for a moment. He knocked at the door. Ellen answered, looked surprised, yet pleased, to see him, smiled and motioned him into the warm, dark room.

At first glance, Ellen looked to be very young. Her hair was pulled back into a neat braid which hung down her back, and she was wearing a simple, blue cotton dress. As she guided him through the kitchen and into the living room, he noticed how shabby, yet neat and clean, the place appeared to be. She led him to a comfortable big gray chair, and offered him a cup of tea. She did not seem at all embarrassed that he was there, and he no longer felt the urge to explain why he had come, although he couldn't have explained it even if she had asked. He told Ellen he had thought about her and her family a few times during the week, and he was just wondering how they were getting along.

"I just feel incredibly sad," she said. "We all feel sad. I'm sure that's normal." She smiled a smile of resignation.

"Have you been out at all?" Lloyd asked. The little flat was warm and dark. He suddenly missed the colorful world he had just been passing through all morning. "Nobody could be sad today," he said. "The colors are magnificent."

"I can imagine," Ellen said, "But it seems so wrong that the world is so beautiful and Timmy's not here to see it."

Lloyd thought of asking Ellen to join him for a carriage ride along the river, but he knew he could not chance being seen, riding along with a young woman in his carriage, so they sat and talked in the dark little room, and later, as he drove home along the river, he pretended she was seated beside him with her hand resting on his leg.

Much time passed before Lloyd and Ellen became lovers. As the river exchanged the golden and red satins for her white ermine stole, they became close friends. Christmas came and went and

Lloyd gave Ellen and her family a large box of chocolates. Soon the river put her winter clothing into storage and got ready for spring. As she became brown and foamy, mischievously ripping up trees and shrubs from her banks just for the hell of it, Ellen and Lloyd became confidants and confessed their love to each other.

It was in the summer, when the river had donned a plain green house dress and was gently playing with the little boats that paddled up and down between the bridges, that Lloyd and Ellen took a trip south on the paddle-wheeler and stayed in a hotel overlooking the river in Harrisburg. Here they became, so to speak, man and wife. That was in the summer of 1902, and the unspoken vows they exchanged would last until death do them part: somebody's death, anybody's death, would do fine.

BE CAREFUL WHAT YOU WISH FOR, SUSAN

Susan had wished for a friend, and her wish had been granted. Mya came into her life and effortlessly replaced Tom, Heather, and all of the old friends in Laurel Hills. She was a delightful companion. She was like a child, and spending time with Mya was like reliving the years when Heather was eight and nine and fascinated with everything in the world.

Their friendship began in early October. Autumn had always been Susan's favorite season, but this was the first year she had spent it in the middle of a multi-colored forest. Mya filled the summer house, as well as Susan's dining room, with huge arrangements of colored leaves and pine branches. In the early morning, she would run in unannounced to add a branch of oak with a few dried acorns, or a piece of curly grape vine, or some fern fronds, to a nearly perfect bouquet, and with a loud "Perfectamente," she would disappear just as quickly as she had arrived.

The only flowers still blooming this late in the season were chrysanthemums. One afternoon as Susan was struggling to scrape years of grease from the oven racks, she looked up and saw an apparition at the kitchen door. Mya stood smiling in at her with an armload of chrysanthemums in yellows, golds, rusts, and varying shades of red and dark pink.

"Those are my favorite flowers," Susan said, as she stripped off her rubber gloves and opened the door.

"That's because you're a Libra. All Libras love chrysanthemums," Mya said in her matter-of-fact tone. "I like them too, but we Aquarians are big daffodil fans. Just wait until spring and you'll see what I mean."

As Mya stood at the sink, arranging the flowers, Susan felt a need to express her curiosity. "You're not going to tell me there's a connection between when you were born and the kind of flowers you like?"

"Of course," Mya said. "Tom's a Cancer, right?"

"Yes," Susan said, wondering how Mya knew that.

"Roses, right?" Mya asked.

"Well, he always buys me roses, but I don't know if they're his favorite flower. I never asked him," Susan said. The silliness of asking Tom his favorite flower, his favorite animal, his favorite color, like a grade school friend, brought a smile to her face.

"Of course roses are his favorite flower. Why else would he buy them for you?" Mya asked.

Susan laughed. "I've only been married to the man for 23 years. How could he possibly know what kind of flowers I like? I don't recall his ever asking me that."

"Any day now, he'll figure it out," Mya added. "Typical man, a little bit slow." And the two laughed quietly at the irony of it all. Susan enjoyed having someone else vicariously criticize Tom.

Sometimes the friends sat at the dining table and sipped licorice tea; other times they followed Kathleen Angel's paths back through the forest. In the early evening, they sat on the dam and watched the sun go down behind the big stone house. And, always, their conversations had a predictable rhythm: staccato retorts, counterpoint, long pauses, and non sequiturs, the philosophical interspersed with the mundane, with a drop of the fanciful and a sprinkle of the absurd added for flavor.

Nothing escaped Mya's curiosity and fascination. She kept track of the phases of the moon, and knew all the constellations and every story connected with each one, and, like a child, she collected pretty stones that caught her eye as she walked along. The heavy brown canvas shoulder bag that she carried was not filled with mirrors, cosmetics, combs and brushes, but with pebbles, an interesting little piece of wood, a bird feather, a walnut, and a displaced sea shell. Mya knew the names of all the plants and trees growing on the estate and could identify an invisible bird from a single chirp in a distant tree.

Mya was not interested only in the natural world and the supernatural world, she was also fascinated with people. Susan took advantage of this to talk endlessly about Heather — Heather as a baby, as a sweet little girl, as a troublesome teenager, and a Heather as she might be all grown up sometime in the future.

"Mother and daughter is the only pure relationship in the world," Mya told Susan, and Susan had to agree.

"I can't wait to experience motherhood," Mya confessed.

Susan felt sympathy for her new friend, 33 years old and no sign of a boyfriend, let alone a husband, and yet wanting a child. If Mya weren't so kooky, she could easily find a nice husband, but, by this time, Susan realized that the kookiness was beyond Mya's control. It was nothing she could turn on and off. If only she could turn it off long enough to snare a man, Susan thought, and then reprimanded herself for being so superficial.

Susan learned that Mya wasn't always kooky; sometimes she was the most ordinary person in the world. As Susan and Tom individually spent more time with Mya, they both learned that she had many faces and personalities. With Susan she talked about recipes, wondered whether she should trim her hair, and complained about working conditions at the Frog. Often she wore a long shirt hanging out over the jeans and tied her hair back with a rubber band. Susan was quite comfortable with her when she was in her ordinary mode. But, at other times, she was fey and exotic, and there was an intensity about her that charged the air with uncomfortable energy. It was this exotic, intense Mya that Tom found stimulating, and when the ordinary Mya sat on the patio with Susan and him in the early evening, Tom excused himself to go to his study to work. She held no interest for him at all besides his curiosity about why she held no interest. It was the same body, face, and voice, but some essential ingredient was missing. The exotic Mya, on the other hand, was so exciting to him that he couldn't be in her presence without wanting to grab her, maul her, kiss her, and fuck her in an effort to try to absorb or tame or share her strange energy.

With Susan she was most often ordinary Mya, a sensitive woman with a delightful sense of humor and a child-like imagination. Mya assumed Heather's role in Susan's life. She and Susan giggled like teenagers over the silliest things. Since Heather was no longer around, Susan found herself saving little observations to tell her at a later date. Now she found herself saving them to tell Mya. Spending so much time alone was tolerable for Susan as long as she could say to herself: "Wait 'til Mya hears about this." Nothing earth-shaking went on in Susan's life on the estate. The days were filled with mundane, routine activities, the cycle broken only by Mr. Edwards' futile attempts to chase a bat out of the attic with his all-purpose chain saw; an ambitious turtle finding his way up out of the creek and onto the bridge, where he had to be rescued; and the discovery of a litter of little wild gray kittens that the mother cat had managed to keep hidden until they were almost as big as she was and were able to fend for themselves.

Of all the people, dead or alive, who fascinated Mya, at the top of her all-time list was Mrs. Angel, and, in particular, Mrs.

Angel's Ghost. When Mya was visiting with Susan in the main house, one of her sensitive psychic antennas was always turning about, searching for signs that Mrs. Angel's Ghost was hovering around. Often, in the early morning, Mya and Susan sat at the dining table, sipping hot wildflower and honey tea, just two ordinary women sharing a few precious moments before the affairs of the day hurried them on to their daily chores. A sudden sound, or a silence, or a slight variation in the light coming in the windows, or a breeze coming through the front door, would trigger a response in Mya, and in a single second, she would change from ordinary and comfortable to exotic and scary. Her body would tense as though a chill had come over her, and her wide eyes would stare at something in the distance. In the silent room, Mya would turn her head from side to side, listening to something that Susan could not hear. After a while, Mya would look from one corner of the room to the other and then speak in a very quiet voice. Susan knew what the topic was going to be.

"Did you sense that?" Mya asked.

The aspect Susan assumed when Mya introduced Mrs. Angel's Ghost into their conversations was one of honest doubt, amusement, tolerance, and an actual interest in what Mya had to say, if only because Mya herself truly believed. She was not pretending.

When Mya first talked about extrasensory phenomena, Susan had listened politely because Susan was a naturally polite person, and because Mya was a stranger. As their friendship grew, Susan felt comfortable enough to express her doubts. Mya did not try to convince Susan, but she also did not refrain from talking about her bizarre interests any time she felt like it. To Mya it was not a question of believing or not believing. It was just another dimension of life, one of which most people were unaware. She felt she was among the privileged few. She was like a person who can type fast, or play the piano well, or knit an Icelandic sweater with no mistakes. She had a gift. It was as simple as that.

In response to Mya's questions, Susan replied: "Well she chose the sconces, and I'm told she designed these cupboards just the way she wanted them. I mean, in that sense, I can sort of feel her presence."

"No," Mya interrupted. "That's not what I mean. Just sit here and try to put everything out of your mind. Breathe in and out, in and out, and don't focus on anything in particular."

Susan put her tea cup on the table in front of her, leaned back in the chair, and folded her hands on her lap. She tried to clear her mind.

Mya shook her head with approval.

Susan closed her eyes. She heard faint irregular bird chirps in the distance, and she thought of something amusing to ask Mya. Did Mrs. Angel, by any chance, know how to whistle? How was she at bird imitations? But when Susan opened her eyes, she saw that Mya was sitting quietly with her legs outstretched, her tea cup resting in her hands on her stomach, and there was no expression at all on her face. Her eyes stared straight ahead at the doors that led to the hall. So Susan saved her funny comment for another time. She tried once again to clear her busy mind. She was thinking that she should remember to put some pork chops out to thaw for dinner. She tried to recall if Tom had said whether he would be home early or working late.

"Did you sense anything?" Mya asked in a soft whisper, without moving a muscle.

"Afraid not," Susan said. "My mind never stops whirling long enough. Did you?"

Mya straightened herself up and set the cup on the table. "Just a bit," she said. "It wasn't strong, or I wasn't receptive enough, I guess."

Mya had a habit of playing with her hair while she talked. She opened her left hand as widely as she could, gathered as much hair into it as she could at the nape of her neck, and then brought it down the front of her left shoulder and smoothed it down to the tips. She completed this ritual twice before she spoke again.

When Mya talked about what she considered to be her field of expertise, she changed from a wide-eyed, silly flake, into a serious savant, carefully choosing her words and organizing her thoughts in an effort to make herself understood. She sat up at the table and pointed with the index finger on her left hand. "There are any number of explanations as to why this phenomenon is occurring," Mya explained to Susan. "I have narrowed it down to two possibilities. The first is that when a body has not been properly buried, the spirit sometimes remains on earth. That might very well be the case here. All those rumors can't be wrong. My second idea is that she might have got trapped on earth because there was something she had left undone, something that was very important to her."

"Like what?" Susan asked.

"I'm not sure," Mya said. "It could be any number of things. I think there's a very strong possibility that she wanted to have a child. Do you realize that she died childless? I mean, she was a Catholic, an Irish Catholic, and she and Lloyd had no children. Do you have any idea what that means?"

"No," Susan shook her head. "Maybe they didn't want children."

"That's not likely in those days," Mya said, "And certainly not a Roman Catholic. Just give me time, and I'll figure it all out."

"How will you go about doing that?" Susan asked. When Mya talked so seriously and convincingly, Susan sometimes forgot she herself was not a believer.

Mya stood up from the table and drank the remaining tea from her cup. She swirled the leaves around in the bottom of the cup, held it under the light, and studied the pattern. "Great. I'm going to make a bundle in tips today," she announced, and then answered Susan's question. "You see, this house has absorbed psychic impressions from every single person who has ever lived in it, and a person who allows herself to be sensitive to these impressions, as I do, can feel them when she is in the house. It's almost like reading a book. I just have to determine which vibes are coming from Kathleen Angel and separate them out from the others."

"I'm just too rational," Susan said. "Maybe too scientific. I'm too attached to the here and now. If I can't see it, I don't believe it exists."

"Everyone has the ability to be in touch with the universal psyche," Mya said. "What you have to do is allow the subconscious signals to reach your consciousness. They're there. You've just got to let them in. All your thoughts and the stuff going on in your head form a big, thick curtain, and the signals can't get through. They're like little rays of morning sunlight bouncing off black velvet curtains. It's like someone knocking at the door when you have your music turned up too loud."

Susan smiled at Mya. "I liked the part about the little rays bouncing off black velvet curtains," she said. "That's a pretty picture."

"You're hopeless," Mya joked, as she pushed the chair under the table. "No, I guess I don't mean that," she said. "You listen. You're very open. Just between Kathleen Angel and me, we're going to make you a believer." She waved at the far corner of the room. "Aren't we, Kathleen?" she asked.

"What did she say?" Susan asked. "I couldn't hear her."

"That's because your mind is too cluttered," Mya teased.

"There are frozen pork chops on my mind," Susan said, as she picked up her cup and headed for the kitchen.

"How do you expect an elegant lady like Kathleen Angel to bother communicating with someone with a head full of frozen pork chops?" Mya asked, as she stepped out onto the patio and headed across the yard.

There were moments when Susan felt as though Mya was dragging her right along into her crazy world. At times it was fun and amusing; at other times, Susan felt uncomfortable. She knew normalcy lay somewhere between Mya and Tom, and her life was a continuous struggle to get back to the fulcrum. After a long afternoon in Mya's world, Susan counted on Tom to toss out a cynical remark to pull her back to center.

"What kind of hocus-pocus did the flim flam lady get you into today?" he asked, as he loosened his tie and pulled his chair closer to the dining table.

Susan carefully placed a steaming, hot casserole dish on a trivet and began to spoon goulash into Tom's bowl. She looked at Tom's expectant face, a smile tickling at the corner of his mouth, as though he knew someone was about to try to pull his leg. As she placed a dollop of sour cream atop the goulash, she said casually, "We tickled trout."

"Tickled trout? Now that's a kinky one if I've ever heard kinky. Did he enjoy it?" Tom chuckled as he raised a spoonful of goulash to his lips.

As Susan sat down, unfolded her napkin, and arranged it on her knees, with a very serious demeanor, she explained Mya's theory of trout tickling. "You dangle your fingers in the water for a few minutes until the trout gets used to them. Then the trout swims up to see what they are. He thinks they're something to eat, of course, and when he swims up, you rub his back, ever so gently at first. He gets mesmerized, and then you just reach in and pick him up."

"Then why are we eating goulash?" Tom asked.

Susan laughed. "It didn't work today. Mya said my rubber glove probably smelled funny."

"Your rubber glove?" Tom asked. "You were wearing a rubber glove?"

"Of course," Susan said. "Don't you know anything? Do you think we wanted to get a finger bit off?"

Tom shook his head in disbelief, and with a mouth full of food, said, "Crazy lady. That Mya is a crazy lady, and she is turning you into another crazy lady." He held up first one finger and then a second. "One crazy lady plus another crazy lady equals two crazy ladies, or is that like trying to add apples and oranges?"

Susan smiled. Somehow being associated with Mya as a crazy lady made her feel like she herself was interesting.

"We're going to have to institutionalize the two of you. I can see it coming," Tom said. "It'll be a sad task, but I think I'll be up to it."

The baffling thing to Susan was that while Tom criticized and made fun of Mya's crazy ideas, he always seemed to want to hear more. He didn't look away and read the paper and utter grunts when Mya was the topic of conversation. He took a lively interest. When Susan didn't mention Mya, Tom found an excuse to bring her into the conversation. He could do this without arousing suspicion by politely and seriously inquiring about Mya's mother. Both he and Susan found the dead mother in the river to be a very humorous topic.

"Anything new going on with Mya's mother these days?" Tom asked, and Susan replied, "I believe she's thinking of moving a little farther down the river. She's having trouble sleeping with all that traffic on the bridge."

"That's a shame," Tom said. "I can't imagine her having to move all that furniture at her age. Maybe we should take the grand piano off her hands, but of course it might not be in such good condition after all this time underwater."

Instead of continuing the conversation, Susan suddenly got up and went into the kitchen to check the oven. More and more often, she felt guilty when she and Tom were making fun of Mya. What if Mya knew they were laughing at her? She had spent enough time with Mya to know that she did have an extra sense of some sort. Susan had known people who were fey, an aunt who could guess who was calling when the phone rang, and a friend who claimed to have dreams of things that were going to happen, and had some stories that seemed to confirm that. But she had never spent time with a person who answered questions before you asked them, and who knew what you were going to talk about before you uttered a word. Mya was very much in tune with what was going on in peoples' minds; that was not so unusual. There are a lot of people who are good at reading other people, but Mya was equally in touch with the workings of the entire physical world. Regardless of what the weatherman said, Mya knew when it was going to rain, how hard it was going to rain, and how long the rain was going to last. When the first snow flake landed on her nose, she knew if flurries were coming, or if a heavy snow storm was on its way. When the river was rising, regardless of dire predictions by the local radio stations, Mya was always able to reassure folks when the river was not going to reach flood levels, and she was always right.

The way Mya was able to read the mailbox was her most impressive feat. Susan often walked down to get the mail with Mya, who left for work at the Frog around ten. Once they had crossed the bridge, Mya placed her hands on top of the Harris mailbox, closed her eyes, and asked Susan: "Are you in the mood for some bills? I mean a lot of bills?"

At first Susan laughed at what she thought was Mya's joke, but when she reached in the mailbox, she pulled out a life insurance bill, a telephone bill, the annual auto insurance bill, and two credit card statements.

"That's the last time I ever walk to the mailbox with the likes of you," she said to Mya.

"Don't blame the messenger," laughed Mya. "I didn't bring the mail. Save your complaints for the mailman."

"I intend to," Susan called, as she turned and walked back up the driveway.

On another morning, as the two reached the far end of the bridge, Mya put her hand on the mailbox and smiled.

"No more bills?" Susan asked.

"Nooooo," Mya dragged out the word as though she were lost in thought. "It's thick." She looked at Susan. "Do you have any friends who write long letters?"

"I don't think so," Susan said, as she began to open the mailbox. 'You're positive it's not just a big fat bill?"

She pulled a single very thick envelope from the box. The return address was Sally's, one of her old friends from Laurel Hills. She tore open the envelope and pulled out a thick packet of yellow lined paper. She glanced at the pages.

"Isn't this cute?" she asked Mya. "They've all written something, all of my old friends."

"That explains it," Mya said, more to herself than to Susan. "I knew it was several letters, but only one envelope. That makes sense."

Susan read the first line and was catapulted back into her old life.

"Enjoy," Mya said, as she headed down the road.

Eventually, Susan accepted the ritual at the mailbox as just an ordinary activity on the Angel Estate. She stood patiently and watched her friend, eyes tightly closed, rub her hand across the top of the mailbox and mumble: "An electric bill. No, it's a different utility. It's a gas bill. There's a personal letter, but it's short, maybe an invitation or something. No, it's a thank you. There's a flyer, two flyers, whoops, no, sorry, three flyers. One's from the new pharmacy. I'm not sure about the other two. Wait, there's one more thing, something little. A late notice from the library. Do you have any books out? No, wait, it's a post card, a picture post card. Someone's on vacation, somewhere out west."

Mya gave a simple explanation for her ability. "Psychokinetics is my forte," she said, "always has been. I can't explain it. Some people are good at PK, and others couldn't do it for all the rice in China."

She might have been talking about roller skating, yodeling, or playing the violin.

Not much impressed Tom, and when Tom was with Mya, it was not her extrasensory gifts that held his interest, but one evening, when he stood looking out the dining room window down towards Mya's house, he was very much impressed by what he saw.

"Damn, take a look at this," he called to Susan.

Susan had been standing in the kitchen doorway, watching Tom staring out the window. He was so engrossed in whatever he was watching that Susan had several minutes to study this familiar, yet strange, man. They had just finished eating dinner and he was still wearing his suit. He never talked much about what he did at work, but whatever it was, his suit never got wrinkled. He looked as fresh as he had at 7 a.m., when he had got into his car and driven away.

Much to Mr. Edwards' delight, Susan had repainted the dining room the proper shade of charcoal blue, and the room had been transformed from a cold, formal, empty room into a cozy blue and silver place with billowy white curtains and a few well-placed plants and baskets. In his immaculate suit, Tom looked out of place, like a Twentieth Century man in a Nineteenth Century drawing room. Realities and truths tumbled around in Susan's mind these days like circus acrobats. Tom had always looked out of place. Even in Laurel Hills, he had seemed like a guest in his own house. Susan's friends were always surprised when they dropped in and found him home. After all those years on the road, he would probably feel more at ease in a motel room, Susan thought. She walked over to the window and stood beside him.

"What's so interesting?" she asked.

He nodded his head in the direction he was looking, and Susan turned her gaze out the window and down across the lawn to the summer house. Mya was sitting on the grass, and all around her were cats, stretching, washing their paws, and playing with each other.

"This is unbelievable," Tom said. "I've never seen anyone get close to those wild little buggers before."

"I guess this is the proof," Susan said. "Mya's not lying about those special powers."

"I'm a believer," Tom announced as he turned away and headed for the stairs. "I'm a believer," he repeated, putting his hands together and bowing his head up and down as he slowly ascended the stairs.

Susan continued to watch the scene from the window. Mya was wearing a long, blue skirt, which she had stretched all around her on the grass. One large gray cat was lying on the edge of her skirt and another sat on the grass beside her, and Mya's hand was gently stroking the compliant friend. Susan saw three smaller cats rolling around and playing nearby.

At first glance, this might not seem to be such an unusual scene, but these were the infamous wild cats, an extended family of predominantly gray and white feral cats that had perhaps begun with some abandoned pregnant ancestor years and years ago.

Not only were these cats unfriendly, but most were not even approachable. On a typical sunny day on the estate, one could see in the distance rangy gray and white cats with pink noses and twisted, crooked tails, lying about the yard on stone walls, on the wide walk way across the dam, and one or two on the warm flat roof of the summer house. Untold others, maybe eight, maybe twenty, lived in the forest near the house and survived on garbage, birds, and wild rodents. If a person walked quietly up the driveway and stood patiently in the bushes at the edge of the dam, he might have an opportunity to watch a skinny mother cat with several half-grown kittens, crawling, climbing, and chasing each other among the vines. These cats were born, lived, and died without names, nor trips to the vet for shots. At times the population would be low enough for Mr. Edwards to comment on their scarcity.

"Wonder where all the cats went? Must be a big cat convention in Baltimore."

Other times, when any number were dropping like snakes from the branches, the dam, the stone wall, and the roof, Mr. Edwards would say to anyone within listening distance, or to himself: "Looks like it's been raining cats and cats," and then laugh loudly at his clever comment.

Over the decades, particularly bold kittens wandered up to the big house, and if they were cute, and if there were children, or cat lovers, living in the big house, they got adopted. These upwardly mobile cats soon forgot their poor relations in the forest and paid them visits only to get impregnated, or to impregnate, a sibling, step-sibling, cousin, or grandmother. Mr. Edwards called them the "cat rabbits." They looked like cats, but bred like rabbits. "Stay away from this place if you're allergic to cat hares, h-a-r-e-s," he repeated to potential tenants. His joke never failed to get a good laugh.

As Susan watched Mya effortlessly, almost magically, befriend the feral cats, she wondered what Mr. Edwards would have to say if he could see her now. She continued to observe the scene, and she settled into thinking what an unusual and special person Mya had turned out to be. Mya helped fill the void left by Heather; she had brought Susan closer to Tom; and she had opened up her narrow world in a dozen directions.

On the other hand, she felt she didn't understand Mya at all. She was like a creature from outer space. Her life style, her values, and her past were all completely different from anything Susan had ever known. Where Susan's other friends had aging mothers and fathers who visited and family and in-law concerns to preoccupy them, Mya had no family at all, except for a dead mother who lived in the river, and Mya was more devoted to this dead mother than any of Susan's friends were to their perfectly healthy live mothers. Although Susan thought most of Mya's ideas were crazy, she envied Mya's blind acceptance of everything life offered, or didn't offer. Nothing seemed to bother Mya. On the surface, she was a poor, unmarried thirty-three year old, living in a shabby summer house without a car, and without most of the amenities of the Twentieth Century. She had never traveled; she had not been to college; and she didn't seem to have any friends her own age. She never got mail. She had no health insurance and never saw a doctor, nor dentist. And this deprivation was all by choice. It was so amazing to Susan that once in a while she couldn't stop herself from confronting Mya about the insecurity of her existence.

"What if you get sick?" she asked.

"I've never been sick a day in my life. Why would I get sick?"

"What about a car, a credit card, a real house, furniture?"

"Distractions."

"Television?"

"It clouds the mind."

To which Susan replied, "But....but....." and then gave up trying to articulate her own philosophy, whatever that was, to a person who claimed to be living a perfect life and seemed to be happier and more contented than Susan could ever imagine a person could possibly be. It was mind-boggling.

YOU'RE IN TOO DEEP;
YOU'LL NEVER GET OUT

Tom's flirtation with Mya evolved quickly into a fascination, and, in no time at all, became an obsession. By the time the trees had shed their golden leaves and the river was trying on new fur coats, Tom sensed that he was in very deep trouble.

Like a slide show, click-click-click, the many Myas passed through his mind as he sat dreaming at his desk: Mya with her long, slim legs stuffed into blue jeans, a simple loose white lace blouse half-tucked in at the waist, feathers and beads and ribbons peeking out from among her long hair; neat, efficient Mya in a simple skirt and blouse with a brown apron tied around her waist and her hair incarcerated into slick, shiny braids, held in place by a variety of bright silver and wooden barrettes; and the best Mya – hold that slide – Mya, naked and warm in her little bed in the summer house, the blankets permeated with exotic odors of sandalwood and patchouli. All the many Myas had one thing in common, a pair of big, wide green eyes that looked directly into Tom's soul and sometimes made him quake with desire, but, just as often, caused him to shiver with dread.

Tom had known many useful and pleasant women when he was on the road. They came into his life for a brief period, made superficial conversation, feigned an interest in him, as he did them, and left after each had got what he or she wanted from the other. None had lasted longer than a few months, and he would have trouble connecting a name with any of the faces. Susan was in a different category from these women. She was a permanent fixture, like the house, the car, Heather, or his parents. There was nothing exciting about Susan. Susan was a daisy, sometimes a carnation, sometimes, even a rose, but Mya was an orchid, a rare one-of-a-kind orchid, perhaps from Hawaii, or some other tropical paradise.

Mya took him to places he had never been to before, places whose existence he had never even imagined. Tom was unsettled by the totally foreign emotions Mya dredged up in him. He couldn't get enough of her, and, worse, she acted as though she could take him or leave him. She always seemed to be holding something back, not just a little of herself, but most of herself. She was an exciting mystery that he wanted to understand, but an ethereal mystery that floated about in the air around him and never lit long enough for him to examine. She was not made of flesh and blood and tears; Mya was the flame of a candle, the song of a bird; she was a butterfly. At times, when Tom sat dreaming about Mya, he thought maybe he was in love with her, and that indeed was terrifying.

He tried to get most of his work done in the early mornings because he knew, as the afternoon dragged on, he would end up staring out the window at the river, the miniature green bridge, and the soft green mountains, trying to sense where in the scene Mya might be. Almost every day he told himself: "I'll not call her today. I'll not see her tonight. I'll stay home and get some things done for a change." He made list after list of things he had to do.

While he was making the list, his mind was not on Mya, but that was only for a few minutes. Mya, warm and giggling, with her long legs wrapped around his waist, replaced the last item on the list, and he crinkled the paper into a ball and tossed it high into the air towards the brass waste basket by the wall.

An irritating thought that wormed its way into Tom's head and gnawed painfully at his brain was that he should stop seeing Mya. He thought about it practically, as a person thinks about giving up smoking. She was something he enjoyed, but something that might be bad for him in the long run. He knew he could not do it cold turkey, and cutting down wasn't possible either. What Tom needed was a patch, permeated with the essence of Mya, to wear on his skin. Every day a certain amount of Mya would be absorbed into his system, and he wouldn't have to chase after her like a teenage boy. But such a patch was not yet available on the market, so Tom suffered on.

To call or not to call. The most frustrating thing was that, after an hour of deliberating over whether or not to call, once he dialed her number, she seldom answered, and that left Tom wondering where she was, what she was doing, and with whom she was doing whatever it was she was doing.

"I've got to get her schedule," he thought, and then smiled at the absurdity of associating Mya with a schedule.

"Control, control, control," she would chant. He smiled to himself at his predicament and at her sassiness, but it wasn't really a smiling matter. For some unknown reason, fate had thrown this woman onto his path, a woman who drove him crazy, literally, and the punishment was that he could do nothing about it. She had no buttons that Tom could push. If he pouted, she ignored him; if he became angry, she left; and if he criticized her, she thanked him and told him he was probably right, but what difference did it make in the long run? Techniques he had perfected over the years to control Susan had no effect whatsoever on Mya.

On the other hand, he felt as though he, himself, was covered with brightly lit and flashing buttons that she was continually pushing, accidentally, rather than deliberately. She made him happy; she made him sad; she made him angry. He loved her; he hated her; he wanted to hit her; he wanted to fuck her. All of his powers had been stripped from him. He couldn't ignore her; he couldn't reprimand her, nor make her behave the way he wanted; and, by his own nature, he could not give in to her crazy ways. He felt like a tragic Greek hero. Worse, he felt like the sad little white horse in a children's book he had read to Heather a million times when she was a small child. The little white horse ran away and ended up stuck in a mud pond, where he sank deeper and deeper, and while he was sinking, the frogs sang: "You're in too deep. You'll never get out. You're in too deep. You'll never get out."

Tom realized that being in too deep was caused by the fact that he had not been able to discourage Mya from moving onto the Angel Estate. He had very mixed feelings about her living not a hundred yards from the house where he lived with Susan. Having Mya on the property where he could keep track of her was at first appealing, but he soon found that keeping tabs on Mya was not a possibility, even if he could see her porch light any time he looked out of the dining room window. It was little consolation to know exactly where the porch light was at all times, but to have no idea of the whereabouts of Mya.

Often he did not see her for days. When he stopped at the Bullfrog and found she wasn't there, in response to a casual, "Mya not around anymore?" he was told she had taken a few days off for R and R. In the late evening, when he stared out the dining room window at the little light in the vast darkness, he felt a loss and a loneliness almost too great to bear, and Tom was the sort of man who could bear anything. On the following day, when he stopped off at the Bullfrog, there was Mya, blowing him a kiss as she floated gaily from table to table with a tray of frosted brown bottles and a basket of chips balanced neatly on her outstretched arm.

"I missed you, Tomas," she whispered as she gently placed a crisp, greasy chip on his lower lip. He opened his mouth like a baby bird and his body felt warm all over.

"I was so worried about you that I almost called the State Police," Tom teased.

"You're so sweet to worry," she said, reaching over and straightening his tie, "But I'm a big girl, and I can take care of myself."

"I know you can," Tom said seriously. "But when a person just disappears for a few days off the face of the earth, anything could have happened." He tried not to sound like a jealous lover. "You should at least let someone know when you're going to be away. What if someone needed to get in touch with you?"

Mya looked at Tom with her big, honest green eyes and asked: "Now who would ever need to get in touch with me?"

"I don't know," Tom said. "I meant anybody."

Mya's disappearances bothered Tom more than he liked to admit, even to himself. Short of having her phone tapped, or trying to follow her, Tom could come up with no solution to his problem. So he merely waited and hoped that some day, he would be given an explanation. One night, as they lay in her warm little bed, exhausted and fulfilled, Mya pressed softly against him, childlike and vulnerable, Tom decided to give it a try.

"I want you to tell me a secret," he whispered into her warm, soft ear. "Where does Mya go when Mya disappears?"

Mya turned her head so that her mouth was damp against Tom's stiff ear, and she whispered:

"Mya was keeping a lonely hunter warm in his little cabin up on Jack's Mountain."

Tom couldn't believe what he thought he heard. He lifted his head up and looked down at her. "What did I hear you say?"

In the same quiet voice, she said, "Oh, Tom, don't start this. There's no way I can tell you where I was." She turned over onto her back and looked up at the ceiling. "What if I told you I was astrotraveling? What would you say to that?"

Of course Tom did not believe in astrotraveling, but he did believe in horny, lonely hunters. Untroubled, Mya lay humming in his arms while Tom fretted and puzzled over her. If a woman had been with a hunter, she would never tell her lover, at least an ordinary woman wouldn't, and astrotraveling was too weird for Tom to even consider.

"If you went astrotraveling, where did you leave this magnificent body?" Tom asked. "I could have used it while you were gone."

"Well, it was right here in bed," Mya said. "Sorry you didn't think to look."

Tom was left with no explanation as to Mya's whereabouts for three nervous days and four sleepless nights.

The person who knew more about Mya's disappearances than she wanted to know was Susan, but she didn't tell Tom what she knew because she didn't want him to have a bad opinion of her friend. And Tom was certainly not going to ask Susan where Mya was. The most he felt he could get away with and still appear disinterested was to comment at dinner that he hadn't seen Mya around much this week.

Instead of explaining that Mya was indeed up in a cabin on Jack's Mountain, blowing some good looking hunter's mind, Susan said, "You know Mya. Probably one of her old grandmas took sick and needed her to help out."

Grandmas were more acceptable than hunters, and more believable than astrotraveling, but Tom was still left in a state of confusion.

Mya's disappearances were just one more unacceptable condition that Tom had to accept if he wanted to be a part of her life. During the times when she wasn't around and he didn't know where she was, he became so nervous and anxious that he did foolish things. One week three days passed with no sign of Mya either at home or at the Frog. Like a lion at the zoo, Tom paced back and forth in his cage at the Kraft Paper Mills. Finally he thought of an excuse to escape. He decided to drive home for lunch. He would check up on the summer house and hopefully get a glimpse of Mya somewhere around the property. Maybe there was a chance she would be there during the day. When he told his secretary, Sandy, that he was going home for lunch, she said his wife must be a very special lady.

"I don't know about special," Tom replied, "but she sure is a lucky lady."

As he walked out of the office Sandy chuckled aloud. She loved working for a man with a good sense of humor.

As Tom drove down Bullfrog Valley Road, a hundred yards or so before the turnoff to the bridge, he pulled off to the side of the road and parked. He glanced over at the summer house, nearly hidden in the forest, hoping to see some sign of life. It was a warm silent day, and the only sound was the quiet purring of the engine. As he sat, he thought of how silly he would feel if anyone knew what he was doing, the big, important VP, hovering in his car, checking up on a crazy young woman, a waitress…. no, worse, a fortune teller. As he sat, pondering his ridiculous situation, the frogs started up a chorus so loud that they drowned out the sound of the car. And Tom heard very clearly what the frogs sang: "You're in too deep. You'll never get out. You're in too deep. You'll never get out."

That's when Tom remembered the book and the little white horse. He hadn't thought of it in 15 years. He tried to recall if the horse did get out. It must have; after all, it was a children's book. But he couldn't remember how. He would have to ask Heather the next time she called.

Tom was not prone to introspection, nor self-analysis. He was a candid, direct man of action, but he shuddered when he heard those frogs, and when he got home, he hugged Susan so hard and so long that she almost asked if anything was wrong.

Tom was home for lunch and he was hugging her. She wanted to think that meant that things were changing for the better, so she hugged him back and didn't say a word.

After a few minutes, he gently released her and looked into her face. "Hon," he said, "do you remember that book that Heather used to love so much when she was little, the one about the pony that ran away and got stuck in the swamp?"

"How could I forget it?" Susan asked. "I probably read it a million times. I used to know it off-by-heart."

"Do you remember how it ended? Did the pony get out of the swamp?" Tom asked.

"Of course it did," Susan said. "The farmer came with a tow truck and they tied a rope around the pony and pulled it out. I even remember the picture." She looked curiously at Tom. "What in the world made you think of that?"

Tom shrugged his shoulders. "I don't know. It just popped into my head this morning, that silly book, and I couldn't remember how it ended."

"He's becoming so sensitive," Susan thought, as she picked a loose thread off the edge of his collar. She smiled an enigmatic smile at the man who still had the ability, although infrequently, to tug at her heart strings and send a tickling shiver down her spine.

"Speaking of tow trucks," Tom said. "do you hear what I hear?"

"Oh, that's Mr. Edwards," Susan said. "He's been out picking apples, and he promised to bring me a bushel so I can make some apple sauce, providing I give him a jar or two, of course."

Tom rattled his car keys. "I won't wait to hear all about the history of apple growing in Central Pennsylvania," he said, as he turned and headed out the door.

From behind the truck, someone tossed an apple high in the air towards him, and he caught it in his left hand and began to shine it on his sleeve. As he waved and called "Thank you," he was surprised to see that it wasn't Mr. Edwards who had thrown the apple. Mya's head popped out from the side of the truck, her hair all wrapped up in a red bandana, a big, friendly smile lighting up her face.

"Did you take the day off to help us make cider?" she called.

"Nope," he called back, "but I'll be home in a few hours to drink some."

All of a sudden, Tom was in an excellent mood. He drove recklessly down the driveway, feeling the need to show off for some reason. As he munched on the crisp juicy apple, he allowed silly thoughts to pass through his mind. He pictured himself waist deep in the middle of the dam, and he pictured Mr. Edwards tying a thick, stiff rope around his waist and pulling him out with the big green truck. In the back of the truck was Mya, wearing nothing but a red bandana wrapped around her head. He couldn't wait until the day was over and he could come home. He had a sudden thirst for a big glass of fresh, cold apple cider.

THE PARLOR

When Mya first mentioned setting up a parlor in the summer house so she could do readings, Susan thought it was surely just a pipe dream. Susan had often seen ads for card readers in the little free local paper, but she couldn't imagine anyone she knew wanting to put up a sign and tell fortunes. There was something degrading about the business. Card readers were con artists and kooks. Mya was unusual, but she wasn't one of them, not a Madame X or a Miss Amber, offering, for a small fee, to predict a stranger's future.

But the pipe dream did not go away. Mya talked endlessly of her plans to turn the front room into a parlor with so much atmosphere that her clients would be transported into an entirely different world, and Susan got carried away by Mya's enthusiasm. Susan loved projects, any kind of project, and particularly one that involved decorating, sewing curtains and table cloths, framing pictures, and painting furniture, so she soon became almost as enthused as Mya about the parlor. By mid-November, the project occupied their minds and imaginations so thoroughly they could talk of little else as they waited for a weekend when the weather was supposed to be decent.

When Susan told Tom she was going to be helping Mya set up her parlor, she expected a nod, a grunt, or a smart remark, but Tom surprised her.

"Let me know if you need any help with the heavy stuff," he said.

"You don't have to go into work on Saturday?" Susan asked.

"Nope," Tom said. 'I've got to stop putting in all that extra time, or they're going to start expecting it of me. Can't let that happen."

Susan was pleased, yet skeptical. "We can really use you, but you're sure you want to help a kooky lady with a kooky project?"

"I said I did," Tom replied.

"That's great," Susan said. "Mya will be thrilled."

Mya was like a child playing with a doll house, and even Mr. Edwards joined in the fun and arrived daily with some antique treasure that he thought might be of use. These old discarded items brought Mya's true magical powers into play. Nothing was ever too far gone for Mya. She was able to repair, restore, or renovate what appeared to be a heap of old rotted brown boards, and with a nail here and there and a little bit of sanding and a coat or two of paint, turn them into a lovely little table.

And when Susan asked: Where did you find this neat table?" Mya replied, "So glad you noticed, Mrs. Harris. It was just one of the antiques that surfaced in the atelier of that famous connoisseur of Early French Furniture, Monsieur Paul Edwards. I'm sure you've heard of him. He's top dog among the collectors here in the Bullfrog Valley."

"You mean to say this table is that heap of old wood that's been lying on the porch?" Susan shook her head in disbelief.

"One in the same," Mya said, running her hand over the smooth surface. "A little nail, a little glue, more than a little paint, and a lot of elbow grease."

"I am impressed," Susan said. "I thought it was fire wood, honestly."

Mya gave no sign that she was aware of the many extraordinary things she knew how to do. Susan thought back to her friends in Laurel Hills, how they would fuss over someone's needlepoint project, or, over a refinished rocking chair. Of course, the needlework project came from an expensive kit ordered from the Museum of Modern Art catalog, and the old rocking chair was taken somewhere to be stripped and made ready for the refinishing, which was then done with an expensive electric sander and stains and varnished purchased especially for the project with much advice from the clerk at the paint store.

Mya, on the other hand, had a shoe box in the kitchen which contained a hammer, a couple of screw drivers, a few sheets of sand paper, and a jar of assorted nails and screws. She frequented the textile outlets, and she was very good at foraging, as she would be the first to admit. Mr. Edwards had several basements and attics filled with things he would never need, and he encouraged Mya to rummage through these places at will. Mya had no doubt that, without spending a cent, she could create the parlor of her dreams, and she was ever so happy that both Tom and Susan were onboard and ready to help.

They chose a nippy, sunny day in mid-November. Mya propped open the front door to the summer house, and the three, dressed in old work clothing and heavy jackets, carried everything out of the big front room and placed it on the lawn. Tom had organized a heavy metal box of tools he thought they might need, and Susan had brought a large thermos of hot coffee and three mugs. They began work early in the morning; there was so much to do.

Tom was in an excellent mood. He pretended Mya and Susan were his lazy, good-for-nothing crew, and he bossed them around and insulted them, and when they complained about his slave-driving, he threatened to replace them with some illegal aliens who were at that very moment swimming across the river to look for work.

The basic plan called for drapes to entirely cover the front wall and window. Mya found a bolt of dark forest green fabric which had been rejected because the dye had been uneven, so she got it for a song, yards and yards of it. It had taken much of their free time during the week before to iron, cut, stitch pleating tape to the top, and then hem the drapes. They made a separate drape to hang across the doorway which led to the living room. Tom's first job was to put up the hardware so the drapes could be hung. He stood on a stepladder, drilling holes in the woodwork, while Mya handed him the brackets and screws. Susan fitted the metal pleaters into the slots in the pleating tape. As she pushed the long brass prongs into the tape, she allowed herself to look in on the scene, as though she were an outside observer: attractive middle aged husband and his wife help friend get started in a new venture. How wonderful it was to see Tom in an old faded navy blue sweatshirt with his hair tousled and his eyes bright. She hadn't seen that Tom in years. It was the Tom she had fallen in love with so many decades ago. That was the Tom who used to juggle little Heather up in the air and put her securely on top of the slide and hold her hand until she got up enough courage to come down.

"I wonder what Heather's going to think of my parlor?" Mya broke into Susan's thoughts.

"I was just thinking of Heather," Susan said.

"I know," Mya said.

"No mind reading on the job," Tom reprimanded.

"Heather will love this room," Susan said. "Did I ever tell you how she was fascinated with Gypsies when she was little? I made her a Gypsy costume for Halloween, and she wouldn't take it off. She wore it everywhere. I covered a beach ball with aluminum foil, and she pretended it was her crystal ball. She was a riot. Do you remember that, Tom?"

"A crystal ball," Mya exclaimed. "That's what I've got to get for this place, a crystal ball."

"Where in the world would you find a crystal ball?" Susan asked. "I don't think I've ever seen a real one in my life."

"They pop up when you need them," Mya said. "And now that I've mentioned it, one will turn up. Just wait and see. In fact, I bet if we looked hard enough, we could find one lying around among Mr. Edwards' treasures."

"If not," Tom said to Mya, "I'll see if I can talk Susan into making you a really nice one out of aluminum foil."

"Oh, Tom, you've got no respect." Mya gave him a smack on the shoulder. "Time for a lunch break," she said to Susan. "Should we invite him or let him fend for himself?"

"Let's give him one more chance," Susan said, as she hurried up to the house to get the nice little lunch she had prepared earlier that morning.

The three sat on the floor and ate ham and cheese sandwiches and drank bitter rose hip tea that Mya had made in a large jar sitting in the sun on the kitchen window sill. Susan listened, amused, as Tom and Mya bickered about the seating arrangements in the parlor.

"You want the client to be totally relaxed," Tom said. "You want her at her absolute best."

"Wait a minute, Mr. Expert," Mya shook her sandwich at Tom. "What in the world do you know about reading cards?"

Tom quickly defended himself. "I might not know much about your particular line, but I know how business in general works. There are certain basic rules that apply in any kind of enterprise."

Susan leaned back against the wall and closed her eyes. She listened to the voices of her best friend and the man she loved. There was no anger in their voices as they argued back and forth. She sensed only teasing and affection.

Tom leaned towards Mya and pressed his point further: "A comfortable, stuffed chair is better," he said. "You want the client to be completely relaxed and able to concentrate on what you're telling her."

"Have you ever had a reading?" Mya asked calmly, as she removed the slice of ham from her sandwich and handed it to him.

"No, but I understand what it's all about," Tom replied, as he took the top piece of bread off his sandwich and placed Mya's ham neatly on the cheese. "It's sort of like a psychiatrist, I would imagine.

Mya turned her head and flashed her eyes at Susan. "Do you believe this know-it-all?" her eyes said. "Watch me knock him down to size."

"I use the cards," Mya explained patiently, "to channel in the client's attention so I can get a clear focus on what's going on in her psyche."

Susan looked over at Tom's face to see his reaction to what he often referred to as gobbledegook, and she was surprised to see him looking serious and respectful.

"So the client really needs to see the cards?" he asked. "You need to have her sitting right there at the table with you?"

"Ummm hmmm," Mya said, taking a large bite out of her sandwich.

"Okay, I see," Tom said. "So we'll put two straight chairs at the table, just across from each other." As he stood up and stretched, he added. "We'll put a comfortable stuffed chair by the door in case someone is waiting."

Mya let out a loud groan. "You're hopeless," she said. "He's totally hopeless," she said to Susan. "Tom, nobody is in the room while I am with a client. This happens to be the most confidential business in the entire world."

Susan closed her eyes once more and allowed herself to doze off to the sound of Tom and Mya's voices. Mya could hold her own. It was amusing to see her knock Tom off balance, again and again. Susan wished she herself could do that. She needed to take some lessons from Mya.

By four the parlor was finished, and Mya was thrilled with the results. Once the drapes were pulled shut, the room became small, dark, and cozy. On the wall which had been covered by the psychedelic mural, hung a large dark velvet square with swirls of colored paint and sparkling sequins, creating outlines of several of Mya's favorite constellations.

A lamp hung from the ceiling over the little table. On one of her many trips back up to the house, Susan had brought down a dark green bulb and a blue bulb for Mya to try in the lamp. First Susan screwed in the green bulb.

"Too green," Tom announced, and Mya agreed. "Nobody can see nothing nowhere no how," Tom said.

Susan carefully lay the green bulb on the table and screwed the blue bulb in. The room suddenly took on a beautiful glow, almost like a gem stone.

"It's perfect," Mya said. She moved around in the semi-dark room. "Look how the blue light changes the color of the drapes. Oh, it's magnificent." She twirled slowly around in the space between the table and the door, and then she suddenly threw open the front door and let a painful burst of gray-white afternoon autumn sunlight into the room.

"Hope for sale," she cried out into the forest, and her voice echoed from the dam, to the bridge, up the hill to the big house, and deep into the dark, green looming forest. "Come and get it. Hope for sale."

Susan was exhausted that night from all of the lifting and bending and running back and forth, but Tom was full of energy and in a great mood. He was the silly Tom she had loved so much some twenty years ago. When they got into bed, they had a giggling session that neither could stop. Tom would start a sentence, Susan would interrupt with something funny, and then they would laugh so hard that he couldn't finish the sentence. They laughed about the parlor and all the crazy people who would now be coming to the Angel Estate to have their dreary fortunes told. Then they couldn't decide if the proper word was told, or read. Do you read the cards and the cards tell the fortune? More giggling. What was particularly funny to both of them was the incongruity of their having helped put the enterprise together.

Tom asked seriously: "What do I say if someone asks me how I spent the weekend?"

They thought of ever so many funny replies to that question, and, still chuckling, they fell off to sleep and both experienced dreams that would have challenged Sister Dory's Dreamcatcher beyond repair.

Although Mya didn't sleep a wink that night, she too dreamed. To have reached this stage of her life was so exhilarating that she felt she might never need to sleep again. She sat at the table and studied her Tarot cards, losing herself in the colored pictures. She got out the cigar box which held her collection of antique thimbles. The glass dome that originally housed them had been broken years ago, but the little thimbles were all intact, each wrapped in a piece of soft tissue paper. She placed the thimbles in a row on a window sill. Once the pink lace cameo sat gleaming in the center of the row, a little bit of her childhood and a little bit of her mother settled into the parlor. She lit several colored candles, for hope, truth, goodness, and love. She burned a fat stick of desert sage incense and brewed a pot of Native American shaman tea, a very special tea that she saved for those rare occasions in life when a dream is in the process of coming to fruition.

When Tom and Susan awakened in the morning, they were both befuddled by what had gone on in their unconscious minds during the night, and they felt uncomfortable, as though something unpleasant had happened and they had not yet heard about what it might be. Had the phone rung at that point, they both would have jumped out of their skins.

Mya, on the other hand, was invigorated by the sleepless night. She danced to the river, crawled up onto her seat on the tree trunk, and sat, happily describing to her mother every intricate detail of the new parlor. She then wandered around the property until she found Mr. Edwards, whom she easily convinced to abandon his current project to come and see the new creation. He was enchanted. For days after, he could talk of little else as he made his way around town to pick up a paper at the newsstand, to get tobacco at the Smoke Shoppe, and to check the convenience store in case there was anyone there who hadn't heard the story.

Mya's parlor was an excuse for Sister Dory to make a special afternoon trip out to the Angel Estate with a bottle of champagne. She was ever so proud of her protégé. And Mya took this opportunity to bring Sister Dory up to the house to meet Susan, and Susan was amazed that this Sister Dory she had been hearing so much about was an ordinary middle-aged woman who could easily have been one of her old friends from Laurel Hills. Later that day when she told Tom about Sister Dory's stylish clothes and beautiful car, Tom came up with so many questions that she became impatient with him. Was Sister Dory able to earn enough money telling fortunes to buy a Camaro? Did she have a second job? Had she inherited a bundle?

"All you think about is money," Susan chided.

"It's my job," Tom said. "It's how I make my living."

It really wasn't about his job. Tom was wondering about the details of Sister Dory's business because he was trying to come up with a plan for Mya's little parlor. Although he himself did not believe in hocus pocus, it seemed as though everyone else did. Magazines were predicting that the Eighties would be the decade of spirituality. Mya was in the right game at the right time, and she could make a bundle, if only she would listen to him. Twenty years as top salesman for Kraft Paper Mills and office walls covered with recognition certificates and wooden plaques with gold lettering had gone to Tom's head. He was certain he had all the answers.

Mya expressed no interest in Tom's expert advice on advertising and marketing, and he didn't dare to approach her with some of his more creative ideas, like a chain of parlors with similar décor, located in little malls and manned by the same women who were now eking out miserable livings reading cards in their kitchens. Fast foods had caught on. Why not fast fortunes? Tom knew he had a million dollar idea. With one general manager and a catchy name, everyone in the business would get rich. He would make Sister Dory the CEO, and he was sure the others would jump at the chance for a regular income and a little security for a change.

But it wasn't time yet to approach Mya with such a progressive idea. Tom was still working on minor details of her own little business, like designing a fee schedule to post by the door, and creating discount coupons to attract new clients and to encourage old clients to come more often, maybe five readings for the price of four, or a free reading for bringing in a new client. Tom was loaded with good ideas.

"How much do you charge for a reading?" he asked Mya, as he sat nursing a drink at his regular little table at the Frog.

"I don't charge a fee for my readings," she replied.

"What do you mean you don't charge a fee? You do this for free?" Just when Tom thought he could never be shocked nor surprised by Mya again, she shocked and surprised him. Like a follower of Chairman Mao, to each of Tom's questions, Mya spouted the party line. Tom thought maybe she had a little red book hidden in her pocket.

"The card reader must not touch the money," she said. "If the card reader takes money from the client's hand, it's a bad omen."

"Bad omen?" Tom asked, trying not to sound incredulous. "What does that mean?"

"It means the client will be back again within 48 hours, and that's not enough time for the reader to recharge from the initial visit. The result is confusion." Mya rattled off her explanation impatiently, as though she thought Tom was deliberately trying not to understand what she was telling him.

"This woman is crazy," Tom thought, not for the first time, and not for the last time. But Mya was not only crazy, she was also beautiful and stimulating, so Tom ignored the crazy.

"So you get no money at all for doing this? Is that what you're telling me?" Tom asked.

"No, Tom. You don't understand. I don't charge a fee, but everyone leaves something."

"How do they know how much to leave?" Tom was curious.

"They leave different amounts," Mya said. "Some are very generous."

"Where do they leave these amounts?" Tom asked.

"Usually on a little table by the door," My replied. "That's how it's done."

Mya's indifference to money was baffling to Tom. He had drawn up plans to standardize the fees and post a fee schedule where the client could see it as she walked through the door. Now he realized he had to throw that idea out. His challenge was to think of a way that Mya could charge, yet not have to talk about money with the client, nor touch any money the client left. This was a challenge that had not been addressed in any of Tom's classes in business school. Tom himself could not believe the amount of time he was spending working on the problem, aware, of course, that it wasn't a problem at all for Mya, but he pretended it was a problem so he would have an excuse to be involved in some part of her life, to make himself needed, at the same time aware and afraid that Mya needed no one. She was totally self-contained.

Tom had no idea how many hours he spent thinking about Mya's business, as he stood at his office window, staring down at the beautiful river flowing on happily without a care in the world. And how many more hours did he spend punching numbers on his calculator and writing up a small business prospective that had nothing to do with the Kraft Paper Mills. If anyone had the inclination to look closely at the balled up papers in Tom's brass waste baskets, he would have reason to marvel at the little figures, odd drawings, numbers and abbreviations. But no one thought of looking in Tom's trash can. He did such a grand job as Vice President of Sales that no one ever questioned how he spent his working hours.

While Tom sat at his desk, creating pages of irrelevant statistics, Mya stopped by Mr. Edwards' place and told him that she needed something for the clients to drop money into on their way out of the parlor. It shouldn't be a cash register, nor anything that looked like it was related to money. Mr. Edwards understood immediately and came up with an empty mahogany Victrola case. When the lid was closed, it resembled a small coffin, but when the lid was open, the inside was lined with maroon velvet. It was quite pretty. He also found a sturdy little table on which it could sit. As he drove Mya and her new financial system home in his noisy old truck, he was pleased to death. He loved old things, and he liked people who appreciated old things and put them to use. When one old thing was put to use, in his mind, it justified his entire collection.

Naturally, Tom learned of Mya's new accounts receivable system by way of Susan.

"It's an old record player. It's very pretty, not a mark on the wood. Mr. Edwards found it for her among all that junk in his attic," Susan said.

"An old record player?" Tom had trouble understanding how an old record player could be an accounts receivable system. He wrinkled his forehead and looked at Susan, waiting for further explanation.

Susan put a steaming baked potato wrapped in foil on his plate and moved the butter dish closer to him. "It's not really a record player," she said. "It was a record player, but it's empty now. It's just a lovely wooden box. Would you rather have sour cream?"

"No," Tom shook his head. "So how is this thing supposed to work?"

"It doesn't work," Susan said. "It just sits by the door and people drop money in it as they leave."

"What if they need to make change?" Tom asked.

"I don't know," Susan said. "You know Mya. She'll just let them make their own change, or tell them to pay next time, or something. We're not talking about large amounts of money here."

Tom finished his dinner in silence. Susan felt as though he seemed angry. She wondered if it was something she had said. She thought back over every word as she ate, and then decided for the millionth time that he was probably angry with her for talking about something as stupid and silly as Mya's latest craziness. The man works hard all day and he comes home and I rattle on about a kooky lady and her kooky projects. He has a right to be angry with me, I guess.

"How was work today, Hon?" she asked, as she placed a bowl of chocolate mint ice cream on the table before him.

"So, so," Tom said.

Susan put a gentle hand on Tom's shoulder and gave him a kiss in his hair. He reached up and put his hand over hers. He felt like crying. So often these days he felt like a small child. If Susan were his mother, and he had been a little boy, he would have wrapped his arms around her waist and sobbed. He had spent hours trying to come up with a perfect solution to what he thought was a problem for Mya. He had even ordered small blue envelopes so that the client could slip a folded bill or two inside and not just toss them in a basket or leave them on the table. He chose the color because he thought it was classy and that Mya would love it. During lunch, he had gone downtown and bought a black metal money box with a combination lock. He paid $48 for the damned thing. Tom sat and watched his ice cream melting in the bowl, and he felt like the biggest fool in the world.

But why the Fool (thoughtless, extravagant, lacking discipline, inconsiderate, unrestrained, and excessive) when, in reality, Tom was the Emperor (action, development, wealth, authority, indomitable spirit, and endurance). All day long people stopped by Tom's office to run things by him. He had a reputation as a clear thinker who could always filter out the bugs and knew how to shoot down worthless ideas with grace, or point out minor changes to salvage a flawed plan. "Run this by Tom," echoed through the corridors of the Kraft Paper Mills. Mr. Flynn joked about having a stamp made that read: "Go ask Tom." At the Kraft Paper Mills, Tom was the Emperor; there was no doubt about that. But when it came to anything having to do with Mya, Tom was incompetent and bungling. He was the Fool, oblivious to the possible consequences of his every action.

As Tom showered and shaved the next morning, the Emperor resolved to the Fool in the mirror that there would be no afternoon drink at the Frog. He had to begin to take steps to get this foolish woman out of his life before she got him into real trouble. The first thing Tom did when he got to the office was to put the money box away where he could not see it. He worked all day long on the new Bates account, did projections for January and February for all the territories, and had Sandy set up a string of appointments for the week. Tom's productive mood lasted for most of the day. The Emperor was in control, and he bore no resemblance to the lovesick Fool.

But, around four, the Emperor began to tire, and the Fool perked up and reminded the Emperor that he had developed quite a thirst from all that hard work. Why shouldn't he be able to stop and have a drink when and where he wanted? Nine chances out of ten, the Fool explained, Mya wouldn't be there anyway. The thought of a cold martini helped coax his car up the drive and into the parking lot of the Frog.

"If she's working," he thought, "I'll just be cool. Hell, I can't avoid her forever."

Mya was working. Tom was cool. But Mya didn't notice. She brought him a martini, made herself an iced tea, yelled to Juan that she was on break, and came over and sat down with Tom at the table.

"Just the man I want to see," she announced.

Tom took a deep swig of his drink. Mya's enthusiasm caught him off guard. He liked being the man she wanted to see.

"Candles and playing cards," Mya said. "I need quantities of candles in every color, and I need regular decks of playing cards, new ones that have never been opened. Inexpensive ones." She picked up a paper napkin and began to write a neat list.

"Can't old Edwards dig some up for you?" Tom asked, sarcastically, but Mya ignored the tone of his voice.

"He only has stuff that's been used," Mya explained. "These cards have to be untouched. They have to be in their original wrappers. Otherwise, there's no way I could know whose life I am reading."

"Okay, okay. I get it," Tom smiled. This serious, professional, didactic Mya was adorable. He reached over and covered Mya's hand with his. "Now just tell me what I can do you for?" he asked, as he gave her hand a gentle squeeze.

She handed him the napkin on which she had written the list.

Tom looked at the list. "What quantities are we talking about?" Tom asked. He could not help but respond when Mya needed something that he could provide.

"That's your department," Mya said. "Aren't you into projections?" She lowered her voice, "Or is it erections you're interested in?"

She glanced over at the door, where five big noisy men were making their way into the room. She stood up, and still holding onto Tom's hand, she asked, "Are you going into work tonight? Because, if you are, we could talk about this later."

Against his will, Tom nodded in the affirmative. "Around 8:30," he said. He watched Mya's firm rear move away from the table, and he had to sit awhile until his hard on went away. Then he left the bar and drove home.

Susan was wearing a new blue blouse and a pair of dangling blue lapis earrings that she had found at the Circle Antique Shop. She felt pretty. She greeted Tom with a hug. "In the mood for some shrimp creole?" she asked. It was one of his all-time favorite meals.

"Sounds great," he said, and that's about all he said for the rest of the evening. At eight fifteen, he came out of his study and announced that he had to go into the office to get more data on something he had to put together for an 8 a.m. meeting. Susan sat on the couch, feeling silly in her new blouse and her new earrings, which Tom had not even noticed.

"Don't bother to wait up," Tom said. "I might run into some complications. You never know what's going to happen with that damned computer."

It was impossible for Tom to hurry when he was making love with Mya. She liked to talk and tease and tickle. She liked to ask him questions that made him so excited he could barely reply. Sometimes she liked to tie him down with long silk scarves and lick him all over slowly with her big warm tongue. "Which is better, down here, or up higher? Slower, or a little bit faster? What about over here? We don't want to neglect that tasty treat." Tom groaned in response to her queries and answered mostly by gently moving parts of his body closer to her mouth. At other times, Mya didn't remove a stitch of clothing, but undid a couple of buttons on her blouse and stuffed a stiff pink nipple into his mouth. "Time to feed the baby," she said. "Oh my, the baby's so hungry. What a hungry baby. Come on, have some more." Mya had the ability to drive Tom absolutely crazy.

During their business meeting that evening, as Mya tried to explain why she needed all those candles and cards, she sat on Tom's lap, facing him with her legs tightly straddling him on either side. She gently moved her pelvis in little circles as she explained that the white candle gives a person faith in what she is planning to do. A pink candle makes grief go away. She didn't tell him that the red, yellow and white candles burning on her table were meant to bring her lover to her bed. Nor did she tell him that if she could get her lover to light the candles for her that he would never leave until she decided he should. By the time she had finished talking about the candles, her crotch was so wet and his penis so hard that they had to pause a moment or they were going to have messy orgasms right there on the chair. Tom led her to the bed, where they undressed each other and followed through with what they had begun in the kitchen.

After the second time Tom came, Mya pulled from nowhere a piece of white silk and rubbed it gently over his sticky wet penis. Then she put the cloth between her legs and held it there.

Tom became very interested in what she was doing. "What's going on down there?" he asked. "What in the world are you doing?"

Mya didn't reply. She rubbed the cloth against his penis again and again until it was once more hard and firm.

"Aaaaahhh, Mya," Tom crooned. "You're forgetting my age. Are you trying to do me in?"

Mya giggled as she pulled herself on top of Tom and arranged herself over the warm, firm penis and began to rock back and forth, back and forth. With her right hand, she carefully tucked the white cloth under the edge of the mattress and then turned her attention back to the groaning man beneath her. The silk cloth would stay under the mattress until she conceived.

Early the next morning, Tom ordered both the candles and the cards from an outlet store which carried some of Kraft Paper Mills' products. They gave him a great price. The candles, which retailed for six dollars in a gift shop, were less than two dollars each. He bought two dozen in each of the colors Mya wanted. And the playing cards were a dollar a deck. He ordered fifty. He carefully wrote on a sheet of paper: "Suggested retail price: candles, $5; cards, $2. Profit of $3/candle and $1 on each deck of cards. On 20 candles, profit of $60; 20 decks of cards, $20 profit." And he drew a little smiley face, just for kicks.

A few nights later, with a silly boyish grin on his own smiley face, he carried two boxes into Mya's parlor, set them on the table, and began to remove smaller boxes from each of them. "Special delivery for Miss Mya Clark," he said.

"What in the world is this, Tomas?" Mya cried. "What are you bringing me this time?"

"Candles and cards," Tom sang. "Cards and candles."

"Oh, this is wonderful. I didn't expect such fast service," Mya said, as she opened one of the boxes and held up a thick yellow candle. "Where shall we put all of these?"

Tom helped Mya stack some of the smaller boxes on a shelf in the parlor, and put the others on the kitchen table to be put away later. Then Tom showed Mya his sheet of profit figures.

"Look at this," he said. Mya glanced at the paper, folded it carefully, and tucked it into one of the boxes. "This man never stops trying," she said. She encircled Tom with her arms and gave him an affectionate hug. As she planted soft, warm kisses on his neck, she said, "You are my savior. You are my patron. What would I ever do without my Tomas?"

Mya was wearing a short, yellow print skirt with a little white top which hung over her breasts and left several inches of her midriff exposed. And as she gave Tom soft kisses that made shivers run up and down his spine and goose bumps appear all over his neck and his face flush hotter and hotter, he was able to reach under the skirt and up under the blouse, and without moving more than an inch or two in any direction, he was able to enjoy what was a very unusual experience for him and a very pleasant one. Mya was wearing no bra and no panties.

"Is this how you treat delivery men?" he asked.

"Some," Mya replied. "Depends."

"I was just thinking of maybe changing jobs," Tom teased.

Mya leaned against him at the door. He wanted to stay longer and repeat in a horizontal fashion what they had just experienced on the vertical, but he had to hurry home. At the door, Mya cleaned his ears one last time with her long, soft tongue, and blew him kisses as he backed away from the door. "Merci, merci, merci," she whispered loudly as he walked down the path to where he had parked his car among the trees.

Of course Mya could not charge her clients for candles and cards, and she certainly couldn't ask for a donation. Most clients, in appreciation for their new sense of purpose and power, dropped generous amounts of money in the mahogany box.

Tom certainly was never going to ask Mya to pay him for the cards and candles. Just as Mya's relationship with a client would be sullied by the mention of money, Tom's casual, constant and comfortable physical closeness to Mya would have been compromised by the mention of money. Tom could easily absorb the loss, and it was worth every dollar he spent for the twenty minutes in the kitchen under the little yellow skirt and the hours of dreaming about those precious twenty minutes.

Without consulting Mya, Tom had business cards printed up for her, simple dark blue cards with Mya written in silver in a beautiful curly script, and on the bottom right corner was her phone number. Tom ordered a thousand, and just to pacify him, Mya kept a small pile on the table near the door. Tom put one of the pretty cards among his other business cards in the leather card holder he carried with him at all times. When he pulled his cards out to look for someone he was referring to or recommending, the unusual blue card inevitably caught someone's eye and peaked their curiosity. "What in the world does this person do?" And Tom was able to reply with a straight face, "She's one fantastic lady." Most thought this Mya person might be a hooker, or a stripper. Only Tom Harris would have the nerve to carry a card like that in his wallet. Only he could pull something like that off and get away with it. What an interesting character he was.

In general there was no need for calling cards, nor business cards, nor fliers in Port Williams. Even in the midst of Twentieth Century technology, news traveled by word of mouth, bad news, of course, traveling a little faster and a little farther than good news. The Port Williams Chronicle was printed daily, but, except for time when the river decided to sink a pleasure boat full of senior citizens, front page news was always happening elsewhere and came to town via the UPI wire. Local news, what there was of it, traveled from tongue to ear to tongue to ear, and during the trip, was embellished and enhanced, as it passed from those who knew people directly involved to those who knew people who knew people involved, to those who had heard of people who knew people involved.

What Mya feared was that the news of her unique parlor would travel so fast that she might be overwhelmed by the number of clients who would want to come, if only out of curiosity. While Tom was desperately trying to advise Mya on how to attract a lot of customers and to find ways to keep them coming back, Mya herself was more interested in limiting the number of clients. Looking into peoples' souls, absorbing their emotional pain, and trying to guide them, warn them, and help them, was exhausting. Not only were there many times when Mya didn't feel up to a reading, but often she needed to recuperate after she had been with a particularly taxing client. And there was no way to predict in advance how deeply she would have to go, so she always had to be at her best, with adequate time to prepare, as well as time to recover.

Clients came to Mya for any number of reasons. Many came out of curiosity; some, from severe desperation; and a few with a specific concern or problem that had been bothering them and that could not be addressed or solved to their satisfaction by a friend, a priest, or the family doctor. There were also a few true believers who used a psychic in the same way one would hire a financial adviser, an interior decorator, or a marital counselor, as kind of an ongoing spiritual consultant.

As the client was walking through the door into the parlor, Mya was already trying to determine what kind of reading it was going to be. She noted the bend of the neck, the tautness of the lips, the way the eyes peered out of the sockets, either looking directly at her, pleading, or avoiding her glance, embarrassed, guilty, or afraid of what they might be giving away. She listened to the shuffle of the soles, or the tap of the heels on the floor. By the time the client was seated across the round table from Mya, there was little mystery left, and Mya's first question often brought everything tumbling right out onto the table, as though a handbag had been dumped out in an angry last effort to find a lost car key.

Those who came out of curiosity were walking and talking advertisements for Mya's parlor. They went home and told their friends and families embellished versions of secrets Mya had somehow known about them, and hinted at mysterious, vague bits of wisdom she had shared with them, things they didn't feel they should repeat, even to a daughter, or best friend. The families and friends eventually made their way to the fascinating parlor on the old Angel Estate so they could experience the phenomenon for themselves. They compared lies and exaggerations and debated whether or not Mya truly had special powers, and, if not, wondered how she could have discovered all the amazing things she apparently knew. A curious client, one who wasn't sure how she felt about psychics, was easy money. She wanted to hear that a lover from the distant past was still thinking about her. She knew exactly who that was. She had seen him at the last high school reunion, and she had picked up on the vibes. She loved to hear that there would be a drastic change for the better in the family's financial situation. She asked practical questions about whether her husband might be getting a promotion, or at least, a raise; if their child was likely to make the Little League All Stars; or if it was a good idea for them to put the old family dog to sleep now that he had lost control of his bladder. Mya shuffled deftly through the cards and brought up hearts and love and diamonds and money and clubs, always protecting her reputation by pointing out preventive cards. These cards meant there was a chance to avert the influence of the previous card, so, if the prediction didn't come true, the client would remember that Mya had forewarned her that it might not. Although the curious themselves seldom came back for a second reading, for months, they sent word-of-mouth referrals to Mya, and the referrals sent others, and a trip to Mya's parlor was on every Port Williams' housewife's to-do list.

The client Mya most enjoyed helping was the middle-aged woman who had reached a point in life where her choice was limited to a Valium prescription, renewable by phone, or another thirty years of angst. Why not pay a visit to Mya's Parlor. She had nothing to lose except a few dollars and an hour of her dreary life. Middle-aged women in Port Williams generally did not work. They had married young, had reared large families, and then found themselves not yet fifty, their children grown and married, and a long stretch ahead of them with nothing to fill the years besides a little garden, some house work, and a tired husband snoring on the couch in front of a flickering television. These women took much longer to decide to come to Mya than the merely curious. In a typical case, the woman heard Mya's name come up in conversation, because Mya had, by this time, become the talk of the town. Later, in a totally unrelated conversation, the woman heard someone tell how her life had turned around as a result of a visit to Mya's parlor. No one, of course, was able to explain how Mya performed her magic, but, regardless, at some point, the woman, now ready to clutch at any straw, called Mya to schedule an appointment for herself.

From the quiet, nervous female voice on the phone, asking too politely if it would be possible for Mya to see her some time, any time, there was no hurry, Mya knew, and she put a little star by the name and was careful not to schedule anyone immediately after. What Mya gave these women was something they hadn't had in years: an hour of undivided attention. She looked directly into their eyes, listened to what they had to say, and asked pertinent questions to make certain she understood what she was being told. Just the fact that someone was listening meant there was hope. For some, it was the first time in decades they had seen hope in person. At what other times in their lives, besides early childhood and the courting years, had these lonely women been given undivided attention? It was uplifting, inspiring, and made them feel they were not in this alone. There was an entire universe of thoughts, symbols, ideas, and dreams to guide them. Even those who didn't believe wanted to believe so very much that there was satisfaction and pleasure in the wanting, even if it was frosted ever so lightly with a layer of skepticism.

Mya's clients came away with much more than what the cards had said. Most had not bothered to drive out to the Angel Estate in years, and it had grown wilder and more mysterious with the long period of neglect. They were charmed and enchanted even before they walked into the parlor, which was exactly the kind of place where one would expect to find a fortune teller. In attempting to describe it, many came up with the same term: "Gypsy-Victorian." Mya had designed everything to eliminate distractions from the outside world. The windows were covered with heavy, dark drapes. The room was lit entirely by candles, and mirrors were placed here and there to reflect the candle light. Some sort of potpourri gave off an odor of lavender, was it, or dried roses, or lilies of the valley, or maybe jasmine, a fragrance that brought back fond memories of a grandmother's bureau drawers. In the middle of the room was a round table, covered with a dark green cloth which reached to the floor. And lying on the center of the table was a thick mirror with imperfections, swirls, and dark areas where the silver had been scraped off the back.

Mya herself was a most important part of the atmosphere. For her readings, she wore some sort of long caftan and a gauze scarf with metal threads running through it. Bits of sparkling stones and silver peeked out from her long earrings and her overlapping, entwined necklaces. In the silent, dark room, Mya became two large green gemstone eyes, a quiet reassuring voice, and ten long slender fingers covered with rings of gold and silver and colored stones, her nails clicking over the round mirrored surface. As she deftly shuffled a deck of cards and spread a few out before her on the table, Mya's serene face and the client's anxious face floated together in the mirror among Kings and Queens and spades and hearts and jokers.

In addition to cost, Mya's advantage over the local Mental Health Clinic was that she was dealing on a plane that people had believed in when they were children and had lost along the way. It was a world of colored gemstones, candle light, witches, dice, incense, and magic, both good and evil. Mya never broke the spell with mundane questions about headaches, irregularity, fatigue and insomnia. She talked of the Queen of Hearts, destiny, the Black Witch, cosmic changes, fools, yearning, and unfulfilled dreams.

For the most desperate, for those exuding such pain that Mya could not bear to look at the gray aura surrounding the body as it crept into the parlor, for those who had been unhappy for so long that they were unable to imagine any other existence, Mya used her worn, familiar, colorful Tarot cards and dealt out a five card spread. Card one reflected the present; card two, the immediate past. The third card spoke of the future; the fourth, of the long forgotten past; and the fifth, of the far-reaching future. To a woman who dwelled on the immediate past, struggled to get out of the miserable present, and yet dreaded the future, the five-card spread gave a new perspective, one filled with hope. Mya could see a physical relief as the client allowed herself to remember that there was a time before the present, and to realize that there will be a time after the present is long gone and has become the forgotten past. Hope had a magic way of erupting spontaneously in the cozy little parlor, often accompanied by the splatter of warm tears onto the mirror, smearing the images into one beautiful colorful palette.

As she wound up the session, Mya didn't prescribe a bitter white pill to be taken with meals and at bedtime, with dry mouth as a side effect. Mya assigned pleasant tasks to her now hopeful client.

"You don't want to just sit and wait for the future to come," Mya said. "There are some things you can do to prepare for it and help it hurry along."

She reached behind her to the shelf along the wall and carefully chose three large candles: pink for hope, yellow for perseverance, and green for strength and courage. These were to be placed in a western window on the second floor and all three lit with a single match just as the sun set each evening. The flame should burn for at least an hour, and in no circumstance should the candles be left burning after midnight. Now the client had in her life an awareness of the sun setting, of midnight, of the dawn, all magical times when special things happen.

Mya tried to give each client a wise little saying to take home with her, one appropriate to her particular situation. Mya had hundreds of them in her mind and could pull one out at a moment's notice. These sayings were so on-target that eventually many people walked around the streets of Port Williams whispering to themselves: "This is my world. There is no other world. If I don't like my world, I must change it." Or "I can appreciate my life, even if it is not perfect. It will become perfect in time." "I must stop living someone else's dreams. I must live my own dreams." "I will concentrate on the newness. I will enjoy the magic of the present moment."

And Mya's clients began to smile more often, dare to wear something completely different from their usual drab wardrobes, and to enjoy their new world, even though nothing had really changed at all, except now they had hopeful, crazy, magic, new perspectives.

Mya was never in a hurry. She refused to schedule readings back to back. There was always time after a reading, if she felt the urge, to offer the uplifted client a cup of tea, loose tea, brewed in an old china pot and served in a cup with a saucer, along with a delicate cloth napkin. During the tea drinking ceremony, Mya opened the drapes and let the outside world come into the room. She suggested the client, now friend, move her chair a little so she could look out the window. The scene was a Nineteenth Century pastoral painting. In the foreground was a small pond with cattails and a dam made of big, gray broken stones. Beyond that, a green lawn led up to a big brownstone house, sitting atop a hill and surrounded by enormous trees. Here and there the artist had painted a patch of orange and yellow daylilies, and, in the background, with wide smooth strokes, she had created smooth, green mountains with a touch of blue sky behind them. The word enchanting automatically escaped from the client's lips. It was the first time in years she had found an opportunity to use the word. It was a lovely word. It felt good on her tongue.

Talk naturally turned to the Angels and tales that had been passed down for generations about the extent of the wealth of Lloyd Angel and rumors about his wife, Kathleen. Mya loved when the conversation took this turn, and soon she and the client were talking about why Kathleen never had children, analyzing the various rumors about how she had met her death, and telling stories of reported sitings of Mrs. Angel's Ghost. Mya repeated what she had come to believe about the Ghost. Kathleen Angel had either drowned herself, or had been drowned, in the river. The fact that she had met a violent death and was not properly buried would account for the haunting. And her continued influence in the town, after all these years, could be explained by the presence of her energy in the river. After all, water traps human energies and thoughts, and moving water spreads them and carries their influence well beyond the immediate vicinity.

Mya was able to explain her farfetched theory in such a way that it even sounded logical to an otherwise rational client as she sat and drank tea in the little parlor, under the influence of her first esoteric experience. It was only after the now uplifted and newly inspired woman got home and repeated the conversation to a skeptical, ridiculing husband that she realized how crazy it all sounded, and she felt embarrassed, then angry with the husband who wasn't going to allow for any change, and then sad, but in the long run, despite the anger and sadness, still a little hopeful.

The post-reading visit, no more than fifteen or twenty minutes long, was a better advertising gimmick than any Tom could have designed. Once her attention turned from the big house on the hill, the client could examine all the wondrous details of the parlor and admire the old pieces of furniture and the rugs and other interesting things Mya had sitting around, mostly on loan from Mr. Edwards' endless collection. And, too, there was time to notice what a lovely creature Mya was, how tall, how elegant, and how unusual and beautiful her eyes were. It was hard to believe she was the same person who waitressed at the Frog, or that she had ever been the pathetic little foster child, Marie Clark. Whether the waitress or the foster child was in the client's thoughts, no one ever failed to leave a ten dollar bill, or a twenty dollar bill, in the box by the door. In the long run, Mya couldn't have set up a fee schedule that would bring in more than she was earning in her haphazard don't-touch-the-money fashion that drove Tom Harris to despair.

MADAME B. COMES TO PORT WILLIAMS

Despite Mya's unwillingness to listen to Tom's advice, she was doing something very unusual for a psychic: she was supporting herself, and she was doing so without compromising a single principle. Someone with less integrity would have charged outrageously for the candles and cards, would have arranged to read for groups at bridal showers and birthday parties, or, as Tom suggested, would have got a 900 number and done readings over the telephone. Many psychics working in Port Williams, as well as many psychics throughout history, did not have Mya's principles.

A hundred years ago, the thing for a struggling psychic to do was to take a long trip to another country, especially to America, to try to make a lot of money in a short time, using any means at her disposal. These psychics often did damage beyond repair.

Madame Bolgoruki, known simply as Madame B., was one such destructive psychic. Although Mya had Madame Bolgoruki's best-selling autobiography sitting on her book shelf, she had never read it, so she had no idea that Madame B. had actually visited Port Williams. She had been invited by Kathleen Angel and had told fortunes in the very same room in which Mya had her parlor.

Madame B., however, differed from Mya in every way imaginable. She was old and fat and disheveled, and she was definitely interested in money. Her goal in life was to accumulate a nest egg so she could retire to her village in the Caucasus and live out her remaining years in comfort and peace. She knew America was the place to work on that nest egg, and thus, she threw all of her energies into a one-year tour, where she told others' fortunes, while she made her own.

Spiritualism was trendy in the late 19th and early 20th centuries. None of Kathleen's acquaintances claimed to be a believer, but several had had their tea leaves read by a Polish Countess in Philadelphia, and others now and again had their palms read by Gypsies passing through Port Williams. These experiences caused no major changes in anyone's life; they merely added a touch of zest to otherwise predictable conversations. They were diversions, and, then as now, every idle, wealthy lady needed diversions.

But none so much as Kathleen Angel. And none was as skilled in providing diversions as Kathleen. One summer she hired workmen to dam up the creek and create a shallow lake. Small floating wooden islands were placed here and there, and row boats were provided for the guests. It took four months to create Paradise Lake, as it was called, and Kathleen held several splendid weekend parties before a tribe of giant beavers moved in and helped themselves to the delicious islands.

Her less imaginative acquaintances anticipated with excitement and curiosity the parties and dinners to be held at the Angel Estate and they were seldom disappointed. Kathleen brought musicians, entertainers, and famous chefs from far and wide to provide memorable amusement and fare on every occasion, and often, for no occasion, but just because she felt the urge.

Once she contacted a medium in Philadelphia and arranged to hold a séance in the summer house on a windy day in March. The eight women she invited were thrilled, while the many who did not receive invitations naturally felt slighted. Kathleen decorated the front room in the summer house in a manner appropriate for the occasion. A round table covered with a black cloth was placed in the middle of the room, and all the windows were draped with dark curtains. The room was lit with heavy white candles, which sat in thick stained glass candle holders. Although the atmosphere was perfect, nothing much happened. The ladies, however, talked about the séance so enthusiastically, with quiet asides about phenomena they didn't want to be generally known, that those who hadn't been there did not know that they had missed absolutely nothing. From the innuendos that peppered all conversations about the séance, they were certain it had been a spectacular event, and the rumor circulated that the spirit of one of Kathleen's ancestors from Ireland had made an appearance at the table, but had spoken some ancient Celtic language that no one could understand. Each of the excluded friends knew Kathleen could not have accommodated all the members of her social set, but nonetheless, each still wondered why she herself had been excluded. No one thought to check names. Kathleen had merely invited the first eight friends alphabetically from her address book, Lucy Adams through Evelyn Carter.

A few weeks after the séance, the next twelve ladies from the address book buried any bad feelings they had over the slight as they opened invitations, written in Kathleen's beautiful curly handwriting, to a card reading, featuring the famous visiting seer, Madame Bolgoruki.

"No sense wasting all the work we put into creating this beautiful room," Kathleen replied, when one of the servants asked if the parlor should be dismantled after the séance. "I'll think of something else to do in here." And she did. She invited Madame B., who was milking Philadelphia, to come to Port Williams by train to spend an afternoon reading for an intimate group of Kathleen's friends, whose last names ranged from D to K. In exchange, Madame B.'s round-trip train fare was paid, a room was reserved for her at the Market Street Hotel, and she was picked up and delivered to the Estate by Andrew in a handsome carriage with two identical shiny black horses. Friends merely wondered at the size of the donation that was expected for a visit of this sort. Whatever it was, the Angels could certainly afford it.

Madame B. was a woman in her sixties, who was so large that her weight, along with layers of clothing, scarves, necklaces, and belts, made her a formidable obstacle to move around from place to place. Andrew had a great deal of difficulty helping her in and out of the black carriage. The experience made him appreciate even more the 110 lb soft, sweet smelling woman that he usually had the pleasure of assisting.

The twelve women assembled nervously in the living room of the summer house while Madame B. was ensconced in the parlor, sitting at the round table. Once again the room was lit by candles, and the window and door covered with heavy drapes. The women whispered encouragement to each other as they took turns, one by one, making their way through the velvet curtains and into the darkened room to hear their fates. As each woman came back out of the room, she was greeted with more whispered questions and quiet giggling as another nervous lady took her turn. Kathleen's newest personal maid, Roberta, all ears, served wine punch and a variety of cookies on a glimmering glass tray to the ladies in the living room. Roberta had been waiting five years for an opening on the Angel staff, and she had discovered almost immediately that being a part of life on the Angel Estate had been well worth the wait. Kathleen promised Roberta that she too could have her cards read, if Madame B. wasn't too exhausted at the end of the afternoon.

It was an unseasonably cold mid-April day, and a small fire had been lit in the fireplace in the living room. Kathleen insisted that everyone go before her into the parlor, even Roberta, and by the time it was Kathleen's turn, she was in a gay and silly mood. The odor of hot, spiced wine punch, mixed with various sweet scents of ladies perfumes and powders, made Kathleen feel a little giddy.

"Wish me luck," she called as she blew a kiss to the ladies and disappeared through the heavy drapes into the quiet, dark and cold parlor. Once inside, she paused, and a shiver passed through her body. Madame B.'s fat, lined face and the odor coming from her thick layers of clothing contrasted dramatically with the fashionable, sweet-smelling, well-groomed ladies in the living room. When Madame B. smiled at Kathleen, her eyes disappeared into the folds of skin on her face, and her stained, irregular teeth glistened brown and gold in the candle light. The fear that Madame B. might be able to read her thoughts propelled Kathleen to walk quickly across the room and seat herself stiffly in the chair across the table from this eerie creature. She gave Madame B. a beautiful rich lady smile, with her lips compressed so that no teeth showed, but she didn't look her in the eye. She focused instead at the flickering candle on the table.

Kathleen was wearing a dusty rose, silk afternoon dress, and much of her auburn hair was piled beneath a small pink bonnet with a wide dusty rose ribbon tied around it. Due to the dampness of the April day, small spit curls framed her face and looked as though they were trying to escape from the bonnet. From each ear dangled three small triangles of pink tourmaline, and a simple strand of tiny, perfect round pearls lay smoothly on her bosom.

Madame B. looked at Kathleen and saw money. There was a time early in her life when she would have looked directly through the pearls and silk and seen discontentment, ennui, and despair, but her growing nest egg blinded her to anything peripheral these days.

Madame B. was also very tired. She had not slept well in the hard bed at the hotel, and her dinner had not set right with her. Nothing much did these days. She had spent eleven months traveling from city to city in America, staying in strange places, and meeting strange people, who spoke a language that was very tiresome for her to try to understand and even more so to try to speak. She was ready to go home. And by the time Kathleen Angel had come into the parlor, Madame B. had just read the cards of eleven similar women, living secure lives, married to devoted and successful husbands. Even if she had been at her best, the cards would still show little of interest. She had deliberately created strange dark men from the past who still dreamed of and longed for the women, and of course, she mentioned that she saw money in every woman's cards, for that was a given in this society. She had thrown in some fevers, a sprained ankle, and a dead horse, purely out of boredom.

She was in this hypnotic mood when she picked up the deck of cards and handed them to Kathleen to cut into three piles; she then took the top pile and dealt out a five card spread. She turned over two of the cards to face Kathleen and said: "I see you have three beautiful, healthy children." She was trying to think of the English words to say that the children were going to bring Kathleen much happiness in her old age, but Kathleen quickly and politely corrected her.

"I have no children," she said.

This quiet declaration awakened Madame B. from her stupor. She never made simple mistakes, no matter how tired she was. She picked up the cards and started over, and there they were once again, two boys and a girl, a baby girl, at that. Had Madame B. not been tired and hungry, she would have merely made a slight change in what she was reading. She would have said three friends, or three sisters, instead of three children, but she didn't. She herself was just as surprised as Kathleen when the children came up once again in the cards.

"Three children," she said.

"My sister Polly has three children," Kathleen said.

"Is she here today?" Madame B. asked. "Perhaps your sister was touching the cards."

"No, she's not here," Kathleen said curtly. Madame B. had touched on two very sore points in Kathleen's life: the first was that she had no children, and the second was that she seldom saw her sisters. They were not comfortable with her new life and friends.

By this time, Madame B. was challenged. She quietly shuffled the cards with her dry, swollen hands, and was pleased to see the bright and cheerful King of Hearts appear on the table. She looked up at Kathleen and smiled. Everyone liked to see the King of Hearts show up.

Kathleen had been lost in thought, and she said: "The only person who might have touched the cards was my husband. I left them on the dining table last night."

As Madame B. carefully removed another card from the deck, the Queen of Clubs, studied it for a moment, and placed it beside the King of Hearts, it became obvious to her that the husband had indeed touched the cards. She smiled at the woman sitting across from her, a woman who had it all. Madame B. noticed the perfect round pearls, each identical to the next. She noted that the bonnet would feed an entire family for a month. Kathleen had the appearance of someone much loved and cared for. The King of Hearts had provided her with jewels and flowers and a beautiful home, but he had given another woman three children.

Madame B. was anxious to finish the reading. Her feet were swollen from sitting all afternoon, and she felt a warm ache creeping up her back and into the base of her skull. She had wasted a lot of time on the mysterious children. Now she felt pity for Kathleen, and she remembered that Kathleen was the one who had invited her and would be giving her the donation for her services. She had a few pat phrases she used when a reading took a wrong turn. She shuffled the cards once again, carefully picked up the three of hearts and put it beside the three of clubs.

"I see a disaster," she said and waited until she could sense Kathleen stiffen. She wanted to divert Kathleen's attention from the children. "It has to do with water." Madame B. flipped the two of hearts down. "It's only a slight disaster, and you will have the resources to weather it. It's a disaster you've experienced before. There will be damage, but this can be repaired."

As she spoke, she noticed she had lost Kathleen's attention, and it was time to end the reading, but as she casually slipped the cards back into the deck, she was overtaken by such a powerful energy coming from her hands that she could not restrain herself from immediately reshuffling the deck and dealing five cards onto the table in front of her. She quickly turned each card over with a gentle snap and watched them form an ugly picture. In the midst of four black spades sat the Queen of Hearts, and there was not a single preventive card in sight. Madame B. had never before seen such a graphic description of anyone's fate. It was the kind of message that a reader, in honor of her sacred profession, was obligated never to reveal, but Madame B. felt she should at least give Kathleen a subtle hint or warning. It was the least she could do.

She waited a few moments for her pulse to slow down and she chose her words carefully. "There is a danger, an evil, in your world that you are unaware of. You will soon learn about it, and it will cause you much grief. But I must warn you to resist any inclinations you might have to act. This is a time to let fate run its course. There is nothing you can do about this danger. Just ignore it, and hopefully, it will go away in time."

Kathleen didn't hear a word the woman said. Once Madame B. had made the painful mistake about the children, Kathleen had lost the little faith she had. She was anxious to get away from the awful smell and back to her friends.

Both women became distracted by the sounds of horses and carriages coming over the bridge to pick up the ladies and take them home in time for dinner. Once again, Kathleen managed a cordial smile and thanked Madame B. profusely for inconveniencing herself and coming the whole way out to Port Williams on the train. Madame B., who was thinking of the envelope Kathleen had drawn from the folds of her dress, said it was a beautiful trip and the countryside reminded her of home.

Kathleen forgot most of the things Madame B. had told her that day, but she did remember the prediction of the disaster when once again the spring thaw came on too suddenly and the river was forced to flood. The bridge on the estate was washed away, and Lloyd had it rebuilt, this time much stronger than before, with three layers of gray stone brought down from Vermont. Kathleen told everyone how Madame B. had seen this in her cards, not two weeks before, but it was generally agreed that a person didn't have to be a fortune teller to predict a flood in Port Williams. If there was one person you could count on to do her job, it was the old river, and no one needed to pay a fortune teller to predict her bad behavior.

When Kathleen mentioned Madame B.'s mistake about the three children to Lloyd, he didn't flinch, but it did make him wonder. The fortune teller was a little off, of course. There were only two children, two sons. However, on the very day that Kathleen told him that Madame B. had mentioned three children, he learned that another was on the way, and he tucked into the back of his mind the fact that it was probably going to be a little girl.

The friends who had been to the séance surprised Kathleen with a lovely gift for the parlor, a blue Austrian crystal ball the size of a grapefruit. It was so beautiful that when Kathleen dismantled the parlor, she put the crystal ball in the dining room window of the big house. The early morning light struck it in such a way that soft blue arrows skimmed across the silver chandelier and brushed warm kisses on Kathleen's cheek as she sat at the table, wondering what she should do that day, what she should do that month, that year, and what she should do for the rest of her life. And sometimes the tears that ran down her cheeks were tinted a very light blue and matched perfectly the Sapphire clip that she wore to keep her hair from falling down into her weeping eyes.

SUSAN VISITS HER DEAR OLD FRIENDS

Susan had enclosed one of Mya's blue cards in a letter to Sally back in Laurel Hills, and Sally stuck the card on the front of her refrigerator with a strawberry magnet. Any inquiry about the pretty blue card naturally led to speculation about Susan's new life, and inevitably, a phone call ensued, and a familiar voice, which Susan used to hear daily, asked: "When are you coming down to visit? You've been gone three months. Don't you miss us all?"

"It's so hard to get away," Susan said.

Another day, another familiar voice: "You're only four hours away, but you might as well have moved to China. We were talking this morning, and we decided to issue an ultimatum. Just tell us when you're coming. We demand a specific date so we can circle it on our calendars."

Susan gave them an excuse she knew they could understand. "It's funny how a house can take over your life," she told them.

"Just go," Tom said. "Anything you're doing around here will be waiting for you when you get back."

Susan chose a date, two weeks off, and let her friends know she was coming.

During the four hour drive, she had sufficient time to feel nostalgic about her old life and to try to put her new life into a form that she could rationally present to her friends. Twice she cried real tears, thinking about her old life, and twice she laughed aloud, imagining Linda's response to trout tickling, ghosts, and astrotraveling.

Once the initial polite exchanges were made and all of the kids accounted for and discussed, and the new family who bought the Harris house appropriately dissected, Susan regaled her friends with tales of her life on the Angel Estate. She was like a breath of fresh air that had blown into town. Nothing of great interest had happened in their lives, and during the long weekend, they made Susan repeat her tales again and again to everyone who dropped by to see her.

Mya was naturally one of the main characters in every one of Susan's tales, and the friends were very curious about her. Mrs. Angel's ghost was dismissed as a joke, but Mya was a living human being, and in every tale, she seemed to be a completely different character.

"Is she smart? I mean, can you have an intelligent conversation with this person?" Ann asked.

"I talk to her every day," Susan said, "and we have lots of intelligent conversations, but we don't talk about books or politics or anything. She's really not interested in what's going on in the real world."

"Does she read at all?" Linda asked.

"She thinks books cloud the mind," Susan replied. "She only reads stuff that has to do with her specialty, I guess you would call it," and they all smiled at the word specialty.

"So what you're saying is that she doesn't read," Linda said.

"I'm sure she's never read the classics, if that's what you're talking about," Susan said. "She's not smart like we're smart, but she's smart in her own way. She can do absolutely everything."

"Well, that might just be a matter of necessity," Sally said. "If she doesn't have a husband or a family, then she has to do everything herself, and she certainly sounds like she's too poor to hire anybody to do anything for her."

Susan wanted to wail, "You don't understand," but she said instead, "That's not what I meant, exactly."

The friends were still waiting, bright eyed, curious, and interested, for Susan to add a brush stroke that would complete the portrait of her strange new friend. These were women who believed in the fine art of communication. If at first you weren't understood, you chose different words, which brought a new set of questions, which elicited different replies, and the process would eventually end in elucidation. Susan became very frustrated.

"I just can't describe her," Susan said. "She's fascinating."

"Fascinating, no doubt," Sally said, "but also a little weird, wouldn't you say?"

Mya was being attacked, and Susan felt a need to defend her. "I don't mean to make her sound kooky," Susan said, a little too loud. She looked at her friends' faces. They were patiently waiting to hear what she actually did mean.

"I never met anyone like her before in my life," Susan said, as a way of apologizing for her inability to paint a true picture of Mya.

None of the women had ever met anyone like Mya either, and they had many more questions, none of which Susan was able to answer to their satisfaction.

"I'll be very honest with you," Susan admitted. "You know as much about Mya as I do. Her life is a complete mystery. She doesn't seem to have a family. Her mother might have drowned. At least Mya thinks she drowned. I mean, every morning of her life, she walks down to the river to visit with her dead mother, and she makes no bones about it. It's just something she does."

"Now you have to agree that's pretty kooky," Linda said.

"Does she have a father, or did she have a father. I hope he's not in the river too," Sally laughed.

"She has never mentioned a father," Susan said.

"What are her other friends like? Have you met any of them?" Ann wondered.

"She doesn't have any friends, except for old foster mothers who took care of her when she was little. They're all in their eighties now. She's always joking about her sixteen grandmothers and how busy they keep her."

"Is she sort of a hippie?" Lisa asked. "I mean, would you describe her as a hippie type, like a throw-back to the sixties?"

"Not really," Susan said. "She sometimes dresses like a hippie, but other times, she wears a sweat suit, or a skirt and blouse, just like us. It's more like she's in her own time warp. She loves old fashioned things, but she's very modern." Susan became even more frustrated by her inability to explain Mya. "She's a hard one to figure out."

"The poor soul," Sally said. "She's so lucky you moved in. Our loss, her gain."

"Oh, no," Susan corrected her. "She's definitely not a poor soul. Nobody would call Mya a poor soul. She's always happy and on top of the world. She worries about absolutely nothing. She's very self-confident, and she's the most productive person I have ever met in my life, absolutely no question about it."

"But all of her productivity seems to have to do with weird stuff, right?"

"She doesn't think it's weird," Susan said. She paused and shrugged her shoulders. Her friends looked on, still waiting for that final brush stroke.

"You know," Susan said. "Mya would tell you she pitied me. In her eyes, I would be the poor soul, not her."

"Come off it," Linda said. "You, the poor soul? You, the lady who has it all?"

As Sally refilled Susan's coffee cup, she rested a hand on her shoulder and looked at the friends sitting around the table. "Dear, dear Susan," she said. "We've got to go up there and see for ourselves what you've got yourself into. We just might have to form a rescue mission to get you away from those ghosts and fortune tellers before they put a spell on you and we lose you for good. As soon as Dan gets next month's schedule, we're setting a firm date."

Susan smiled as she sipped at her coffee. These friends would never understand. They were all sealed up in a world of children, husbands, schedules, and in-laws. She felt for a moment she was lucky she got away. She glanced over at the sink and saw a pair of pink rubber gloves lying on the counter. On the refrigerator was taped "A Long List of Dumb Things I Gotta Do." She looked for a chain coming out from under the stove. It was there, she knew, but it was invisible. She was seeing her friends through Mya's eyes, and she pictured herself telling Mya funny tales of Weight Watchers Gift Certificates, security systems in the shape of dog bowls, and the avid neighborhood campaign against bug spraying.

One last time she tried to explain her dear friend Mya to the ladies. "When you guys meet Mya, you'll understand more. She marches to her own drum beat."

"Don't tell me she's got a drum," Sally said. "It fits perfectly. I can just picture her out in the forest, drumming all the bad spirits away."

The friends laughed uproariously at the image, but Susan did not join in. "No, she's not like that at all," she said quietly.

"Well, we're definitely going to meet her," Linda said. "We're going to all pile into my car and drive up. Do you think you could convince her to do a group reading while we're there?"

"Maybe. I'll ask her," Susan said, but she thought, "They don't understand a thing."

Then Sally asked a question that Susan could answer. "What does this Mya person look like? Does she have long black straight hair? A pointed nose covered with warts?"

Susan leaned her chin on her hand and tapped her fingers against her cheek. "Let me see. How would I describe Mya? She's about 5 foot 8 or 9, maybe 10. She's very tall. She's as tall as Tom. She probably weighs….it's hard to tell how much she weighs. She's not really skinny, but she's certainly not overweight. She's very firm and strong. She walks a lot. I mean she walks everywhere."

Susan paused. She had never thought about Mya objectively before. Mya was a presence and a force. "She has very long brownish, kind of golden hair, about down to here." She pointed to the top of her hip. "But she always has it braided or twisted up on her head with clips and ribbons and beads and stuff. And the best thing about her are her eyes. She has the most unusual shade of light green eyes, and they're very wide, like they go the whole way across her face."

"Is she attractive?" Linda asked.

Susan looked at her friends sitting around the table. They were attractive, each in her own way. They had controlled, fashionable hair, pleasant faces with just a hint of make-up, colorful blouses and skirts, and expensive, yet inconspicuous jewelry, a gold chain, a simple silver watch, and a wedding band. If the word attractive described them, what word could she use to describe Mya. She was surprised at what came to mind.

"She's beautiful," Susan said. "In fact, in the right clothes, she would be absolutely stunning, a knock out."

"Beautiful or not, she sure sounds weird," Linda said.

The group began to break up. Ann wanted to run to the store.

Kids were due home. Everyone took a few minutes to hug Susan, who was going to head back north before dark. Each friend had something funny to say about Mrs. Angel's Ghost, the haunted house, and the fortune teller. As her old friends hurried down the walk, Susan stood in the doorway with Sally, waving and calling goodbyes to them. Just as they stepped back into the house, and Sally was about to close the door, Ann shouted from the sidewalk.

"Susan, I forgot to ask the million dollar question."

"Shoot," Susan yelled back.

"What does good old Tom think of this kooky lady?" she asked.

"He loves her," Susan yelled.

"Then she must have special powers," Ann called back. "I don't think he ever loved any of us."

MYA KEEPS AN EYE ON TOM

Tom and Mya spent the entire weekend in bed. They hadn't planned it that way. It just happened. When Susan announced her decision to go back home for a visit, Mya arranged her schedule so she could be off work Friday, Saturday, and Sunday. She and Susan had coffee early Friday morning, and Mya told her it was going to be very quiet and lonely without her. Susan told Mya to keep an eye on Tom.

"If you hear any loud music or see signs of wild parties going on up at the house, don't hesitate to call the police," Susan said.

"If Tom throws a wild party," Mya said. "I'll be the last to leave, and you'll be the last to know."

As she was about to lock the door, Susan called Tom and told him about the salami and rolls and the container of tuna salad in the fridge. He told her to have a great time and to say hello to their old house for him.

As soon as Tom hung up, he walked out of his office, his hand pressed against his forehead. "I've got the most incredible headache," he said to Sandy. "Got any good drugs?"

Sandy looked in her middle desk drawer and pulled out a small metal pill tin and shook it. With a long, red fingernail, she pried it open. There was one white pill inside. "Will this help?" she asked.

"I doubt it. With a big head like mine, I'd need about a hundred of those little things." Tom walked back into his office, closed the door, and picked up the telephone receiver.

As Mya waved goodbye to Susan, she heard her phone ringing in the distance and sprinted up the path to her house.

"I'm here," she said into the phone.

"Be there shortly," Tom said, and they both laughed and simultaneously hung up.

Moments later, Tom dragged himself out of his office, carrying his briefcase. "Sandy, I've got to get out of here before this turns into a blooming migraine. I'll go home and lie in a dark room for a couple of hours and see if I can shake it."

"Hope you feel better," Sandy said.

"You hold down the fort," Tom replied. "I'll try to check in later."

He walked slowly down the hall and out into the parking lot, his shoulders rounded, and his head leaning a little to the side. He took his time unlocking the car door, climbed into the front seat, and leaned over the steering wheel for a few minutes. He crept out of the parking lot, but, by the time he reached Sawmill Road, the car was in fourth gear and he was definitely exceeding the marked 35 mph limit. He flew down Bullfrog Valley Road, bumped across the bridge, parked the car along the driveway and ran across the dam to the summer house. The freedom of not having a wife in the vicinity made him giddy. He planned to pop his head in Mya's front door and call, "I'm home, dear," but when he opened the door, he saw that it was pitch dark in the summer house and Mya was nowhere to be seen.

As he stood for a moment in the silence, he heard her voice calling from the bedroom: "Finders keepers."

Tom felt his way down the hall and paused in the bedroom doorway. The room was lit by candles. Mya lay on her side on the bed, naked except for a tiny pair of yellow satin bikini panties. Her hair was brushed out and hung loosely over her shoulders, breasts, and arms. Her teeth, her eyes, and the yellow satin glistened in the candle light. At first Tom felt scared, but Mya's husky voice kept him from running out of the room and back to safety. "Oh, it's you, Tomas. I was expecting the meter reader, but I guess he's busy today. You'll have to do. Come on over here." She patted her hand on the bed beside her. "Think you're qualified to do the meter reader's job?"

It was only Mya, sassy, smart, teasing Mya. There was nothing to be afraid of. She watched with her big green cat eyes while Tom slipped out of his clothing. She moved back on the bed a few inches and welcomed him in.

Hours later, when the outside world has become dark, and the room had become even darker and smelled of warm bed clothing and melted wax, Tom lifted his head and asked: "Where in the world have I been?"

"With me," Mya said. "I took you to a special place I know about. Did you have a good time?"

Once again Tom felt a strange kind of fear. Mya was wound around him like a warm, strong python. He couldn't tell where he began and she left off. She put her mouth over his mouth and began to breathe with him and for him. He felt as though he was going to suffocate, and he pulled his face back and shook his head.

"Scared?" Mya asked. "Scared of what you're feeling?"

Tom hadn't the words to talk about what he was feeling. All he could say was: "It's strange. I never felt like that before."

"It was complete, wasn't it?" Mya asked.

Tom didn't want to talk. He felt a frantic need to remove the python and get out of the room, and go off somewhere alone so he could try to figure out what had just happened to him.

"I'm starved," he said. That would have worked with Susan. She would have been out of bed, wrapping her robe around herself and hurrying down to the kitchen. But Mya wasn't Susan. She locked her legs around his legs, bent back, and reached down to the floor. She swung the yellow satin panties on her index finger. She rubbed the soft satin on his face and around his ears and neck and then began pushing the panties into his mouth.

"Here's a good snack," she said, and Tom was aroused and disgusted at the same time.

Eventually, they got dressed and went up to the big house, where they made sandwiches with the tuna salad and drank an entire bottle of wine. Then came more love-making in the living room on the floor before the fireplace, on the foyer with the moonlight filtering through the pastel windows, and in the bedroom on the second floor in Susan and Tom's bed, where they fell into a deep sleep under the disapproving eyes of Kathleen Angel.

The weekend passed by quickly, and yet Tom was aware of every single moment. He had never felt this close to anyone in his life. He was absorbed in Mya's long, smooth hair, in the slightly salty taste of her skin, in the sweet and sour odor of her body, and in the pure green depths of her eyes. He couldn't get enough of her.

Early Monday morning around 4 a.m., Mya crept out of his bed and made her way down the yard to the summer house. When Tom awakened at six, alone in the bed, physically and emotionally exhausted, he lay and thought, or tried to think, about what he had experienced over the weekend. Trying to make sense out of something so mystifying caused Tom to become nervous and anxious. Something had caught hold of him and twirled him around and tried to suffocate him and to choke him and had confined him and absorbed him. It was all so wonderful, and yet all so terrifying. It was so good and yet so evil. It was satisfying and at the same time upsetting. It felt so right and so wrong, all at the same time.

Before he left for work, he raced around the house, trying to make certain there were no signs that anything unusual had gone on while Susan was away. The bed was a wrinkled mess and the sheets smelled of sex. He thought maybe he should wash them, but he didn't want to arouse suspicion. He had never washed sheets in his life. Instead, he smoothed the wrinkles with his hands and folded the spread down so fresh air could get to them.

He left for work in a daze, but by the time he drove into the parking lot, the emotional energy of the weekend had been converted into healthy enthusiasm and he couldn't wait to get to his desk and attack anything that was waiting there for him. This was a world where he knew what was happening and why.

"Headache all gone?" Sandy asked, as she handed him a stack of folders.

"What headache?" Tom asked.

"You left on Friday with a terrific headache. Don't tell me you forgot," Sandy said.

"Oh that," Tom said. "I just told you I had a headache to try to get some of your stash."

"What a cad," Sandy said. "Just for that, I left a few dozen messages on your desk."

"Ah, sweet revenge," Tom sang, and Sandy laughed as she walked back to her desk.

Mya spent most of the day at the river with her mother. At four she headed for the Frog. She was in an excellent mood.

Susan drove across the bridge at seven that evening and paused for a moment to look up and admire the estate. This was truly her home now. She looked over at the summer house. There was no sign of life. She'd have to wait until morning to tell Mya about the visit.

Tom heard her car and met her at the door. He gave her a quick hug and asked, "How did it go? Did it make you want to move back?"

"I had a great time," Susan said, "but it's so nice to be home."

"It's good to have you back," Tom said. "I nearly starved to death."

"Don't tell me you haven't eaten yet?" Susan said. "Just give me a second and I'll whip something up. I could use a bite myself."

"You don't have to cook anything," Tom said. "You must be tired from all that driving."

"Not at all," Susan replied. She hung her jacket in the hall closet, rolled up her sleeves, and went into the kitchen. Tom stood in the doorway and listened to the news about the old neighborhood while Susan fried salmon cakes and put together a nice green salad. It felt so good to be home, and she could tell that Tom had missed her.

THE OLD FRIENDS COME
TO CHECK UP ON SUSAN

In time, Susan's friends were able to juggle their schedules and select a date that was convenient for four of them to come and visit. They made arrangements for husbands to come home early from work, got friends to do any necessary car pooling, and planned to make the visit in one very long day. Susan had mailed a nice clear map with a note telling them how much she was looking forward to the visit. Sally made a last minute call to remind Susan to ask Mya if she would read their cards.

"I'll see what I can do," Susan said. "She wanders around a lot and she isn't always here, so there's a chance you might not get to meet her."

"No way," Sally said. "We have to meet her. She's the real reason we're coming. You're just an afterthought."

Susan was afraid that might be true, and she wasn't certain she wanted them to meet her wonderful, yet strange, friend. Mya was so different that Susan could only anticipate an awkward, uncomfortable visit. She already knew her friends would judge Mya and probably laugh and talk about her for days and weeks afterwards. It was only natural. That's what she herself would have done in her previous life. And, naturally, Mya, who was totally nonjudgmental, would either say nothing at all about the friends, or, if pressed, would claim she found them to be very interesting. Mya found everyone to be very interesting.

Susan was aware that this was a problem of her own making and no one else would be bothered by it. Both her friends and Mya, as different as they were, were absolutely certain of their values. Neither would be threatened by the other. It was Susan who floated from one world to the next and didn't belong anywhere. Mya had explained that this was a problem common to Libras, but that was little consolation to Susan.

It was only in desperation that Susan decided to consult Tom about her dilemma. One night, as they were lying in bed, side by side, each with a magazine, Susan said to Tom, "Hon, you're going to think this is a really dumb thing, but something's bothering me and I need your expert advice."

"Shoot," Tom said. "I'm all ears." He didn't look up from his magazine.

"You know Sally and Linda and the girls are coming up Thursday."

"The Tupperware Quartet," Tom joked. You certainly do have a problem.

"They want me to get Mya to read their cards," Susan said.

"Great idea," Tom said, putting his magazine down. "Even if she charges them, say, ten dollars, instead of fifteen, you know, because they're your friends, that's an easy forty dollars."

Susan was used to Tom's way of thinking. Often the businessman leaped out when she was trying to discuss emotions. She had to chase the businessman away before she could proceed.

"No, Tom, that's not what I'm getting at." Susan put her hand on her forehead. "How do I say this?" She looked across the pillow into Tom's totally confused eyes.

"So what's the problem?" Tom asked. "Just spit it out."

"You'll never understand," Susan said, and then she blurted out the first thing that came into her head, the truth.

"I guess I'm embarrassed," she said. "Mya's so weird and kooky, and Sally and the girls, particularly Ann, are so straight and normal. They're just going to hate each other. Well, not hate each other. It's just going to be so uncomfortable." Susan's voice was rising and getting louder, and she was gesturing with both of her hands.

Tom lay on his side, composed and cool. "If you're embarrassed about your friends," he said, "just make sure they don't run into Mya. That shouldn't be all that hard to do."

Susan sighed. When she and Tom tried to talk, she always ended up defending herself. 'I'm not embarrassed, but I honestly think the big reason my friends are so anxious to come up here is to meet our resident fortune teller."

Tom put his finger on the end of Susan's nose. He pushed gently. "And who was it that told them about the fascinating fortune teller in the first place?" he asked.

"Well, she lives here and she's interesting. There wasn't any reason not to talk about her." Susan defended herself.

"I think the first thing you should find out is whether Mya is going to be around on Thursday, because, if she isn't, then you don't have a problem."

She's always around at least part of the day," Susan said. "A person can't go very far on foot."

"She might be planning to spend the day in a hypnotic trance," Tom joked, "or maybe she's taking a little astrotrip down to Miami."

"You're no help at all," Susan said, and she turned away from Tom and buried her head into her pillow.

Tom raised himself up off the bed and leaned on his elbow, looking down at Susan's hair. "You know, I think maybe I can help you out," he said. "But you'll owe me." He rolled onto his back and looked up at the ceiling. "Didn't you tell me Mya is dying to go down to Bellsburg to see all those little antique shops?"

"Yes, she's always trying to talk me into driving her down there for a day. Why? What's that have to do with anything?"

"Well, I've got to go out of town one day this week, any day. It doesn't matter which. I have to meet with the new owners of the plant in Lewistown."

Susan lifted herself up off the pillow. "That's just a stone's throw from Bellsburg." She sighed with relief.

"A couple of miles," Tom said. "So, we drive down there. I drop her off in Bellsburg. I see my men while she shops around, and by the time I pick her up and we drive back here, your friends will have come and gone."

As Tom talked, Susan felt her anxiety dissipate. "You're brilliant," she said, and she placed a kiss on his forehead.

"I'm not going to give you an argument about that," Tom said.

"What would I do if I didn't have you to get me out of these awful messes I'm always getting myself into?" Susan asked. "I'll talk to Mya in the morning and see what she thinks."

"Ready to go to sleep now?" Tom asked, as he reached over and turned the light off. He curled up around Susan's back. It was a comfortable position they had come to assume after twenty years of sharing the same bed. Susan gave his hand a kiss and pushed her rounded back closer into him. She soon felt his deep regular breathing and heard light snoring. This was always her best time for thinking. In her warm, secure cocoon, Susan lay for a long time, making a mental list of all the things she would need to buy to make a special lunch for her friends: crabmeat for a quiche, mushrooms, salad greens, and rolls, and ingredients for miniature cheese cakes. She went to sleep with a peaceful mind. Everything was going to work out splendidly.

Early the next morning, Susan tapped on Mya's kitchen door. "I have good news for you," she said. "You know the shops you've been wanting to see down by Bellsburg?"

"Ummm hmmm," Mya shook her head. "Come on in."

"I think I got you a ride. Tom's got to go down that way on Thursday, and I told him you might want to….."

Mya didn't let her finish the sentence. "I can't go on Thursday," she said. "Your friends are coming. Don't tell me you forgot?"

Susan could think of nothing to say.

"They're still coming, aren't they?" Mya asked.

"Yeah," Susan said. There was no way she could lie to Mya. "I didn't know you'd be that anxious to meet them," she said. "I mean, they're just a bunch of ordinary ladies."

"But they're your friends, and that makes them special," Mya said. "I've had to hear about them for six months now. I believe I've certainly earned the right to meet them."

"Hold this," she said, as she handed Susan the very end of a long, skinny braid, and while Susan held the braid, Mya wrapped a thin blue satin ribbon around and around it and then tied the ends gently in a little bow. All of the anxiety that had built up in Susan from the day before resurfaced as she sat and watched Mya do one last braid. There were ten in all, each wrapped on the end with the same bright blue ribbons. Mya took the first two braids from the front and connected them on top of her head with a longer blue ribbon and let the ends dangle down among the braids. Mya then shook her head gently so that the perfect shiny braids arranged themselves just as she had planned. Digging through an antique basket full of ribbons and trinkets, she pulled out two long blue crystal earrings and fastened them onto her ear lobes. She smiled at Susan and flicked the earrings with her fingers.

"I made these a long time ago when I was in my crystal stage," Mya said. "Like them?"

"They're lovely," Susan said. "They match your ribbons perfectly."

"I'll make you a pair," Mya said. "Just let me know what color you'd like."

As Mya put the basket of ribbons and trinkets on the shelf above the table, Susan began to think aloud.

"Sally's hair will be cut very short. She doesn't like to fuss with it, so she keeps it short. Linda's is kind of long, and she pulls it back into a pony tail thing, that is, unless she's going out somewhere special, and then she takes the time to curl it. Ann has a shoulder length curly perm, and I haven't seen her with it yet, so I don't know what it looks like. She says it makes her look like a middle-aged housewife, which she is, of course, but she doesn't want to look like one."

Mya gave Susan a curious smile. "Why are you telling me this?" her eyes asked.

Susan had no reply for the wide eyes. She had merely been thinking aloud. She looked confused.

"I'm going to like them," Mya said, "no matter what kind of hair they have. I'm going to like them because they're your friends and they love you, you love them, and I love you, so I'll love them too, right? Isn't that how it works?"

Susan couldn't help but laugh at Mya's naïve silliness. She continued smiling the rest of the way up to the house. She smiled at her silly friend. She smiled at Tom and her ludicrous attempt to solve a problem that probably wasn't a problem at all. Silly Tom. Silly Susan. Unpredictable Mya. Susan couldn't wait until Tom got home so she could tell him how their plan had flopped. This was something to laugh about, even though she felt more like crying.

"The only thing predictable about Mya," Tom said, "is her unpredictability."

"Who said that?" Susan asked. "Ralph Waldo Emerson?"

Tom didn't crack a smile. Everything was set up for Thursday so he could spend the entire day with Mya. He had created a brilliant story for Mr. Flynn. He told him he would be making some cold calls on the folks down around Bellsburg, just to get an idea of the potential market. If it turned out to look like it was worth the effort, they'd go after it. If not, what would they lose but a few hours of his time.

Mr. Flynn thought it was a stroke of genius. He reiterated Tom's brilliant idea aloud: "So this rather sharp fellow from Kraft just happens to be in the area and drops casually by to see what kind of operation they're running. They'll be blown away, of course, and they'll show you the works. So, a week or two later, when one of our reps calls, we've already got a foot in the door. Cunning strategy, Tom, you're a genius."

Instead of spending the day with a genius, Mya chose to spend the day visiting with a bunch of silly women that she had never met and with whom she had nothing in common. Tom couldn't decide who was the bigger fool.

"I don't know whether I should invite Mya to have lunch with the girls," Susan interrupted Tom's thoughts, "or just ask her to come over later."

Tom was of no help. "Go ahead and ask her to lunch. If you want her to come, she'll refuse," he said, "and if you don't want her to come, she'll be here with bells on."

"What a cynic you've become," Susan said. "Mya has driven you to cynicism."

"Better than drink," Tom said, "speaking of which." He went to the liquor cabinet and fixed himself a strong one.

The friends arrived and nothing went as planned. Things went much better than planned. Sally, Linda, Ann, and Lisa were gay, silly, and enthusiastic, ready to thoroughly enjoy a new experience. They noticed and commented on every detail of the enchanting house, the enameled door knobs, the silver sconces, the patterns of the hard wood floors, the leaded glass windows, and the multitude of closets and pantries.

Mya had told Susan she wouldn't come in time to join them for lunch, that she would rather come over later after they were all talked out. Susan informed her friends that Mya would be over after lunch, and then she got too involved in the visit to worry any longer. She relaxed and began to enjoy her old friends.

Mya's timing was perfect. The girls had helped clear the table and Susan was serving a tray of miniature cheese cakes with dollops of sour cream and smears of a variety of colors of jelly on the tops.

"Now I remember why we miss you so much," Sally laughed, as she took a cheese cake from the tray. "I haven't had these in so long."

"Too long," Lisa said, as she tried to choose between a pineapple and a raspberry cheese cake. "I guess I'll take them both," she said. "They're small."

"I really shouldn't," Ann called, as she reached for a second.

"Look, someone's coming," Sally whispered, pointing out the dining room window.

Everyone looked because everyone had been expecting Mya and everyone was very curious, even Susan. She didn't know if Mya would appear in a simple pair of jeans and a peasant blouse, in gauze, in the black linen Tyrolean dress with embroidery she had found at the thrift shop last week, or in a ball gown. Would her hair be tamed, wild, braided, curled, or hanging down straight with tiny beads attached to the ends? Which Mya would come to meet her friends? A part of Susan wished for an ordinary Mya, but another part hoped she would look exactly like the resident fortune teller. One thing for sure, Susan knew, she had no way to predict which Mya would appear. Like the others, she could only wait and see.

The Mya who appeared was a Scandinavian princess in yards and yards of lavender gauze. She wore a beaded headband and eight silver bangles on her wrist, and her hair was combed out, silky and golden.

"She's barefoot," Sally whispered loudly.

Once Mya was in the dining room, seated across from the women, staring with her huge, wide eyes, it didn't matter that she was barefoot and looked like someone out of a Norwegian fairy tale. When she opened her mouth to speak, she sounded like a graduate of a young ladies finishing school.

"Susan has talked so much about you that I feel I have known you all of my life," she said to the ladies at the table. Susan thought she detected just a touch of a foreign accent, but she couldn't place it and she had never heard Mya use it before. Mya was utterly charming and fey. She surprised even Susan with the way she remembered the friends' children and husbands, and how she connected all the right facts with the right families. Susan suspected her friends wanted to inundate Mya with questions, but they were trying very hard not to be rude, so they stuck to pleasant, polite conversation.

"I love your dress," Ann said. "It's so billowy."

"Thank you," Mya said, fingering the sleeve. "I made it this morning. I wanted something new to wear for this special occasion."

Susan felt smug, like she herself had scored a point. Here was living proof that Mya was some sort of wizard.

"You made the headband too, right?" Susan asked.

"I made that a while ago," Mya said, "when I was in my beading stage. It just accidentally matched this fabric, so I slipped it on today."

"I wish I had talent," Sally said. "I have trouble sewing on buttons."

Mya shrugged her shoulders. "I have a lot of time on my hands," she said, "and, besides, I don't have a husband and children to use up my energies, and I also don't have a lot of money to spend."

They laughed nervously at her modest explanation. "Talent by default," Ann said.

Now it was time for Mya to ask some questions. "What do you think of Susan's new home?"

They answered in unison, "Lovely, interesting, unique, charming, and, most of all, enchanting."

"Did Mrs. Angel come out at all during lunch?" Mya asked.

The ladies perked up at the mention of Mrs. Angel. This is what they had been waiting for. "Nope, she's not been around," Susan replied casually.

"Just watch. These cheese cakes will disappear one by one," Mya said, picking a tiny cake up gently with her fingers and peeling the paper cup away, "and none of us will have eaten a single one. There's the proof, even if no one gets to see her."

"Have you ever seen her?" Ann asked. "I mean, actually seen her?"

"Not with my eyes," Mya replied. She turned to Susan. "Do you think your friends might like to come over and see my humble abode?"

Before Susan could reply, the friends quickly began to get up from the table.

"If you would like," Mya said politely, "I could read your cards."

It was the invitation they had been hoping for, and they all answered at the same time. "We'd love that. What a wonderful idea. You're sure it's no trouble?" They quickly drained the coffee from their cups and began to help remove the dishes and silverware from the table and carry it into the kitchen.

"I'll clean up," Susan said. "You guys go on ahead with Mya."

"You're sure you don't need help?" Linda asked.

"Go, go, go," Susan said, shooshing them out of the room.

Mya strode out the door and down across the lawn to the summer house, her lavender gauze blowing in the breeze and her golden hair glimmering in the sunshine. The four ladies trailed along behind, smiling silly smiles and sending vague enthusiastic messages to each other with eyes and lips and shoulders and hands.

As Susan washed plates, she thought of how everything had turned out so right. Mya had been spectacular; her friends had been enchanted; and her own image as the lady who had it all was preserved until the next crisis.

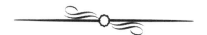

ADD A VICTORIAN CONSULTANT
TO THE MIX

Like hope, civic pride was not an abundant commodity in Port Williams. As soon as children had mastered the art of whining, they began to complain that nothing interesting ever happened in the dreary old town, and every young person had plans to leave as soon as he or she finished high school. But, if and when that time came, a few had somehow become pregnant; others had married; and most had in one way or another become so woven into the fabric of the town that they were unable to extricate themselves, even if they just had a poor paying job that they hated at the local gas station, or worked as an aide at the nursing home. Certainly there were a few who managed to move away, but more in evidence were those who had tried to get away and couldn't. There was a beauty operator who moved to Florida, where she found that the people weren't nice. She missed her old friends so much that, in less than three months, she was back among them for good, swearing never to leave again. A rare young couple with a small child made a brave stab at starting out somewhere new, driving distance from Grandma and Grandpa in Port Williams, of course. With frequent trips home, they lasted a few months before they were back, reassuring their friends that it was strange out there, different and uncomfortable, not at all like home. It felt so good to be back that nobody left twice. In the most unsettling and mobile of times in America, the natives of Port Williams stayed right where they belonged, and complained endlessly.

Mya was one of the few who lived in Port Williams because that was exactly where she knew she was supposed to be. She and a small handful of other enthusiastic natives bore the burden of civic pride for the entire population of the town. Mya was pleased to see Susan's growing affinity for the town and for the wonderful old things it contained; she delighted in having someone to whom she could show off the particular wonders she herself had discovered over the years in Port Williams. She became Susan's own personal tour guide and took great pains to introduce her to the many interesting facets of the old lumber town.

Their favorite excursion was a three hour walking tour of the mansions that lined Queen Street from Fourth to Twelfth. Even looking out through a dirty car window, a drive down Queen Street transported a person back to an era when life was slow and peaceful and there was time and money to hire a famous Italian architect to design the mansion of your dreams, a bit larger and a bit fancier than the ones on either side of it. There were in all thirty huge structures with turrets, stained glass windows, wraparound porches, wrought iron fences, carriage houses, and formal gardens with fountains. Each mansion was different from the next. A twenty-room white and brown Tudor sat beside a dark red and gray Victorian lady with high sharp gables and eleven pink porches. Her neighbor was a heavy, boring, unadorned gray stone Romanesque castle, and next to her stood a red brick Federal with fat white columns holding up the porch roof. They called the style "eclectic renaissance." Many of the homes were built by the same architect. Once he designed a house, he threw away the plans, and with nothing but a sharp pencil and a piece of blank paper, he started another.

Although these lovely ladies were entering their second century, they still looked splendid. They had survived man's continuous fiddling with the basic rules of beauty. They had endured modernization and renewal, when several sisters were dismantled in broad day light and replaced by convenient, sterile, low, brick buildings. They had wept as sisters were raped of copper bath tubs, stained glass windows, and crystal chandeliers. They then sat for years, ignored and taken for granted, until one day renovation came to call. Although this was a kinder concept, it still entailed minor cosmetic surgery, and more than one unlucky sister who hadn't taken care of herself was gutted and stripped of her charms.

At the time Mya and Susan came to call on these charming old ladies, restoration and preservation were in vogue, and, at last the sisters could relax and enjoy life. No more bloody, painful face lifts; no need for an uncomfortable, stylish wardrobe that pinched at the waist; no strenuous aerobics classes. Some mansions had been converted into office buildings; others had been divided up into apartments; and two had been turned into bed and breakfast inns. Six were open and available to the public, and these, along with various gardens, gates, and architectural details that could be observed from the side walk, filled the three hours of the tour.

Mya had taken the tour so often that the guide had become a personal friend. "Wait 'til you meet Gladys," Mya told Susan as they walked toward the corner of Queen and Fourth. "She's been doing these tours for eighteen years."

Susan anticipated meeting another very old lady. For some reason, Mya seemed to love old people, and she knew more old ladies than anyone Susan had ever met.

"There she is." Mya took Susan's hand and hurried her along.

Susan looked up ahead and saw a true Victorian lady in a long, red silk dress with a matching hat and gloves. She carried a small red and white brocaded and fringed parasol with a carved ivory handle. She wasn't an old person; she was ageless. She greeted the two with a big smile, hugged Mya, and asked why she had not seen her for eons. When Mya explained that she had moved from Queen Street and was now living on the Angel Estate, Gladys literally swooned. Mya then introduced Susan as the mistress of the big house. Gladys took her hand and smiled at Susan as though she were meeting her favorite celebrity.

"A surrogate Kathleen Angel," she said. "You lucky, lucky lady. You and I will have a lot to chat about today."

As the others began to collect on the corner, Gladys greeted each as though she was an old friend. The group consisted of a young woman, accompanied by her visiting mother-in-law; two elderly sisters from Pittsburgh, who were passing through; and six members of the East Pennsfield Victorian Society.

"We'd better get a move on," Gladys said. "Any stragglers will just have to catch up. We have so much to see in one afternoon. She carefully opened her parasol and gave it a gentle shake to align the fringes. "Come along now, Dearies," she called.

Already charmed by the elegant Victorian lady, the group huddled together like a class of kindergarten kids and followed her down the street. She paused on the sidewalk before each of the first three houses and pointed her parasol at the intricate floral design of a wrought iron gate, at a cupola that was damaged in a violent wind storm, and at a carriage house that was brought over in pieces by ship from Ireland. She interspersed architectural and historical details with charming tales of the eccentric inhabitants of the big homes, past and present. She prefaced each remark with "In fact," or "Rumor has it," or "Off the record, just between you and me." Some of her information was hearsay, she admitted, but most of it was the Gospel truth.

They reached the fourth house on the right, still chuckling over a tale of a woman who was such a snob that she wanted her house to be torn down when she died lest it fall into the hands of someone from the lower classes.

"Hearsay," Gladys said. "Remember, it's only hearsay."

They turned into the Hudson Castle, and without pausing, Gladys opened the gate and led the ladies up the flagstone walk and onto the porch.

"We're welcome here," she said. "They're serious history buffs."

Using her hip, shoulder, and leg, she pushed open the heavy front door and motioned for the group to follow her into the parlor, where they stopped and looked around and were delighted to find themselves somewhere back in another century.

"Make yourselves comfortable," Gladys told them, and they tried, but it was difficult to relax on Gothic Revival chairs, and impossible to sit for any length of time on a medallion back sofa with lumpy, firm horsehair seats. They sat stiffly and selfconsciously on the edges with their backs nice and straight and their feet flat on the floor. Gladys smiled with approval.

"Victorian women never slouched," she said. "They always maintained proper posture and manners wherever they were."

A fireplace framed with pastel ceramic tiles and topped with a heavy, gray marble mantel, took up one wall of the parlor. Gladys pointed at a log resting on the grate. The log was an artificial one from K Mart, still wrapped in red paper.

"Juxtaposition," Gladys laughed. Juxtaposition always made her laugh.

She moved quietly through the parlor, pointing out that the crystal light fixtures had been converted from candle to electric, and that the three dimensional wall paper was reproduced by a company in Maine that specialized in Victorian wall paper patterns.

"Look closely at those tiles," she said. "Each tile is a picture of a Greek god. The Victorians loved the Greeks."

"Hearsay," Gladys lowered her voice. "The owner was offered twenty thousand dollars for the lot of them by some rich Texas millionaire. Of course he refused to sell them. They are invaluable. How could anyone put a price on such irreplaceable treasures. They are priceless." She clicked her tongue at such crass materialism.

Someone began to play a mazurka on the pianoforte in the library, and the music and the furniture seemed to be trying to pull the ladies back into a time before their time, but they were holding too tightly to the present to be able to go. They asked Gladys what the Lincoln rocker would be worth today, and wondered how the double steeple clock would look in their own homes. Gladys led them on through the dining room, pointing out the original Beleek china and silver flatware of the French Revival style, forty place settings of each. "And they didn't get it with green stamps," she chimed in.

She continued on through the ballroom, decorated in olive green and light rose. She told of fancy balls, dinner parties, sleigh rides, fox hunting with imported horses, and dancing masters who came to the homes to give lessons to the entire family. She said they often had live music at their dinners and parties, and as they passed back through the library, she nodded at the young man seated at the pianoforte in blue jeans and a black tee shirt, playing music from four hundred years ago.

"Juxtaposition," someone whispered, and Gladys laughed and said, "I see there's a fast learner in this crowd."

As they passed through the room, she pointed down at the carved lion's feet on the heavy ornate legs of a table beneath the window. "Be sure to notice the little mother of pearl claws," she said. "And now to the room that ladies are always most interested in, and I don't mean the powder room either."

The kitchen, which had not been modernized at all, shocked everyone and brought them back to the present.

"The kitchen at the Angel Estate looks exactly like this. Am I right?" she asked Susan.

"My kitchen is much worse than this," Susan replied. "The sink is on one side; the counter is on the opposite side; and the stove is on a wall about a mile from both of them, not to mention the refrigerator is in the basement. To make a simple sandwich, I have to walk five miles and risk my life on a flight of ancient rickety stairs."

"My dear, there's a simple solution to all that," Gladys said. "You must get yourself a cook and a few servants."

In the meantime, Mya was off to the side, looking at things on her own. She was not interested in Beleek china nor French Revival flatware. She was trying to feel vibrations of emotions recorded in the house. While Susan was feeling a semi-sweet romantic nostalgia for something she had never experienced, Mya was rubbing her hand along a French Ivory cosmetic tray, trying to connect with the historic life force of the house.

For a perfect ending to the afternoon, they were served tea at small wooden tables on a wrap-around porch. The tables were draped with yellow linen cloths; the cups were china; and the napkins, small cloth triangles, trimmed with lace. On each table was a crystal vase of miniature dahlias in white and yellow. While the group lingered over tea, Gladys questioned Susan and Mya about the Angel Estate, almost as though it were an old friend of hers who had come upon bad times. She was worried about the friend, and her conversation was filled with words like shame, heart-breaking, and tragic.

"Someday," she said. "Our Historical Society is going to get its hands on that place. There are only two things standing in our way. One is that old eccentric, what's his name, and the second is, of course, what else, money." Then Gladys came back from her sad musings and smiled at Susan and Mya and said: "It seems as though the place is in good hands now. I hope you lucky ladies take advantage of your privileged responsibilities."

As Susan was sitting with Gladys and Mya at the little table, sipping the most delicious tea she had ever tasted, she felt inspired. She resolved that she was going to try to do something more about the condition of the Angel Estate. She had seen how healthy and happy a lovely lady could be when she was given a little attention. There was more, much more, she could be doing. It was true, the house could not hold a torch to some of her sisters on Queen Street, but the Angel Estate possessed other charms. The Queen Street mansions were built side by side in the middle of town, and although the houses were enormous, there was no land at all around them. The Angel Estate had hundreds of acres, and, in addition, there were the pond and the carriage house and the bridge, and many other attributes, almost too many to mention.

Gladys interrupted her musings with a very pertinent question: "Susan, how did you enjoy meeting our Lovely Ladies this afternoon?"

Susan confessed that, although she was very impressed with all she had seen, she still preferred the Angel Estate. "The house itself isn't as elegant or interesting as some of these," she said, "but I'm an outdoors kind of person, and I like the forest and the streams and the big lawn and all the gardens, even in their wilderness state."

"It seems the Angels were under the influence of the Italianate Villa concept," Gladys explained. "And my dear, it sounds like you too are an aficionada of the concept." She placed a red silk hand on Susan's arm. "The Italianate Villa was very popular in the early twentieth century, but people can no longer afford that sort of life style. You must realize you're a very privileged woman to be able to live on the Angel Estate. Only a few very fortunate beings are ever given such an opportunity. You must have done something wonderful in a previous life to have earned the privilege."

Susan had a greeting ready for Tom that night. "Sir," she said, "You are looking at an Italianate Villa aficionada."

"I am?" Tom asked. "How'd that happen?"

"I just found out today, as I was peeling the historic psychic layers from the mansions on Queen Street," she said. She walked into the kitchen and came back, carrying a steaming dish of something wonderful.

"What'd that set you back?" Tom asked.

"Three hours, five dollars," Susan replied, as she scooped a pink and green concoction onto Tom's plate.

"That's a bargain if I've ever heard bargain," Tom said, sniffing at the concoction and smiling.

"And I got a free consultant in the bargain," Susan said.

"No such thing," Tom said, as he pushed up his sleeves and picked up a knife and fork.

"The tour guide, Gladys, said she'll answer all my questions, give me any advice she can, and will help me solve any problems I come upon if I decide to try to get the Angel Estate back into its original condition." Susan sat down and looked pensive for a moment. "And I told her I would take her up on it."

Tom looked down and asked his plate of corned beef and cabbage a very serious question: "What in the world am I in for now?"

While Mya was anxious to explore the psychic milieu of the Angel Estate, Gladys, on the other hand, had waited an equally long time for an opportunity to be involved in the physical restoration of the neglected and abused old property. She had shed many a tear into her little lace handkerchief, thinking about the sad state of all the irreplaceable artifacts that Kathleen Angel had so lovingly collected for her beautiful home. Under Gladys' guidance, Susan's list of things to do changed radically. The purpose was no longer to merely make the place comfortable and functional, but rather to restore the ambience that Kathleen Angel herself had created some seventy years ago. This meant Susan could not simply weed a flower garden and plant some petunias from the K-Mart. She had to spend endless hours in the musty historic room of the Port Williams Library, looking through old landscape plans, and then carry home a stack of heavy books on Victorian gardening and flowers native to Central Pennsylvania.

An early morning call from Gladys might mean driving to Lock Haven to an auction and sitting all day on an uncomfortable wooden folding chair, waiting for a cast iron patio set to be called up, one that dated from the early Twentieth Century, and, of course, needed scraping, rust removal, and painting, which entailed another trip to the library to get a book on restoring wrought iron furniture. The finished product was worth every bit of the effort and time Susan had put into it, and wasn't Gladys thrilled when Mr. Edwards came up with a matching plant stand to complete the set.

Mr. Edwards had reached a stage beyond Great Guns. He had died and gone to Heaven. Although he claimed to be working on his own very long list of yesteryear, he took frequent breaks so he could come by and check on what kind of mischief the girls were getting themselves into. With Mr. Edwards' advice, Mya's energy and enthusiasm, Gladys' expertise, and Susan's persistence, projects that seemed overwhelming slowly came to completion, one by one. Bits and pieces of Mr. Edwards' collections were dragged out, repaired, refinished, and found comfortable niches here and there in the big house and surrounding property. Tom greeted each new finished project with a smart remark, which Susan repeated for the amusement of her friends. As they scraped red enamel off a metal-lined old pie keeper, they tried to anticipate what Tom was going to come up with when he saw this strange old piece sitting proudly in the kitchen. Tom didn't disappoint them.

"Pie keeper?" he asked. "Why would anyone ever want to keep a pie? There's no keeping involved when it comes to pies. You put a pie on the table and it disappears, just like that. But what do I know about old things?" But then another thought came to mind. "Maybe the wife of the guy who invented this was a really bad cook. She couldn't make a decent pie for all the blueberries in Maine, so the husband had to invent a place to keep all the bad pies. Are you sure it's not called a bad pie keeper?" From then on, they always referred to that particular piece of furniture as the bad pie keeper.

Gladys was a genius at locating the perfect item to add the finishing touches to a room. If it couldn't be found at an auction, or at a yard sale, or among Mr. Edwards' collection, rather than use a reproduction, she substituted something from a different time period. Reproduction immediately followed the word razing in Gladys' x-rated list of vocabulary words. Gladys believed that if a person looked long enough for something and wanted to find it badly enough, it would eventually appear. Under Gladys' influence, Susan's horizons expanded in every direction, and it was only natural that in time they would expand across the driveway and into the little carriage house that heretofore had not interested her at all.

SOMETHING TRULY HORRIBLE MUST HAVE HAPPENED IN THE CARRIAGE HOUSE

The carriage house was a white wooden cottage that was set into the hillside along the curve in the driveway, about 100 yards from the main house. The upper part was covered with white wooden lattice and on the lower level were three doorways, each large enough for a carriage to be driven in and out. A second floor porch extended out over the ground floor and provided a protected area for the loading and unloading of the carriages and wagons. The big white doors had been boarded up for years and there was no way for a curious person on the outside to see in through the opaque filthy windows.

Who knew what wonders the carriage house contained. "Probably old tack, maybe some rusty tools, a dead horse or two, and a nice family of rats," was the way Mr. Edwards described it. "I'm going to go through it one of these days when I get time," Mr. Edwards' father had said, and Mr. Edwards himself often repeated the same words. For over forty years, he had been curious about the contents of the carriage house but had never got time to look inside.

Mya, too, had been curious, and all Susan had to do was mention that Gladys thought there might be some things they could use in there for Mya to arrive one morning with a "bon idee."

Mya's "bons idees," as she called them, included everything

from dragging salt licks deep in the forest for the deer in order to counter the negative karma caused by the hunters, to building a shelter of pine branches for the now not-so-wild cats. Although Mya's bons idees involved work, they often turned out to be a lot of fun.

"Are you game for absolutely anything?" Mya asked.

"Before I say yes," Susan replied, "can I have just a little hint of what I might be getting myself in for?"

Mya opened her big green eyes as wide as she could and nodded her head in the direction of the carriage house. "I thought it was time for us to take a little look-see and find out if Gladys knows what she's talking about."

"Do you think Mr. Edwards would mind?" Susan asked.

"Do you think Mr. Edwards would notice?" Mya asked. "We're not exactly going to vandalize the place. We're just going to carefully, very very carefully, remove the boards from the back door and go in and take a quick inventory."

"You twisted my arm," Susan said. "Let's go."

"It wasn't all that hard to do, now, was it?" Mya jumped up from where she had been sitting on the stone wall. "Would you by any chance have a great big claw hammer we could use?"

"Yep," Susan said. "Be back in a second." She hurried down the cellar steps to the workroom where she had been storing all the old tools she came across, and returned to the kitchen with a medium sized hammer and a much larger one. She handed the larger one to Mya.

"How about a flashlight?" Mya asked.

"No problema," Susan said, as she reached under the counter and handed Mya a heavy black metal flashlight.

Mya clicked it on and off a few times and shook her head. "Onward," she said, and the two began marching across the yard towards the carriage house, hammers resting over their shoulders, singing, "Hi ho, hi ho, it's off to work we go."

Mya led Susan directly up the stone steps on the side of the carriage house and around to the back door, which had a large board nailed across it at an angle.

"Anyone could break into this," Susan said.

"Who'd want to?" Mya asked.

"Who besides two crazy bored ladies in search of treasures," Susan said.

Mya laughed as she put the claws of the hammer under the board and began to tug. The board was so rotten that it crumbled away from the rusty nails, which remained stuck in the frame. As Mya turned the black enamel knob on the door, she discovered the door was not locked, only swollen shut from dampness and time. With her shoulder and hip, she pushed on the door as hard as she could, and it scraped along the floor until the opening was wide enough for Susan to squeeze herself in sideways. Mya was soon beside her in the dark, pointing a narrow band of light around the room. It took a moment for their eyes to adjust. The room hung heavy with the smell of dust and mold and old things from centuries past. Susan was nearly overcome with claustrophobia and panic. She wanted to bolt back out into the sunlight, but Mya's quiet voice arrested her.

"Can you feel the sensations?" Mya asked in a whisper. "They are so strong I can hardly stand it."

"It's creepy," Susan said.

"Something very important must have happened in here," Mya said, "or maybe it's just that all of her things are in here together, giving off horrendous vibes."

Rays of dusty light landed here and there on rolled up carpets and ancient trunks. Lace curtains lay in crinkled heaps and held inches of fine dust in every fold. Susan looked up at Mya and saw that her eyes were glazed as though she were in a trance. She was staring in the distance, above the boxes and trunks, through the walls, and into the world beyond. Susan looked down to where the light was shining on a black trunk near the wall. The hinges were dull and tarnished, and the leather was green with mold. She thought of how nice the trunk would look once it was polished and cleaned. She wondered if she would ever be able to get the smell out of it. Mya's quivering voice interrupted her thoughts.

"Come on, let's get out of here," she said. "We'd better not disturb anything. This was a mistake."

By now Susan's claustrophobia had totally disappeared and she was anxious to start digging through the stuff. She was certain there were lots of things in here that would go perfectly in the big house. "Let me see if that trunk is locked," she said, taking a step forward.

Mya grabbed her sleeve. "No," she said. "Come on. Let's get out of here. Now!" She grabbed Susan's shoulder and steered her forcefully out of the opening in the doorway. Once they were outside, Susan looked into Mya's face for an explanation, but Mya didn't speak. Her face was white, her lips were tightly pursed, and her hands were shaking as she arranged the rotten board back over the rusty nails and pushed it tightly into place.

As they walked quickly and silently back to the house, Susan tried to understand Mya's reaction. Mya obviously had claustrophobia even worse than she had. It was creepy to go into an old place like that. It was like stepping back into another time period. There was the fear that you could get trapped there and not get back to the present. As they walked down the driveway, each dangling a hammer along her side, Susan was amused by the image they must have cast. As they paused on the little cement stoop outside the kitchen, Susan waited for Mya to speak, but Mya remained silent, as though her mind was someplace else entirely. Susan again thought of how funny they must have looked, two grown women with claw hammers, hurrying frantically away from the carriage house, being chased away by dust and dirt and rust and mold, and perhaps even by an angry ghost.

Susan gave a short giggle and looked up at Mya. "Don't we look like a pair of fools?" she asked.

In response, Mya handed Susan the hammer. "I have to figure this out," she said. "It might be that the carriage house is where the astral body has chosen to reside. She certainly makes it very clear that she doesn't want anyone in there."

Susan could think of nothing to say in reply.

"Something truly horrible happened in there," Mya continued in the same flat voice.

As the two stood on the damp cement stoop in the silence with only the faint sound of doves cooing in the eaves, Susan thought, not for the first time, that perhaps Mya was insane. Most of the time she was somewhere within throwing range of normal, but once in a while, she seemed like she was going off the deep end. As she took the hammer that Mya was handing to her, Susan suddenly felt afraid of this strange woman. She wanted to snap her fingers in front of Mya's face to try to make her come back in touch, but she couldn't. It was as though Mya was in a trance. Without even a goodbye, Mya walked across the lawn to the summer house, and Susan went inside and felt edgy all day long.

Later that afternoon, a composed and cheerful Mya came by to try to explain what had gone on that morning. "So many strong emotions, not just bad ones, but good ones, like love and happiness, are recorded in all those old things in the carriage house. When someone who is extra-sensitive, like I am, gets around them, the emotions reproduce themselves in me, and it is overwhelming, almost like I got nuked.

Susan could think of nothing to say.

Mya tried to explain it further. "What if six radio stations were all trying to broadcast from one spot on your dial? No, that's not a good example. There's no emotion involved." She thought a moment, chewing on her bottom lip and staring into space. "What if you had ten children and they were all in trouble. No, not all. Some were in trouble and some were fine, and they were all calling and shouting at you from ten different locations in a big field. Some were laughing and some were screaming. Can you imagine that?"

"Yeh,"Susan said. She nodded her head.

"Didn't you feel weird in there?" Mya asked.

Susan tried to inject a bit of the rational into the conversation. "I felt cooped up, and it smelled bad and everything, but I wasn't scared. I didn't feel like I had to get out of there."

"Well, just consider yourself lucky," Mya said.

Susan didn't know whether she was lucky or Mya was the lucky one. Mya's world had so many more dimensions than Susan's world, and Susan didn't know whether to envy her or pity her.

"I don't think we'll be able to go in there again," Mya said. "Sorry if you're going to miss out on some treasures. You'll have to make our apologies to Gladys. She'll understand, if anyone does."

Susan put the carriage house out of her mind and promised herself she would explore it someday when Mya wasn't around. Her immediate goal was to finish as many projects as she could in order to have the house, and maybe the estate, absolutely perfect by summer, which was only a few months away. In less than one year, one determined lady with a shoe box full of tools had performed miracles. Of course she had the help of a tiny wise adviser in an antique red silk dress, one enthusiastic resident psychic, Mr. Edwards and his chain saw and his old green truck, a very approving and engaging ghost, and Tom's check book. Regardless, the results were entirely disproportionate to the efforts. The place looked grand, splendid, lovely, and charming; in other words, enchanting.

KATHLEEN FINDS A PURPOSE, AND MORE

It had taken Kathleen Angel, the architect, and a few dozen workers seven years to complete the estate. They worked incessantly through the heat of summer and the snows of winter until the last tree was planted, and the missing piece of trellis nailed onto the kitchen porch. Only then did the workmen with their ladders, tools, rigs and wagons move across the bridge and onto another site. Like magic, the dream that had existed only in the mind of Kathleen Angel had become a reality that everyone could enjoy. The Angel Estate was perfect. Every brass lock on every window gleamed; the closets were papered to match the walls in the rooms; Wedgewood plates with charcoal blue trim peeked from the French cupboards in the dining room. The green velvet lawn was trimmed with small circular beds of portulaca, peonies, hyacinths, sweet peas, and orange poppies. At some point, after seven years of designing, planning and building, a fairy wand had magically touched the Angel Estate and proclaimed that it was perfect at last.

Kathleen wandered through the house, touching things, looking at small details, studying the way the big gray stones fit together perfectly to make the living room fireplace, and marveling at it all. Her small reliable staff was able to keep everything in order and running smoothly, and in no time at all, Kathleen felt empty once again. And who could Kathleen talk with about emptiness?

Her sisters were struggling to provide for growing families and had little sympathy for a wealthy, idle sister, suffering from ennui.

Once she confessed to sister Rebecca, "Lloyd doesn't pay enough attention to me," and Rebecca had no sympathy at all. "What are you saying? Lloyd doesn't pay enough attention to you? Are you crazy? He only builds you the grandest house in Port Williams. Kathleen, you'll never be satisfied." And that was pretty much the general feeling of her entire family. Her mother listened sympathetically to Kathleen's problems, but she too was not as understanding as Kathleen would have liked. "You can't have everything, Kathleen. You have more than most. Be thankful for that."

It was during this period of the post-house building doldrums that Kathleen's mother died quietly in her sleep. To the funeral came all of the pathetic, hard-working women that she had lived with in the West End. Most had outlived their husbands, and many came accompanied by grown children with children of their own. What struck Kathleen was that the grown daughters were following in their mothers' footsteps. Kathleen was the only one who had moved into a completely different world. She looked at her wrinkled old dead mother lying in the white satin coffin, her worn hands folded together on her breast with a white pearl Rosary entwined among her fingers. The women expressed their condolences to Kathleen and her sisters with quiet humble respect. Every single one mentioned that Jennie Hannigan was a saint.

"Your mother was a special servant of God," Father John said to Kathleen. "We are going to miss her here in the parish. God doesn't often send me a helper like your mother."

For days after the funeral, scenes played around in Kathleen's mind. She couldn't stop thinking of the poor women, dressed in their best, gray and white hair pulled back into buns and clipped tightly into place, their bodies sagging and lumpy, their fat feet stuffed into shoes that no longer fit and were brought out only for church and funerals. She thought of their quiet, humble way of speaking, how truly sad they were to be losing Jennie, how they sincerely wondered how they would get along without her. Kathleen remembered these ladies from her childhood when they were young women full of energy, with large families to care for, and she remembered how they shouted back and forth to each other from their little back porches with loud and strident voices. She remembered how boring and dirty it had all seemed to her then, but now, when she looked back on those times, her neighborhood seemed like a pleasant place, and for the first time in her life, she missed it.

After her mother's funeral, Kathleen returned to the old neighborhood to visit with her mother's friends. Talking about her mother made her feel less lonely. But the women did not seem comfortable having her there. They no longer thought of her as one of Jennie Hannigan's daughters; they thought of her as Lloyd Angel's wife. Their discomfort bothered Kathleen. When she dropped in unannounced for a cup of tea, they dropped what they were doing and fussed as though royalty had come to visit and not the daughter of an old friend. Yet she wanted to be a part of their lives, and she soon came up with an idea. She decided it would be her obligation to try to fill at least a part of the void left by her mother's death. She approached Father John with her plan.

"Remember when you told me you would help me find something meaningful to do with my life when I was ready?" Kathleen asked.

Father John looked perplexed. "That's quite a promise. You're sure I told you that?"

"Yes," Kathleen said. "No wonder you can't remember. It was several years ago. I told you I had been to a séance and you said

I was flirting with danger, and that for an afternoon's amusement, I was willing to jeopardize my everlasting soul. I never forgot those words."

"I believe I remember now," Father John shook his head.

"I know I've taken a long time to come around to this," Kathleen said, "but I just feel I need to do something for the people of the West End."

"We each help in our own way," Father John said. "Your generous donations to the parish are more than enough."

"But I want to do something personally," Kathleen said, "like my mother did."

Father John restrained a sudden wince. "Your mother lived among these women all of her life," he said. "She was one of them, and they were her friends. She understood their needs, even better than they understood them."

True to her nature, Kathleen would not take no for an answer.

"What harm can she do?" Father John asked himself. He told Kathleen if she truly wanted to help, she could work with the Home Mission. The Home Mission was made up of twenty or so women who visited families in their homes when a child was born, or when someone was ill, or having bad times, to determine what they needed and what the Church could do for them.

"These people are very proud," Father John warned Kathleen. "They don't always come to us with their problems. We mingle among them and try to discover their needs for ourselves. That was what was so wonderful about your mother. She lived among them and she always knew when someone was sick, or when a husband had gone on a binge, or when somebody needed to talk. A living saint, your mother."

Kathleen felt inspired. She dressed in her simplest black mourning outfit and tied her hair up under a small gray bonnet so that barely a curl peeked out on either side. She wore no jewelry except for a simple gold wedding band and a small gold cross hanging from a delicate chain around her neck. She spent a long time looking at herself in the mirror, pleased with the piety she was able to create by sucking in her cheeks, breathing very softly, holding her lips closed, and allowing her eyes to focus somewhere in the distance. She felt saintly.

She had Andrew drop her off several blocks from the West End, and she walked gracefully into the neighborhood, feeling pure and full of purpose. Andrew sat and waited for her, enjoying all the attention Bay Swallow and the buggy caused in a part of town where such fine trappings were a rarity. When anyone stopped to admire Bay Swallow and pass the time, Andrew proudly explained that his mistress, Mrs. Lloyd Angel, was doing charity work, and he was waiting to take her back home to the estate. His explanation duly impressed everyone. He was proud of Mrs. Angel, and he felt, in a just world, and Andrew thought it was a just world, that Mrs. Angel's Christian efforts with the poor people of the West End somehow, in the big picture, might make up for her husband's philandering.

Andrew wasn't the only one pleased with Mrs. Angel's latest activity. Her stages were documented and discussed by all of her admirers and critics alike. "Did you hear about what Kathleen's doing down at the West End? Isn't it wonderful?" asks one friend. "Oh, yes, I heard, but I wonder how long this one will last," replies the second friend. "You know Kathleen." Lloyd was supportive of her new activity. He liked to see Kathleen busy. She was easier to live with when she had her mind set on something in particular.

The fact that she was Lloyd Angel's wife had opened many doors to Kathleen, but in her new capacity with the Home Mission, the doors were opened to her because she was Jennie

Hannigan's daughter. As Lloyd Angel's wife she had made them uncomfortable, but as Jennie Hannigan's daughter, she was better able to fit right in.

As she sat in tiny, warm kitchens and drank tea whose strong flavor transported her directly back to her youth and made her miss her mother terribly, she found there had not been many changes in these women's lives since she was a girl. The rest of the town had spread out and grown up. People prospered. But, except for a few, like herself, most of the West End people were right where they had always been, and right where they belonged, according to some. The men still drank; the women worked too hard; and the children arrived too often.

Two days a week, Andrew drove Kathleen to the Church to visit with Father John before she started her rounds. Father John was pleased with her. Once he realized she was going to stick with the Home Mission and that it was not just a whimsical reaction to her mother's death, he allowed himself to think that this experience was going to be very good for Kathleen. She had always been a difficult and proud young girl, and she had moved on to become a frivolous and extravagant young woman, but she had always been a doer and a planner. Maybe these traits would be helpful now that she was becoming older and more responsible.

Months passed and Kathleen was more content than she had ever been, and thus, everyone on the Angel Estate benefitted indirectly. And the Home Mission was ever so much more effective with a fresh and energetic worker among its ranks. So, ironic it was then that during this beneficent period of Kathleen's life, the first time when she was truly putting other's wishes before her own, that she became aware of a devastating turn of events. If she hadn't been working selflessly for the Home Mission, she would never have found herself on Dutch Hill, face to face with the mysterious children who had once surfaced in a deck of Madame B.'s cards.

Yes, it was ironic that Kathleen was doing charity work when she discovered that Lloyd Angel had another family. There was no question in her mind when she set eyes on the two handsome, dark-haired boys that they were somehow related to her husband. The boys, ages four and six, were staying with an aunt in the West End because their mother was at that moment giving birth to a third child.

Later, Kathleen wondered what had brought her into the particular house where the boys were staying. This family did not belong to the parish. She had dropped off a parcel of clothing for Mrs. Overton's growing daughters, and, as she stepped out of the door, she noticed a young woman standing on the porch of the house next door. Kathleen greeted the woman and remarked that her flower boxes looked lovely. The woman turned out to be very friendly and invited Kathleen to step over to see a new litter of kittens her old mom cat had hidden on the porch. Kathleen spoke to the two little boys, who were stooped over the box of kittens.

"Aren't you boys lucky. What are you going to do with all these kittens?" Kathleen asked.

"They're not ours," the eldest boy said. "We don't live here."

"These are my cousin's children," the woman explained.

Kathleen looked from the box of gray and gold and white furry bodies to the boys, who had stepped away from the box and were standing side by side, looking down at her. They were dark, healthy boys, well dressed, and not at all like the pink, sickly children who ran about the streets of the West End. She had a sudden eerie sensation. These boys looked exactly like Lloyd's nephews in Maine. They looked just like what her sons would have looked like if she and Lloyd had been able to have children. The youngest had Lloyd's hair, with a smaller version of Lloyd's cowlick; and the eldest had Lloyd's expression on his face, the big dark eyes, and the heavy brow. Kathleen took a small gray kitten into her trembling hands. "Where does your cousin live?" she asked.

"She has a nice little flat over on Dutch Hill by St. Benedicts," she explained. "I've got the boys because she's expecting a baby this week."

Kathleen put the gray kitten back with the mother and picked up a soft warm little tiger. She held it under the chin. Then she handed the tiger to the youngest boy, and the older boy gently handed her a little ball of white fur with a pink nose. She looked more closely at the boy's dark brown eyes. He had Lloyd's thick black lashes.

"What's your name?" she asked.

"I'm Danny," the oldest said, "and he's Patrick."

"Now which one of you was named after your daddy?" she asked, "Patrick, or Daniel?" She was hoping it would be one or the other.

"We don't have a dad," Patrick said.

Daniel corrected his brother's statement. "We have a dad but he don't live with us."

The woman interrupted with a quiet explanation and a look of embarrassment that the boys had spoken out of turn. "My cousin is in an unfortunate situation. The father of the children is in no position to marry her. He's a very kind, nice gentleman, and he supports her nicely, as you can see. It's a shame, but there's no talking to her, and it's too late now."

Kathleen said nothing. Her big eyes expressed a dozen questions that she was afraid to ask.

"The boys are hoping for a little sister," the woman said. "Truth of the matter is, we're all hoping for a little girl."

A little girl. For a few minutes Kathleen rubbed her lips along the kitten's little white furry head and thought.

"We have a lot of children's clothing, particularly for newborns," Kathleen said. "They hardly wear them before they grow out of them. Do you think your cousin would like some?"

"I'm sure she would," the woman said. "You never have enough clothes for a new baby, especially if she turns out to be a spitter."

Kathleen was amazed at her ability to remain calm. "Where does she live?" she asked.

"She lives in the first little gray house beside the St. Benedict's Church," the woman replied. "But you could leave the clothing here if it's more convenient. I'll see that she gets them."

"I might just do that," Kathleen said, as she carefully put the little white kitten back into the nest and stood up to leave. "I'll bring them here, unless I happen to get over that way."

Kathleen arrived home in acute distress. She paced about the house and out into the yard, feeling as though something horrible was happening, but she was not certain what it was. She tried to figure out why a vague hint of something with no proof at all would upset her so, and she silently cursed the stupid fortune teller. Two children and one on the way, probably a little girl.

By the time Lloyd got home that evening, Kathleen was outwardly calm. She told him about part of her day, and he told her the railroad company was going to start having a daily train to New York City, instead of the weekly one. Kathleen said that was very good news. Lloyd said it would bring more people to town, and there was talk about building another hotel. Everything was always changing, Kathleen was thinking, changing, but not always for the better. She wished it would stop for just a moment so she could catch her breath.

Early the following week, Kathleen was back in the West End again and just had to stop by and see the kittens. She learned that the cousin had delivered a perfect little girl, and both the mother and daughter were doing well. Kathleen felt a sudden pain in her heart. A baby girl. Two boys and a girl. The three children that Madam B. could not exactly place.

Andrew was very surprised to see her walking quickly back towards the carriage. She had been gone for barely a quarter of an hour. On the surface, she appeared calm, but Andrew knew her well enough to sense a storm beneath.

"First to the Church," she said, "and then we're going to deliver some baby clothes over to Dutch Hill."

"Dutch Hill?" Andrew asked. It took all the self-discipline he could muster not to blurt out: 'Not Dutch Hill! Any place in the world but Dutch Hill." Dutch Hill was a bone in Andrew's craw. The only part of his job that he hated was the trips back and forth to Dutch Hill. It had always been the voice of Lloyd Angel that commanded: "Dutch Hill." It didn't sound right when it came from Kathleen.

"Dutch Hill," Kathleen repeated, and in a quiet, strange voice, she added, "A woman there has had a lovely little baby girl, and we're going to take her some clothing to keep it warm."

When she added the directions, "We're going to the first little gray house beside St. Benedict's Church," Andrew's hands began to shake, but he carefully guided the horse down Market Street and headed north on Lincoln. Ordinarily he would have sat proud and tall, enjoying glances of admiration at the immaculate horse and the elegant trap, but this time, he huddled down and tried to control his frantic thoughts. He could think of no way to protect Mrs. Angel from the pain that might await her on Dutch Hill. And that wasn't his job, he told himself. But it was his job, his self argued back. His job was to protect Kathleen Angel. His job was to deliver her in perfect condition to wherever she wanted to go, whenever she wanted to get there. That was the catch.

As soon as St. Benedict's tall brass bells appeared up ahead, Kathleen directed Andrew to park the carriage in the lot behind the Church and to wait there for her. He tried once more to intervene. He reached over and tugged at the bag of clothing in her arms.

"You mustn't be carrying that," he said. "Let me take it in for you."

Kathleen held the bag as tightly as she could and gave Andrew a kind, yet scornful, look. "No, you wait here," she said so sharply that Andrew stepped back and remembered his place. "I won't be long at all."

Andrew rubbed his cheek along Bay Swallow's smooth neck and whispered into the horse's ear: "Our Kathleen's in trouble, old friend. Perhaps we'd better do some praying here by the Church." As his voice tickled the horse's ear, Bay Swallow thrust his head so hard that he hit Andrew on the nose and forced him to lean against the big warm horse until he gained his composure.

Kathleen walked deliberately and quickly to the gray house next to the Church. She tapped on the door, and as she waited for someone to answer, she felt such anxiety that she could barely control herself to keep from bolting off the porch and running back to the carriage. She shifted her weight and clutched at the soft bag of clothing.

A pretty blonde woman in a simple blue cotton dress answered the door and said "Hello," just as though she were expecting her.

"I'm a friend of your cousin Patty," Kathleen said. "She told me you just had a new baby, and I'm with the St. Stephen parish, with the Home Mission, and we have lots of extra new born clothing. I told Patty I would bring some to you, and she thought that was a good idea."

"She told me you might be coming," the woman said. "Come on in."

Kathleen handed her the bag she was holding. "She said you only had boy things and you might need these."

The woman motioned for Kathleen to follow her into the kitchen, where she put the bag on a chair and asked Kathleen to sit down.

"I'm Ellen," she said.

"Call me Kathy," Kathleen said. "Nice to meet you, Ellen. I met your boys over at Patty's, and they are lovely little guys."

"Well, thank you," Ellen said. "Would you like to meet their new little sister?"

"Could I?" Kathleen asked, gently pulling a soft gray leather glove from each of her hands.

"Of course," Ellen said. "She's not at all breakable, although the boys seem to be trying." She gently placed the warm, live bundle into Kathleen's arms.

Ellen began to remove the clothing from the bag, one piece at a time, holding each piece up, turning it about, and then folding it neatly and placing it in a pile on the table. "These are lovely," she said. "They're almost brand new. They'll certainly come in handy."

Kathleen looked into the baby's face. She didn't look like Lloyd. She was too new to look like anyone yet. Kathleen examined the perfect little hands. The baby looked up at Kathleen with gray-blue baby eyes, and Kathleen's eyes began to shed warm tears, which ran down her face and dropped into the thick white bundle and disappeared.

Ellen examined the stitching on a tiny yellow cotton shirt. "I can't wait until she grows into this," she said. She held up a bonnet with three lace ruffles around the edge and two long white satin ribbons hanging from each side. "Look, Rachel," she said, "You'll wear this when we go out walking."

Although Kathleen continued to look down into the baby's face, Ellen couldn't help but see the tears slowly making their way down her cheeks and the damp spots that were growing on the blanket.

"Do you have children?" she asked. She thought perhaps the memory of holding her own baby for the first time might have brought on the tears.

Kathleen could not speak. She shook her head. Ellen felt embarrassed and angry with herself for having asked the question. She tried to undo the damage. "Sometimes I think I have three too many," she smiled. "Children are a lot of work."

Whirling around inside Kathleen were anger and love and hate and sorrow and revenge, which all became blended into a large vat of confusion. She felt compelled to speak, and when she finally forced the lid on the boiling cauldron inside, she chose a safe topic.

"My mother, God rest her soul, had eight children," Kathleen said.

"Oh, my," Ellen said. "I can't even imagine that. My mother had four, but she never got to see them grow up. She died right after my brother Timmy was born."

"How sad," Kathleen said. "I'm sorry to hear that."

Ellen began talking about her family. "Dad had an awful time." She picked up the pile of neatly folded baby clothing. "I ended up raising my brother and sister, and I was nothing but a kid myself."

Ellen walked into another room, leaving Kathleen frozen in a chair, gently holding a warm bundle which might or might not be Lloyd's baby. She began a fierce argument with herself. She knew that it wasn't unusual for a woman to be raising a family without a husband in the West End. Sometimes men abandoned their families and returned to their original homelands, or because an altercation occurred and they had to leave town in a hurry, or just because there was a job somewhere else in the country that held great promise, and they went off with plans to send for their families once they got settled. Some workers were killed while building the new hotels and bridges in town. Kathleen remembered many times when her mother had been collecting household items and clothing and money for an abandoned mother, or for a widow who was unable to provide for her family. On the other hand, this mother, Ellen, did not seem to be in great need, and the cousin, Patty, had indicated that there was a father in the picture and that her situation was a matter of choice, rather than tragic circumstances. Kathleen wondered why she felt so certain that Lloyd was that absent father, and that this was Lloyd's baby that she was holding gently in her arms. Because the boys looked exactly like Lloyd's family, she explained to herself. The older one has a dimple in his chin, exactly like Lloyd, and both have his hair, thick and brown, which falls in the front just like Lloyd's. The younger one's eyes are exactly like Lloyd's eyes, and when he looks up, it's with the same expression she often sees on Lloyd's face. Their father is a man married to someone else, no doubt, and even if that were all coincidental, there was still Madame B.'s awful mistake about the three children who appeared in the cards.

Kathleen felt a desperate desire to know the truth, but even in her distress, she was aware that a direct question –Are these Lloyd Angel's children?—would be a crazy thing to ask. Yet, in her confusion, she made a comment more indiscreet than she would have otherwise dared.

"Your cousin told me the children's father is, I forget exactly what she said, that he's living out of the area, or something," Kathleen mumbled, sorry she had introduced the subject.

But Ellen did not seem to be upset at all. She spoke in a direct, simple manner. "The children's father is unable to live here with us at the moment," she said. "He's a very good man."

That was much too vague to satisfy Kathleen. "Does he have to go back to the old country?" she asked. That was a very common excuse, or reason, for an absent father or husband in the West End.

"No," she said, as she folded a soft white blanket and held it up to her nose. "The children's father is, unfortunately, already married," she said, and she shrugged, and the shrug told the rest of the story.

"That's very sad," said Kathleen.

"Well, it's almost like we're married," Ellen explained. "He's very generous and the children and I want for nothing, and he comes to see us as often as he can. He's a very busy man."

"What about his wife?" Kathleen asked. Talking about herself in the third person was a new experience.

"I've never met her," Ellen said. "She's a very prominent woman in town. There's no way our paths would ever cross, and I really wouldn't want them to."

"How did you meet the children's father?" Kathleen asked, but then corrected herself, "I'm sorry. That's such a personal question."

"I don't mind talking about it," Ellen said. She stood in the doorway, holding the stack of neatly folded baby clothes against her chest. "It's not exactly a secret. We have no secrets here in Dutch Hill. Everyone knows everything."

Ellen looked into the sympathetic eyes of her guest, a Home Mission volunteer, an obviously privileged woman, giving up her time and energies to help out her fellow creatures. At least that's what Ellen thought she saw as she began to tell her story.

"My father had actually worked for this man for years. He built all these houses in this neighborhood for his workers. He had a lot of people who worked for him. I had heard his name but I had no idea what he looked like or who he was. I met him at a really awful time." She paused, searching for the right words. "It was the day my little brother Timmy died, and I had to go and get Dad, and that's when I met him. He was so sympathetic. I was incredibly young at that time." She stopped musing and began moving towards the bedroom to deposit the stack of clothing. As she came back into the room, she stopped a moment and shook her head. "It just all happened," she said. "It's hard to explain how those things happen."

Kathleen continued to hold the baby and watch Ellen as she moved around in the little kitchen. She had many more questions to ask, but she did not trust her voice. The oldest boy is about six, she thought. Ellen must have known Lloyd for at least seven years. After having had three children, Ellen probably looked older than she actually was, but Kathleen judged that she was not yet thirty. She was very attractive, and she probably would have no trouble finding a husband and father for these beautiful children. There was a disproportionate number of unmarried men working in the lumber industry and in the building trades in Port Williams, many probably hoping to find a nice woman to share his life.

As though she were reading Kathleen's mind, Ellen said, "I know this kind of situation isn't generally acceptable among nice people, and I can't bear to think of what my poor old mother would have said about it, but I intend to spend the rest of my life with this man. I adore him. We belong together."

For a brief second while she was listening, Kathleen strangely found herself feeling sympathy for Lloyd and Ellen. It was a moment when she herself didn't exist, and all she saw were two people in love, but kept apart by someone else, two people with three beautiful children, who should rightfully be able to have a life together. Fortunately, Ellen was busy at the stove and didn't look over at Kathleen, sitting in a trance, holding the baby, and looking out into a world where she did not exist, or, at least, should not exist. If it were not for her, Ellen and Lloyd could be man and wife. As though the pain that was creeping through Kathleen had escaped her body and made its way through the blankets she was holding, the baby suddenly began to cry. Ellen carefully picked her up out of Kathleen's arms, and Kathleen was suddenly empty and alone and chilled to the bone. All of her connections to the living world had been severed.

Ellen sat down in a chair across the room and began to arrange the front of her dress to nurse the baby. She gently folded the top of an apron across her shoulder.

"I hope you don't mind," she said to Kathleen, "but she's starving."

"Not at all," Kathleen said. "It's time for me to be getting on my way."

"I am so happy that you came to visit," Ellen said. "I hope you'll come again and see how Rachel is getting long. Thank you so much for all the lovely things you brought."

It was all so kind and sincere that Kathleen had no reply. She sat a moment longer, watching Ellen feeding Lloyd's daughter, and as she watched the scene, her empathy slowly dissipated and was replaced by bitterness, anger, and an intense feeling of injustice. While Ellen got the love and affection, Kathleen got the quiet indifference. Kathleen got hard, cold jewelry; Ellen got soft warm children. Life was so unfair. As Ellen carried the baby into the back room to change her, Kathleen stood up to leave, and as she quietly made her way towards the door, she placed on the table one ivory vellum calling card with thick violet script: "Mrs. Lloyd Vaughn Angel."

As Kathleen stepped out onto the porch, a cold wind penetrated her clothing and blew her hair right out of her blue sapphire hair clip, which came dangling down onto the floor. As she reached down to retrieve it, a second gust attacked her and she had to lean against the railing to get her balance. Andrew had been too nervous to wait in the parking lot, and the moment he sensed a sudden change in the air, he drove the carriage to the front of the house that Kathleen had entered. He kept his eyes glued to the door, and he jumped down the moment he saw it open and ran to help Kathleen as she stumbled across the porch and down the steps to the street. Andrew lifted her up into the carriage, tucked her in, and then signaled Bay Swallow to head for home, as fast as he could go.

Kathleen felt no cold, no rain, no snow; she felt nothing. When they reached the estate, she hurried into the house and up to the bedroom, ignoring Roberta's efforts to help her remove her coat. As she riffled through her husband's pockets and examined objects sitting on his bureau, the calling card never left her mind. She pictured Ellen picking it up, reading it, and standing in the little kitchen in utter shock. It's not that Ellen didn't know that Lloyd had a wife. It was more the idea of having the enemy right there in the camp. She pictured Ellen frantically glancing around the room to see what the elegant Kathleen Angel had seen. Was the floor clean? Were the windows shining? She pictured Ellen looking into the mirror to see if her hair was neat, tightening her apron strings to pull in her thickening waist, and noticing there were stains on the baby's chemise.

But this all happened only in Kathleen's imagination. The card lay on the table unnoticed. Ellen changed the baby and put her down for a nap. A few minutes after Kathleen had stepped off the porch and hurried towards the carriage, the boys pushed open the front door and barged into the house, hurrying to get away from an oncoming spring storm. Coats and hats were removed and the door remained ajar, a fierce wind blowing through the kitchen. By the time Ellen put the baby down and came out to reprimand them for the unnecessary rowdiness, the calling card was face down on the floor under a chair, a muddy footprint on the clear ivory.

Ironically, it was Lloyd who noticed it a few hours later when he stopped in to see the baby and to warn Ellen about the approaching storm. He noticed something white on the floor, and, without thinking, reached down to pick it up. He recognized what it was immediately, but it took several seconds for his mind to register the implications. It was something very familiar to his eyes, but it was in the wrong place. He held it in his left hand and waited for Ellen to say something. He dreaded what she might be going to say.

Ellen didn't notice his concern. She gave Lloyd a quick hug and hurried into the bedroom to get the baby. She took a few moments to arrange the soft little form in a white crocheted blanket, and she carried her out and handed her to Lloyd, a wonderful honest smile on her face, her eyes completely innocent. "Sit down and hold the newest little Angel," she said.

Lloyd quickly lowered himself into a wooden chair and took the small warm bundle in his arms. Ellen gave Lloyd a kiss on his forehead and walked to the stove to put on the tea kettle.

Lloyd mumbled something that Ellen couldn't understand. Then he repeated it very slowly and carefully: "Was Kathleen here today?"

Ellen turned and looked at him. He seldom mentioned his wife's name. "Kathleen? You mean your Kathleen? Why in the world would she come here? I mean, what makes you think she's come here?" As the words came out of her mouth, the picture of the lovely woman from the Home Mission flashed before her eyes. Kathy from the Home Mission. "Do they call her Kathy?" Ellen asked.

Lloyd shook his head. "No," he said. He could not imagine how Kathleen's card got on this floor unless Kathleen herself put it there. He thought maybe he shouldn't upset Ellen. On the other hand, he knew what Kathleen was capable of and he felt Ellen should be warned. "Did someone named Kathy come to visit you today?"

Ellen didn't reply. She stood, staring at Lloyd and the baby, completely confused by the thoughts that were swirling through her mind.

Lloyd opened his left hand and dropped the card onto the table. "I found this on the floor as I came in," he said.

Ellen picked up the card and studied it. The elegant writing on the card, just the combination of Mrs. and Lloyd and Angel, and the shade of purple ink, fit the lovely lady who had come calling. Ellen suddenly understood. She looked at Lloyd, her Lloyd, handsome, big, gentle, holding their baby, Lloyd who had been her husband, so to speak, for nearly ten years. And she thought of the lady from the Home Mission. Even Kathleen's simplest black dress was elegant by Dutch Hill standards. Ellen shuddered. In all these years, she had pictured Lloyd's cold wife as possibly beautiful, thin, and well groomed; yet she had never tried to imagine the sound of her voice and she had never wondered whether she would be a warm, affectionate person with such a lovely laugh. She thought of the tears in the woman's eyes when she nestled the baby against her and said, "I have always wanted one of these."

Ellen didn't feel anger; she felt incredible sadness. Lloyd and she were no longer alone in the room and never again would they be alone anywhere. Ellen sensed that the spirit that had taken up residence with them was a gentle, vulnerable lady; Lloyd knew the spirit was someone unpredictable, morose, and potentially evil, such a danger that he could not, dared not, put into words.

A SUDDEN SPRING STORM

Sudden spring storms can still take one by surprise in Central Pennsylvania. Just at the point when a person is certain the last snow flake has fallen, the snow tires can be safely removed, and the shovels and salt can be put away, a late storm arrives. And, although it has happened year after year after year, everyone is always surprised and no one is ever prepared.

Susan endured and sometimes enjoyed the long winter months, but was happy when March arrived with a bit of sunshine to warm up the chilly spring breezes. She no longer had to worry about gloves and boots and head scarves; she could go out of doors wearing just a thin jacket and a pair of light shoes and her favorite pair of jeans. Daffodil and crocus leaves were peeking up through the grass, and the birds had become utterly boisterous. From dawn until night they chirped, sang, mated and fought in the trees and on the lawn near the house. And Mr. Edwards and his infamous truck, which had miraculously survived yet one more winter, appeared more frequently on the property, intending to begin work on the long list of unfinished projects from the year before, and the year before that, while at the same time, adding to the list all the things that had not survived this last winter intact.

One chilly March afternoon, as Susan stepped out the back door to check the weather, the old truck came chugging and thumping up the drive. It was a sunny day, but the air was quite cold. Susan shivered in her sweater. Mr. Edwards stopped the truck and got out and walked around to Susan. Mr. Edwards never greeted a person formally, or informally, for that matter. There were no "hello's" or "hi's" or "how are you's." As soon as he spotted a potential audience, he began to entertain. He had such a quaint way of talking that Susan tended to pay more attention to the way he said something than to what he was actually saying.

"I thought I'd chopped up my last log of the season. Who knows how long this storm's goin' a last?" He pointed at a few dark gray clouds high above the mountains on the north. Susan had not even noticed them. She was in the habit of checking only the weather close to the house.

"What storm?" Susan asked. As usual, she wasn't sure when Mr. Edwards was joking. It felt like a typical March day to her, a little wind, a slight chill, and a touch of sun. "What kind of storm?"

"A snow storm, one of them late snow storms we get around here." He settled back against his truck and began to expound on the impending storm, and reminisce about past storms. Susan stepped into an area with more direct sunlight. She shifted her weight to one foot and crossed her arms in front of her. When Mr. Edwards started a monolog, one never knew how long the journey would take, nor where it would lead. If one couldn't escape, it was best to settle in and make yourself comfortable.

Later, as Susan walked to the mailbox and returned to the house, she thought about the importance of imagination when one lived in a place where nothing happened. In order to keep from going crazy with boredom, a person had to have a good imagination. Small, insignificant things that a normal person would never even notice took on great importance to Mr. Edwards.

"Tom probably didn't even see those little gray clouds as he drove to work this morning," she thought, while Mr. Edwards did not only see them, but realized that they forecast impending doom. The dam might break. The river might flood. Children will be washed away. Memories of all the disasters of the past sixty years were wrapped up in those little gray clouds. Susan planned to spend the afternoon sewing pillow covers with some pink calico that had surfaced during the move. Mr. Edwards, on the other hand, would spend the day frantically cutting wood in preparation for a big storm that he was certain would hit right after dinner. Same world; funny world.

Susan lost herself in her sewing project, which was giving her all sorts of frustrations with the tension on the sewing machine and the thread in the bobbin breaking every few minutes. Thus she was pleased to be interrupted a few hours later when Mya tapped on the door and poked her head in and called: "Can you believe it's snowing? Come on out here and see it. It's beautiful."

Susan stepped out of the doorway and reached her hands out to catch the big white flakes that were drifting slowly down from a very dark gray sky. Mr. Edwards' small gray clouds had expanded to cover the entire sky.

"Come on in," Susan said.

"Only for a sec," Mya replied.

"This is the last time I'll ever belittle Mr. Edwards' wisdom," Susan said, and she repeated the conversation they had had earlier in the day.

"It's not only Mr. Edwards," Mya said. "All they could talk about at the Frog was the big storm. I don't think a single person walked through the door without announcing the arrival of a major spring storm." Mya stepped back, hung her fingers on the sides of her jeans pockets and spoke in the low gruff voice she used when she was imitating the men who came into the Frog.

"Big storm comin'. Big fuckin' mother storm comin'."

"I guess these people are like cows and dogs," Susan said. "They rely on their instincts. Civilized people like us need the weather report. I had no idea there was going to be a storm, did you?"

"No," Mya said. "I had no idea, but I'm going to go right home now and get ready to enjoy every last flake."

"Only you could enjoy a storm," Susan laughed. "Won't you feel guilty what with all those children about to be washed away, and all those old people drowned in their rocking chairs, and the poor bridges cracking up and falling into the river?"

"Not my concern," Mya said. "The storm wasn't my idea." As she stepped across the flagstone patio, which had a very soft covering of white flakes, Mya turned back and asked: "Did you start dinner yet?"

"No, I was busy fighting with my sewing machine," Susan said.

"Well, you'd better start dinner," Mya said. "I'm sure your doting husband will be home early. Remember, there's a big mother storm comin'." She walked down across the lawn with her head bent back and her mouth wide open, catching big white snowflakes on her tongue.

By the time Susan heard Tom's car on the drive, the flurries were coming down fast and thick. Minutes later, Tom was stomping the thick wet snow from his shoes in the hallway. "That was shear hell," he announced as he gave Susan a quick wet hug.

Tom was in excellent spirits. It seemed as though the storm and the challenge of the drive home on the slippery roads innervated him. Susan imitated Mr. Edwards, leaning against the imaginary truck, describing every snow storm that had hit since 1901. Tom assured her that Mr. Edwards wasn't the only one intrigued by the storm. No one had done a lick of work all day long because of the storm. Sandy had seen the first invisible flakes at 10 a.m. and she spent the day running back and forth to the window, reporting storm warnings to everyone who stopped in or called.

"I told her maybe she could get a job with the weather bureau," Tom said. "I finally had to send her home early. She was totally useless."

As soon as he finished eating dinner, Tom got up from the table and headed for the hall closet. As he pulled on a pair of big snow boots that Susan had never seen him wear in his life, he said, "I'll bring in a load of wood so we can have a nice fire."

Susan was delighted with his plan. "I'll make some hot chocolate," she said, "with real whipping cream, and maybe tiny marshmallows, if I can find some."

"We'll have a great evening," Tom said. "If we can't fight this damned storm, we'll just enjoy it."

As Susan cleaned up in the kitchen, she could hear Tom thumping in and out the back door, carrying logs to the fireplace in the living room. She felt happy. She had not seen Tom in such a good mood for a very long time. After dinner, he usually read, sometimes paced, went to his study to work, and often went back to the office around eight or nine for a couple of hours, if he had a particularly important project in the works. She thought of all the years when she imagined how nice it would be to have Tom home in the evenings with her. That turned out to be a joke. Once he stopped traveling with his work, she was even lonelier than before. When he had been on the road, and she knew he wasn't going to be home, she made plans, did things with Heather, wandered to a neighbor's to watch a special TV show. But now that Tom came home every night, she ended up sitting and waiting for someone who was home physically, but not emotionally.

But tonight was going to be different. They would build a fire, probably curl up together on the couch, and make love to the sound of the storm trying to blow the house away.

A tap on the window above the sink startled Susan. Tom pressed his face against the glass. "I'm going to move the car down by the road," he mouthed. "It'll be easier to get out in the morning."

Susan went upstairs and changed her clothes. She put on a blue satin bra with skimpy lace cups and deliberated over whether she should wear matching panties, or none at all. She anticipated Tom's groan of appreciation as he reached up under her robe and felt bare skin.

She looked at herself in the mirror as she brushed her hair. She tried to force the lady in the mirror to lighten up, to think about the present and not about bad memories. For the past few years of her marriage, when she and Tom made love, she had compared herself with unknown, faceless women everywhere. There was often the ghost of another woman sharing the bed. "Get over it," Susan whispered to herself. "Just get over it." Susan brushed her hair loose, put a dab of perfume under her right ear and on both wrists, wrapped her white robe around her and walked slowly downstairs.

Kathleen Angel had designed the house in such a way that each room was an aesthetically pleasing unit, even before rugs, pictures and furniture were added. Susan's gaze rested on the wooden curved mantle, the woodwork, and the windows with brass knobs. The wooden floor boards shone in the candle light. The doorways on either side of the fireplace led into a second living room, but Susan kept them closed to save on heat, and on either side of the long room were windows with many panes, some looking down onto the front lawn to the dam and the summer house, and others facing up onto the vineyard and the mountain above the house.

The living room was quite large, yet very cozy. Susan looked out the back window and saw that the snow had already covered Tom's car tracks and footprints. There was no sign that he'd been home at all. She walked across the room and tried to look down the smooth white lawn, but all she could see were heavy snowflakes falling in the porch light. Susan stood and watched the falling flakes and thought: "This is what life is all about, snowflakes, beautiful old houses, and anticipation of love." For a moment she remembered poor Mya over in the little summer house all alone, but it was impossible to pity Mya for long. She was probably fine. Susan couldn't even guess how someone like Mya might enjoy a storm. She was probably involved in some weird project, arranging her magic thimbles, or writing in her journal, or sifting through her Tarot cards.

Susan was so enjoying setting the mood for the evening that she didn't mind that Tom had not yet returned. It had been a long time since she'd had a nice romantic evening with Tom. From time to time, they did make love, but it was like a reflex that just happened when they were lying side by side in bed.

Susan lit the two candles in the brass holders on the mantle and three more candles in little red glass cups around the room. She turned off all the lights except for a small lamp in the corner. The world was silent, like Christmas time in a children's story, and then she thought of music. She wanted appropriate music. She put Bach's Mass in B Minor on the stereo and adjusted the volume. She sat on the sofa to wait for Tom, for the fire, and for the evening to begin.

The sound of the back door being forced open, followed by giggling, teasing voices, interrupted Susan's thoughts.

"Look who I found wandering around, out lost in the storm," Tom called to Susan as she stepped out into the hallway to see what was going on. Following behind Tom was a person, all bundled up in a big jacket with boots and a woolen cap pulled down and covering most of the face. The figure was too tall to be Mr. Edwards, but it did look like a man. The two were covered with snow, almost like they had been rolling in it, and as Tom bent down to remove his boots, the other figure took off its hat and shook loose a head of long golden hair.

"It's only me," Mya said.

Susan pushed her disappointment to the back of her mind and smiled. "I was just wondering about you, Mya. I was going to call and see if you wanted to come over and share our fire," she lied. She didn't ordinarily lie to Mya because she was afraid Mya could see the lie in her eyes, but the hallway was not well lit and Mya was concentrating on pulling off her boots.

Tom slicked his wet hair back with his hand and stood up tall. He pointed to Susan: "You, make some hot chocolate, and be snappy about it." He pointed at himself: "You, Tom, get that fire going, and you, Miss." He pointed at Mya. "You sit down and make yourself comfortable. You're our guest."

As Susan heated water, then milk, in a pan on the stove and beat heavy cream with her egg beater, she felt like crying. Then she thought of the sexy blue bra she was wearing and she felt like laughing. What a fool she was. She could hear strains of Bach in the distance, the sounds of the wind trying to get in the kitchen door, and faint sounds of Mya and Tom's voices coming from the living room. Her best friend, her husband, a beautiful house, the world's most delicious hot chocolate, and a lovely snow storm and a fire, Bach, candlelight…what more could a woman ask for? As Susan carried a tray of steaming mugs into the living room and placed it on the table in front of the sofa, she felt empty and sad. She had a sudden rush of that familiar feeling that nothing ever turned out the way she had hoped it would.

"What a lovely fire," she said to Tom.

"You never told me you were married to an Eagle Scout," Mya said. "First he rescues a lady lost in the storm, and then he makes a fire that would earn him a badge in advance kindling. Is there anything this man can't do?"

Susan looked at Tom's beaming face as he absorbed and appreciated Mya's words of admiration.

"Cheers," Mya said, lifting her mug up in front of her and sniffing at the sweet steam that was rising above it.

Carefully, Tom tapped his mug against hers and then against Susan's. They each took a swig and stood, licking whipped cream from the corners of their mouths.

The three friends sat down and prepared to enjoy the evening, each in his own way. Tom was pleased to have an opportunity to be spending the storm with Mya, while, at the same time, not neglecting Susan. Susan was arguing with herself over whether she had the right to feel disappointed and chastising herself for not being able to seize the moment. Mya sat quietly on the floor before the fire, trying to put herself in a receptive mood to tap into the psychic reservoir of memories in the old house. Strains of violins, crackles from the roaring fire, and the periodic howling of the wind created an atmosphere where she could allow her mind to flow back into the eternal now. But as peaceful as she herself felt, warmed by the heat of the fire and satiated by the sweet taste of chocolate, the energy she was able to sense was entirely negative. It was the same familiar anxious, unhappy and discontented ambience she always picked up on in the house. Mya could detect no remnant sensations of intense violence. If anything terrible had happened, and Mya was certain something had, it had not happened in the house itself. What she felt was more like quiet despair, long-term despair, the kind of despair for which there is no cure except for death, and death itself is not always the cure, as the haunting by Kathleen Angel well proved.

Mya's habit of looking back into the past made her short-sighted about the present. Her fascination with Kathleen Angel prevented her from suspecting that the negative energies might be coming from someone in the present, someone sitting in this very room with her. She looked over and gave Tom an enigmatic smile; she then blew Susan a kiss; and she stretched out on the floor and closed her eyes and drifted back into the 19th century to see if she could make some sort of contact with the spirit whom she thought was causing such despair.

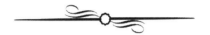

MYA'S DIARY

During the times in Susan's life when she felt the need to keep a diary, her biggest concern was where to hide it so that Tom or Heather wouldn't be able to read it. The fact that Mya kept a diary didn't surprise Susan, but she was shocked to learn that Mya kept it right out in the open where anyone could pick it up and read it, and Mya's diary was just the sort of artifact that someone would want to pick up and examine. It was a small, thick, antique book with a padded ivory silk cover, and the cover was decorated with an embroidered basket of lavender flowers. The book was very old and smelled sour and musty. It always lay in the same spot. Mya had placed it at an angle on a circular crocheted doily on top of a bookcase by the door in the parlor. Beside it was a green fountain pen, wrapped with fine filigree gold, and the pen stood upright in a matching green holder. Susan had picked up the pen more than once and marveled at the exquisite filigree, so fine, so beautiful, and still shiny and bright after years of use.

"It was given to me by a dear old friend of my mother's," Mya explained.

"It's probably worth a lot of money," Susan said. "There's not a single mark on it. Do you think this might be 24 carat gold?"

"Don't have any idea," Mya said. "It was given to her by a great aunt. I can't even begin to figure out how old it is, probably over a hundred years maybe. And this is my journal," Mya said, picking up the ivory book and handing it to Susan. "It's also very very old."

Susan took the book in her hands and ran her finger over the knotted lavender flowers. "It's lovely," she said. "Another gift from an old lady?"

"No," Mya said. "I got the cover at an antique shop. It was in horrible shape, but I managed to clean it pretty thoroughly, without tearing it even once. Then I bought paper pages and cut them to fit. "

"I can't believe you keep it right out in the open with clients coming in and out all the time," Susan said. "What if someone decides to read it?"

"I only write very important things in it," Mya said, as she straightened the doily and replaced the book at the exact angle where it had been lying. "It wouldn't make sense to anyone but me."

Mya's diary was just another bit of strange behavior for Susan to report to Tom at dinner.

"Do you know where Mya keeps her diary?" Susan asked Tom.

The words Mya and diary gave Tom cause to shudder, until he glanced over at Susan and saw her looking perfectly calm and innocent. He didn't say the first thing that came to his mind – "Why are you asking?" Instead, he chewed slowly and swallowed. "I can't imagine that Mya is the sort of person who keeps a diary," he said.

"Every sensitive woman nowadays keeps a diary," Susan said. "But Mya keeps hers right on top of that bookcase by the door, right there where anyone could pick it up and read it."

"What sort of person would pick up someone else's diary and read it?" Tom asked.

"Anybody could," Susan said. "I think it's a normal thing to do, particularly if it is out in the open."

"I don't know what kind of normal people you know," Tom said.

A familiar flush of guilt and insecurity spread through Susan's body. A simple interesting conversation had turned into an opportunity for Tom to criticize, and, as always, she felt judged and found wanting. She sulked as she cleared the table. She resolved, as she did every day, not to try to start conversations with Tom, and she further resolved, as she did every day, to speak only when spoken to, and, under no circumstances, to joke about her best friend's unusual ways.

Tom didn't notice nor care that Susan was sulking. He had something else on his mind. So Mya had a diary sitting out on a shelf where anyone could read it. Lots of her clients were kooks, and some of them were wives and sisters and mothers of the very people he worked with at the Kraft Paper Mills. Not to mention, of course, that Susan went in and out of Mya's parlor all the time, and she obviously didn't think there was anything wrong with reading someone else's diary if it were lying around.

After dinner Susan took a long, hot bath, soaking in a blanket of coconut bubble bath in the gray tub in Kathleen and her favorite bathroom. She analyzed the conversation that had taken place at dinner. She chastised herself for bringing up the topic of the diary. Why had she done it? One reason was that it was becoming more and more difficult to talk with Tom, and Susan naturally thought that the story of the old antique diary, sitting on the book case, would be amusing to him. She often used tales about Mya to amuse Tom, and just as often, she felt guilty for doing so. As the bubbles slowly evaporated and the water became cool, her final thought on the matter was that she was being duly punished for making fun of her friend. In reality, she envied Mya. She herself would like to have an antique ivory book that she had found and restored, and she would love to own a gold filigree pen that had been given to her by someone dear to her mother. Mya's life was touched with beauty and meaning. Susan's life was a useless void.

If Susan had had a diary that night, she would have written her resolution to appreciate her friend Mya more and to never use that friendship as a means to initiate conversations with Tom. But she had no old antique journal, and she had no filigree pen, and she had no thoughts worth writing down, so instead, she cried herself to sleep under the sympathetic and watchful eye of Kathleen Angel.

For a day or two, Tom was obsessed with the existence of Mya's diary. He told himself he had to make certain there was nothing incriminating about him in the book, but the truth was he wanted to pry into the mystery of Mya, and what better way to do this than to read her most personal thoughts.

On Wednesday at noon, he called Susan from work. It was a casual call to say hello and ask what she was doing. Tom seldom called her during the day, and Susan was surprised to hear his voice.

"Did I get you from somewhere?" he asked.

"No," she said, pausing to give him a chance to explain why he was calling.

"I was just sitting here looking out the window," he said. "It's such a great day. I was just wondering if you and Mya were outside enjoying it."

The thought that he was at work wondering about her caused a flush to slide through Susan's body.

"It's a beautiful day," she said, "but it's still a little chilly. I'll probably take a walk later. Mya doesn't get home until three."

"So, what are you doing? Sitting on the couch with a book?" Tom teased.

"No, I am not sitting on the couch with a book," Susan said. "I'm about to start a major project."

"Major project? That sounds serious," Tom said.

"Yep," Susan said. "I'm going to wax all the floors in the hall and on the landing."

"Wow," Tom said. "That'll take hours. It makes me tired just to think about it."

"I just want to get it done, once and for all," Susan said. "I just want to cross it off my list."

"Have a good time," Tom laughed. "I'd better get back to the grindstone. See you around six."

Susan smiled as she hung up the phone. Maybe Tom felt guilty for being so critical of her last night, she thought, and she felt good the rest of the afternoon, as she waxed and rubbed and admired the results of her hard labor.

With Mya at the Bullfrog and Susan occupied, Tom left for a long lunch and drove towards home. He parked some distance from the house along the road and began to walk towards the bridge. If anyone stopped, or if Susan came out, he planned to say he was on his way home with a migraine and the car had stalled when he went to turn into the drive.

His plan was so simple. Without seeing a soul, he walked across the bridge and up through the forest to Mya's back door. Naturally, the door was unlocked. Mya didn't believe in locking doors. "If you can't trust the world, who can you trust?" she had often repeated.

Tom walked into the dark, quiet room, and saw the diary lying on top of the bookcase. Before Tom touched the diary, he noted the angle it made with the top of the bookcase and approximately how close it was to the edge. He gently picked up the heavy soft book and sat down in a chair by the table. As nervous as he had been while he was walking down Bullfrog a few moments ago, nothing compared to the anxiety he felt as he opened Mya's diary. Perhaps he would learn the truth about their relationship, and maybe he was going to find out if his suspicions of other men had any foundation. With the book resting on his hands, he paused and wondered if he was perhaps going to learn things he really didn't want to know. He was scared, too scared to open the diary. He sat quietly for several minutes and ran his fingers over the flowers. He smelled a faint odor of mildew mixed with a sweet perfume. It smelled awful. One of the reasons Tom hated old things was because of the way they smelled.

Sitting in Mya's parlor, surrounded by her Gypsy possessions, holding a hundred year old diary, Tom didn't know whether to laugh or cry at his predicament. "Oh, hell," he said aloud, and he opened the book. Several pages were filled with Mya's beautiful flowery handwriting, and what he could read made no sense at all. He skimmed each page, looking for his name, but he saw no names at all.

"I must always be careful to distinguish the within and the without," he read. "Attain the necessary level of consciousness to tap the cosmic reservoir of memories." He flipped through a few more pages and looked for Tom, Susan, or anything familiar. "The past, the present, the future are illusions. We live in an eternal now."

Tom carefully put the diary back on the shelf. As he walked quickly down the forest path to his car, he felt relief. His initial reaction had been right. Mya was discreet. She wasn't the kind of person who would sit and and write incriminating thoughts in a diary and then leave it out for anyone to read. Every time he doubted Mya, she came out okay. He felt secure. His little indiscretion wasn't going to be discovered. He had worried for no good reason. By the time he reached the office, he was in such a gay mood that Sandy wondered aloud whether it had been a two martini, or three martini lunch.

"Just call it a multi-martini lunch," Tom laughed. "Give or take a few." He was tempted to tell her about his bizarre, ironic experience, and get a good laugh out of her, but reason prevailed and he just went into his office and got to work.

As he drove home that evening, he created an amusing story about his afternoon. He put someone else in the main role. It seems an acquaintance of his was having an affair with a fortune teller, and he found out through his wife that the fortune teller kept a diary out in the open for everyone to see. And this friend got so worried about this diary and about everyone in town reading it that he sneaked into the fortune teller's house when she wasn't home and he read the diary. What a joke on him. There wasn't a word about him, or about any other men, in the diary. It was all gobbledegook. And here he had to sneak out and get away without anyone seeing him. What a story. But it was not a story for Sandy, nor for Susan, nor for anyone in Port Williams for that matter. Tom would have to save the story for another place and another time, perhaps over a multi-martini lunch with a colleague in some other state, a colleague with a good sense of humor, one who appreciated a good story. And it was a good story, no doubt about that.

Susan herself had resolved never to mention the diary again, so the book lay at an angle on the doily, self-contained and unaware of the turmoil it had caused. Mya picked it up from time to time and wrote in its pages some tidbit of esoteric knowledge that she might someday need to guide her on her journey through life.

THE LOVE-STRUCK FOOL

Tom had lost all control. Despite his daily resolution to go directly home after work and not stop to check on Mya, he was unable to do so. It seemed there was a large magnet in the Bullfrog parking lot with a powerful attraction for his car, and the important Vice President found himself unable to drive on past the dark lane that led up to the Frog.

"I'll just stop in for a quick drink and tell Mya I'm not going back into work later, that I'm not going to see her tonight. I have more important things to do," he told himself.

Whether or not the Love-Struck Fool followed through with the plans made by the Emperor depended entirely on Mya. If she dropped what she was doing and hurried over to him, right there and then his plan changed. But, if she was occupied with customers and didn't immediately break away when he came in, the plan remained firm.

On one particular day, although the place was no more crowded than usual, Mya was so busy she barely had a chance to speak to him as she set his drink on the table. She delivered the second drink in an equally big hurry.

As she placed the glass on the table, Tom reached over and touched her arm. "Wait a second," he said, "I just wanted to let you know that I won't be going into work later tonight." He felt good when he said it. He was in charge. He was the one who was making the decision not to see her. He felt relief. But, as usual, Mya surprised him. Suddenly, she was no longer in a hurry. She dropped herself into a chair beside him and said, "That's fine, Tom. I already have some plans for this evening, so it will all work out great."

She gave him a big, innocent smile and began to make small talk. Tom was having trouble listening because he was wondering about her plans. Was she going off to spend the evening with an old sick lady friend? Was she taking another advanced hypnotism class at the Spiritual Center? What he truly wondered was whether she was going to be with another man. Did she have a date? But he didn't dare ask.

Mya continued making small talk, while Tom watched her. She was vibrant. Her cheeks were flushed, and her lips full and red, as though she had been kissed and kissing. Tom had not been with her for three nights. On Friday night someone came in from out of town, and he and Susan had spent a long, dull evening entertaining. On the weekend, Mya was nowhere to be seen. She often made herself scarce on weekends. Tom suspected she did it to force him, or enable him, to spend time with Susan. Mya was very considerate of Susan. In fact, Mya was very considerate of everyone, unfortunately. At that very moment, she was talking about how Juan, the cook's helper, sent most of his wages back to his family in Mexico, and how the poor fellow had to work two jobs and live in a single room with four other people.

"It must be tough," Tom said.

Mya yawned, and Tom noticed that her eyes were glassy. She looked as though she hadn't been getting much sleep lately. "There's something going on," he thought.

Mya leaned on her elbows and grinned at Tom. "What's you thinkin' so hard about?" she asked.

Tom allowed her to look directly into his eyes. He wanted her to see what he was wondering about. With his eyes he asked a simple question: "Who have you been fucking?"

Mya had no trouble reading the question, but she chose not to answer it. "I've got to get back to work," she said. "For some reason, the boys are particularly dry today." She put her hand on Tom's. "What's your big important plan for tonight? You taking Susan out some place special, I hope. It's not fair that she's home alone all the time."

She had done it again. Without a second thought, she had thrown Susan into the conversation. Tom squeezed his glass so hard he was surprised it didn't crush in his hand. He wanted to pick it up and throw it at her. He watched her approach two couples sitting at a table, scribble something onto her pad, and make her way towards the kitchen, pausing to collect an empty glass and plate off the bar and to exchange a few words with a young man sitting alone, nursing a beer.

Tom focused his eyes on the young man. Was he the one? "Probably not," Tom decided. He was a puny looking guy, and Tom remembered he had seen him before, sitting with a girlfriend. Tom's eyes scanned the room, and as they paused at each table, he wondered about every single man. Before he had finished his inventory, Mya came back into the room from the kitchen and began floating from table to table. She paused and laughed with absolutely everyone. She could be fucking every man in the room, or she could be fucking none, or one, or two, or seven, or all of the above, or none of the above. The Love-Struck Fool was completely overwhelmed.

Tom left a twenty dollar bill folded in half under the empty glass. He hoped she would get the message. Before he reached his car, he was sorry he had left the insulting tip, but he was not going to walk back inside to retrieve it. He had to get away from that place. He had to get away from her. Tom was not comfortable in situations where he didn't know the rules, or, as seemed to be the case more and more in his present life, where there were apparently no rules at all.

Once he was home, the anxiety of knowing he was not going to see Mya that night began to gnaw at him. As he and Susan sat at the table, he waited for Mya's name to come up. He desperately wanted to talk about her. As he sat quietly chewing on a piece of sausage, a crazy idea came into his mind. He wanted to ask Susan what she truly thought about Mya. Susan had a good sense about people, and he had often relied on that sense.

"What does Mya think about me? Does she talk about me? Do you think she likes me?" he didn't ask. Oh to be a teenager once again, to be hanging around with a gang of friends, analyzing, criticizing, predicting, confessing, and lying about your latest romantic interest. But Tom could not even bring up her name, let alone talk about her with anyone at all.

After dinner he lay on the couch with his arm over his eyes and told Susan he had a bit of a tension headache. Once Susan had finished the dishes and sat down at the table with a new copy of Victoriana that had arrived that afternoon, he got up off the couch and sat at his desk in the study. He couldn't concentrate on anything. He wondered who had been kissing his Mya. Of course he had no right to care, but whether or not he had the right to wonder, it was driving him crazy.

Susan did have something amusing to tell Tom about Mya that evening, but she held off. She didn't want to bother him with one of her silly stories when he had a headache. She would share it with him later when he felt better. He was going to just die when he heard about Mya and her latest interest. Susan had almost died herself when she heard about it.

Early that morning Mya had waltzed over with the biggest grin on her face.

"You look like the cat that ate the canary," Susan said.

"You're close," Mya said, "More like the cat that ate the fox." She came in and plopped down at the dining table.

Susan automatically went into the kitchen and brought Mya a mug of hot strawberry cinnamon tea, their latest favorite. "Let's hear all about it," she said. "I love animal stories."

"I just couldn't wait to tell you," Mya bubbled. "I don't even know where to begin. You're going to die when you hear about it."

"You're getting to be as bad as Mr. Edwards," Susan said. "Just spit it out."

"Well, did you hear about the Male Fox Review?" Mya asked. "Did I mention they were in town?"

"Nope," Susan said. She shook her head. She had no idea what Mya was talking about.

"They're male dancers," Mya explained. "They were at the Frog last night."

"Oh my God," Susan exclaimed. "Male dancers at the Frog? Wait til Mrs. Angel's Ghost hears about that. I can smell the place burning already."

"Please don't mention it to her," Mya whispered. "And, also, don't tell her this, but I've got a date with one of the dancers tonight. I am sure she would not approve."

"They're doing another show tonight?" Susan asked. "You mean enough people like that sort of thing? I can't imagine it."

"No, they're not doing another show," Mya said, "And I'm sorry, because I know you really wanted to get a chance to see them. It's just that one of the dancers is staying around for a few days, and I promised I would meet him again tonight."

"Are you telling me you have a date with a male stripper?" Susan asked. She shook her head in disbelief, disbelief that Mya was still able to come up with such surprises.

"If you'd seen him in his little silver sequined jock strap, you'd be wanting to go out with him yourself," she teased. "He's called the California Schemer."

Susan felt her face grow warm. "Only you, Miss Mya Clark, would have a date with a guy with a name like that. I hope you get what you deserve," she teased.

"I hope so, too," Mya said. "In fact, I'm looking forward to it."

Susan chuckled to herself all afternoon about Mya and the California Schemer. She usually made a point of never telling Tom anything that would make Mya seem cheap or trashy, but this was too good to keep to herself.

After a while, Tom got up off the couch and began to wander around the house, walking from room to room like a lost soul. It was hard for Susan to concentrate. "You don't want to go to a movie or anything, do you?" she asked when he came into the living room for the third time. "We could catch the nine o'clock. I don't know what's playing."

"I'm not really in the mood for a movie," Tom said.

Susan found an interesting article on reproductions of Victorian crystal chandeliers. She heard Tom dialing the phone in his study, but she couldn't hear his voice. She wondered who he was trying to call at this hour. She heard him go upstairs, and she heard him come back down. He walked into the dining room and stood, looking out the window. As Susan watched him, she felt the nervous feeling creeping from him across the room and into her. She put the magazine aside and walked over to him. She stood quietly beside him and peered out into the darkness. One small porch light was gleaming above the door of the summer house. The rest of the world was pitch black.

"Are you upset about something, Tom?" she asked. "I haven't seen you this fidgety for a long time."

Tom rested his arm lightly on her shoulder. "Just restless," he replied.

Susan moved closer and leaned her head against his chest. She felt sympathetic. Poor Tom. She decided this might be a good time to tell her funny story and get his mind off whatever it was that was bothering him.

"I wonder how Mya is making out with the male fox," she said aloud to herself.

Tom perked up when he heard the word Mya. "A fox?" he asked.

Susan laughed. "Not a real fox," she said, "an exotic dancer type fox."

"She's taking dancing lessons?" Tom asked. Like Susan, he was always ready to be shocked by anything Mya happened to be doing. Dancing lessons, why not?

"Lessons," Susan said. "Well, not exactly." And she began to tell Tom an edited version of the Male Fox Review and the California Schemer with the sequined jock strap.

In the darkness of the room, she did not see Tom's face change from disbelief to pain to anger. As Susan finished the story, she added one more idea, thoughtlessly using words with barbs so sharp it was surprising Tom didn't bleed profusely onto the rug.

"Mya's always talking about having a baby. Maybe this California Schemer would be the perfect father. He's a hunk, and he's probably got good genes, and he certainly wouldn't hang around afterwards and make any demands on Mya's life."

Tom stared out the window, hypnotized by the amber light in the distance. He said nothing. Once again, Susan realized her timing was off. She had wasted a good story. She should have saved it for a time when Tom was in a better mood. She didn't think he had heard a single word she said. She picked up the magazine and went into the living room and curled up on the sofa. She finished the article on the chandeliers and folded the corner of the first page. She couldn't wait to call Gladys in the morning and tell her about the latest tacky reproductions. Gladys would be sending a letter of protest off to the editor as fast as she could fill her ink well and coax her quill pen into flowing properly.

She heard the door slam and the sound of the engine turning over and she listened as Tom's car wound around the drive, down the hill, and across the bridge.

"Tom always said the thing he missed most about his old job was driving around, listening to music," she thought. Whatever Tom's problem was, he was obviously trying to work it out on his own. There wasn't anything more she could do, so she might as well stop wasting time thinking about it.

"God, I'm beginning to sound like Mya," she said aloud. She tossed her magazine on the couch, stretched her arms high in the air and began to dance around the room.

At first when Tom went back to work in the evenings, Susan was not comfortable alone in the big house. Things creaked, clunked, scratched, bumped and sighed, and Susan had trouble determining whether the noises were friendly or unfriendly. She walked from room to room searching for the sources of the noises, and, in time, she learned to distinguish the forest noises from the house noises, the attic noises from the basement noises, and she began to enjoy the strange symphonies emanating from her home.

She was relieved when Tom left for his drive and took with him the anxious, uncomfortable vibrations he was exuding. She danced into the kitchen where she poured a water glass full of white wine, turned off all the lights, and then went upstairs. She was looking forward to a nice, long soak in the tub.

Kathleen Angel had obviously loved bathrooms, and she had seen to it that anyone who wanted to take a nice, long, hot bath could do so with style. There were a total of six bathrooms in the house, but it was the one on the second floor, adjacent to her bedroom and sitting room, that most appealed to Susan. It was an enormous room, and arranged around the inside wall were a bidet, a regular sink, a deeper sink for hair washing, a tub, a toilet, and a large, glassed-in shower with eight nozzles at different heights from the floor to the ceiling. Everything in the room was pink and gray. Pink swans floated peacefully on the gray ceramic tiles, and pink frosted glass shades covered the bulbs and cast a soft, romantic light about the room.

Susan filled the tub with very warm water, sprinkled lavender bath crystals under the faucet and gently lowered herself into the water. She lay in the tub, sipping her wine, and thinking about the past, not her own personal past, but the magic, enchanting past that was captured in this house, and now, more and more often, in her own life.

As she stepped out and rubbed herself dry with a big towel, she wrapped a smaller towel around her head and looked at her reflection in the steamed mirrors. She imagined she was Kathleen Angel, trying to decide what to wear for the evening. She pretended Lloyd Angel had invited some of the lumber barons and their wives over for a dinner. Susan pictured handsome, rich men and lovely, petite women sitting at the dining table while servants in black and white suits passed around steaming silver dishes filled with roast venison and quail. Susan put on an old fashioned white cotton night gown that Heather had sent her for her birthday. "Wear this, and you will be in tune with the house," Heather had written on the card.

Susan lit a candle by the bed, and, instead of reading, she lay there thinking about how silly life was. Here she was, a grown woman, pretending she was an elegant lady who had died seventy some years ago. She looked up at the picture and saw that Kathleen too was amused. Tom was somewhere driving around worrying about something, probably a big order that got fouled up. And Mya was off having sex with the California Schemer. Susan thought of how nice it was not to have to worry about work, and she was glad she wasn't in Mya's shoes, because she would never enjoy sex with a one-night stand. She tried to think of what it would have been like to have been Kathleen Angel and to have had to manage the estate and live in a house with servants and maids. While Susan was lying in her big soft bed, half asleep, dreaming and fantasizing, she felt so content. She realized for the first time in years that she was glad she wasn't anyone else or anywhere else. As she blew out the candle and rolled over to go to sleep, she thought, "This house really does things to your mind. This is the first time in my life that I've ever been glad that I'm just plain old me. Whoever that is," she added with a quiet snicker.

She had been asleep for hours when Tom crawled carefully into the far side of the bed. She never awakened and was surprised to find him there in the morning. He had had a very long and exhausting night.

When he left the house, he headed north on 15 into New York state; he then turned east on 17 and drove for a couple of hours, and then turned south again on 441. He drove over 200 miles, and as he drove, he held a conference with himself aloud in the car.

What exactly is going on here? Admittedly, there is a problem, but what is the nature of this problem?

The problem is Mya.

The problem isn't Mya. The problem is that you are stuck in that damned office and you don't have time to work things out anymore. When you were on the road, you had plenty of time to figure out what was going on and to stay on top of things and put them into perspective. Now so many things happen that you don't have time to deal with them.

Mya is not the problem. Mya is not the problem. Mya is not the problem. If he repeated it often enough, he might even come to believe it.

The idea of Mya making love with a male stripper was no problem at all, Tom argued to himself. He tried to picture Mya with a male stripper, but he had never seen a male stripper. He was forced to substitute a random customer from the Frog. He tried to picture a naked Mya sitting astride a faceless man, and he found it impossible to conjure up such an image. Mya kept disappearing from the scene, and he was left with a man, lying on his back, wearing nothing but a red and black checked hunting jacket and his underwear.

Tom's Mya, in her own eccentric way, had class. She was discriminating. Tom was unable to believe that she could be in love with a man of his caliber, and at the same time, be fooling around with an exotic dancer from California that she barely knew.

Once he had eliminated the possibility that Mya was off screwing the male dancer, he was able to rationalize an explanation of the story Susan had been telling him. Mya loved to shock and to joke, and even Susan admitted that you had to take some of Mya's tales with a grain of salt. Too many preposterous stories came out of Mya for them all to be true, and furthermore, Susan didn't always get her facts straight either, so, obviously, Mya had told Susan about the dancer just for shock value, and Susan had swallowed the whole tale. Poor Susan would believe anything. Tom could see that in a day or so, Susan would be telling him about how that imp Mya had fooled her once again. Tom was angry with his dumb wife, and he was even angrier with himself for getting caught up in this kind of hysteria.

It was nearly 2 a.m. before he had it all worked out and finally felt ready to drive home and go to bed. After five hours of thinking and stewing in the car, he had come to another conclusion.

Regardless of what was going on with Mya, the move to Port Williams had been a major mistake. He would never fit in with these hicks. They chose to live in some long past period of time, and they selected from the Twentieth Century only that which they could not resist: snowmobiles, four wheelers, VCRs, and exotic dancers. They were stuck in a time warp, and there was no way that Tom would ever be able to relate to them and all their crazy ways.

While Tom was driving around thinking about time warps, Mya was learning that she herself had not kept up with the times. She was accustomed to horny Pennsylvania country boys. If one became a little rough, it was due more to clumsiness and drink than to any sadistic inclinations. Mya taught any number of these boys to slow down and remember they had a partner underneath them with needs of her own. Mya was not inexperienced in the ways of love and she had enjoyed a variety of partners over the years. But the California Schemer was in a league of his own. He was incredibly good looking, tanned, blond, and very well built. During the performance at the Frog, although Mya was busier than she had ever been, she still managed to make eye contact with him, again and again, as he thrust his pelvis in and out and wiggled his butt and paused while frantic women stuffed bills under his sequined jock strap. By the time the crowd had thinned, without a word, the two knew they would be spending the night together. Even in the back of a van on an air mattress, sex with the California Schemer was better than anything Mya had ever imagined.

But on the second night, in a hotel room, Mya learned that the California Schemer was incredibly strong and determined, and that he had proclivities that to her were unnatural. He was not a Pennsylvania country boy, and Mya was not able to talk her way out of what had become a dangerous situation. She was scared. And when her fear and discomfort reached a point where she began to protest loudly, he clasped one big strong hand over her mouth, and she felt as though she was going to choke.

When she realized it was useless to struggle, she deliberately allowed herself to slip quietly into a trance. Since childhood, she had been able to use this technique when she wanted to escape from boredom or discomfort, but this was the first time she had to use it to escape from danger. When the California Schemer felt the fight go out of her body, he took his hand off her mouth and released her. At first he thought she had fainted, but when he saw her staring up at him with her big green eyes wide open, yet not seeing, like a dead person, he was afraid, and all sexual excitement drained away. He began to shake her by the shoulders.

"Hey, you okay? I didn't mean to hurt you. I just got carried away." He gently slapped her cheeks with his hand.

Mya felt herself float up to the surface, saw the strange man's concerned face looking down at her, and decided to play possum until she could think of a way out. He felt her wrist for a pulse. He put his ear close to her mouth to listen for her breathing. He left her lying there for a moment while he hurried into his clothing and gathered hers up from around the room. Mya heard him pulling on his jeans and stepping into his shoes. When she sensed him moving towards the bed, she peeked through her lashes and saw that he was fully dressed and was holding her clothing in his arms. She felt it was safe to pretend to wake up. She moved her head from side to side and blinked her eyes as though she was trying to clear her thoughts.

"Are you okay? You must have fainted," he said. "Can you get up?"

Mya got up and slowly and methodically dressed herself. He was visibly scared, and while he was scared, she knew she was safe.

"I want to go home," she said as softly and slowly as she could. "I want to go home now."

The only thing he wanted to do was to get her out of the room. He picked up his car keys off the bureau.

"I'll take a taxi," she said.

"Does this burg have cabs?" he asked. "I don't think I've seen any. Do you need money?"

"I'll be okay," Mya said in her quietest voice, as she opened the door and stepped out into the hallway. "I'm okay," she whispered once again.

"You're sure?" he asked.

"I'm sure," she repeated, as she pulled the door quietly closed behind her and ran down the hall and out into the street. She had spent a lot of time getting dressed for the evening. She was wearing a yellow gauze dress with full, ruffled sleeves and a wide loose skirt that reached to her ankles. It was not the best outfit for running. The skirt gathered between her legs and slowed her down. She took off her sandals, and with a combination of running, walking fast, and floating, she headed towards home, two miles away. It was 2 a.m. when she reached Bullfrog Valley Road and finally felt comfortable enough to slow down. But just as she was beginning to relax and breathe normally, she heard the sound of a car and she slipped quickly into the trees along the road, just in case the California Schemer had decided to follow her home.

At exactly 2 a.m., Tom turned down Bullfrog Valley Road, still pondering over the strange idea of people living so many different life styles at the same time in the same place. Here he was, a rational, educated man, living in a society where people believed in ghosts, and talked about them like they were live people. The very instant that thought passed through his mind, a light billowy dress appeared up ahead in his car lights, and then disappeared into the trees. It was a moment like no other moment in Tom Harris' life. Reality was held in suspension. He did not believe in ghosts, and yet he was actually seeing a ghost.

He couldn't decide whether to slow down and look, or speed up and escape. But Tom didn't have to make the decision. When Mya recognized Tom's car, she ran out of the trees onto the road and waved, and when he realized it was Mya, he screeched to a stop. She opened the door and leaned in.

"What in the world are you doing out here at this hour?" Tom asked.

"Just taking a walk," Mya replied calmly. "Might I ask the same question of you? What are you doing out here at this hour?"

"Just taking a drive," Tom said. "Hop in and I'll give you a lift."

Although they both appeared to be calm and subdued, the car was immediately filled with a strange energy. Tom was so glad to see Mya. He felt he had been lost in a cave for hours and had finally seen the distant light of the entrance. Seeing Mya in the flesh meant she was not at that moment in the arms of a male dancer.

Once Mya was seated in the warm, secure car with familiar, harmless Tom, she felt extreme relief. Tom's anxiety, concern and confusion mixed with Mya's fear and distress, and the resulting energy could not be ignored. This was not a time for small talk. Mya was suddenly in his arms and he couldn't get enough of her. As one arm held her closely to him, the other ran through her hair and down the sides of her face, around her breast and around her rib cage. And Mya did the strangest thing. She began to sob, deep sobs that racked her body and made Tom hold her closer than he had ever held her before.

"Are you all right?" he asked.

"I am now," Mya said, and she knew she was.

As a result of that fateful night, many resolutions were made. Mya decided she was through with one night stands and sex with strangers. She could have been killed, and then what about her powers, her future, her baby? It was time to start thinking about the future. From now on she was going to belong exclusively to Tom, at least until the baby came.

After holding Mya in his arms in her utmost vulnerable state, Tom decided he could not give her up. He had never felt anything like this for anyone in his life. He couldn't help himself. He was in too deep; he would never get out; and that was all right with him.

Susan decided she was tired of worrying about Tom all the time. If he had problems and he didn't tell her what they were, then it was hopeless to always be trying to cheer him up. She wanted to enjoy life for a change and not have to fall into a pit every time Tom came home with a long face. She loved this big old house, and she loved all the new things she was learning about the history of the house. Gladys had suggested that she join the Port Williams Historic Society and volunteer to help with the house tours. There was so much to do and learn. Susan was finding an exciting niche for herself, and she didn't have time nor energy any longer to fret over Tom. He was on his own.

During the next few days, it seemed like the world had been washed with a fine warm spring rain. All the tension was gone and everyone was in a good mood, a starting over mood. Tom was relaxed and happy. He no longer fussed over whether or not to see Mya. Mya was there for him in a new way. And when Susan wasn't traipsing along after Gladys on Queen Street, she was holed up in the Historic Section of the Library, or digging around among Mr. Edwards' collections.

Mrs. Angel's Ghost was particularly content and idle. The transmission on Mr. Edwards' truck was working like it was brand new; the river skipped a spring flood for the first time in ten years; the trees and flowers on the estate were growing and blooming; the gypsy moths had not made their annual visit; and even Heather, who was eight states away, got promoted to Sergeant months before she ever expected it.

THE DUTCH HILL TRAGEDY

For anyone with the time or inclination to listen, Bullfrog Valley Road itself had many interesting tales to tell, some amusing, some boring, and some so sad and tragic that they would linger in the listener's mind for years to come. The night of the storm was one of the latter.

Andrew dropped Ellen and the children at her cousin's and hurried home to the estate. The horse seemed to sense that danger was imminent, for without any encouragement, he hurried along as fast as he could go. Light rain was beginning to fall, but the air was so cold that Andrew knew the rain would soon turn to ice and snow. It was five o'clock in the afternoon, and darkness was already descending.

Kathleen stood shivering in the shadows of the carriage house, and when she heard the sound of the buggy on the bridge, she stepped out onto the driveway. Andrew was surprised to see her there, small and frail, and wearing the same long damp gray cape she had worn to Dutch Hill earlier in the day. This sad figure had totally occupied his thoughts during the ride home. He didn't know what was wrong, and it was not his place to ask, but he felt anxious and worried about her.

As he jumped down from the driver's seat, he said, "You must go inside and get out of those wet clothes. You're going to catch your death of a cold."

Kathleen didn't listen. She pushed him aside in order to climb up onto the carriage and settle herself into his recently vacated seat. She reached down and took hold of the reins.

"I need this for a while," she said.

Andrew was confused. "Is there some place I can take you?" he asked. Andrew never argued with Mrs. Angel. No one ever did. Yet a terrific storm was on its way, and Mr. Angel had told him to get the horse and buggy home as fast as he could.

"Mr. Angel asked me to….." he began.

"Where is he?" Kathleen shouted down, as she tugged the reins tightly to the left to turn the horse back down the drive.

That's when Andrew realized what Kathleen was doing. This cold, shivering, beautiful creature was going to find her husband and bring him home to safety. The injustice of it all was too much for Andrew to bear. He grabbed the horse's bridle and brought the buggy to a momentary halt.

"Mr. Angel's all right," he said. "I just left him a little while ago. He'll find shelter in town until the storm's over."

"Where is he?" Kathleen shouted.

"I left him near Dutch Hill," Andrew said without thinking.

The familiar name, Dutch Hill, echoed in the frozen air. Kathleen whipped at the tired, cold horse until he reluctantly began to trot down the driveway where he did not want to go. Andrew was worried about Kathleen, but he was also concerned about Bay Swallow. He was one of the best horses in Lloyd Angel's stable.

"Bay Swallow is exhausted," he yelled after Kathleen, but she could no longer hear the voices of humans.

There was nothing more Andrew could do, so he turned his attention to tasks over which he had some control. He made certain everything was neatly stacked and hung in the carriage house and the doors tightly closed against the storm. After all, that was his job: he was paid to take care of the horses. The humans on the Angel Estate, unfortunately, were responsible for taking care of themselves.

Kathleen and Bay Swallow met men on horseback, as well as those driving carriages, everyone in much too big a hurry to acknowledge anyone else. Perhaps that is why no one recalled seeing her on the road that night. It was established that Andrew was the last person to have seen her alive, and he said he thought she was going to pick up Mr. Angel at one of the work sites. He didn't mention Dutch Hill. Upon further questioning, Andrew expanded his story. He said that Kathleen had been waiting for him when he returned with the carriage. She had asked where Mr. Angel was, and Andrew had told her. When he realized she was going out in the storm to find him, Andrew had tried to convince her that he should go instead because there was a tremendous storm coming, but Mrs. Angel, who was, as everyone knew, very strong-willed, had insisted that she take the carriage, and she had headed off down the driveway to go and find her husband, and there was nothing Andrew could do to stop her. He recalled that she seemed to be very distraught. Everyone knew how much Kathleen Angel adored her husband, and she was obviously insane worrying about him.

It was a night when so many bad things happened that it was difficult to concentrate on any single event. The winds blew for hours before the storm actually hit. A tremendous fire broke out on Dutch Hill, and several houses were burned to the ground. The St. Benedict Church was nearly destroyed, and some thirteen people had died in the fire.

The rain, and then the snow, did not arrive in time to put the fires out and the winds had ample opportunity to whip the flames about and spread them from house to house. By the time the Fire Department was alerted, enough snow had fallen to make it impossible for the fire wagons to be hauled across town.

A tired, wet, cold horse, harnessed to a carriage, was found, huddled against a pillar beneath the Lark Street Bridge. He was led to the carriage barns on Market Street, where a young man recognized him immediately as one of Lloyd Angel's animals. They rubbed him down, bedded him, but weren't able to get in touch with Mr. Angel until the roads were cleared, several days later.

During the week, some of the details of the night of the storm began to emerge. The fire had started in the house next to the Church. Several people were missing and some eventually turned up at friends' houses where they had sought shelter; a few had spent the night in the Trinity Church, a few blocks away. By the week's end, Kathleen Angel was still among the missing.

As days passed, hopes diminished. Friends and family began to muster around Lloyd. Everyone pretended to be hopeful. Kathleen was a force; she was a survivor; and she was an inherent part of the Angel image. No one could imagine Lloyd Angel without Kathleen at his side.

Over the weeks, and then months, and then years, Lloyd continued to live in the house, and nothing on the surface of his life was altered. His business concerns, friends, and his role in the town did not change. He did not remarry, and those who thought they knew him well were certain he would never get over the loss of his Kathleen. Andrew and he never spoke of the tragedy. Andrew never spoke to anyone about that night, except once in a long while, he looked into Bay Swallow's big brown eyes and asked: "Don't we sorely miss the dear, fine lady?" And Bay Swallow shook his fine big head and seemed to blink away a tear or two.

Every time Lloyd Angel tried to head towards Ellen's new place on Walnut Street, he sensed Kathleen's spirit hovering beside him. Often he was unable to cross the Lark Street Bridge, and he parked the carriage by the river and sat staring into the distance. Poor Lloyd Angel, sitting by the river, mourning the loss of his beloved wife, was a familiar sight. He spent less and less time with Ellen and the children, and eventually, he avoided going to Ellen at all, and instead, sent Andrew weekly with an envelope addressed to her. Their love was reduced to the silent glare Andrew focused on Ellen as he handed her the envelope at the door, and to her polite response of appreciation.

"Tell Mr. Angel I said thank you," Ellen said. "Tell Mr. Angel I appreciate his thoughtfulness." "Tell Mr. Angel the children and I are doing fine." Andrew never delivered a single message. He felt it would have been disrespectful to the memory of Kathleen Angel.

Time passed. The real Kathleen Angel faded and was replaced by a more romantic portrait. Her beauty was exaggerated; her style and taste were held up as paragons; and her kindness and charitable acts became almost legendary. The magnificent house sat as a monument to her glory, and as years went by, it seemed Lloyd himself could not do enough to preserve Kathleen's memory. He had always been a generous man, donating land and money to every project that came and asked, but now to the land and money, he added Kathleen Angel's memory. Simple kneeling cushions at the Baptist Church were dedicated to the memory of Mrs. Lloyd Angel, although Kathleen would not have been caught dead in a Baptist Church. The restoration of the stained glass windows of the St. Stephan's Church was done in memory of Kathleen Angel, and the chimes of St. Benedict's that have sounded twice a day for over seventy years do so to the glory of Kathleen Angel. No one hears them anymore; sirens, automobiles, and televisions drown out the soft metallic notes. Even in Port Williams, life has become too busy and frantic for chimes, but when they first began to sound, during the Christmas season of 1913, no person could help but pause and remember the beautiful, dead woman, and the sad, adoring husband that she left behind. The chimes brought tears to many an eye. Then, as now, everyone loves a sad story. There's nothing quite like someone else's tragedy to make one feel connected to the forces of life and content with one's own fate.

But time dilutes tragedy. The tour guide on the bus driving slowly down Dutch Hill points to the St. Benedict Church and reports: "There was a big fire here about fifty or so years ago. I believe a dozen or so people died in it." In the same breath, he points out the unique design of the wooden carvings on the immense entrance door.

When local history books mention the great Dutch Hill Fire of 1913, they focus on the near destruction of the St. Benedict Church, and the fact that a new, more beautiful church was built on the site, one that still stands today. The reader comes away thinking that the fire wasn't such a bad thing after all. History cares nothing for despair.

It is impossible to try to estimate or measure the amount of sorrow unleashed the night of the Dutch Hill fire. The deed itself was so evil that God felt he had to cover it up with a soft white blanket to hide it even from his own forgiving eyes. At times quiet and trembling, at times sobbing and wiping her nose on her cold, damp sleeve, Kathleen Angel was a missile loaded with fuel, shot off at a target by some unknown force. The missile was disguised as a beautiful woman; the projector was a black four-wheel carriage, drawn by a black thoroughbred horse, imported from Ireland; and the target, #24 Elm Road.

Kathleen Angel never had a clue as to the source of her lifelong discontentment. Over the years she tried to blame any number of things: her parents, their poverty, her childlessness, Lloyd's indifference, and often, just the inexplicable nothingness of life. When she met Ellen and the children, she was irrationally certain that she had something tangible to blame for her despair. Nothing could have stopped Kathleen that night. Had Bay Swallow collapsed, she would have run the rest of the way on foot.

By the time Kathleen reached Dutch Hill, both she and Bay Swallow were drenched, cold and shaking. She pulled up into the yard beside the church, nearly fell out of the carriage, and scrambled across the small strip of land which separated the church from the first small house on Dutch Row. Kathleen had no strategic instructions on how to carry out her mission, no small packet slipped to her in a crowded airport. Before her was a back porch with a pile of neatly stacked wood, an old shelf, a basket full of rags, and a box containing paper and trash. With sheer will Kathleen quieted her trembling long enough to light four small fires among the clutter. As the fourth fire came to life and yellow flickering tongues began to lick a brown paper bag, Kathleen's last bit of control left her and she tripped down the steps and ran to the carriage. She collapsed onto the seat, gave Bay Swallow his head, and once more on that miserable stormy afternoon, he began to trot towards home, hay, water, and warmth, or so he thought.

Kathleen and Bay Swallow made it only as far as the Lark Street Bridge. Had Kathleen been rational, she would have driven home, claimed she was out looking for Lloyd, gone to bed with a fever, and, in a few days, gotten up and continued her life as before. But Kathleen knew her life as before was gone. She did not feel remorse. She felt a mixture of anger, hate, and disappointment, not only with Lloyd, but with herself, and mostly, with life in general. Between the waves of rage, lucid thoughts passed through Kathleen's agitated mind. She thought of all the effort and energy and years she had put into the estate and into herself, and it had all been for nought. Instead of sitting in a velvet covered Queen Anne's chair in front of a marble fireplace, Lloyd preferred a wooden chair in a stuffy, cluttered double with a glass of beer and a plate of potatoes. Lloyd was a complete stranger. She was married to a complete stranger, and she never wanted to see him again.

The river was having a ball that night. She loved storms. She and the wind were playing a game where the wind gave her such a big push that she nearly washed completely out of her bed and up onto the road. She giggled and screamed all the while like a silly teenage girl, but when she settled back into her bed, she dared the wind to do it again and again. She was like a child on a swing, scared but excited all at the same time. "Push me higher, higher, higher," she called.

But the river was never having so much fun that she wouldn't take notice when a distressed soul neared her bank. Thus, when she heard a carriage racing down Lark Street, she paused in her play to listen. She shimmied a little to reflect some brightness on her waves, and gurgled like a happy baby in the midst of the howling winds. Kathleen heard the gurgle and saw the glimmer. She jerked poor Bay Swallow's head so sharply that the carriage nearly toppled off the road. The cold, tired, confused horse fought against the bit. He was suddenly sick of taking orders. He was determined to get himself home once and for all, but how can one poor horse's determination compete with the forces of fate that were driving Kathleen at that moment. Bay Swallow, carriage, and mad woman half tumbled out of control off Lark Street and onto the flat bank below. The terrified horse used all of his strength to avoid ending up in the frothy water. The river was disappointed. She hadn't had a horse in a long time.

Kathleen suddenly became focused. As the horse frantically braked with his heavy front legs, every muscle in his body straining, Kathleen calmly crawled down from the carriage, up the bank, onto the road, and along the bridge to dead center, where she stood for only one second, part of her wanting to still her thoughts, but a stronger part forcing her on. The river shoved all the branches and logs to the side and made a nice clear spot, but Kathleen could see nothing through her tears and the rain and sleet that were now pouring down on her face. The world was pitch dark, windy, wet, and cold. She heard the happy gurgle and felt a light spray of refreshing water. Kathleen was thinking of her favorite room, a brightly lit sitting room with moss green carpet and peach-flowered chintz chairs, with a marble fireplace and a large oil painting of a vase of pale blue and white lilies hanging above it. She could feel the warmth of the fire as her body hit the cold, churning water beneath the Lark Street Bridge.

The river welcomed Kathleen with the same indifference with which she welcomed anyone who chose to join her on her eternal journey to Baltimore. She tossed Kathleen Angel's body along with the logs and broken tree branches, and when it got hung up on a rock, or was heading too close to the bank, she gave it a gentle push back to the center. Kathleen thrashed around in the water, her cape, gown and petticoats at first buoying her up, but soon weighing her down and dragging her along with the raging currents.

It was as though someone had tossed a bundle of old rags into the river. At first Kathleen bobbed where she landed, thrashing with her hands, trying to keep her head from going under. The hat went first, dancing from wave to wave down the dark and turbulent river. Then one by one the clips and pins became detached from the beautiful auburn hair, which streamed out in all directions. She may have cried out, but there was no one there to hear.

The river juggled Kathleen for a few moments, trying to decide whether to keep her or to toss her back up onto the bank where someone might find her and bring her back to life. Like a cat playing with a mouse, tossing it, catching it in its jaws, batting it with its paws, the river played with Kathleen. And while the river played, Kathleen's soul ascended to a more peaceful realm. Her body, clothing, a silver hair clip, a strand of black pearls, three small golden bracelets, and a broach in the shape of a butterfly with ruby wings were left behind in the wild and turbulent water.

Kathleen's silver and pink tourmaline rosary beads remained in a deep pocket of her underskirt where she had stuffed them earlier in the day. She never went anywhere without her special rosary beads. They kept her safe.

Strong emotions can be recorded in matter. The deposit can afterwards affect a sensitive person and cause similar emotions to reproduce themselves in that person. That's why Mya loved old things. She owned nothing new. The possessions she acquired at the thrift shops and yard sales contained the emotional and spiritual energies of their previous owners, a tiny smidgeon of the universal psyche. In particular, treasured items given in love carried with them a positive energy. Mya collected old wedding bands, which was ironic, since she never intended to marry. An old wedding band contained love, anger, remorse, despair, contentment, security, and sometimes even sexual energy. Mya could close her eyes and read the history of a marriage by gently rubbing the wedding ring across her lips and then holding it in the palm of her hand until it warmed up and began to excrete the emotions and sensitivities it contained.

Her very special silver filigree hair clip with the blue stones gave off an array of emotions that was equivalent to a double dose of LSD. She wore it on every important occasion, and it had never let her down. One of her ongoing projects was to try to read its history. But the hair clip turned out to be more complicated than a simple wedding band. It was like trying to read a novel in a language of which she knew only a few words. She sensed only that when she piled her golden hair atop her head and fastened it with the blue clip, she felt charmed. The lovely clip garnered compliments from everyone who noticed it, and good things happened when it was fastened lovingly in her hair.

Kathleen Angel had a full head of thick auburn hair that hung to her waist, and she chose her personal maid solely on her ability to arrange that marvelous head of hair. On an ordinary day, when she took the carriage into town to visit the dressmaker, the hair could be brushed out and pinned up under a bonnet in thirty minutes. But for an evening at the opera, or at the Grand Victorian Ball, it took two or three hours to arrange the small braids and clips and curls and feathers in a way that pleased Kathleen. Styling Kathleen's hair was the main duty of her personal maid, and no one envied her that duty.

Kathleen had a collection of elaborate hair clips and combs of silver, gold, ivory, and tortoise shell, each adorned with gems and crystals of every color and size. Her favorite piece was a silver filigree clip, covered with blue sapphires, which Lloyd had got from an Argentine ship captain in exchange for some mast beams. The clip was priceless.

After Kathleen's death, Lloyd thoughtfully distributed her jewelry among her many sisters and nieces, but fine jewelry was an extravagance for working class families, and what was not sold to replace a horse, or to help the family through hard times, was sold during the depression for considerably less than it was worth. Eventually, Kathleen's collection, including her elaborate hair clips and combs, fell into the hands of clever goldsmiths who melted them down, removed the stones, and created pendants and broaches, or set them in rings, doubling and sometimes tripling their worth.

The blue clip Kathleen had fastened into her hair the fateful day of the Dutch Hill fire was made of intricate Argentine silver filigree, and the head of the comb was delicately tooled and decorated with rows of small blue sapphires. The overall shape of the piece looked like a big tooth with five long silver roots that were pushed deeply into the hair. A fine silver bar and clasp at the top of the roots tightly fastened the clip. Although it was of greater value than her other hair ornaments, because of its secure clasp, Kathleen wore it often.

On the tragic day of the fire, the reliable clasp held through the frantic carriage ride, through the scrambling and running in the church lot, and during the ride back to the river and the climb up onto the bridge. But it was not strong enough to resist the prying fingers of the cold river, and it was pulled off and carried away by the greedy currents. At that point, Kathleen was beyond caring.

There was something charming and childlike in Mya's habit of picking up stones whose glitter caught her eye, hoping to find a diamond. "Anything is possible," she always said, and she believed it.

Fourteen years after the river had taken Kathleen Angel and treated her and her possessions so carelessly, a nine year old boy with an eye for glitter spotted something silver along the shallow bank of the river, two miles south of the Lark Street Bridge. When he picked it up and rinsed it off, he saw that it was a ladies comb. He thought it was quite a find and took it home to his mother, who showed it to everyone who came into the house over the next few days.

"Look what our Jimmy found."

"Isn't that interesting? Looks like it might be worth something."

The clip sat on the kitchen table for all to see and then joined a collection of shells, bones, and rocks in a box on a shelf in Jimmy's room. It eventually made its way into an older sister's dresser drawer, where it grew dull.

"It might be worth something," was a common observation any time it was taken out and cleaned during the years that followed.

The sister, who never threw anything away, kept the old comb among her things for forty years. Eventually, she gave it to a young woman with a thick head of auburn hair who was living with her and helping to take care of her husband who was recovering from a stroke. The young woman, Pauline Clark, shined the comb, had the clasp repaired, and wore it often.

Some of Pauline Clark's possessions were kept in two sturdy boxes which moved with little Marie from foster home to foster home. Marie had gone through the boxes a hundred times and knew every item intimately: a bible from Pauline's grandmother, letters, notes, a glass ballerina, gray leather gloves, four delicate embroidered and tatted handkerchiefs, and some rings and necklaces, old fashioned stuff that no one wanted anymore.

The most interesting treasure in the box was a silver comb. Mya cleaned it up and shined it until it glimmered and the stones sparkled, and over the years, she wore the clasp any time she wanted to feel special. She never wore it to the Bullfrog, however, because there was a rule that long hair had to either be kept in a net or neatly braided. It was the Bullfrog's one salute to hygiene: no hair in the food. Mya either wore one long braid hanging down her back, or smaller braids arranged on top of her head. The only times she wore the clasp to the Frog was during that brief period when Sister Dory was seeing the blue aura when Tom Harris was about to come into her life.

How often Mya had worn it when she was sitting around visiting with Susan. How often Susan had remarked on how lovely it was. Mya had taken it out of her hair and shown Susan how intricate it was, how the blue stones sparkled, and how ingenious the clasp was, and they marveled together over it and said no one made beautiful things like that anymore. They held it up to the sunlight coming in the window and were enchanted with the flickering blue rays that danced all over the dining room walls.

"Wouldn't it be funny if this clip once belonged to Mrs. Angel?" Susan asked.

"Anything is possible," Mya said, and she held the clip out to an imaginary being in the corner of the room. "Was this yours?" she asked the invisible being. "Was this a gift from your doting rich husband?"

A cascade of blue lights swirled angrily around the walls and settled on the silver chandelier, where they blinked once and disappeared.

"There's your answer," Mya said to Susan, and Susan felt a shiver creep slowly down her spine.

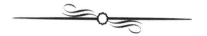

ONE YEAR ANNIVERSARY

A day arrived in July when Susan baked a devil's food cake, iced it with pink fondant, and put one small candle in the center. It had been one year since she and Tom had moved onto the Angel Estate. Mya was invited to join them for cake and Asti Spumante. Each held a pale blue crystal wine glass with an intricate curly capital A etched on the side. Susan had found the glasses in a collectible shop on Route 15, and she hoped and pretended that they had once belonged to the Angel family.

"This auspicious occasion calls for a toast," Tom announced, as he held his glass out in front of him. "Gentleman before ladies," he said.

Susan waited for a smart remark, but as he was beginning to do more and more lately, on this occasion, Tom surprised her.

"To one of the most interesting years of my life," he proposed.

Susan waited for a post script. She watched as Tom took a sip of his drink, swallowed, and looked over at her. "Next."

Susan held her glass up to the light and looked at the bubbles disappearing into the glimmering swirls and design of the elegant goblet. Then she studied the hand that held the goblet, long delicate fingers covered with antique silver rings, one with a cluster of white and gold stones, one with a large blue aquamarine, and plain silver bands, and sparkling pinkie rings. The hand she studied seemed not to be her own; it was the hand of a wealthy, elegant lady. This new Susan had begun to collect estate jewelry. She wished she had thought to wear a pair of lace gloves, and smiled at the juxtaposition of lace gloves with the corduroy pants and sweat shirt she was wearing.

She lowered her gaze and looked first into Tom's face and then into Mya's big green eyes. "I want to propose a toast to Kathleen Angel, who made it all possible," she said.

"A toast to the ghost," Tom said, as he took a slug from his glass, picked up the bottle, and refilled it.

Mya smiled and shook her head. She highly approved of toasting Kathleen Angel. She then lifted her glass high and looked through it first at Tom and then at Susan. "To the year when all my dreams came true." Then she corrected herself, "almost all my dreams."

On hearing the words, Tom felt his face grow warm and turned his head so no one would notice he was blushing. And Susan stood with the glass resting on her lower lip, wondering. It was the year when all of Mya's dreams came true, and the most interesting year of Tom's life. Hyperbole seemed to be the order of the day.

To break the silence, Tom offered a second toast: "May my life continue along its present path," he said.

"You've become so poetic, Tom," Susan said, and she repeated his toast. "May my life continue along its present path."

They both turned to Mya. "May my one last dream come true," she said.

No one in the bright, happy dining room that night was aware that Mya's simple toast negated those of Tom and Susan. There was no way that their lives could continue on the same path if Mya's one last dream came true.

All winter long, as Mya dreamed about her baby, Sister Dory shuffled through her cards and advised: "Hold off. Wait a little longer." She wasn't entirely pleased with what she was seeing in the cards, but she didn't want to alarm Mya. Once spring came, Mya began to grow impatient. Everywhere she looked on the estate, new life was being created. Crocuses and daffodils pushed green shoots up through the ground to catch a dose of the warm spring sun; birds chirped love songs as they built nests and found mates. Even the wild mother cats magically deposited litters of the tiny, gray and white and black furry kittens in nests on the porch. Mya tried to feel vibrations when she sat by the river, tried to sense what her mother was thinking. All the signals she received were positive. Everything was giving her the go ahead. She calculated the best time for the baby to be born, astrologically, as well as seasonally, and she came up with May. The pregnancy would not impede her during the hot summer months, nor during the cold, snowy months. And she would have five months of warm weather when the baby and she could sit out of doors on a blanket in the yard. The baby would be a little Taurus. She would grow up to be a tall woman; she would be a solid, practical thinker with her feet planted firmly on the ground; and she would seldom be restless. Mya dreamed of the little heifer, frolicking in the flowers in the sunshine. She would tame a wild kitten for her. And she would name the baby Paulette, after her mother.

Often the subject of babies came up when Susan and Mya were talking. Susan loved to talk about the glorious years when Heather was a baby and then a charming little girl. Susan thought it was absolutely normal and healthy for a 34 year old woman to want a child, but she was bothered by the fact that Mya did not want a husband. Mya only wanted a child.

"But it's so much easier if you have a man around to help," Susan said.

"That's the conflict," Mya said. "I want a child, but I don't want a man to complicate my life. I am sure I can take care of one little girl all by myself."

"You've just never met the right man," Susan said. "You just wait. Any day now, Mr. Right will come along, and you'll know what I'm talking about."

"I doubt it," Mya said. "I've had lots of opportunities, but I've always known I would never marry, no matter how wonderful some man might seem to be."

Susan tried to see all sides of every situation. She herself could never have a child without a husband, but the times had been different when she was younger. Besides, Mya was a very unique person, and she lived in a very unique world. She made her own rules, and even though that impressed Susan, she still felt that Mya wasn't always as practical or wise as she should have been.

"What if the baby gets sick?" Susan asked. "I mean, a short stay in the hospital can be thousands of dollars. It's that kind of thing that's scary."

Mya, the eternal optimist, replied: "As your brilliant husband would say, statistically, what are the chances of my baby ending up in a hospital with a serious illness? I've never been sick a day in my life."

Susan laughed. "As my brilliant husband would also say," she said. "It takes only one to make a statistic."

Susan knew her voice of reason would not alter Mya's decision if she were really serious about this crazy idea, but deep inside, she wasn't sure Mya was all that serious. Mya was always excited about something or other. She talked about and discussed her current obsession non-stop for a few days or weeks, but then moved on and became equally enthused about something else. But as time passed, Susan came to realize that the baby was something different. This was one crazy idea that didn't seem to be going away.

Susan found it very difficult to make conversation with Tom. She was never sure when Tom was going to ignore her or not hear what she was saying, or when he was going to inspect every word with a microscope and then ask a dozen questions that she couldn't answer. It was never easy to tell Tom something, so she tended to keep things inside until they refused to stay there any longer. She had known about the potential baby for weeks and had not said a word. She had no intention of telling Tom, but then, one evening at dinner, when she looked up at Tom and giggled as he tried to nibble the end of a green bean that was dangling from his fork, for no good reason, obviously the time had come, she impulsively announced: "Mya is going to have a baby."

It was fortunate for Tom that he had that string bean to contend with. He spent a few more seconds aiming with the fork before he caught the elusive creature, guided it to his teeth, and crunched it, bit by bit. It was obvious to Susan that he wasn't interested in hearing another of Mya's hare-brained ideas, so she changed the subject and asked: "Do you like the way I did these string beans?" Not waiting for him to reply, she added: "I fixed them with soy sauce and oil in the oven. It's incredibly easy. I think even cold they would be delicious."

Tom's mind was not on the recipe for cooking string beans. "What is this, some kind of immaculate conception?" he asked.

"Nope," Susan said. "I guess she's always wanted to have a child, and this is the first time her life has been settled enough. You know Mya. She doesn't do anything in the conventional way. She said she looked for a man who had the qualities she wanted in a father for her child. He had to be born under a certain sign and all that. You know Mya. I guess she found him."

"Where? Up at the Bullfrog?" Tom gave a nervous laugh, as another stubborn solitary string bean evaded the prongs of his fork.

"She didn't say. You know Mya. She's very discreet when she needs to be," Susan said.

"So she actually told you she is pregnant?" Tom asked.

There was a hint of disgust in his voice, and Susan had her usual fear that he was going to be critical of her best friend, or of her just for talking about it. "I don't think she's pregnant yet," Susan said.

"Then how is she going to have a baby if she isn't pregnant?" Tom asked, sarcastically. "I know she claims to have special powers, but nobody's been able to do that yet."

It would have helped if Tom had listened more carefully and caught that important little word "yet."

Susan assumed a different demeanor, part narrative and part ridicule, but soon, the ridicule slowly crept up to the surface and took over. The serious narrative became very humorous.

"Mya feels that she has an obligation to see that her powers are passed on and remain on earth after she dies. So, she could teach them to someone that she knows has the gift, or inclination, but it would be better to teach her own child, because the chance that her child will have inherited her special abilities is very good. She could start even before the child was born, and she wouldn't have to fight off any established ideas and biases that the child already had." Susan surprised both herself and Tom by adding, "It kind of makes sense, in a way."

"Did you say it makes sense?" Tom asked in a loud voice. "Did I hear you right? You think it makes sense?" He shook his head back and forth in disbelief. "Susan, you're getting to be as crazy as she is."

"In her scope," Susan tried to defend herself. "Considering the way she thinks and lives, the way she functions in the world, yes, it makes sense, even if you don't think so."

"It makes sense for someone without a husband, someone who lives hand to mouth, someone who hasn't got a relative in this world, to be thinking of bringing up a child?" Tom sounded angry.

"When she needs to go away somewhere, will she leave it down by the river for her mother to watch? Or will she summon Mrs. Angel's Ghost to push it around in a stroller?"

Tom's reaction surprised Susan. He was criticizing Mya, yet it seemed to be Susan herself whom he was angry with. She was torn between defending Mya and defending herself. The best she could do was fling an arrow at Tom, and she did so without checking to see how sharp the barb might be.

"Regardless of whether you and I agree or not, Mya will do what Mya wants to do. There's no use arguing about it. It's none of our business."

"We're not arguing," Tom said in his loud, angry voice.

"Just the same. It's none of our business." Susan tried to be calm, so Tom would calm down. This was a new trick she had learned from Mya. Mya had told her that as a Libra, she had great influence on the people around her. She was the one who created the balance. When people were angry, she was the calming factor, and when people were too calm and indifferent, it was her role to excite them and bring them back to the middle.

"Nobody knows the power of the Libra," Mya had told Susan. "In any sticky situation, it's the Libra who determines the outcome."

Although Susan wasn't a believer, she took Mya's information to heart and felt she had gained a new power. It was like the feather that enabled Dumbo to learn to fly.

Susan got up from the table and said, "I got a surprise for you," and went into the kitchen before Tom had a chance to ask what it was. He thought he had already had enough surprises for one day.

Susan cut Tom a piece of the glorious black forest torte she had baked that morning. It was his favorite, and she knew it would cheer him up and make him forget the argument. As she poured coffee into two white mugs and got the creamer out and filled it, she toyed with the awful realization that Tom was becoming more and more difficult, and that she never knew when a simple discussion was going to turn into an argument. Every day she added one more topic to the list of things that she'd better not mention. Some days he was open and friendly and some days he was closed and preoccupied. She changed her mood and stories accordingly. Being a Libra was a very difficult job. Mya said it was one of the most important signs, and if it weren't for Libras, the whole world would be in constant turmoil.

How Susan wanted to quote Mya on that as she watched Tom take a large bite of the torte and heave a loud sigh of pleasure, but she held her tongue. She'd talked enough about Mya for one day.

AN IDEAL TIME TO HAVE A CHILD

Mya had an unusual method for becoming pregnant. She didn't keep track of her periods, nor take her temperature each morning. In late July, she wrote the name "Tom Harris" on a small piece of paper and tucked it into her left shoe, face side up. She did this every day for thirteen days. Then she waited for nature to take its course.

One night in mid-August, Susan had to run to the mall to buy some special soaps and creams to put in a box she was sending to Heather.

"Want to run along to the mall?" Susan asked Tom.

"Nope. I'll beg off this time for a change," Tom laughed. Tom hated to shop, and, in particular, he hated to shop at the mall.

"I won't be long," Susan said. "I'll be back in a couple of hours."

Less than five minutes after Susan had driven down the driveway, Tom hurried over to spend the gift of time with Mya. He tried not to seem as though he was in a hurry, so when Mya asked him to light the two red candles that were sitting in the window, he obliged, and took time to make sure they were both burning nicely. He thought Mya was as usual creating a sensuous atmosphere for love-making. What he didn't know was that Mya had had those candles ready for days, waiting for this moment. When a person wants to become pregnant by her lover, they must make love by the light of two red candles which the lover has lit with his own hands.

The love-making which followed was not as amazing as usual because Tom was preoccupied with the idea that he might not get back up to the house before Susan returned from the mall. He was figuring out in his mind how long it would take her to drive to the mall, how much time she would spend shopping, and whether she had mentioned stopping at the grocery store on the way back, which would add another 15 or 20 minutes to her trip. He didn't want to get into trouble, but if he wasn't back up at the house, he could say he had taken a walk in the woods. What the Fool did not realize was that while he was worrying about little trouble, he was in the midst of creating very big trouble.

Mya knew she had conceived that night. She became suddenly aware that a second soul was inhabiting her body, but, just to be absolutely certain, she made herself available to Tom five more times that week. She did unheard of things like change her work schedule, allow Tom to take her to a motel one afternoon for a few warm, sweaty hours, and even take a chance on having sex in the car parked down a dirt road by the river. By Friday, Tom had a constant tingling in his pelvic region, and he couldn't get enough of Mya. He made love to her eleven times in five days and had quick sex with Susan six times in between. He amazed himself. He wished he were back in the high school locker room so he could brag to the other guys about his prowess.

Regardless of how or why or when a woman gets pregnant, the moment she realizes she is pregnant is an exciting one. Whether she wants to be pregnant or not, a miracle has happened right there in her body, and it is hard to keep a miracle a secret. There is a need to tell someone. In Mya's case, it was natural for her to tell Susan. As much as she wanted to blurt it out or shout it across the lawn and into the forest, instead, she teased Susan a little. She did one of her imitations of Mr. Edwards when he had something to say. He always took a very indirect route through a dozen non sequiturs and then ended up by surprising the listener with news that had nothing to do with anything he had been talking about.

"I'm going to be getting a roommate," Mya told Susan with a silly grin on her face.

Susan's immediate reaction was that a guy was moving in with Mya. There would be nothing unusual about that, but Susan's first reaction was one of disappointment. If Mya was living with someone, she wouldn't be able to spend as much time with her.

"She'll be arriving in May," Mya added, and Susan became confused.

"She? I was just going to ask who he was and where you met him," Susan said.

Mya laughed at her predictable response. "She," Mya said, rubbing her hand across her flat stomach, "is a baby girl."

"You're not pregnant, are you?" Susan asked.

"I told you I was going to do it," Mya said.

Susan couldn't believe what she was hearing. "Have you been to a doctor?" she asked, and realized it was a stupid question the moment it came out of her mouth.

"Of course not. I'm only a week pregnant," Mya said.

"Oh, you mean your period's late," Susan said, almost with relief.

"No, I'm not late," Mya said. "I'm pregnant."

"The father?" Susan asked. The question slipped out before she had decided whether or not it was an appropriate one to ask.

"Of no importance," Mya said, just like that.

Susan tried to force herself to see this through Mya's eyes. The father was of no importance. The father would never know. It was mind-boggling.

Susan was dying to tell Tom that it had really happened, that Mya was indeed pregnant, yet she was hesitant to mention it because of the way he had reacted the last time she had brought up the subject. But it was in the front of her mind and on the tip of her tongue, and she was dying to tell someone, and Tom was the only one around, and Tom had been in a very good mood for a few weeks now, and what did she have to lose?

Tom was lying on the couch on his back, holding a magazine above his face. Susan pulled the magazine down an inch, peeked into his eyes, and announced: "Mya's pregnant."

Tom didn't seem to be interested at all in the news. He pulled his magazine back to where it was and read for several minutes before he spoke. This gave Susan ample time to rue her decision to share the news with him.

When he did speak, he said, "I don't know why they can't cut the cost on these air bags. I mean, why would anyone want one for the driver's seat and not the passenger's. That doesn't make any sense at all. It's the passenger who's most likely to get killed."

"That's why they call it the suicide seat," Susan agreed.

Tom continued to read the magazine, and when his arms got tired, he turned onto his side and then onto his back again and then onto his stomach, leaning up on his elbows and resting the magazine on the pillow. Every time Susan looked in at him, he was in a different position.

"Wouldn't you be more comfortable in a chair?" she asked.

"Hmmmmmm," he answered. "I guess so." He sat up and stretched his arms out and groaned. "She know who's the father of this kid?" he asked so casually that Susan thought at first he was talking about something he had been reading.

"The father is of no importance whatsoever." Susan automatically spit out a direct quote from Mya.

Tom hopped up suddenly from the couch. "I think I'll take a little walk and work the kinks out of my back," he said.

Susan was disappointed that she had got such a mild reaction from Tom. She decided to sit right down at that moment and write to Heather. She would enjoy the story. "News Flash," she wrote. "Seeress about to give birth. Father unknown. Child to be female and a Taurus. Grandmother in river allegedly thrilled about the news."

As Susan sat at her little desk, trying to think of funny ways to phrase her news for Heather, Tom was confronting Mya in the summer house and he was not trying to be funny nor clever. Tom had never been so angry with Mya. He was so furious that he wanted to smack her across her face. He stomped into the parlor and shouted at her. "What in the hell do you mean telling Susan you're pregnant?"

Mya was dumbstruck. She stepped back and looked at Tom in disbelief. She had never seen this side of him before. She hoped Paulette wasn't going to get a temper like that.

"Do you want to go out that door and come back in like a human being?" she asked.

"Are you pregnant?" he asked in a less angry voice.

Mya took him by the arm and led him into the room and closed the door. "Yes, I'm pregnant," Mya said. "It's a very special event, and I wanted to share it with my best friend."

"Is it mine?" Tom asked.

"No," Mya said. "She's mine."

Tom was very impatient. "Mya," he said in a voice he had never used with her before, deep and low and forceful like a heavy iron probe. "Cut the garbage. I am asking you a simple question. Am I the father of this baby?"

"An individual soul is about to enter the world, using my body as a conduit. It has nothing to do with you, nor even with me for that matter," she said.

Tom, who generally felt little, and always controlled what he felt, suddenly contained a whirlpool of conflicting emotions.

Mya continued: "It was your seed, Tom, that was planted so this new life could grow, if that's what you mean, but it is not your baby."

Tom hated this woman who was standing there beside him in this dark, moldy, oppressive little room. He realized, not for the first time, how vulnerable he had been. Not once during the past year had he anticipated this dilemma. Mya was 34 years old and very sophisticated in the ways of love. She had probably had more men than Tom could imagine, and certainly she knew how to avoid getting pregnant. The great thing about Mya was that she just seemed to enjoy fucking for the sake of fucking. Commitment was never an issue. And now this change of events. She had obviously, deliberately gotten herself pregnant, and Tom saw himself as an innocent victim, and he stood silently, asking himself: "Why me? Why is this happening to me?"

"Are you all right, Tomas?" Mya interrupted his thoughts. She stepped closer to him and began rubbing the sides of his face with her palms. He began to relax. He looked into her face. She was totally calm and more beautiful than he had ever seen her. He suddenly wanted to take her in his arms, but she was pregnant to him, and she had told Susan that she was pregnant, and she had not told him. There was a perversity to it that Tom could not comprehend. He felt as though he was going to cry, and he hadn't cried in years.

"Poor Tomas," Mya said. "Sit down." She pulled a chair up and sat down across from him. She reached out and took his hands in hers. She spoke in a quiet, steady voice, as though she were speaking to a small child. "This isn't a problem, Tom, not for you, and not for me. I've wanted a child for a very long time. This is the first time I've been settled into a place where I belong, and it's the first time I've been making enough money to think about having a child. It's an ideal time, as far as I'm concerned."

It was so out of line with the practical, normal way Tom thought about life that his mind could not grasp what she was saying. "You're going to keep it?" he asked.

"Listen to what you just said!" Mya held his face firmly between her hands and looked into his eyes. "Of course I am going to keep her. Do you think I'd give my baby away?"

"And you're going to continue to live here in the summer house?" Tom asked.

"This is my home," Mya said. "If I have my way, I intend to live here forever."

Mya rubbed her hands up and down his arms and then began to circle his ears with her fingers. He wanted to push her away and smash her up against the wall. He had been trapped by a crazy lady and he was terrified that he would never be able to get away from her. At the same time, he was aware that he didn't want to get away from her. He had to swallow and hold his breath to fight back the tears that were about to fall.

"Are you going to tell Susan I'm the father?" he asked, pathetically.

"Why would I ever do anything like that?" Mya asked. "There's no need to hurt Susan."

"What if it's a little boy and he looks exactly like me?" Tom asked.

Mya laughed. "Just because you think you're the center of the universe doesn't mean you have all the dominant genes. Actually the baby is a she and I'm sure she'll look exactly like her mother."

Fortunately for Tom, he had not had a lot of adversity in his life, but, unfortunately, he had never had to develop any coping mechanisms. He could beg, but he knew that wouldn't help, and he wasn't good at begging. He could offer Mya money to go away, but he knew she wouldn't accept that, and the truth was, he didn't want her to go away. He wanted the baby to go away. He wasn't at all tired of Mya yet. As he sat, feeling the comfort and warmth of Mya's hands rubbing up and down his arms, he calmed down. He realized he was going to have to sit this one out, hoping Mya would lose the baby, which he somehow knew would not happen. Knowing Mya, she probably had herbs to prevent miscarriages, herbs she had found down by the river where her dead mother lived. When he opened his eyes, his warm, familiar Mya was leaning over him. When he closed his eyes, the awful feeling of distress returned. What had he gotten himself in for? If worse came to worse, he and Susan could move away. That thought brought with it even more distress.

Mya began to play with the top buttons of his shirt. He reached over and felt her breast beneath her loose gauze blouse.

"Careful, they're sore," she whispered, and that excited him so that he forgot all about how upset he was.

As she pressed her warm body into his on the little bed, and he felt his body responding, he asked himself, "Is it worth it?"

Mya slipped up on top of him so that one warm nipple hung down and touched his lips.

"Yes, it was worth it," he decided, as he began to lick the nipple with his warm wet tongue and press his hard penis up between her legs.

Later, when she leaned against him in the doorway and told him goodnight, Mya said, "I'm happier than I've ever been in my life, Tom. Please don't ruin it for me."

Tom closed his eyes. He was more confused than he had ever been in his life, and it seemed there was nothing he could do about it. He held her familiar warm body as closely as he could for a few moments. "I won't ruin it," he promised. "I'm sorry I behaved the way I did. Do you forgive me?"

"Of course I do," she said. "You're forgiven, now let's be happy. Deal?"

"Deal," Tom replied, as he gave her hand one last squeeze and turned to walk across the bridge. The frogs commemorated the deal by not making a single sound, and Tom himself was so quiet when he walked back into his house that Susan couldn't read his mood at all. He stopped in the doorway to the living room and looked over at her, curled up on the corner of the couch, doing a crossword puzzle.

"Just the man I need," she said. "A funnel shaped estuary, three letters."

"Let me see," Tom said. He took the folded paper from Susan. "What do you have here for 48 across, snubbed-nose dog?"

"Pug," Susan said. "That's right, isn't it?"

"Yeah, I guess that's right," Tom said.

They settled in with the crossword puzzle, and Tom found an error. For a "tack article," Susan had put saddle instead of bridle, and that opened up a whole new section. Tom handed the paper back to her, along with her pencil. "Here you go, Hon," he said. "Now you can probably finish the rest of it on your own."

"Thank you, Tom," Susan said. "What would I do without you?"

It wasn't a question. She didn't expect an answer. It was just one of those comments people make without thinking. Ordinarily Tom would not have given it a thought, but now he began to wonder: What would Susan do if I weren't around? As he showered, he thought about good old Susan, quietly working on a crossword puzzle, cooking special treats for him, never making demands on him, just always there. Then he put Susan in a back corner of his mind and began to think of Mya. Quiet unobtrusive Susan hadn't a chance against the energies and emotions that Mya released in Tom. He stayed in the shower a long time, allowing the warm water to wash Mya off his skin, and wishing the water could penetrate his skin and wash her out of his mind and heart and nervous system.

By the time Susan joined him in bed, he was feigning sleep; yet, during the night, Susan was awakened again and again because Tom was curled so closely around her, trying to absorb security from the only stable thing in his life.

Tom spent the next morning at his desk, drawing little numbers and circles on yellow legal pads, tracing over them, tearing up pages, starting new pages, and staring out the window at the depressing, gloomy mountains and at the fat gray river, which looked like she too might be pregnant. It wasn't impossible. In this crazy world of Port Williams, where Tom Harris was trapped, anything was possible.

With Mya as his lover, Tom had spent his days fantasizing and his evenings living out those fantasies. He hadn't neglected Susan. She never needed much attention, and now that she was so obsessed with the house and all the historical stuff, she needed even less. Tom was on a roll. But wasn't it amazing that all it took to turn his paradise into a hell was for Mya to become pregnant. He could not for the life of him figure out exactly why it made such a difference. Mya was the same person; he was the same person; but this potential child threatened everything in his life.

In the course of a day at his desk, he could think of nothing but Mya, Susan, and the baby. He could not bear the thought of losing Mya, but he could also not bear the thought of Mya living next door with his child. There were many sensible solutions, but none was acceptable to all the involved parties. He and Susan could move away, but he wasn't ready to leave Mya just yet. The simplest solution would be for Mya to have an abortion. Things could then get back to normal. If she would agree to do this for him, he would promise to marry her later, after he had had an appropriate amount of time to separate from Susan. He couldn't divorce her on the spur of the moment, but he was sure he could work it out if he could just have a few months.

In the late quiet evenings, as Susan sat reading in the living room, and Tom stood mulling by the dark windows, morbid black thoughts crept into his mind. He thought of ways to get Susan out of the picture. He found that planning on doing away with his wife made him so uncomfortable that he had to change his plans from an actual murder to something he could feel more comfortable with, maybe a fatal accident. A scene that came to him again and again was Susan falling down the rickety steps to the basement. How often she herself joked about falling down those steps. She ran up and down a dozen times a day to get meat from the freezer or canned goods from the shelf. Tom wondered if he had the courage, or guts, to push her? He imagined her turning and looking into his face as she fell. It was probably a better idea to loosen a stair tread, or put a flat, slippery board on one of the top steps and hope that she would fall when he wasn't home. It definitely should happen when he was at work. That way, he wouldn't be a suspect. But what if she lived but was crippled. Then he would never be able to leave her. He would be stuck forever. During the hours he spent making plans to eliminate Susan from his life, he wondered what kind of person would be able to even think of doing such a thing.

While evil black thoughts were creeping about in the recesses of Tom's mind, he couldn't hug Susan, nor look in her eyes, and when she asked a question or tried to make conversation, he shrugged or hummed. He was beginning to hate her, but he hated himself even more. None of this was her fault, but it irked Tom to see her going about her daily activities without a worry in the world. He hadn't seen her this happy and busy in years, and she was keeping him from being happy. It wasn't fair. The only topic that diverted his attention from his morbid obsessing was Mya.

"What a brave person Mya is," Susan said. "She's an inspiration."

"I'm not too impressed with someone who deliberately complicates her life and ends up tied down taking care of a kid without a dad."

"You know what might happen," Susan said kindly, pleased that Tom had joined the conversation. "Mya is a beautiful person. Someone very special will come along and marry her someday. It won't matter that she has a child. Those things aren't that important anymore. Her mother wasn't married, and Mya told me that she had lots of boyfriends and she could have married anyone she wanted. It didn't matter that she had a child."

"So, she's just like her mother," Tom said, "and doesn't she always go around saying she'll never get married?"

"She says that," Susan laughed, "but she's young. Every woman wants to get married eventually."

Susan had inadvertently shot another dagger at Tom, and when it hit, a sharp pain passed quickly through his heart. The thought of Mya with someone else always had that effect. Without a word, he got up from the table and headed for the back door to take a little walk. No longer did he even think of saying to Susan that he would be back soon, or that he just needed a breath of fresh air, or that he needed to walk off a piece of pie he had just eaten. He desperately had to get away from her. She interfered with his thoughts. She tortured him, and he was certain he was beginning to hate her. She was the reason he could not be with Mya.

It was painful for Susan to admit to herself that Tom didn't want to be around her. She blamed his behavior on stress at work, the move, depression, and even the onset of male menopause that she had read about in a magazine. After all, she was doing everything she could to make his life comfortable. There was nothing more she could do. During the years when he was on the road, and she saw him only on weekends, she did not consider him to be a moody person, but now that she saw him every day, she was aware of his continual shifts from happy to sad, from quiet to talkative, and from cynical to enthusiastic. As a Libra, she was good at adjusting her behavior accordingly. If he joked and teased, she joked and teased back. If he buried his head in the paper, she picked up a book and read. If he crept silently into the house so that, had she not heard his car coming up the drive, she wouldn't have known she was home, Susan avoided him, served him a quiet dinner, and respected his need not to be bothered. She patiently waited the moods out as they changed from day to day.

In late September, a mood had descended on Tom which didn't seem to want to pass. Days went by and then weeks. Tom was quiet and edgy, jumpy, and unpredictable. Just when Susan had decided he was settling in and beginning to enjoy a normal life in Port Williams, something had happened. Tom was a bunch of nerves, and Susan absorbed the uneasiness and felt nervous herself. How could she settle down and have a nice quiet evening while Tom paced, slammed doors, shut himself in his study for hours, and then drove off without telling her where he was going. Tom was upset; thus Susan was upset. She tried to talk with him about it.

"Is something bothering you?" she asked.

"No, why?" he replied.

"You seem so jumpy lately," Susan said, "like you can't relax."

"Things are just getting to me," Tom said.

"What sorts of things?" Susan asked.

"Everything," Tom snapped.

"You mean work?" Susan asked, and she waited for an answer that never came.

Mya was always in tune with people's feelings and she naturally picked up on the unhappy vibrations in the Harris household.

"Susan, you seem nervous," she said. "Is anything wrong?"

"I guess I am nervous," Susan said. She looked down at her hands and saw that she was peeling the leaves off a long, green fern she had picked up along the path. She and Mya were taking the baby for a walk, the baby which was now in its second month of gestation.

"I suppose it must be age," Susan said. "Tom's all crazy too, and his moods affect me. Maybe it's that male menopause thing. He's just going through it early."

"It's you I am worried about," Mya said. "Maybe you should go down and visit your old friends again. Do you think that would help?"

"I was thinking Tom and I should get away together for a few days," Susan said. "I can tell that work is really getting to him. He's not used to the stress of dealing with the same people day after day."

"If you think the negative vibrations are coming from Tom," Mya said, "You shouldn't allow yourself to go away with him, because those bad vibes will go right along with you. You should go away by yourself for a few days and get yourself centered so when you come back you'll have the inner strength to combat the negative energy that Tom is exuding."

"But I worry about him," Susan said. "I couldn't just go away and leave him when he's like this. He would never admit it, but he needs me."

"You shouldn't let Tom's problems affect you so," Mya said. "You can give him your love and support, but he is the one who has to deal with his own problems. He's a big boy."

"Mya, it's not like that when you're married. Everything Tom does affects me. There is no way I can be calm and happy when he is upset."

Mya stopped to pick a black eyed Susan from along the path. She handed it to Susan. "Here's your sister flower," she said. "She will cheer you up. I can't bear to see my best friend sad when I am so happy."

Susan felt once again how lucky she was to have found such a friend. They walked silently down the path through the wood. Susan stepped on the pine needle carpet and then onto the soft green moss. She pulled a branch from a birch tree and peeled away the sweet tasting bark with her teeth. Mya talked, and Susan tried to concentrate on what she was saying. Her voice was soothing. She was giving Susan advice, but it was abstract advice. It sounded like she was reciting poetry.

"You have to pay attention to what is and not what should be. Be empty. Get rid of all your old reactions and responses and make yourself empty. Yield. Yield," Mya chanted. "Yield. Let it go. Just let it go."

"I shouldn't do anything at all?" Susan asked. Since she didn't have any idea what she could do, it wasn't such bad advice.

"You can't solve another person's problems," Mya said. "Center yourself. Do exactly what you feel like doing and don't change your behavior because of Tom. You're allowing him to pull you off track."

"How did you get to be so sensible, Mya?" Susan asked. She did feel at this moment that everything Mya was saying made sense.

"It's logical," Mya said. "You should never love anything or anyone more than you love yourself."

Mya's historic perspective pulled Susan out of her narrow confines. She began to feel better as they walked along the quiet pathway. And she hurried up to the house, savoring the mood and trying to make it last. She put Bach on the stereo and turned up the volume. The music floated about the house and out the windows into the surrounding forest. Susan's mood stayed with her as she tore lettuce and chopped carrots and celery and sliced little round red radishes. When she heard Tom's car coming up the drive just a little after six, she was centered and she was not going to let anything knock her off track. When she heard the door open, she began to walk over to give Tom a greeting to set the mood for the evening. But Tom did not come into the dining room; he walked straight to the stereo in the living room and switched it off in such a hurry that the needle scraped across the record, sounding like the cry of a dying animal.

Susan ran upstairs and shut herself in the bedroom. She took the oval frame down off the wall, and she began to tell the sepia eyes how she felt. She cried as she talked, and Kathleen Angel looked back at her with sympathy and compassion. When she had finished talking and crying, Susan felt much better.

Next morning she told Mya what she had done. "I think I'm going crazy," Susan confessed. "I spent last evening telling all my troubles to Kathleen Angel."

Mya was of course very interested. "How did she come to you?" she asked.

"She didn't come to me," Susan said. "I talked to her portrait. I don't know why. Tom upset me so much that I needed someone to talk to and she was the only one there."

"It's like group therapy," Mya said. "You're having problems with Tom, and she obviously had problems with Lloyd, and maybe they were similar problems, who knows?"

"The important thing is that I feel better," Susan said. "I don't know what's bothering Tom, so I can't do anything about it. I'm just going to take your advice and not worry about it anymore. You're right. He's a big boy."

"It sounds like Kathleen agreed with me," Mya said. "I'm sure whatever's troubling Tom will soon be over. Remember how unhappy you were when you first moved here. Now you say you're happier than you've ever been in your life."

"You're so old and wise and philosophical," Susan said.

"It all comes with motherhood," Mya said, and she called to Susan as she walked across the dam. "Speaking of motherhood, shouldn't Heather be home on leave soon?"

"She hasn't written anything about it," Susan said.

"I just have a feeling," Mya yelled. "A good feeling."

Susan was pleased to have something positive to tell Tom that evening as he crawled into the living room and sank into a chair.

"Mya thinks Heather might be home on leave soon," Susan said.

"God, that's all we need," Tom grumbled.

And Susan ran upstairs to tell Kathleen how mean and awful Tom had become.

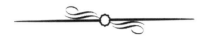

GO ASK TOM

As Tom sat at his desk and mulled over his predicament, he doodled cryptic symbols on a yellow legal pad. He was so embarrassed at the thoughts he was entertaining that he was unable to write words down to describe them. Instead, he drew diagrams: a box with an S in it on one side of the page; T & M & b in another box on the other side of the page; and a cryptic list of "+" and "-" entries. A second diagram showed M & b in one box at the top of the page and T & S in another. The most desirable scheme in Tom's mind was a big box with T & S and a small box nearby with only an M, and no b anywhere in sight.

Tom thought he was assessing the situation critically, analyzing each prerogative, and trying to come up with the best solution for all parties involved. He was using the same approach he used for any major problems that cropped up at work. First, he identified the problem. That was half the battle. Second, he listed all the potential solutions and analyzed each, using positive and negative columns. Ordinarily, his third and last step was to carefully look over the entire picture, and nine times out of ten, the appropriate action or most expedient solution jumped up at him in 3D.

"Go ask Tom" echoed through the halls of the Kraft Paper Mills. Sometimes a problem involved an unknown that made it more challenging than usual. Perhaps a small company was bought out by a new owner from out of the territory, and the new owner was the unpredictable element until they got to know his strategies and intentions. In the present case, Tom was very much aware that the high priority problem that he was spending endless hours of Kraft Paper Mills' time on had one major unpredictable, and her name was Mya.

The S would be okay. She would quietly resign herself to anything. She had got over her sadness about Heather's leaving, and she had adjusted to life in Port Williams, far from all of her old friends. In fact, she seemed to be thriving in the new environment. She would be fine. If T left with M, S would be a bit devastated for a while, but S wouldn't do anything rash because of H and because she didn't have the gumption to harass T and M. T optimistically saw a future where S might remain friends with T and M. She always spoke so highly of M, called her a best friend, and T had to admit that M did have special powers when it came to handling people. What an imagination T had.

The most convenient and expedient solution that jumped up in 3D was the AB solution, but M would never agree to that. There was no doubt about it. M was the problem here.

Tom spent five hours drawing the little boxes and making lists, and by the end of the afternoon, he had the beginnings of a severe headache.

"Don't interrupt me for anyone," he had told Sandy at noon. "I'm working on the big one."

At five, Sandy buzzed Tom: "I'm about to leave. How's the big one coming along?"

Tom managed a chuckle. "What I didn't tell you, Sandy, was that the big one was a migraine, and it's coming along great. Thank you for asking."

Tom didn't stop at the Bullfrog on his way home. He didn't want to chance a drink with a headache coming on, and he wanted to be at his best when he confronted Mya later that evening. As he walked in the front door at home, he announced to Susan that he had a terrific headache.

"Susan put her hands on his shoulders and gave him a kiss on the forehead. "You never used to get headaches, Tom. This might sound crazy, but I bet it's that darned computer."

"You might be right," Tom said.

"I've read about kids getting sore necks and wrists from playing computer games, and women getting cataracts from doing word processing all day long. Now there's you and your headaches. Do you want to lie down a bit before dinner?"

"Good idea," Tom said, as he headed towards the stairs. "I'm not really all that hungry anyway."

"Then it's worse than I thought," Susan teased.

As Tom slowly ascended the stairs, briefcase in hand, jacket draped over the other arm, Susan called up a message from the foyer. "One funny thing to report, Hon. This might cure your headache."

Tom paused and looked down at Susan's smiling face.

"Mya has come up with a name for the baby," she said.

For a second Tom forgot his headache as his stomach tried to come up into his throat. He feared the name might be Tomas. It would just be like Mya to do something like that.

"What is it?" he whispered, closing his eyes and seeing all the little boxes with b, AB written inside. Why would anyone be naming a dead baby?

"Paulette. It means little Pauline, after her dead mother in the river," Susan called. "It sounds nice, doesn't it?"

"Her mother must be thrilled," Tom said. "And if it's a boy, what then? Paul?"

"Mya knows it's a girl," Susan said.

Tom gave Susan a look of utter disgust. "How exactly does Mya know it's a girl?" he asked.

"Who knows how Mya knows anything," Susan said. "Maybe a bird told her, or a wild cat, or maybe she saw it in the cards." She held her head up and stood tall, trying to imitate Mya when she was expounding: "All we know is that Little Baby Paulette is due May 7th. She is a Taurus. She's going to be tall and beautiful and she's going to have Mya's special powers. So there." She smiled up at Tom as she delivered the punch line: "This afternoon, I began crocheting a little pink blanket for her."

"You'd think that would be a job for her grandmother," Tom grumbled into the carpeting on the stairs, as he fairly crawled past the stained glass windows on the landing and up the remaining stairs to the bedroom. "Then, again," he said to himself, "I guess the yarn would get all wet."

He managed a weak, half-hearted smile, as he threw himself down onto the bed and flung an arm across his eyes to keep out the light. Diagrams flitted through his mind. Now that the baby had a name and a pink blanket, there was no possibility of AB as a potential solution. It would have to be T&M&P in one box, and S in another. It was hard to think with the headache shooting sharp pains through his temple behind his right eye. If only he could sleep for a little bit, maybe the headache would go away. He turned onto his side and closed his eyes, but something felt wrong. It felt like there was a presence in the room. He felt as though someone was watching him. He opened his eyes very slowly and saw above him on the wall an oval frame with a picture of a woman wearing a big hat. He had never noticed her before. Who in the hell was she? She was probably someone's old relative, maybe Mr. Edwards' mother. No, people like Mr. Edwards didn't have mothers. It was probably no one in particular, just a picture Susan and that awful Gladys lady found somewhere in a junk store. The woman looked directly at him, through him, into his thoughts, and he had to close his eyes to get away from her searching eyes. As he drifted off to sleep, he thought about how strange everything in his life was becoming. He and Susan never used to like old things, and now she was cluttering every room in the house with old junk and doilies and now things like this awful picture. Susan was a simple person, and obviously Mya and Mr. Edwards and that Gladys lady were having an influence on her. Tom was certain the picture had something to do with one of them. They were all against him, all lined up on one side, these crazy people, and now Susan was lining up alongside them. She knew he didn't like old things, but that didn't seem to stop her anymore. She was out of his control. Maybe it wouldn't be so bad not to have her in his life any longer.

With that thought, Tom fell into a deep sleep and didn't awaken until the alarm went off at 6 a.m. His headache had vanished, and he was starving. Susan was particularly quiet at breakfast, and Tom talked to fill the silence. He even gave her a hug at the sink.

"I'm going to try to stay away from that evil computer today and see if it helps. I think you might be right about it causing my headaches," he said.

"Have a good day," Susan said. "I'm glad you're feeling better." And she was, because whatever Tom felt Susan felt whether she liked it or not, and no one enjoys a headache, especially a vicarious one.

BABY PAULETTE

Mya didn't sit at a $3,000 cherry desk and draw diagrams on yellow legal paper with a gold pen with her initials on it. She did a five hour shift at the Frog and got $24 in tips, excellent for a weekday lunch shift. From 3 until 6, she read cards for four different clients, one old and three new. She earned $60, plus a $5 donation for an astrological wall chart. She fixed a ground almond roast for dinner and ate a slice, along with some green beans and an apple. While she was eating, she read about natural pregnancy and natural childbirth. Mya was happy beyond how a human being should be happy, ever.

As Paulette moved into her third month of gestation, Tom was not yet frantic. He was worried, but not frantic. There was a problem, he had to admit, but he did not yet see it as a problem without a solution. It would merely take time to find a solution that would satisfy all parties concerned. After he had spent several mornings shuffling little boxes around on the page, he felt he was ready to make a stab at what he considered to be his best hope. He called Mya Friday afternoon and asked her if she would like to go for a drive with him on Saturday. He decided not to advise her that his intention was to have a serious talk with her; he told her it was the week before peak foliage and he had a yearning to see the leaves in upper New York State before the crowds arrived. They could leave early Saturday morning and either drive back late that night or stay over and come back Sunday.

"Oh, Tomas, how you tempt me with your lovely ideas," Mya crooned. "But Saturdays are my biggest days, and, as much as it's against my nature, I must be practical from now on."

Tom hadn't anticipated a refusal. He paused to think of a convincing argument.

"Maybe we could take a walk back in our very own woods," Mya said. "It's every bit as beautiful here as in New York State."

"How much will you make on Saturday?" Tom asked.

"I don't know," Mya said. "I'm going to work both the lunch and evening shifts. I might make as much as a hundred dollars with all these people out driving around to see the leaves."

Because his plan was being thwarted, Tom couldn't think straight. He forgot that he was trying to reason with a person totally indifferent to reason.

"What if I gave you a hundred dollars to come with me instead?" he asked.

Mya laughed. "Oh, Tom, you sound so desperate. Why don't you just ask Susan to go along with you. She would love it. She never gets away from this place, and I'm sure she wouldn't charge you a cent."

Tom was silent. He never knew how to respond when Mya tossed Susan into the conversation. It always stopped him in his tracks. What Mya said was true. Susan would probably love to go for a nice drive. And Mya was right about his being desperate, but it was not to see the leaves.

"I want to be with you," he said.

"Listen, Tom, I'm very flattered. I truly am. But there's no one to cover both shifts for me even if I could take off. I really can't get away."

"How about Sunday?" Tom asked.

"Sunday's already taken," Mya replied. "I promised to have lunch with Auntie Edna, and I'm sure it's going to be a long one, knowing her."

"Who's Auntie Edna?" Tom asked.

"One of my grandmas," Mya said. "She's a fantastic lady. I mean, she's in her eighties and she can still fix the most elaborate meals you can imagine. It's her birthday, and she's having me to lunch, and she is cooking the meal and baking the cake. That's the kind of lady she is."

Tom heard more than he wanted to hear about Auntie Edna. "Couldn't you put her off until after the leaves have gone?" he asked foolishly.

"It's her birthday," Mya repeated. "It would break her heart if I couldn't come."

Tom was so frustrated that he let down all of his defenses. It was very unlike Tom to beg. He had little experience begging, and he was not good at it.

"Your job comes before me, and your old friends come before me, and your clients come before me. It seems like there's no place for me in your life." Tom hated Mya for making him beg.

"Just because I'm not with you every minute of the day does not mean I'm not thinking about you," Mya said.

Again, still, Tom remained silent.

"How about tomorrow morning?" Mya asked.

Tom suddenly remembered his reason for calling in the first place. Leaves, or no leaves, he needed to have a serious talk with Mya.

"Okay," he said. "I guess I'll have to take what I can get. When? Where?"

"Eight thirty on the log bridge," Mya said, "And don't be late."

"See you then," Tom said, as he hung up the phone.

Early in the morning, the forest was still damp and the trees looked as though someone had just brushed them with dripping gold and orange paint. The sun had a plan to dry off the paint, a soon as she could find a good parking place high in the bright blue sky. Tom wished his mind could be clear enough to appreciate the forest, but, instead, his thoughts were filled with diagrams, lists, priorities, and plans. Once this was all behind him, he would start to live again and enjoy things like autumn leaves and nice walks in the forest.

Mya looked radiant in a blue silk tunic hanging loosely over her jeans. She hugged Tom and gave him a lingering kiss, which he couldn't appreciate because he needed to get on with the business at hand, but he couldn't brush her away and take a chance of slighting her, so he waited patiently for Mya to release him. He let his hand slide through her long, soft hair and down her breast to remind himself that once business was taken care of, he would be able to once again enjoy this lovely body, but not until.

Tom took Mya's hand and they walked slowly down the path into the forest. It turned out to be a very short walk. Tom learned that talking with a beautiful fey lady in an orange and gold forest was quite different from making a presentation before a group of rational, intelligent human beings in three piece suits. His favorite words – support, inevitability, prioritize, assets, deficiencies, prognosis, and feedback—were inappropriate, and he felt himself ill equipped to debate in a foreign language whose principal words included soul, spirit, universe, child.

"How are you feeling?" he asked, just to get onto the subject.

"Wonderful," Mya said. "I have never felt better in my life."

"So, you're still planning to go through with this?" Tom asked, "having this kid, I mean," but he realized kid sounded harsh and changed it to baby.

Mya corrected his correction. "Paulette," she said. "Do you like the name?"

Before he could entirely eliminate Plan 1, AB, from the picture, he felt he had to at least mention it, as hard as that might be.

"You wouldn't consider an abortion if the money was available?" he asked in a voice louder than necessary, but when she didn't respond, he added, "You could have the baby at another time, a more convenient time."

Mya dropped his warm hand and turned to face him on the path. What he had no way of knowing, and what Mya was absolutely certain of was that an embryo immediately after conception and long before it develops inner ears, starts to record all conversations in which its mother participates. So Mya replied in a voice as loud as Tom's. She was speaking to both of them, Tom and Paulette.

"I love little Paulette more than anything in the world. She's my very own special child, and I will die for her if necessary, but I would never allow her to die for me."

"This is just not a convenient time for all of this to be happening," Tom said. "There can be other Paulettes in the future, when things are different."

"Convenient time for whom?" Mya asked. "I couldn't ask for a more convenient time, and there can't be other Paulettes. Every human soul is a unique entity."

Tom knew it wouldn't do to make Mya angry, so he reached over and took her hand again. "I should have known how you would feel about that," he said gently.

"Don't even use the word," Mya said. "I don't want Paulette to hear that word." She put her hands on her stomach to cover Paulette's ears.

Tom lowered his voice. He now felt there was a third person listening, and he had to be very careful what he said. "There are other alternatives," he whispered.

Mya shook her head. She didn't want to hear about other alternatives. She looked into Tom's eyes and read his mind.

"You could pay me to move away and then you could send me money to stay away," she said. "I think that's what some men would do in this situation."

"Oh, no," Tom shook his head. "That wasn't what I was going to say."

"Number two," Mya said. "You could leave Susan and marry me." She ticked off number two on her second finger.

Tom wanted to discuss that one, but Mya was not to be interrupted. She had taken over the conference, and she wasn't going to give up the floor.

"That's not an alternative for me because I love Susan and Susan loves you. We're not going to hurt Susan just to make things easy for ourselves." Mya looked into Tom's eyes with what appeared to him to be disgust. "Any more alternatives I haven't guessed?"

Tom closed his eyes and turned his head so Mya couldn't read the other two alternatives, thoughts he had been too ashamed of to write down on paper.

"No more alternatives," he said. "You win."

"Tomas, there's no win. There's no lose. This isn't a ball game. I'm going to have a little girl, Paulette, and I'm the happiest person in the universe, and if you love me, as you say you do, then you'll be happy for me too."

"I am happy for you," Tom lied. "I think it's great." He smiled. "You're sure a baby won't cramp your style?"

Mya nuzzled her face under Tom's chin and flicked her tongue on his neck. "Not my style, but it sure might cramp your style. No sex for seven months."

"I would certainly call that cramping my style," Tom said. A little spark of hope began to grow in his heart. "Is something wrong? Did a doctor tell you not to have sex?"

"No," Mya said. "It's just good policy. The fetus is much more sensitive than most people realize. The excessive emotions the mother experiences during sex are too powerful for a tiny child to absorb. You've got to keep everything peaceful when you're carrying a baby."

The Battle of Angel Woods was officially over. Tom was defeated; Mya, victorious. Not a single volley was shot during the battle, but after, as Tom and Mya were walking back down the path towards home, some foolish hunter began to shoot in a new rifle, and the autumn forest was disturbed by the sounds of death.

"That has got to stop," Mya announced. "I'm going to speak to Mr. Edwards tomorrow about it. I'm not going to raise my child in a place where people are slaughtering poor innocent animals."

She continued her harangue as she walked ahead of Tom down the path. He could not hear what she was saying, and once more, he didn't care what she was saying. He was wondering how he had allowed this crazy, crazy woman into his fine, secure, comfortable life. And he wondered again and again as they rustled along the thick crackling layer of colored leaves on the forest floor: What in the world am I in for next?

A BLUE CRYSTAL BALL

It was becoming harder and harder for Susan to talk with Tom. It seemed as though the more interested she became in something, the less interested he became. The only subject that was still guaranteed to get a rise out of Tom was the bizarre activities of their neighbor.

"Mya's decided she's not going to do any astrotraveling at all until after Paulette's born," Susan told Tom one night at dinner when he seemed to be in a slightly receptive mood. "She's afraid they'll get stranded some place and won't be able to get back home."

And the funny old Tom resurfaced for a moment with: "She'll have to travel by bus from now on, although that's still no guarantee she won't get stranded."

Susan laughed. What a crazy world it was. And, as far as she could see, it was getting crazier. But the strange thing was that the crazier it got, the more relaxed and happy Susan became. Only a year before, she would have been shocked at the bizarre things that were going on, but now she felt right at home.

The Angel Estate had a life of its own, and Susan got sucked right up into that life. Each morning, she sat down and made a list of things to do, but she was aware that making the list was merely an exercise in automatic writing. All of the items on her list were related to the estate, and her list was just a miniature version of Mr. Edwards' endless, continually growing, all-time list. And both lists were dictated by some higher power with motives of her own.

In her previous existence, Susan's list included "Make dental appointment, have car tuned up, check on home owners' insurance policy." Could those have been written by the same hand which now writes: "All dandelions must be removed from front lawn; check with Mr. E. about Angel family portraits for living room wall; check with Mr. E, or G, re KA desk; do something about hunters."

Susan had become a woman with a mission, and with Mya and Gladys spurring her on, the house slowly began to change. The transformation had begun with the arrival of the portrait of Kathleen Angel. Soon antique crystal drinking glasses replaced plastic cups in the bathrooms. Wrought iron and brass andirons appeared by each fireplace. Victorian lace curtains now hung in the dining room. At all times, some piece of old furniture was being refinished in the basement, and the smell of varnish and shellac offended Tom's sensitive nostrils as he walked into the house each evening.

One morning Susan attacked the mustard weeds along the drive to the west of the house, removing the roots with a sharp trowel. It was back-breaking labor, but it had appeared on the list and it had to be done. She took frequent breaks in order to reach her arms up to the sky and stretch the kinks out of her body. And during every stretch, she looked over at the carriage house, hiding along the drive and she felt it was beckoning to her, hinting of secret treasures, tempting her to come and take a look. She remembered the time she and Mya had taken a peek in there and how upset Mya had become.

She heard Gladys' voice: "My heart breaks when I think of all those authentic pieces buried away in there, being eaten by mice and woodworms, victims of neglect and time."

Then she remembered Mya's voice: "Obviously the astral spirit resides in the carriage house. Something horrible must have happened in there."

The carriage house was not on Susan's list. It was on Mr. Edwards' all-time list, right down near the bottom, alongside clearing the little graveyard, but it was not on hers and had never been. But the urge to check through the place quickly, just to see what was there, hounded her all morning long as she worked along the drive. Her stretches became more and more frequent, and she lost interest in the mustard weed and went into the house for a drink of water. As she stood by the sink and slowly drank a glass of water, for no good reason, she pulled open a drawer and saw a small silver flashlight lying among screwdrivers and hack saw blades and other junk. She felt an urge to pick it up.

"Someone wants me to take a look in the carriage house," she said to herself. "Might as well. What harm can it do?"

She walked across the yard and tried to look in the windows of the carriage house. They were darker than ever and all she could see were huge gray shadows looming inside. She walked around to the back and checked the board that Mya had removed that awful day last spring. The board was barely resting on the nails. Susan took that as a sign of permission from somewhere, or someone. She lifted the board off, leaned it against the porch wall, and pushed the door in, just a little, just enough for her body to squeeze through sideways.

Once inside, she pointed the flashlight into the corners and all along the wall. The room was familiar and she did not have any eerie feelings. She just felt curious.

"I guess I need Mya around to help me with the eerie dimension," she thought.

She stood in one spot long enough for her eyes to adjust to the dark and then she carefully began to explore, one step at a time. As she lifted up bits of heavy, dusty, leather harness, cold rusty metal tools, and broken jelly jars, she realized she wasn't having nearly as much fun as she would have if Mya were here with her. The magic was gone. All she was finding was a bunch of someone's old discarded junk.

She made her way among the clutter to the wall, where a huge black trunk sat waiting for her. There was an inch of undisturbed dust on the top, and the brass latches were dark green. Susan carefully lifted the lid and saw that the trunk was filled with folded pieces of cloth, perhaps old sheets and curtains. She was feeling disappointed. She thought of how much more exciting the dream of what she would find was than the actual stuff she found. Wasn't it just like life? Reality can never live up to the dream. Hidden treasures and valuable antiques turned out to be rags, broken bottles, and pieces of rotten leather. She flashed the light around the room one last time to see if there was a brass lamp or a mirror, something beyond the reach of time's mindless destruction. Nothing in the sweep of light caught her eye until she pointed the light once more into the trunk and realized that she might have found at least one useable treasure, a bundle of old lace curtains. There were endless windows that needed covering in the house, and if she could get the smell out of some of these curtains, surely she could put them to use. As she reached down among the fabric, trying to feel for lace, her hand came upon something soft and smooth. She jerked her hand out and uttered a small uncertain shriek. She thought she had found the nice family of friendly rats that Mr. Edwards was certain dwelled in the carriage house, but she soon realized what she had touched didn't feel like a living rat; it was a piece of thick soft cloth. She shook her head and laughed at herself. It was just another funny story to tell Mya.

When she pulled the soft cloth out, it turned out to be a thick sack made of maroon velvet, and it contained something very heavy. She felt around the fabric for an opening, found a tight draw-string, worked it loose, and folded the top down to see what the sack contained. It was a solid round glass ball. When Susan held it up towards the dusty window, she could not believe her eyes. It was a crystal ball, and even in the dusty gloom, it shot off soft blue rays in all directions.

"Oh my God," Susan said aloud. "Wait til Mya sees this. What a find."

The ball was a bit bigger than a grapefruit, and it had a bluish tint to it. Susan couldn't wait to get it out into the light and inspect it more thoroughly. The lace curtains by now totally forgotten, she held the ball closely to her body as she stumbled over things in a hurry to get it out into the sunshine. She was excited and pleased with her find. What a treasure. In a million years she had not expected to find a crystal ball. It was what Mya had always wanted. She had mentioned it a dozen times. Now Susan would be able to surprise her friend and give her a gift worthy of all the happiness and support their friendship had brought to her. Mya was always the one to come up with wonderful surprises; now it was Susan's turn, and the crystal ball would be the greatest surprise of all.

She held it close to her chest with both arms as she hurried to the kitchen to wash it off and shine it with a fresh, clean linen towel. As she washed it carefully with warm water and soap and then rinsed it again and again and dried it with the towel, she wondered how she should present it to Mya. Should she wrap it up as a gift and leave it on Mya's table in the parlor? Should she put it on her own dining table and wait for Mya to notice it, and then tell her it was a gift from Mrs. Angel's Ghost?

Susan gently carried the crystal ball into the dining room and held it up in front of the windows. Blue waves swirled through the ball and light blue arrows darted throughout the room, where they bounced from the silver sconces and caressed the silver chandelier as though it was a dear old friend. When she looked directly into the ball, Susan saw tiny figures dancing about, but she didn't even think to look closely at them to see if they were perhaps people she knew. Some claim a person can see both the past and the future in a crystal ball, but Susan was too excited about the find itself to pay much attention to anything but the present. She was so excited that she couldn't even wait until Mya came home. She wrapped the ball in the dish towel, held it tightly against her ribs with her right arm, and hurried down the driveway, across the bridge, and up Bullfrog Valley Road.

Port Williams was experiencing a record high for October. The sun beat down as though it was a July afternoon, but the constant chilling breeze coming from every direction reminded Susan that it was indeed late October. Bullfrog Valley Road was lined on one side with tall, leaning conifers, and the other side was bordered with lower bushes and tall grass with an isolated pine tree here and there. In the shadows of the trees, the air was very cold, but in the open areas between the trees, it was unbearably hot. As Susan rushed along, she was first hot and then cold and then hot again. Since the big house and its environs was always much cooler than the world around it, Susan had taken off on her errand wearing a heavy shirt and sweater. It wasn't until her initial excitement waned that she began to notice the heat from the glaring sun along the road, and suddenly the crystal ball felt very heavy. She paused and put it carefully on the ground while she took off her sweater, tied the sleeves around her waist, and let it hang down behind her. Then she switched the crystal ball from hand to hand every few yards as she hurried up the road.

She soon came to the curve in Bullfrog Valley Road where the lane to the Inn turned off. She had seen this lane so many times, but she had never gone up. In the beginning, Tom had said that they would have to go for a drink some night just to check out the place, but, for some reason, they had never managed to do that. Susan paused at the lane and switched the towel to her other arm once again.

"This is crazy," she thought. Her enthusiasm had lessened as she grew tired from the long, hot walk. To think poor pregnant Mya does this twice a day, she thought. She slowed down, but she didn't stop. In the distance she saw a clearing and headed towards it and soon found herself at the edge of a large parking lot where a dozen or so cars were parked at random, and straight ahead she saw a large, gray rectangular building.

Susan was disappointed. Although Tom had told her the Frog was as ugly as sin, she thought, just from the silly name, that it might be at least quaint. She was not expecting a big, wooden warehouse with no windows. As she studied the place, she decided the door with the old neon metal beer sign above it was probably the main entrance, and she didn't want to walk into the main entrance because she was not accustomed to walking into bars alone, particularly in the afternoon. She had no idea what she might come upon. So she walked around the building to see if she could find another way to get in. On the opposite side of the building she came upon a little porch, covered with trash cans filled and overflowing and cardboard beer cases and broken bar stools. She thought if she could just slip through this entrance, she might be able to see Mya and signal to her to come to the door for a minute so she could show her the surprise. It was hard to tell how many people would be in the bar. Susan felt nervous.

The door was very heavy, and she had to push with both her hip and her shoulder in order to open it wide enough to slip through. The room was dark, and until her eyes adjusted, Susan could not make out a thing. Slowly the place came into focus. The room was enormous. In the distance were tables and chairs with a few people seated at some of them. She stepped closer to the bar and stared into a big, green fish tank that cast an eerie glow in all directions. In the light of the tank, she saw a man wiping off the bar with a white rag. Music was blaring from the far corners of the room, and Susan heard the sound of pool balls rolling and clicking. She edged up to the bar, clutching the towel in her arms.

"Excuse me," she said to the man.

He leaned his head closer to her in order to hear and looked at her mouth to see what she was saying.

"I'm looking for Mya Clark," she mouthed. "Is she working today?"

He shook his head quickly up and down and pointed off into the dark with his cloth. "She's on break over there with one of her boyfriends." He dangled the cloth on the end of his extended arm. "Over there."

As Susan peered into the darkness in the direction in which he was pointing, she saw two figures at a table in the farthest corner of the room. Their heads were nearly touching, and one had a hand on the other's shoulder. As Susan stared, the scene became clearer. The first thing that came into focus was Mya's golden hair. It was twisted on top of her head. Susan couldn't make out the features of the other person, but his movements, the way he held his head, the way he moved his hands, were very familiar to her. It was someone she knew very well, but she knew it could not be that person. Not in the Bullfrog Valley Inn, and not in the middle of the afternoon.

Susan saw Mya's hands reach up and her fingers gently play around the man's ears. His head was drooping and he looked sad. It was the same hang-dog look Tom assumed when he wasn't getting his way. Susan could still not see his face. He was wearing a suit, and in his dark head of hair were some little gray streaks, which were picked up by the dim, indirect lighting.

The bartender had wandered away, and except for two big gray lumps at the other end of the bar, Susan was alone. She forgot what she was carrying; she only knew that it was something incredibly heavy. She leaned on the bar stool, and with her other arm, automatically readjusted the towel. And as she rearranged the towel, her hand touched the cold, smooth glass of the crystal ball. She looked down to see what it was that she was carrying and saw a smeary reflection of her own familiar face, looking lost and distressed,. All she could think was that she needed to get that pathetic person away from here as quickly as she possibly could.

If a friendly drunk had staggered up at that point and asked Susan what was wrong, she wouldn't have been able to tell him. Something bad was happening, but she didn't know if she was causing it, or if someone else was. A crime was being committed, and she desperately needed to get away from the scene. That's all she knew.

She was so frantic that she felt any moment she was going to crumble to the floor. She had to get outside. She wanted to see the sky and the trees, to be reassured that the world as she knew it was still out there, waiting for her. With one quick movement, she flew to the door, pushed it open with her body, squeezed through, and leaned against the porch wall. The towel and whatever she had wrapped up in it dropped onto the cement floor, and as she went down the steps, she tripped on one, caught herself on the second, and then lost her balance completely and landed on her knees on the gravel. Up onto her flat feet she got and down the road she ran as fast as she could go. When she reached the end of the long driveway, she stopped and bent over to catch her breath. She looked behind her to see what she was running from and saw only a quiet roadway leading up into the forest. Several deep breaths later, she relaxed a little and was able to float slowly down Bullfrog Valley Road towards the safety of the Angel Estate, the place where nothing bad could ever happen.

What the people driving down Bullfrog Valley Road saw that afternoon was a middle aged woman out for a walk. She looked like any ordinary woman, probably trying to firm up and get her figure back after a few years of child bearing and rearing. No one gave her a second thought. No one noticed that her shoes were not touching the road, and that she was floating gracefully in the air.

Susan didn't know what she was doing. Her thoughts were churning. She was trying to make sense of what she had seen in the Bullfrog. Why would Tom be there with Mya? Was it possible that this was a horrible coincidence, maybe the only time he had ever come to the place at all. But, statistically, what were the chances that she would go there for the first time in her life on the same day Tom chose to go there, and at the same time. The bartender had called him Mya's boyfriend, but maybe he said that as a joke. Susan tried to come up with an explanation that would allow her not to believe what she had seen with her very own eyes.

Lovers, that's what Susan saw sitting at the table at the Bullfrog, lovers bathed in an intensity so strong that the rest of the world was entirely shut out. How long had it been going on? When? Where? How often? Susan thought of all the evenings Tom went walking. She heard his polite refusals when she asked to join him. But his walks were only for a few minutes, at most, half an hour, certainly not time to make love. And he worked all day. Susan called him at work sometimes, and he was always there when she called. He worked in the evenings sometimes, or else he was at home. And Mya would never do anything to hurt her. Mya was the kindest person she had ever known. Susan argued with reality. There was no time for Tom to have an affair, and Mya wouldn't do it, not with Tom. Not Mya. Not Tom. It wasn't even a possibility.

As she floated along Bullfrog Valley Road, she reminded herself that Tom and Mya didn't even like each other all that much. Tom made fun of Mya and laughed at her, and Mya looked for every opportunity to criticize Tom and to point out to Susan how thoughtless and inconsiderate he was. Tom and Mya were the two most important people in her life now. She trusted them and relied on them totally. She loved the two of them, enjoyed their company and fussed over both of them endlessly. And when Tom said Mya was a kook, Susan defended her. When Mya criticized Tom, Susan defended him. She wondered if all those people at the Frog knew what was going on. What a fool she was. There was a fool floating down Bullfrog Valley Road, but no one noticed, for a fool will often disguise itself as a middle-aged woman out for an afternoon walk, a middle-aged woman without a care in the world.

Although it was a warm October day, as the afternoon grew later, the air became cold. Susan slowed down until she felt her feet touch the ground. She noticed for the first time that the birds were collecting on the telephone wires in long black chains, getting ready to leave for the winter. If only she could turn herself into a black bird. If only she had allowed Mya to teach her to astrotravel. She wanted to go someplace far away, but she could think of no place to go. She decided to go back to the house and sit with a calendar and try to figure out what had happened and when. How long had they lived in the house? When had she gone on that trip down to visit her friends and asked Mya to keep an eye on Tom? Could she ever ask them when it began? Would they lie? Of course, Tom would lie, but Mya never lied about anything. Who should she confront first, Tom or Mya? Did she want to hear the lie first and the truth second, or did she want the truth first and the lie second. It was a difficult choice.

She thought of another option. She could pretend she knew nothing, and she could observe them and maybe catch them in the act, so to speak. The thought of Tom and Mya making love was such an unsettling thought that she actually shook her head back and forth as hard as she could to try to get it out of her mind.

Before she realized where she was, she had reached the mail boxes, and she couldn't recall if she had got the mail that morning. She looked at their mail box, innocently leaning on its wooden stand. If it was true about Mya and Tom, there would be no such thing as mail for the Harris family. There would be no such thing as the Harris family at all. As she stood looking at the gray metal box, she thought of Mya placing her hand on top of it, closing her eyes, and saying: "There's a flyer. It's from the grocery store. No, it's a photo shop advertisement. There's a reminder card from either the dentist or the doctor. And there's a letter, not a fat letter, and it's from some place out west." Susan opened the box and it was empty. She began to cry.

As she walked across the bridge and looked over at the summer house, more tears ran down her face and onto the front of her shirt. Through the tears, Mya's home was a blur of green and gray and black camouflage. She squinted and several wild cats came into focus. They were curled together in two's and three's on the dam, trying to keep warm.

"Now, I'll be like a wild cat," Susan thought. "I'll have no home. I'll be alone and loose in the world, and I'll have to depend on strangers for food and love."

As she headed up across the front lawn towards the house, she heard in the distance the whining sound of sirens, and the whining became louder and louder. It was the sound of unexplainable despair, and Susan broke into a run to try to escape, but it was everywhere, coming from all directions, and she could not get away from it.

The dark branches of the trees were etched against the dull gray afternoon sky. Farther on, the deep green pines filled in the background, and the sirens continued to scream from all directions. Susan felt totally alone in a new and terrifying world, a world where everything and everyone could change in a second, and a person could do nothing about it. She sat on the stone bench on the hill and looked out across the lawn with teary eyes, wide, but not focused on anything, not on the ancient green hemlocks that sheltered the summer house, and not on the opaque gray sky. Susan was a blind person, aware only of the cold creeping up into her body from the stone bench.

The bench was purely decorative. Nobody ever sat on it deliberately, for even in the summer, it was cold and hard and uncomfortable. When Kathleen Angel had designed the bench, she had in mind an illusion. The bench was constructed of heavy brown stones, solidly and permanently cemented together to last until eternity. It formed a symbolic vantage point where she could sit and look over the estate. The person sitting on the bench would be captured in the painting, and yet, at the same time, would be able to observe the painting. Susan opened her bleary eyes and looked across the lawn to the pond, the summer house, the hemlocks, and beyond to the deep green forest. She turned and glanced behind her at the big brown stone house that she loved so much. Everything was in its place. All was peaceful.

Minutes passed. Maybe an hour passed. Now the sky was dirty gray and the sun a circle of painful white. Cold shadows crept from under the stone house and settled about the yard like big gray wolves. Susan became a part of the landscape, a few last minute sloppy brush strokes added by a painter who felt the picture needed a human element, someone to feel, to enjoy, to suffer.

The sirens had long since ceased whining, and early evening silence descended. Susan closed her unseeing eyes and pulled her arms closer around her knees. She felt like a tired soldier in a cold, wet trench, thankful that the firing had abated. The soldier fell asleep in that muddy hole, oblivious to the physical discomfort and appreciative of the cessation of the psychic discomfort, but the sleep would be short-lived. The ominous sound of whirling helicopter blades were impossible to absorb into a dream.

Susan jerked to wakefulness and saw above her head in the darkening gray cloudless sky a single white helicopter with red lettering on the side. She watched it whirl its way across the sky, nearly touching the hemlocks and then rising to clear the low green mountains beyond. She recognized it as the Life Flight helicopter that took people to big medical centers in Philadelphia when they couldn't be cared for at the Port Williams Hospital. The helicopter reminded her that elsewhere life was still going on and that someone was very sick, and possibly dying, but that was no consolation to her. She stood up from the bench, reached back and felt how cold and damp the back of her pants were, and walked stiffly down to the house.

THE FIRE

The regular clientele of the Bullfrog Valley Inn didn't pay much attention to the outside of the bar. When they found themselves in the vicinity of the Frog, as they frequently did, they were either thinking of an uplifting cold drink, or a friendly face. They walked from their car or truck to the bar in a hurry and didn't notice much of anything. It was only the atmosphere inside, where they would spend the next four hours, that was important. If the owners of the Bullfrog had spent thousands of dollars to scrape away the flaking paint on the exterior and cover it with a bright new coat, the effort would not have brought in a single new customer. It was better policy to spend money on a good country band, bigger amps, or a second show of the all male exotic dance troupe that was such a hit.

It would take more than a little trash and clutter to keep the regular customers away. Since some of the oldest of the clientele could remember, broken bar stools and pool cues had been piled against the back of the building, along with cases of empty beer cans and bottles. It was part of the charm. The stuff on the porch was mostly paper trash from the cans inside. The guy who was supposed to clean the Frog on Sundays usually burned that in a barrel out back, if he had time, but he hadn't showed up for a couple of weeks, so it was piling up and some had spilled out and blown around the side of the building. No big deal. He'd get to it one of these days and clean it up.

Susan noticed the trash when she walked up to the door; she thought it looked awful, but she expected nothing else. Everyone always said the place was a dump, and it was. And it just wasn't a bad day or a bad time for her to come there. It was a typical Friday afternoon at the Frog. Mya was waitressing, but she was on her break and sitting at a table with Tom, who had left work early to stop by and try to pin her down to a specific time to talk with him later that night. He was distraught; Mya was frustrated and angry. Tom's immature behavior was something she had not anticipated. He was happily married and settled, and very experienced with women, so his sudden anger and concern over her pregnancy was baffling. She would expect behavior like this from some of the local guys she had dated, but she expected more understanding from Tom.

Mark, the weekend bartender, had come in around noon and planned to stay until closing. A second waitress was due to join Mya around five and overlap until the dinner crowd thinned out. One of the owners would come in around 8 and hang around, helping out, until closing. There were twelve cars and trucks in the parking lot. Three guys were playing pool; two men sat at a table arguing over a contract to join a hunting camp; one old man, quite drunk, sat on the very last bar stool, bumping his head gently against the wall; and two men, each with a draft beer and a sandwich plate, had pushed their chairs back a little to watch the action at the pool table.

A little after four more patrons would dribble in for a Friday afternoon beer, and some of those would sit for hours, having one more for the road with old friends they hadn't seen in a couple of days. There would be a lull between 6:30 and 9, when the band was due, and when a younger crowd would come on the scene for dancing and drinking. The place wouldn't clear out until two or three in the morning. Every Friday was the same, except for the Friday that Susan came to the Frog to deliver a special present to her dear friend Mya.

As Susan was tripping down the cement steps, she was unaware that the crystal ball had cracked and broken quietly into hundreds of pale blue shards. Had she looked back, she would have seen a beautiful light show. As the sunlight hit each fragment of the crystal, blue rays and beams flashed and swirled before they settled into a soft blue glow. And the blue glow reflected on the wrinkled paper napkins and potato chip bags that cluttered the porch. The same hot sun that beat down on Susan beat down on the porch. The floor was warm; the paper, dry; and, in a short while, as the thud of Susan's feet against the dirt road grew softer and softer, smoke and small hungry, flickering flames licked at the papers on the porch, liked what they tasted, and reached up for more. Potato chip bags, napkins, a cardboard beer carton and a newspaper were devoured and soon the flames were licking against the dry chips of paint on the wooden wall and dancing up the wood shingles and onto the roof, climbing along the edge of the roof, carefully burning each dry pine needle that lay among the shingles.

It was 4:30 in the afternoon. All over Port Williams, regulars were beginning to think it was about time to put away the tools of the trade and head for the Frog to get a jump start on the weekend. Down the air vent and into the bathroom came the braver flames, riding along on hunks of wooden shingles. They landed on the bathroom floor that Mya was going to sweep up when she got a free moment. The bathroom was a banquet table, all set up and waiting for a party of hungry flames. The trash can was filled to the brim with tissues and paper towels, used once and crinkled up into just the right shape to be imminently flammable.

In the kitchen, Mark was making himself a steak sandwich because he knew he wouldn't have a chance to eat once the place got crazy. He noticed wisps of smoke leaking through the wall above the stove and thought the hot splattered grease was beginning to smoke. He watched it for a moment, and when the first flame flicked its tongue at him and withdrew, he got scared. He had never seen that happen before. He assumed the fire was confined to the kitchen, and before he realized the extent of the blaze, he ran to the big sink and began to draw a pan of water. During those few seconds, the fire had time to spread in both directions, and when Mark turned around, carefully trying to balance the pan of water, he faced a wall of flame.

"Where's the fuckin' fire extinguisher?" he yelled. There had to be one, but he couldn't remember ever having seen it.

The fire had begun at the back door, spread across the roof and down into the bathrooms beside the front door and into the kitchen. At this point, people began to ask each other if they smelled smoke, smoke other than that coming from their cigarettes. As they held their noses up and sniffed, the roof broke through in several places and large chunks of burning wooden shingles fell down onto the wooden tables, igniting paper place mats and paper napkins, and bounded down onto the wooden floor.

At 4:45 p.m., a dispatch came into the Port Williams Fire Department: "Structural fire in Bullfrog Valley."

"Is it the Frog? Jesus Christ, is the Frog on fire?" The dispatcher forgot to keep his voice calm and controlled.

"I'm not Jesus Christ, but yep, it's the Frog all right, and it's a big one."

"Dammit. I knew that was going to happen. I knew it was going to go up someday."

"Didn't we all?"

Volunteer firemen were toned out in their beepers and simultaneously the sirens began to sing. At 4:55 p.m., fire trucks arrived at the Bullfrog, and by 5 p.m., three fire companies had been paged for mutual aid and had responded, along with the paramedic vehicle, two ambulances, and the squad vehicle. More ambulances were called to the scene.

"Definite multiple injuries. Known dead." There was no more joking by the dispatchers.

At five o'clock, while Susan was curled up on the stone bench, feeling as though her world had ended, two modern warriors in fire retardant suits and self-contained breathing apparatuses, carried a man's crumpled body from the building and placed it on a long board, covered him with a sheet, and slid him into the ambulance, which headed slowly down the lane. There was no need to hurry.

Two more warriors carried a woman out of the Frog. She was rapidly assessed by the paramedic, found to be in severe pulmonary distress and in shock. Within seconds, she was covered with a blanket, immobilized on a long board, and placed into an ambulance, which sped down the long dirt lane and onto the main road, where the driver turned on the siren and sped towards the Hospital. The first ambulance, carrying the man, pulled over and allowed the second to pass by with a polite exchange of siren chat.

The woman had no identification on her body. A nurse in the Emergency Department recognized her as the waitress at the Frog, what's her name, the one with the weird name, the nice one.

"Well, find out who she is," the doctor barked, "because it looks like we're going to have news for the next of kin."

After a cursory examination, he said, "Maybe not," and arranged by phone for a transfer.

The Life Flight helicopter arrived on the pad in moments and the woman was sent off to a Burn Unit in Philadelphia.

In another cubicle in the Emergency Department, a paramedic took a black leather wallet from the man's suit jacket pocket, shuffled through a stack of credit cards, and found a driver's license, and radioed the local police. They needed someone to advise a family of a death.

The doctor covering the shift that afternoon became a bit famous for having taken care of the victims of the Frog fire. He got sick and tired of everyone asking him about it. Some asked such inappropriate questions.

"Wasn't that waitress beautiful?"

All the doctor could remember was the smell of burned hair.

"She had such magnificent big green eyes."

"I never saw her eyes," the doctor said.

"Such a shame."

The rumor of the fire spread almost as fast as the fire itself. A pilot flying a small aircraft just to the east of town wondered about all the vehicles heading out towards the Bullfrog and he made a quick turn and soon saw the smoke. He radioed back to the airport, and the people boarding a flight for Chicago were able to spread the news all across the United States, before the next of kin were even notified.

In Port Williams they could talk of nothing but the fire. Of course everyone claimed to have predicted it, and no one was surprised.

"The place was a tinder box waiting for a match."

"Miracle it didn't happen years ago."

"Do you think he did it for the insurance?"

Optimists said it was excellent timing for a fire. An hour later and the place would have been packed.

Regulars moaned: "What will we do without the Frog? It's like an old friend up and died. Where are we going to go when we need a little lift?" "They'll rebuild it. They always do, every time it burns."

"But it won't be the same. It'll be too new and clean. We'll be able to see what we're eating. No one would want that."

"Oh, don't worry. It'll dirty up fast enough. Give us a couple of months and we'll turn it right back to its original condition."

"But what about Hugo? They'll never be able to replace Hugo."

The story was passed around that Hugo was cooked right in the tank. Someone threw an onion in and some green peppers, and it was the best fish soup anyone had ever tasted.

"Poor old Hugo."

"Poor old Frog."

And there were a few who resigned themselves to the fact that Mrs. Angel's Ghost had finally got rid of that old dump, and there were others who thought it was just about time. Bully for her.

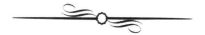

WHATEVER GETS YOU
THROUGH THE NIGHT

Susan stood inside the door and closed her eyes and shook. She didn't know what to do. Where do you go when you are uncomfortable in the world? How can a person escape from this world that she's trapped in? She poured herself a large glass of whiskey, gulped it down, washed the glass out, and went into the living room and lay down on the couch under a soft white blanket to wait for the drink to take effect.

As she lay there, she spun romantic yet tragic yarns in her imagination. She would go away and not tell Tom where she was. He would search and search and when he found her, he would beg her to come back to him. But the truth kept breaking into her dreams, the new truth that she hadn't yet absorbed nor understood. Soon drums began to play in her ears. They faintly tapped out the words Tom's baby, Tom's baby, Tom's baby. Then another sweet dream floated by. Mya goes away and has the baby and someone else moves into the summer house, a new friend, a nice friend. Then more drumming. Tom hates me. Tom hates me. Tom loves Mya. Mya loves Tom. Tom and Mya are going to have a baby.

Even Heather tried to creep into her dreams, but Susan couldn't deal with Heather, not now. Tom's baby would be Heather's sister. The longer Susan lay there, the crazier she felt. Go away. Stay here. I have no place to go. I can't stay here. He doesn't want me here. Stay here and watch what's going on, but don't let them know you know. Then things will just continue the way they are, but I'll hate both of them, and I probably won't be able to keep up the pretense.

By the time Officer Elkins and his buddy, Officer Samuels, met at the Emergency Department and talked with the doctor and then began to make their way out to the Angel Estate, it was after seven. Susan had been lying on the couch for more than two hours. The pillows were damp with warm and cold tears. As the officers parked the car and walked up to the door, they were certain no one was at home. All of the lights in the house were out except for the outside flood lights that had come on automatically at seven.

"I'll give it a try," Officer Elkins said, as he tapped the door with the metal knocker. "Just in case." The night was totally silent. "One more time," he said.

"This is a beautiful old place," Elkins said to Samuels. "Isn't it?"

"It's peaceful," Officer Samuels said. "It's a peaceful place."

"I think I hear someone coming," Officer Elkins said.

When Susan heard the car come up the drive, she thought it was Tom, so she stayed where she was on the sofa. She would pretend she had fallen asleep, and that way she would not have to talk to him nor listen to him nor confront him, because she had no idea how to go about addressing the new reality that she was trying to come to terms with. But when she heard the knocker, she knew it wasn't Tom. Maybe it was Mr. Edwards. It would be nice to see Mr. Edwards. Maybe he was bringing her a gift. She walked over and opened the door.

What goes through a person's mind when she opens a door and sees two police officers standing before her?

"Heather," Susan thought. "Heather has been in an accident."

The problems of the afternoon slipped to the back of her mind. She said nothing. She opened her eyes wide and waited for the policemen to speak.

Both officers held their hats in their hands before them. "Are you Mrs. Thomas Harris?" Officer Samuels asked.

"It's not Heather," she thought. "It's Tom. Something must have happened to Tom."

"Yes, I'm Susan Harris," she said, and there was a note of relief in her voice. They hadn't asked if she were Heather Harris' mother. "Tom's not here. He's probably still at work. Is there something wrong?"

"May we come in?"

"Certainly," Susan said. She snapped the hall light on and held the door wide open. "Come this way," she said as she led them into the dining room and turned on the light. They stood in the doorway. Susan still did not have any idea why they were there.

"Would you like to sit down?" she asked, and she wondered if she should offer them coffee, but first she needed to know why they were here.

Officer Elkins sat on the edge of the chair. This was never an easy job, but at least this time he didn't know the woman, hadn't grown up with her husband and played high school football with him, and didn't know every relative she had, which was usually the case. The lady looked disheveled. He wasn't close enough to smell alcohol, but she certainly didn't look like she was on top of the world. She wiped her nose with a tissue, straightened her sweater, and patted nervously at her hair.

"I've a bit of a cold," she said. "I was just lying down." It looked to the men like something more than a bit of a cold.

Officer Samuels got tired of waiting for Officer Elkins to broach the awful subject they were about to share with this lady.

"Mrs. Harris, did you know about the fire this afternoon?" he asked.

"The fire?" Susan asked. "No." Then she remembered the sirens wailing and wailing. "I heard sirens a while ago, but I didn't know there was a fire. I thought maybe there was an accident."

"Well, there was a big fire down at the Bullfrog Valley Inn," Officer Elkins said.

The strangest thought passed through Susan's mind. Do they think I set the fire? It was the only time in her life she had been to the Bullfrog, and it had caught fire. Had anyone seen her going there? She tried to focus on this new concern and warned herself to be careful what she said.

"There were so many sirens going off that I had to come into the house to get away from the noise," she said. "I was here all afternoon. I was working in the yard."

"It was quite a fire," Officer Elkins said. "The place burned to the ground."

"How terrible," Susan said, but she was glad the old place burned. Now Tom and Mya would have to find another place to sneak off to, she thought.

Both officers were quiet. Susan still didn't know why they were there. They surely didn't come the whole way out to the estate to tell her about the fire. She couldn't tolerate the silence. She had to speak. "That place was an institution in this town. I mean, I've never been there, but I've heard so much about it." She was becoming animated. "I just said I'd never been there," she thought. 'Why in the world did I lie." She was covering up, but she wasn't certain why she needed to.

Officer Elkins and Officer Samuels were so busy concentrating on exactly how to break the news that they paid no attention to Susan's confusion.

"My husband," she began to say, and then she paused. She planned to say "My husband was always going to take me there for a drink someday," but she remembered that she was no longer going to be able to talk about her husband, and the joke was on her. Tom never intended to take her there for a drink. That was Mya and his cozy little nest.

The mention of her husband gave the officers an opening. "That's what we came to talk to you about," Officer Elkins said, "Your husband."

"Tom?" Susan asked. Now she was confused, yet relieved. It wasn't Heather and it wasn't an accusation of arson. "Is Tom in trouble?" Susan asked. "Is there something wrong with Tom?"

Officer Elkins looked at Officer Samuels. "How do you answer a question like that?" his eyes asked. Officer Samuels was sick of the delay. Even though Elkins was the senior officer, Samuels decided to take over and get this done with.

"We just came from the hospital, Mrs. Harris." Officer Samuels paused to see if she was going to catch on. Her eyes were blank. "I hate to be the one to bring you such dreadful news, but your husband was in the Frog when it caught fire this afternoon. I'm sorry to tell you that he died in the fire. He didn't make it out."

They were prepared for hysteria, prepared to restrain her gently until she cried it out. They were prepared for tears and wailing. Officer Elkins had put a clean white handkerchief in his pocket before he left the station. But what they got was absolute silence, and it was very difficult to sit in that room for nearly twenty minutes while the woman sat and stared into space.

"Are you all right?" Officer Elkins asked.

Susan didn't answer. She didn't hear.

"Do you want me to get you some water or something?"

It was a challenge to sit and wait. Officer Elkins shifted in the chair. Officer Samuels picked at his nails and adjusted his watch on his wrist. They exchanged glances. Officer Elkins shrugged his shoulders. Officer Samuels held his hand up to signal: Give her a little more time.

Eighteen minutes passed. Officer Samuels put his hand on Susan's arm and asked, almost in a whisper: "Is there anybody you'd like to call?"

No response.

"Do you have a doctor here in town, a family doctor?" Officer Samuels broke in. "Do you have a minister? Would you like to call your minister?"

Officer Samuels stood. "I know how you feel, Mrs. Harris. You must be devastated. It was a terrible, terrible accident. A thing like that should never happen to anyone ever."

And the woman said the strangest thing, not to anyone in particular, but into the space before her eyes. She said: "There's no such thing as an accident. An accident is merely a coincidence. It's a coming together at a certain point in time and space of various forces so that a certain pattern is formed." She stood up from the chair and said, "That's what a friend of mine always says."

"Would you like to call your friend?" Officer Samuels suggested.

"It's not something I'll ever be able to do again," Susan replied.

The officers were so relieved to hear her talking that it didn't matter that what she said made no sense at all.

"If you'd like to freshen up a bit, we'd like you to come along with us down to the hospital and make the proper identification.

There'll be someone there to talk with you about arrangements and what you need to do."

"I'll just be a moment," Susan said as she headed for the pink powder room by the back door.

The officers shook their heads and made eyes at each other.

"You never know," Officer Elkins whispered.

"I'm glad it's over," Officer Samuels said. "Wasn't that strange?"

"To each his own," Officer Elkins said. "A person's gotta do what a person's gotta do."

"Whatever gets you through the night," Officer Samuels agreed.

Susan closed the door quietly behind her and stood for a moment in the small, warm bathroom. She held her hands in front of her and squeezed her fingers. It felt consoling, as though someone was holding her hand. She reached up and clicked on one of the pink frosted glass lamps on the wall above the sink. She put her face close to the mirror and stared at the familiar stranger looking back at her. It was an old peach-toned mirror in a metal frame which someone had painted with gaudy gold enamel. The mirror had been hanging there since the house was built. The silver backing was chipped along the edges and wide gray streaks that looked like water marks swirled across the glass. A million wipes with window cleaner and a soft cloth had not removed them. Thoughts of replacing the old mirror with a new one lasted only long enough for a lady to notice how pretty she looked in that old mirror. Everyone looked beautiful in the mirror because the defects were on the mirror and not on the face looking in. A shiny new bathroom mirror accentuates every wrinkle, every broken capillary, every blemish. New mirrors make people feel ugly, but this old mirror had been around for so many generations and had seen so much of life that it felt nothing but kindness and pity for the anguished, despairing faces that looked into her.

It was this very same mirror that reflected back to Kathleen Angel the fact that she was a beautiful woman, and it made Kathleen wonder why, if she was so lovely, she was so filled with angst? No matter how reassuring the mirror tried to be, Kathleen often stood before it, weeping over the emptiness of her life and the agony of her soul.

Now another soul in despair was looking into the mirror, a woman not as beautiful as Kathleen Angel, but a kind and gentle woman who had asked so little of life that life felt no need to give her anything at all. The lady in the cracked mirror looked back at Susan, nonjudgmental, and asked, "What now?"

"Arrangements," Susan answered. She remembered a day a few years ago when Tom and she had gone together to the lawyer's office to write a will. When the lawyer asked, "Do you have a cemetery plot? Tom grinned at Susan and said, "Welcome to old age."

"I guess we've skipped old age," Susan said to the lady in the mirror. "Welcome to death."

Susan walked out of the house with an officer on either side of her in case she collapsed. She knew she was not going to collapse, but it was nice to have them there. Before she stepped into the car, she looked across the lawn at Mya's place. Her numbness was pricked by a thought of revenge. She thought of how bad Mya was going to feel. Mya's baby now truly has no father, Susan thought with sad satisfaction. Susan did not wear revenge well. The awful thought came to her that Mya might be with Tom right now. Mya might have accompanied him to the hospital and been with him when he died. All these morbid possibilities were settling down in Susan's numbed and frozen brain, but she wouldn't ask about Mya. That might make the officers suspect that she had been at the Bullfrog. She sat silently in the front seat, while Officer Elkins drove and Officer Samuels filled up more than half of the back seat of the sedan. It was a very quiet car.

As they pulled down the driveway towards the bridge, Susan noticed how dark the world had become, and as they started to cross the bridge, in the darkness they saw one bright headlight turn at the mail boxes and head towards them. As he rolled down the window, Susan could hear the familiar rattle and clank of the old truck. Mr. Edwards stopped the truck, turned off the motor, and ran over to the police car window.

"Hello there," he said to Officer Elkins, as he nodded to Officer Samuels in the back seat, and then he turned to Susan.

His familiar face in the window of the car brought Susan back to life. It was as though her kind mother had appeared and opened her arms to let Susan into the warmth and comfort of her loving embrace. For the first time since she had known him, Mr. Edwards was speechless. They looked at each other and communicated without words. He said that he never had any idea that something like this would happen. It was beyond his wildest imaginings. They both sensed that this was something much bigger than either of them and something no one else would ever understand. He reassured her that she had done everything right, and nothing was her fault. Someone else must have surely done something awful to bring such a tragedy on all of them. He told her she could stay there for as long as she wanted and not to worry about the rent, but he was afraid she wouldn't want to stay there, not after this.

"Is there anything I can do for you?" he asked, and as the question hung between them in the air, a splendid idea came into his cluttered mind and dug its way past piles of half formed ideas and landed squarely on the tip of his tongue.

And Susan smiled at Mr. Edwards and said: "I can't think of anything, but I'll let you know if I do."

He interrupted her with a question: "Have you decided where you're going to bury Tom?"

Susan didn't reply; she just shook her head back and forth. "No idea," she whispered.

"Well, I was thinkin'," Mr. Edwards said. "You know where my dad's buried, don't you?"

"Yes, he's in the little graveyard up at the end of the property. I've seen his marker."

Mr. Edwards began to ramble on about how he had to get permission and they didn't think he would be allowed to do it because you can't just bury a person on any old piece of land, but it turned out the Angel cemetery was registered, so it was legal to bury him there.

"If you want to bury Tom up there," Mr. Edwards aid. "I don't think that'll be any problem at all. You could visit him any time you wanted," and he couldn't keep himself from adding: "He'd be in good company. You know all those other ones that are up there too."

"What a wonderful idea," Susan thought. She shook her head and smiled at Mr. Edwards. "Thank you. Thank you," she said. "You've saved me a lot of grief. It's a wonderful idea, and Tom will love it there."

Mr. Edwards was pleased. He backed away from the window, nodding his goodbyes to the officers, crawled up into his truck, and in a few minutes, he was grinding in reverse across the bridge and onto Bullfrog Valley Road.

Mr. Edwards' appearance relaxed the tense air in the car. The officers began to joke.

"In all seriousness, I should have given that guy a ticket for driving with a burned out bulb," Officer Elkins said.

"He should get a fine for taking that rattle trap out on the road at all," Officer Samuels replied.

"I didn't notice any inspection sticker, did you?" Officer Elkins asked, and they both chuckled quietly.

Officer Samuels tried to bring Susan into the conversation. "That truck is famous in this town. Everyone's got a story about old Edwards and that God-awful truck," he said. But Susan was lost in thought and didn't reply, so he turned his attention back to Officer Samuels and they discussed what an eccentric old fellow Mr. Edwards had turned out to be, and laughed loudly at the fact that he couldn't hold a torch to his father, the man for whom some say the word eccentric had originally been coined.

TOM WOULD HAVE LOVED
HIS FUNERAL

In today's world, chaos has become a normal event. It takes its place along with the tides, the phases of the moon, and the seasons, as an integral part of life on earth. Chaos is now a comfort, instead of a stress, and Susan discovered this fact for herself after the fire. She filled out forms; talked with strange, kind people; and actually enjoyed shopping for a coffin, feeling the smooth, rich wood with her finger tips and deciding Tom would like cherry rather than pine and that he would look particularly handsome lying against dark green satin. She called friends and relatives, and she answered the telephone every few minutes all day long. She talked with a local minister that someone recommended and told him about a man named Tom who had a wonderful sense of humor, was a great father, and was a most thoughtful husband and friend to her. She smiled sadly as she dabbed at her eyes with a handkerchief. Susan tried on all the dark colored dresses in her closet, chose two that were appropriate, and hung them in the bathroom and let the shower drip to steam out all the wrinkles.

During the year that Susan had lived in Port Williams, she had not met more than a handful of people. All of a sudden, she received calls from dozens of people Tom worked with at Kraft Paper Mills, neighbors she had waved at and met once or twice, people who heard her sad story from Mr. Edwards, and others who were just obsessed with the tragic fire at the Frog and wanted to express their sympathy and concern. Susan was magically able to meet all sorts of new challenges, and everyone offered to pitch in and help in any way they could.

And, best of all, Heather was flown in by the Red Cross the morning after the fire. Much to Susan's delight, there was no sign of the denim-clad teenager who had left for the service; instead, Heather was a polite young lady in a navy blue uniform with perfectly shined black leather shoes and a sensible purse. She held Susan's hand as they stood beside the closed coffin and asked: "How are we going to get by without Daddy?" And Susan reassured her: "We'll miss him, that's for sure, but we'll be okay. He would expect us to go on living and enjoying our lives."

"You mean, keep on truckin'," Heather said, imitating Tom.

"Right. That's more like it," Susan agreed, and her eyes filled with tears.

During the first few days, there had been no sign of Mya anywhere near the summer house, but Susan didn't trust herself to ask anyone about her, so she patiently waited for someone to mention her name, but most people were careful not to talk about the fire at all when Susan was near, and thus, several days went by before she had a chance to learn about her old friend. She overheard a woman say that the waitress had been taken by helicopter to a burn center somewhere.

"Is the waitress going to be all right then?" Susan asked the woman.

"It's hard to tell, but if she's going to make it anywhere, she's in the right place," the woman replied.

"Mya was in the right place, as usual," thought Susan, and she felt relieved.

Around 10:15 on Tuesday morning, a procession of cars followed a shiny black hearse down Bullfrog Valley Road, past the Angel Estate, and up the tiny road to the cemetery. Friends, family, and employees of the Kraft Paper Mills all came to pay their last respects to Tom. Most of the locals had not been to the cemetery in decades, and Mr. Edwards himself had not bothered to clean it up in years because he said the place gave him the heebie jeebies. "Tidy up graveyard" was as far down on his list as it could go and moved one notch lower every time a new chore was added.

The long-neglected graveyard was a small, rectangular area, set back a few hundred feet from the road and surrounded by a lop-sided wall of irregular field stones, placed randomly by anonymous hands over the decades and held together by stubborn clinging vines and mosses, woven and plaited by generations of little furry creatures who lived, bred, and died in the graveyard. Wild flowers and weeds grew rampant. Among the unruly vegetation sat eleven old, eroded markers, leaning this way and that. Two tall gray stones stood in the very center and leaned towards each other as though they were trying to touch, two eroded markers with a vestige of worn flowery lace trimming the curved tops, meeting a weeping willow design which flowed down on either side of the stones and ended in the earth somewhere.

"Lloyd Vaughn Angel, b. January 5, 1865, d. March 25, 1931. 66 yr, 2 mo, 20 dy. How vain this world, how few its joys, yet God creates and he destroys. He lived beloved and lamented died."

And on the marker that was reaching for him was carved: "Kathleen Elizabeth Hannigan Angel, wife of Lloyd Vaughn Angel, b. November 7, 1872, d. 1912. She came forth as a flower and was cut down." And at the bottom of the stone, so worn that only those with much patience could feel out the message with finger tips aiding squinting eyes: "A soul in repose," a blatant lie if there ever was one, and everyone knew it.

One interesting unusual vine had taken a fancy to Lloyd Angel's stone and had nearly covered it with small green and gray leaves and tendrils that had braided, coiled and twined themselves into a lace cape. At the point where his marker leaned closest to Kathleen's, the vine had sent a fresh green tendril across the space, where it tried with every fresh breeze, to attach itself to Kathleen's stone. No doubt, Lloyd was wanting to know if his beloved wife had arrived and was lying there beside him.

In an appropriate dull gold and gray setting, figures in dark clothing stumbled around in the cemetery, trying to get their footing, heading for the newly dug grave near the stone wall.

"Where did all these people come from?" Heather whispered to Susan.

Susan herself was surprised at the turn out. "Most from work, I guess," Susan said. "Everyone loved your dad."

The minister's talk was brief, according to Susan's instructions, and there was a moment of levity when Mr. Edwards drove up in his noisy truck a few minutes into the ceremony and snorted his way through the crowd to come and stand by Susan.

As the mourners one by one politely nodded farewell to Susan and reminded her to call if she needed anything, and in slow motion, walked to their cars and drove away in low gear, Mr. Edwards stood in the background, looking like he had something to say.

To every offer for a lift down the little road to her house, Susan replied, "We're going to stay here and keep Tom company for a while. I'm not ready to say goodbye." Everyone understood.

When Mr. Edwards finally approached Susan, he looked nervous for some reason, and Susan waited patiently for him to speak. He looked down at his feet, and he looked into the distance at the forest beyond the little graveyard. Finally, he met Susan's eyes with his own and said, "She died this morning. I'm so sorry."

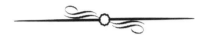

BE KIND TO MYA'S MEMORY

Although she had been wondering and worried about Mya for days, it had never entered Susan's mind that Mya might die. She let out a pained sigh. "No, it can't be. Are you sure?" she asked Mr. Edwards, and he shook his head up and down and reached out and patted her arm with a gentle hand.

"Who is it, Mom?" Heather asked. "Who died?"

"A friend," Susan said. "A dear, dear friend."

A new set of challenges arose.

"What should we do?" Mr. Edwards asked. "They got in touch with me, but I don't know anybody to call. She didn't have no family that I know of, at least none among the living."

"There were lots of people she knew," Susan said. "She talked about them all the time. I can't think of them now. Let's go back to the house."

The new crisis eliminated her plan to stand by Tom's grave and mourn with Heather. They squeezed themselves into the front of Mr. Edwards' dirty truck and sat stiffly, worrying about their clean clothing. He chugged slowly down the road towards the bridge, spinning out to Heather's fresh ears the long, sad tale of Pauline Clark's mistake.

Susan tuned out the familiar story to concentrate on people Mya had mentioned. From time to time, she felt the need to interrupt Mr. Edwards' tale.

"There's a fortune teller friend I met a few times. Sister Dory. She lives in town somewhere. She and Mya were very close."

"Not much of a friend and not much of a fortune teller if she didn't warn her about something like this," Mr. Edwards said, and Susan and Heather giggled in spite of themselves. Mr. Edwards returned to his tale.

Susan interrupted him once more. "She had a lot of old lady friends with names like Bertha and Rose that she visited, but she never mentioned their last names, and I don't have any idea where they might live."

"I probably know every old lady in town," Mr. Edwards said, "but what's an old lady going to for her at a time like this? They're probably busy making their own funeral arrangements."

Heather, until this very day, an innocent to life and death, asked: "What would they do if there's nobody to claim the body? Where would they put her?"

Mr. Edwards said something so inappropriate and flip that both Susan and Heather were shocked. "They'll probably toss her into the river with her mother," he said.

"Eeeeeeee," Heather said. "How dreadful."

"No, it isn't dreadful," Susan thought aloud. She craned her neck to look over at Mr. Edwards. "That's a wonderful idea. That's exactly where Mya would want to be."

Mr. Edwards issued a half chuckle snort. "The river can take as many as she pleases, but there's laws about someone else throwing a dead body in there."

Susan was already steps ahead of him. "I wasn't thinking of the body," Susan said. "Couldn't Mya be cremated and her ashes sprinkled in the river?"

This new and startling idea caused obvious discomfort and confusion to Mr. Edwards. "Can you just do that to someone? I mean, is it legal? Can you just cremate someone? Does something have to be written down or signed by somebody? I'm not sure you or I can make a decision like that. We're not family."

"I'll look into it," Susan said.

This did not satisfy Mr. Edwards. Half in jest, he said, "If worse comes to worse, she can have my spot up there," nodding his head back in the direction of the graveyard. "I'm not planning on using it for a long, long time.

Susan had a fleeting image of Tom and Mya, buried side by side, and in a hundred years, the vines twining back and forth between the stones. "No, we can't put Mya in the ground," she said. "Mya would want to be free."

Because the truck was almost as wide as the bridge, Mr. Edwards came to a complete stop, put the gear shift in neutral, and revved the engine a few times to try to move into a contrary first gear. Every time he put it in first, it slipped back to neutral, and he revved the engine for a few seconds and tried again. Susan was making eyes at Heather, who was acknowledging with her own eyes that she now understood that her mother had not exaggerated when she wrote about Mr. Edwards' antics in her letters.

There came a sudden jolt as the truck leapt into the first gear and started across the bridge. Susan and Heather tried to keep from giggling aloud. On the other side of the bridge, Mr. Edwards once again braked to a sudden stop.

"You wouldn't want to go in there now and look around a bit, would you, and see if you could find any letters from cousins or something?" he asked Susan, as he looked over at the dreary little summerhouse. Then he thought better of his suggestion. "I guess that's not such a good idea at a time like this."

"We don't have a lot of time," Susan said. "I'll go in and look around and see if I can find an address book or some phone numbers written somewhere that might help us."

"You're sure you don't mind?" Mr. Edwards asked.

"No, I don't mind. This is something that has to be taken care of. This will not wait," Susan said. "Will you take Heather up to the house. Someone's got to be there for the phone." To Heather she said, "I'll be up in a few minutes."

Susan stood on the edge of the walkway above the dam until the truck crawled up the driveway and disappeared behind the house. She walked slowly across the dam, placing one black flat shoe in front of the other. The board that formed the make-shift path looked wet and slippery. She felt she had to be extra careful. Disasters and tragedies always seem to occur in clusters, and she at this moment was indispensable. Important duties had been entrusted to her, and she was the only person in the world who could perform them. She paused midway on the dam and looked down into the water. The world was completely silent. Something was missing. The frogs were gone. There were no little plopping sounds like they made when they hit the surface of the water.

In Susan's present state, where time, even life, hung suspended, she had trouble remembering what day it was, and when she tried to think about anything besides the immediate task at hand, she became confused. Standing on the damn, she focused all of her attention on the problem of trying to figure out what month it was. It wasn't summer any longer because the trees were no longer green, and the air was chilly. That's why the frogs had gone. They buried themselves when it got cold. It must be winter. But we haven't had Christmas yet this year, she thought. Heather will be home for Christmas. No, Heather is home now, but that's because Tom died. Heather is home because Tom died. It isn't winter yet. It will soon be winter, she decided, as she reached the other side of the dam and stepped safely onto the damp ground. At this point she noticed there were no cats around. Where would the cats go this winter? One of Mya's bons idees last winter was to make nice warm cat nests on her back porch. Susan herself had donated old blankets and towels. Mya said they were helping God because sometimes he got too busy to take care of everything. Susan was suddenly and acutely aware of the absence of Mya. What would the cats do without Mya, she wondered. What will I do without Mya? I'll have to be the one to help God, all alone.

She held the door knob in her hand and tried to concentrate. She was here to find out if there was someone who could take care of Mya's body. She already knew there was no one and that she herself was going to have to do what needed to be done. She knew she was really here to take the opportunity to snoop, and she'd better hurry before Mr. Edwards and Heather began to worry about her. Later she would examine the place in greater detail, but this first cursory inspection was to look for notes in Tom's handwriting, any tangible evidence that the two had indeed been lovers. Until she knew there was something to be forgiven, how could she begin to forgive?

The parlor was dark. As Susan pushed open the door, the acrid odor of burned logs and mold offended her nostrils. There was no incense nor fruit scented candles burning to mask the odors. She snapped the switch and brought the parlor into light. Without Mya, without the flickering of candlelight and the exotic scent of smoldering incense, the parlor became a smelly old room full of shabby, broken things that belonged in the trash.

Susan had no time to wonder about the transformation. She remembered her mission and headed for the diary sitting on the shelf beside the door. Even the old ivory book looked shabby. She noticed for the first time that the silk was stained brown around the hinges and some of the pearls were missing, while others dangled precariously on loose threads. The book gave off an odor of mold and mustiness mixed with sweet cheap perfume. The lace was coming undone. Susan carefully took the book in her hands and sat down at the table. She was filled with dread and anxiety. Until this moment, she was able to believe, or convince herself that she could believe that there was a possibility that Tom was meeting with Mya at the Bullfrog for some totally innocent reason that she herself was incapable of discerning. She so desperately wanted to believe there was an innocent explanation that she argued with herself over the wisdom of opening the diary and finding out otherwise. But her morbid curiosity was not to be denied, and she randomly selected a page half way through the book and began to read.

"Unlimited insight into the secrets of men's hearts can be constructive or destructive," she read. "You can appreciate your life, even if it is an imperfect situation."

"The summons of the celestial is heard and answered from within," was written in Mya's neat hand. Susan read it aloud. It made no sense, but it sounded nice. She read it again.

She flipped through pages and pages of similar entries, looking for mention of Tom, or of herself, but there were no names in Mya's diary, only ideas and theories that made little sense. As she carefully paged through the diary, she came upon an entire page devoted to death. She whispered Mya's favorite word, serendipity, as she flattened the page with her hand and began to read. "The dead are alive....Individual consciousness exists after death....The dead are invisible, but not absent," and then Susan read with great interest: "Burial is a waste of time. Funerals are for the living and not for the dead."

Susan put the ivory book back exactly where it was on the shelf and made certain it was lying at the same angle. Then she smiled at herself. Nobody cared if she read the diary. Mya was dead. "The dead are invisible but not absent," passed through her mind, but she herself did not believe that.

"Mya, are you here?" she asked aloud. No one answered, and her words were absorbed by the heavy curtains. "Are you dead, Mya?" she asked, and once again the answer was silence. "Mya is dead," Susan announced for her own benefit. "Mya is dead."

Instead of silence, she heard a noise at the kitchen door, and she began to tremble. What a freaky state she was in. As she moved towards the kitchen, she heard a woman's voice at the parlor door, and she saw flashing quickly by the window, a tall, blonde woman in jeans. Her heart stopped beating and she covered her mouth with her hand to try to prevent a loud scream from escaping.

"Mya," she called, and at the same time a voice answered back, "Mom, Mom, are you in there?"

It was Heather. Susan was smacked back to earth so hard that she began to laugh and couldn't stop. Since laughter is infectious, Heather began to laugh too, although she had no idea why she was laughing, and every time she managed to stop long enough to try to ask Susan why they were laughing, Susan laughed even harder and Heather laughed harder, and then they cried and then they laughed, and they laughed and cried at the same time. Finally, like two people coming out of a fit of some sort, they settled down and looked around.

"My God, what is all this junk? What is this place?" Heather asked.

"It's Mya's parlor," Susan said. "I'm sure I wrote you about it."

"I know you did," Heather said. "I just didn't expect it to look like this. You said it was beautiful. I pictured it so different." She began to walk around the room, touching things and examining things. "This is wild," she said. She spotted the shelf of books above the fireplace. "Look at these." She pulled one book down and examined it. "Did she read these books? Did she believe in this stuff? Was she kind of crazy, Mom?"

"No, she wasn't crazy," Susan said "She was just different. She didn't think like other people. She was special."

Susan picked up a worn deck of Tarot cards from Mya's shelf. She flipped through and looked at the pictures on the cards. She studied the "Laroue de Fortune," with naked blind justice spinning the wheel, a man and woman trying to keep their balance, while a third man falls to the ground. She pictured herself holding onto the wheel while a man and a woman fell off and were lost in the universe. As Susan studied the cards, Heather fired questions at her. "How did she ever get interested in this stuff to begin with? Did she really believe all this hocus pocus? Did you ever let her read your cards?"

Susan found herself defending Mya. "She thought everything was possible," Susan said. "She believed in absolutely everything."

While Susan was answering Heather's questions, which were the same questions she herself had once asked, a decision was made, the decision to be kind to Mya's memory, the decision to take a pair of scissors and clip the end off the movie reel of her time with Mya. She would clip it right before she found the crystal ball; no, even before that. She would clip it right after the picture where the three friends had made their wishes on the first anniversary of their life together on the Angel Estate, right before things began to go wrong.

Heather interrupted her mental editing. "Look at these tiny little thimbles, Mom," she said. She sounded like a small child. "They're so pretty. Look at the little windmill."

"Those were very important to Mya," Susan said. "I'll tell you a story about those someday when we have more time. She always claimed they were the original source of her powers."

"Spare me," Heather said. "Did you find what you needed? Let's get out of here. It's depressing."

Susan put the cards back and picked up the ivory book, along with Mya's pen and ink bottle that sat beside it on the book case. "I have what I need," she said. "Let's go up to the house."

When they reached the big house, she left Heather downstairs in charge of the phone and told her she was going to her room to lie down and rest for a few minutes. She closed the bedroom door and sat at the little mahogany desk by the window. At first it was difficult to get used to writing with a fountain pen. She hadn't used one in years. She made circles and rainbows and slanted lines, exercises she remembered from elementary school. Once she felt comfortable with the pen, she practiced a page of letters that looked somewhat like the letters Mya wrote, both capitals and small.

Susan found a nice clean page in the middle of the book and began to write Mya's instructions on what to do in case of her death.

MYA JOINS HER MOTHER IN THE RIVER

The river had never been as lovely as she was on the day of Mya's funeral. For the important occasion, the river had chosen a dark gray satin number, subdued, yet not depressing. She was calm and smooth, except when a ripple erupted here and there on her surface like a giant tear.

A small group stood on the bank: Heather, whose pretty young face over the past few days had become sadder and wiser; Mr. Edwards, as always; Sister Dory, who could have been mistaken for a suburban housewife in her black rain coat with a black scarf tied around her head, and wearing a pair of designer sunglasses that nearly covered her entire face; Gladys in a gray silk mourning dress, circa 1890, with a matching gray feather bonnet, fine black veil, small silk lace gloves, and with a tiny black parasol dangling gently from her wrist and a satin bag hanging from her arm; and Susan, in a long black dress, carrying a blue willow ceramic urn, lovingly wrapped in a lavender silk scarf. Lavender was one of Mya's favorite colors and she wore it often.

In her entire life, Susan had never heard of such a ceremony, and she certainly had never officiated at one, but the power and the knowledge came easily to her and she felt very comfortable. She placed the urn on the scarf on the river bank, and the friends stood in a circle around it, as Susan read selections from the ivory diary. The pale November sun provided solemn faint yellow lighting, and the river gargled and swallowed and lightly splashed out an old funeral song to accompany the words. Although Susan merely read quotes at random from the ivory book, an order somehow came into being and the reading came across as a simple, yet beautiful, philosophy, indicative of the way Mya had lived her life.

Susan looked up from the book and began talking about Mya. She described how Mya was able to create beautiful things from the most humble resources. She was totally self-sufficient, and she treated everything in the world as though it were sacred. She appreciated the simplest things, and she truly celebrated life. Susan recalled how she had met Mya for the first time in the summer house. She told the little group of celebrants how lonely she had been, and how, when she prayed for a friend, Mya had magically appeared. She talked about how Mya had influenced her and made her appreciate all of the little things in life that she had forgotten were so important. Mya had changed her from a discontented idle woman into a happy productive human being. She paused at this reflection, amazed at what she had just heard herself say.

Sister Dory took advantage of the pause to tell how a quiet, awkward young woman had been directed to her door by some higher power, and how, over the years, this same woman had changed from an abandoned foster child into a gifted psychic.

When it seemed like it was Mr. Edwards' turn, he merely repeated a bit of the tale of Pauline Clark's mistake and told of how surprised he was to find her at his door when she came to rent the summer house.

Heather joined in. She said although she had never known Mya, her mother had written about her in almost every letter. Heather wished she had been able to meet Mya. She was certain Mya was a very interesting person and she knew that her mother was going to miss her desperately.

As each person finished, Gladys dabbed under the veil at her tearful eyes and nodded that she was unable to speak.

While they stood with their heads bowed, the river had her say, and a few birds chirped in their opinions, and a breeze stirred the bushes beside the bank. Then the river became impatient and began to fill the silence with gargling and slapping sounds, and she created glistening little whirlpools here and there. The friends standing on the bank shared the feeling that Mya's mother was anxious for her to come and join her in the river. The feeling was not an uncomfortable one; rather, it was reassuring.

Tom's voice of reason suddenly broke into Susan's thoughts, as it often did these days. "It's only the goddamned river making the same goddamned sounds a river always makes."

The spell was broken for Susan and she reached down and picked up the urn and began to head up the path with the others following silently behind her. A few yards up the river, they came to a large tree growing out of the bank and leaning towards the water. The trunk had formed a nice curved seat where a person could sit comfortably and dangle her feet. The bark on the tree was eroded and smooth, as though someone had often sat there in times past. Susan looked at the tree and knew immediately that this was the spot Mya meant when she said: "I think I'll go down and visit with my mother for a spell."

"This is the spot," Sister Dory said. The group came to a halt. Each carefully took a handful of ashes from the urn and tossed them gently into the air above the river. Then Susan emptied the remainder of the ashes and rinsed the urn out with river water. She dried the urn on her big full skirt until it was shiny and clean.

The ceremony was over and it was time to return to their normal lives. Sister Dory said she was going to walk down along the river and say hello to Charles while she was in the area, and she invited Gladys to join her. Gladys said she would love to go along. She was glad to have an opportunity to meet Charles at last. She leaned against a tree and exchanged her fine slippers for a pair of white tennis shoes, which she had been carrying in her satin bag. As she trailed off behind Sister Dory, she turned, pointed down at her shoes, and mouthed to Susan, "Juxtaposition!" and Susan could not help but smile.

Susan carried the urn back up the path, and she was followed by Heather, who was marveling at this new person her mother had become. Mr. Edwards snorted on ahead of them. Winter was coming and his list of chores was now three pages long and growing.

For weeks Port Williams could talk of little else but the fire. Several regulars who had intended to go to the Frog that afternoon, but who had been held back by a phone call or a slow gas station attendant, saw Divine Providence in what would at any other time have been an ordinary frustration and a justifiable reason to take the Lord's name in vain. They speculated on how the six who had died happened to have been in the wrong place at the wrong time, and the tale of the impressive behavior of the wife of the biggie from the Kraft Paper Mills was repeated again and again. The officers told how she had sat for an hour, quietly collecting herself and praying, and how she had then begun to make burial arrangements like she'd been doing it all of her life. The story of how she took care of the waitress, paid all of her medical expenses, and arranged a beautiful ceremony for her at the river was shared and elaborated on by all. Many made resolutions to imitate her behavior if and when the occasion ever arose in their own lives. She was indeed an inspiration.

Sometimes the challenge of death – someone else's death, that is – brings the best out in people.

Lloyd Angel, for instance, discontinued his affair with Ellen once Kathleen was gone. It wasn't necessarily a moral decision; it was just the fact that being with Ellen became a discomfort, for Kathleen never left them alone. Without Kathleen and without Ellen, Lloyd Angel immersed himself in his business concerns, and his fortune doubled, then tripled. He became a philanthropist partially because it was trendy, and partially because he had so much money that he didn't know what to do with it. During the years from Kathleen's death in 1912 until his own death in 1931, he donated large sums of money and buildings and land to any good cause that came to his attention.

And it is this Lloyd Angel whose memory survives and is reinforced by local history buffs and tour guides in Port Williams. At present, the politically correct story is that Lloyd Angel was a handsome, wealthy man, whose wife was suddenly and tragically taken from him. So devastated was he that he never remarried and he spent the rest of his life alone in their mansion, sleeping in the same bed that he and Kathleen had shared all their years of wedded bliss.

Similarly, Tom's death and Mya's death forced Susan into a role for which she was eminently suited. She became the bereaved widow of the Kraft Paper Mills now famous vice president, and the sole and only friend of the late Mya Clark. Heretofore the role would have been an impossible one, but Susan discovered she had excellent guidelines, not only for dealing with death, but for dealing with life. All of the crazy ideas Mya had expounded danced about in Susan's head. Susan did not necessarily believe any of it, yet they were the only guidelines available to her, so she followed them to a tee and never questioned a one. For weeks after the deaths, she read Mya's ivory book daily. It was all there, everything she needed or wanted to know. And, in addition, she received much needed help from Mya's very own mentor, Sister Dory.

Within a few days after Mya's funeral service, Susan received a note from Sister Dory. The note was typed on thin white computer paper. Susan was both surprised and pleased. Sister Dory wrote that Mya's service had been one of the most sensitive celebrations she had ever attended and Mya was fortunate that Susan had been a part of her life. She thanked Susan for all she had done for Mya.

"Our Mya was a child of the universe, a spirit loose in the world, vulnerable and alone. Your friendship was of great importance to her. She told me many times, and I can see from the sensitivity you displayed at the service that Mya had an irreversible influence on you as well."

Susan wrote a simple thank you for the lovely note to Sister Dory, and she was surprised to find another note in her mail box that week. "We're becoming pen pals," she thought. "Pen pals with a kook," Tom's imaginary voice chirped in.

Sister Dory wrote: "If you would like help taking care of Mya's things, I would be glad to come over sometime and give you a hand."

Susan replied that she would like that very much, and if Sister Dory would call her, they could set up a date. She felt very old fashioned, sitting with her pen and paper, writing notes back and forth to a woman not two miles away, who answered her notes on her word processor, neatly typed. Juxtaposition, once again.

Sister Dory was close to Susan's age, was fey like Mya, but clever and practical like Tom. She reminded Susan of the best parts of Mya and the good parts of Tom. She felt that she and Sister Dory were destined to become very good friends. They soon found they had a lot in common. For starters, each had a dead husband. It had been years since Sister Dory had lost her Charles, but she still had much good advice to give to Susan on how to cope and how to adjust to the loss of Tom.

"You're going to be depressed for a while, so don't make any major decisions for the first few months. Just hibernate your way through the coming winter like a big black bear, and by spring, you'll find yourself feeling more like your old self and ready to get on with your life."

She told Susan that Christmas was naturally going to be a very hard time, and she offered to come spend the holidays with her.

At that moment, Susan was not pleased with the promise of spending Christmas with a strange woman, but by the time the holidays rolled around, the two had become such good friends that Susan couldn't imagine spending it with anyone else. Heather came home. Mr. Edwards dragged in not only pine cones and holly branches covered with little red berries, but the biggest hemlock tree Susan had ever seen. Gladys shared her patterns for Victorian Christmas tree ornaments, which they made from starched lace and velvet and cinnamon sticks. They burned bayberry and pine candles, and Susan baked all of Heather's favorite Christmas cookies.

"This is the most wonderful Christmas I've ever had," Heather confessed.

"Me, too," Susan said.

Then they both felt guilty that Tom was not there to share Christmas with them. Sister Dory had cousins and old friends whom she brought by to see what Susan had done with the house. Gladys twice brought girls from the Society to see what a true Victorian Christmas was like. She was thrilled to have an opportunity to wear her green velvet Victorian afternoon dress, circa 1904, and a sable cape that had belonged to the great grandmother of the President of the Pennsylvania Preservation Society. Mr. Edwards said he wasn't much for Christmas, but he stopped in now and then, nonetheless, to enjoy the cookies and the audience. One evening he brought along a gallon of very old homemade cider, and everyone got quite a buzz, including Mr. Edwards himself. People from the Kraft Paper Mills did not forget Tom Harris' widow. Susan received lovely plants and flowers and several cards and phone calls. All the old friends from Laurel Hills phoned to see how she was doing and to wish her a happy holiday and a healing New Year.

Mostly it was the big house itself that exuded the spirit of Christmas. The sconces and the chandelier seemed to enjoy playing with the candle light, and the windows competed to see which could create the most elaborate reflections of the colored lights from the tree. A Christmas Eve snowfall covered everything with sparkling white diamonds and marshmallow fluff. Mr. Edwards found an old set of sleigh bells among his collection, and he hung them precariously above the front door, where the wind periodically came along and practiced old Norse melodies in minor keys that brought shivers down the spines of all who happened to be listening.

YET ANOTHER PERFECT TENANT
FOR THE SUMMER HOUSE

The summerhouse sat vacant for months, waiting for an appropriate tenant to come knocking. For the first time, Mr. Edwards was going through the bother of screening the people who inquired about renting the place. Since Susan had not mentioned anything to indicate that she might be thinking of moving out anytime soon, Mr. Edwards was trying to be very careful not to bring someone into the summer house who might scare her away. His self-imposed edict that there would definitely be no hunters and no party boys eliminated most of the applicants. He had no idea how to find a tenant who would be an appropriate neighbor for a grieving widow. He had been mulling over this problem for weeks when the dilemma resolved itself, as dilemmas often do.

Susan and Sister Dory called him in one afternoon to join them for a cup of hot chocolate. He happened to be very hungry at that moment, and he was pleased to accept the invitation. He had no inkling that the girls had an ulterior motive.

"Put several kinds of cookies out," Sister Dory advised.

"Absolutely," Susan replied. "And I've got extra whipped cream for his chocolate, and some bittersweet curls to sprinkle on the top. Fill that silver dish with cashews. They're his favorite."

They sat at the table with the chocolate and the cookies and the cashews and looked out the window at the dark little summer house in the distance. Naturally they began to talk about Mya, how much they all missed her, and about the parlor and what a shame it was that all her work and effort was going to waste.

"Have you got anybody interested in renting it yet?" Sister Dory asked.

Mr. Edwards said he wasn't having much luck this time around. There hadn't been a single applicant who would have been pleasing to you-know-who, the one who still cares about this place.

And Sister Dory said, "Well, do you think another person like Mya would be pleasing to you-know-who? I think she liked Mya a lot, don't you?"

"A resident fortune teller," Mr. Edwards thought aloud. "That's not a bad idea. All that fixin' up wouldn't go to waste." Then he looked discouraged. "Are there many of those fortune tellers wandering around looking for places to live?"

That was a cue for Susan's line. She turned to Sister Dory and asked: "Are you looking for a new place by any chance?"

And Sister Dory acted ever so surprised. "I never thought about it, but that's not a bad idea. You mean I would come here and live in the summer house and do my readings in Mya's parlor?"

Tom Harris was laughing smugly in his grave.

The world of the occult was changing dramatically, and Sister Dory was riding along on the forefront. Fast foods – fast fortunes. Tom's marketing ideas were coming to pass. For $2.95 per minute, a person could dial a 900 number and have a card reading. "Sister Dory is standing by with her cards, waiting for your call."

Sister Dory was a natural at marketing. Tom Harris would have been so proud. She had a whole packet of ads that she ran in all the local papers. She tried to target every audience: "Become your total self. Never be without a man again. Guaranteed results." She sprinkled her ads with convincing statistics: 98% accurate. Increase your chances of winning the lottery by 1000%. Immediate results or your money back.

Sister Dory had no compulsion about getting a 900 number, advertising in every newspaper in the 500 mile radius, consenting to interviews on radio programs, and creating a little shop in the corner of the parlor where clients could buy candles, cards, astrological charts, crystals, dice, incense, voodoo dolls, and Peruvian silver healing bracelets, all marked up as high as she dared without looking greedy. Stapled to the back of the door was a list of her fees, and she scheduled clients back to back and had an answering machine so she wouldn't miss a single prospect. One of her most popular items was a gift certificate for one reading. She advertised it as the perfect birthday gift for anyone. Discount coupons were available at the counters of every convenience store in Port Williams, and on laundromat bulletin boards, where people in need of hope were likely to see them.

Sister Dory was a practical woman. The rent at the summer house was half of what she got for renting out her nicely furnished ranch house. That provided a little cushion, which, it turns out, she did not need. In addition to inheriting most of Mya's clients, she brought along all of her regular clients. The story of Mya's death was a very effective advertisement. So many new clients called that Sister Dory was forced to put them on a waiting list, which made her readings even more in demand. Mya had given her a new start on life, logical pay back for the help she had given Mya over the years.

Sister Dory had lost no time in convincing Mr. Edwards of the benefits of having the Angel Estate included on the Port Williams historic tour. She pointed out that he could charge the Historic Society twice as much as he charged the Hunting Club. He would not only make more money, but the karma of the place would be totally improved. She of course pointed out that Kathleen

Angel would surely have preferred groups of polite tourists to beer-drinking, gun-toting hunters, and Mr. Edwards was wise enough to acknowledge the truth when it was going to bring in more money and make Kathleen Angel happy.

There were other important changes to be made. Mya had claimed to be an advocate for Mrs. Angel's Ghost, but she was all talk and theory. She had never really done anything concrete to improve the image. The ever pragmatic Sister Dory set right to work on this important image. She engaged Susan in her PR mission.

"If we can come up with a suitable ending to Kathleen Angel's life, perhaps people will stop telling such dreadful tales about her," she said. "Okay, maybe she wasn't perfect, but what person ever deserved to be described as being dragged under a train in Turkey, unrecognizable because the gravel tore away all of her beautiful features. Or what about her husband murdering her? Some say he pushed her off the train in Turkey and then didn't report her missing until a day or two later. Who needs that kind of slander? No wonder she can't rest in peace."

"It certainly doesn't do the memory of Lloyd Angel much good either," Susan agreed.

Sister Dory was big on brain-storming. "We'll put our thinking caps on for a few days," she told Susan, "and surely, two bright ladies like us will be able to come up with something workable."

"How do we put Kathleen to rest?" Susan found herself wondering as she walked to the graveyard to put a fresh bouquet of violets and dandelions on Tom's grave.

She paused and rested her hand on Kathleen's stone. "Where are you, dear Kathleen?" she asked. "Where do you want to be? It's up to you now. Just give me a sign."

She sat on the wall and waited, but it was obvious that Kathleen Angel was nowhere near this graveyard. She had never been here, and it wouldn't be right for Sister Dory and Susan to put her there just for the sake of cleaning up her image. A discontented woman who couldn't be happy in a 17 room house should not end up in a 6 foot pine box, or, rather, a mahogany, or cherry, or teak box.

"She's somewhere else," Susan thought, as she crawled down from the stone wall, gave Tom's stone a goodbye touch, and headed down the road. It was a lovely April day. There was not a cloud in the robin egg blue sky and the air was as fresh as God could make it. Susan wanted to walk to the end of the earth. She headed down the path to the river. Maybe Mya had an idea about helping create Kathleen's new image.

When Susan reached the tree along the bank, it looked to her as though the river was trying to clean up her image too. She was softly sweeping up broken limbs and the debris of the last winter storm and singing a pleasant gurgling river song as she worked. Susan reached down to touch the water, and the river splashed fondly at her hand like a puppy. Sometimes the river could be so gentle and kind. Susan crawled up onto the tree trunk and made herself comfortable. She closed her eyes and tried to think of Mya in the river. Then she thought of Mya's mother in the river. It was a pleasant thought, the mother and the daughter together in the river. The river must be a pleasant place to be, so much nicer than the graveyard, Susan said aloud to herself. Perhaps Kathleen Angel would like to be in the river, Susan thought.

"Would you girls like some company?" she asked, and her question was answered with a spray of fresh water on her cheek.

She climbed down off the tree and ran up the path toward the estate. She walked down the lawn towards the summer house. Sister Dory had repaired the walkway across the dam because she didn't want to chance a lawsuit when some spastic client slipped on the old board and fell and broke her neck. Susan tripped lightly across the sturdy, new walkway and tapped on Sister Dory's front window.

Sister Dory pulled the curtains aside and looked out. Susan motioned that she had something to tell her, and a moment later, Sister Dory appeared at the side door.

"How about the river?" Susan asked.

"That's inspired," Sister Dory said. "Yes, I do believe she drowned in the river."

"Accidentally," Susan added.

"Of course, accidentally," Sister Dory said. "So her body was not properly buried and thus her spirit roams about her old home that she loved so much. It's logical."

"Yes, it makes sense," Susan added, and immediately thought she heard Tom's laughter somewhere deep in the fading memory of a previous life.

HERITAGE WEEK

Once again spring was a busy time on the Angel Estate. Mr. Edwards and Susan helped Sister Dory get the parlor set up and going, and the three of them worked to get the main house ready for the summer tourist traffic. The big deadline was the first week in June, Heritage Week, when all of the old mansions were open to the public, freshly squeezed lemonade sold on street corners, arts and crafts booths set up in the downtown area, and an old fashioned trolley available to transport people from site to site. Since Mr. Edwards had agreed that the Historic Society could put the Angel Estate on its list, it was arranged that the trolley would make four daily trips out Bullfrog Valley Road to the estate.

Susan sent flyers to her friends in Laurel Hills and invited them to come up and visit during Heritage Week. They responded immediately. There was no way they were going to miss this opportunity to come up and check on their old friend. They had no idea what to expect and were dying of curiosity.

They spent the entire four hour car ride speculating on the tragic state in which they would find their friend. No one could imagine Susan without Tom. Susan without Tom almost made one believe in the old Hindu custom of cremating the widow when the husband died. They went through a box of tissues crying about how awful it would be if any of their own husbands died, particularly in a fire. They anticipated how awkward the visit was going to be. They wondered if they should mention anything about Tom and the tragedy, or if they should wait for Susan to bring it up. They had not resolved this issue by the time they arrived at the estate, patted at their hair, gathered their belongings, and got out of the car in the driveway.

Linda gave one last admonition: "We'll just play it by ear. Don't mention anything until she brings it up."

And weren't they surprised when they were met at the door by Susan looking better than they had ever seen her. She was wearing a deep blue-gray Victorian dress with a black velvet hat, trimmed with ostrich feathers, nonetheless, and black lace gloves without fingers. An intricate lace veil covered her face.

Linda was the first to get control of her voice. "Is this the infamous Kathleen Angel?" she asked, as she gave Susan a gentle hug.

"Not quite," Susan said, and she hugged her back and then hugged each of them carefully, not wanting to muss her dress. She gathered them ahead of her like a flock of chickens and swooshed them into the house. "I have a tour beginning in a few minutes," she said as she led them into the living room where a small group of seven people stood waiting.

Susan had her spiel, as she called it, down pat. As she led the group from room to room, she interspersed historic and descriptive information about the furniture and the architectural details with facts about Kathleen Angel's Ghost and about ghosts in general. She used the same voice to describe the bull's eye leaded glass window and to tell of psychic vibrations so strong in the carriage house that sensitive people were known to faint upon entering it.

When asked whether she had ever been approached by Mrs. Angel's Ghost, she gave a direct quote from Mya. "Some people are afraid of ghosts and some aren't. People who really believe in ghosts find them benign; people who don't, fear them." She pulled a black lace fan from a pocket somewhere in her costume and carefully waved it before her face. "I regard Kathleen Angel as a very dear friend," she said, and eyebrows were raised.

She made a point of leaving each group with a provocative thought from the writings of Mya, from her books, which Susan now perused, or from something she remembered Mya saying. "Are the five senses the only means by which we get our information about the world?"

Her friends were torn between wanting the old Susan back and appreciating the empowerment of the new Susan. They couldn't wait until the tour was over and the people left so they could sit and talk with their old friend, but when the tour was finished, Susan didn't change her clothes, and as long as she was wearing the Victorian dress with the full skirt and the long sleeves that met the black lace gloves, and as long as she was wearing the feather hat, although she had pushed the veil back off her face, it was impossible to talk about the ordinary cares of life.

They had wondered endlessly about Susan's plans now that Tom was gone. They were all certain she would move back to Laurel Hills; after all, she had lived there for 17 years, and it's where her best and oldest friends were still located. Ann waited for an appropriate break in the conversation to ask if Susan knew when she would be moving back down home again.

Susan was no longer a spontaneous chatterbox. She took a few moments to ponder the question. If she moved away, who would take care of Tom's grave? Who would walk by the river and visit with Mya? Sister Dory would be all alone, and Mr. Edwards would miss her sorely.

"I'm probably not going to move anywhere," she told her friends. "I think I've found my niche right here on the Angel Estate.

The friends could think of nothing to say. Personal appearance was a safe topic. "Are you letting your hair grow?" Linda asked.

Susan thought about that question. Her hair had grown very long during the year of tribulation, purely because she had not taken the time to get it cut. Now she was able to wear it pulled up on the back of her head, clipped neatly in place with the blue hair clip she had found among Mya's things. She reached up and removed two black pearl hat pins from the feathered hat and carefully lifted it from her head. She unclasped the hair clip and allowed her hair to fall down her back. She turned around to show her friends how long it had grown. But it was not the hair, but the clip, that caught their attention.

"What a beautiful hair clip," Linda said. "Is that something Tom got for you?"

It was the first time Tom's name had been mentioned. They waited nervously for Susan's response.

"No," Susan said. "Don't I wish Tom had had such good taste. It used to belong to my friend Mya, and to her mother before her. It's very old, and Mya thought it might have at one time belonged to Kathleen Angel." She held it in her hand for her friends to see, and the blue stones glittered and the silver gleamed and her friends were speechless.

Susan was glad to see her friends leave that afternoon. She was dying to be alone so she could think about the day. Still wearing her lovely Victorian dress, she slipped into a pair of sneakers, whispered "juxtaposition," and started off for a nice long walk. She stopped by the graveyard and sat listening to the insects playing their harps and violins. She smelled the roses. She brushed some cobwebs from Kathleen Angel's stone, and paused a moment to rest her hand on Tom's squeaky clean marker. The graveyard was so peaceful; for a moment she almost envied him for having such a nice place to rest. Maybe someday she would join him there in the peaceful graveyard. She immediately thought better of that idea. It would be much more fun to be with the girls in the river. She was thankful she didn't have to make that decision right then and there. She'd think about it later when she had more time.

Now she wanted to hurry down to tell Mya how the day had turned out. It was a warm June evening, and the path was as familiar as the back of her hand. She stepped quickly along, holding to the sides of her voluminous skirts, being careful not to let the berry bushes catch on the fine voile ruffles. Even more carefully, she crawled up onto the tree and arranged her skirts around her until she was sitting comfortably on the smooth flat trunk. Below, the river gurgled a little welcome, and cleared her throat as though she were about to speak.

"You be quiet," Susan said to the river. "It's my turn to talk." She began to tell Mya all about how perfect the day had turned out. She told her how nervous she had been about the tour and how well it had gone off. She thanked her for the quotes and for the wisdom. She told her about the friends who came from Laurel Hills to see how she was doing and how strange they seemed to her now. She guessed she had outgrown them.

Heritage Days ended with a formal dinner cruise down the river on the paddle wheeler. Reservations had to be made months in advance, and many were disappointed not to get the opportunity to join in this gala event. Dresses were designed and created during the long winter months, and fifty couples were finally able to enjoy the special cruise.

As Susan sat on the tree, chatting with her best friend Mya, the paddle wheeler chugged by on the opposite side of the river, and the couples standing on deck looked over and couldn't believe what they were seeing. It was a magic evening, and dusk was beginning to fall. They saw a woman in a beautiful long dress, a woman from another century, sitting in a tree on the other side of the river. The brightest and most rational among them thought it was a clever part of the ceremony. The woman was probably getting paid minimum wage to sit in the tree and add a little atmosphere for the suckers on the cruise. Others weren't sure what they were seeing, and a few believers, as there will always be believers, knew that they had at last seen the Ghost of Kathleen Angel, and they were now among the privileged of Port Williams.

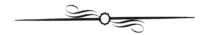

EPILOGUE

The Angel Estate is a site highly recommended for anyone in the mood for a visit to the peaceful and charming life of bygone days. If you find yourself in the Central Pennsylvania area and have a little time on your hands, take a trip to Port Williams. After a luxurious lunch on the paddle wheeler, enjoy a three hour tour of the mansions on Queen Street, and then catch the trolley out to the Angel Estate to put the finishing touches on your visit to yesteryear.

The estate is a charming old place, built some hundred or so years ago by a lumber baron, Lloyd Angel, for his lovely wife, Kathleen. The grounds have been cleaned up and the Port Williams Historical Society has placed wooden benches and tasteful verdigris metal trash bins here and there for the convenience of the visitors.

Sister Dory, the resident fortune teller, is ensconced in the charming summer house with her Tarot cards, astrological charts, and computer. She is often booked up for readings, but tourists are welcome to visit the gift shop, which is filled with fascinating esoteric paraphernalia.

Susan Harris lives in the big house. She was recently chosen to be President of the Historical Society for the fifth year straight. She spends the winter sewing period costumes and making hats, and, in the summer, she is very busy with the groups of senior citizens and Victoriana buffs who stop by to see the estate. She wears elaborate old fashioned costumes, which she designs herself, and serves tea and homemade cookies in the dining room as she regales the guests with tales of Lloyd and Kathleen Angel. She is so enthusiastic and sincere that you would think she had been a personal friend of the lumber baron and his wife.

The alleged haunting of the estate has ceased, and the pleasant atmosphere is disturbed only by the sound of Mr. Edwards' old truck, coughing, sputtering, and choking its way up the drive. Sister Dory and Susan scheme endlessly to try to find a way to discourage his noisy arrival during tour hours, but he doesn't seem to be able to take hints, subtle or otherwise. What can they do? After all, he owns the place. They are mere tenants.

When Sister Dory and Susan sit together in the evenings, they often try to think of a way to get enough money to purchase the estate, but they know that even if they had the money, Mr. Edwards would never be willing to sell. Sometimes, while they sit together on the patio, sharing a nice cool bottle of Zinfandel, they become very silly and admit that they must face the fact that there's only one way they're going to get their hands on the place and that's for one of them to marry Mr. Edwards. They laugh hysterically over which one is going to have to make the sacrifice. Susan thinks it should be Sister Dory because she's been widowed longer, but Sister Dory thinks Mr. Edwards should be given the choice, in which case, they both know it would be Susan. There's no doubt about that. He's got quite a crush, and it's obvious to everyone.

Sister Dory offers to read Susan's cards to see if she can get a handle on how fast this thing's going to go and when the big event might take place, but Susan absolutely refuses to have her cards read. She's not really a believer, but, regardless, she doesn't want to take the chance of getting mixed up in any kind of hocus pocus, just in case.

From time to time, during an evening visit to the graveyard, she mentions to Tom that Mr. Edwards has a bit of a crush on her. She tells Tom that Sister Dory thinks she should marry Mr. Edwards so she would always be able to live in the big house. She asks Tom what he thinks about the idea. She's only teasing him, of course, but, nonetheless, she hurries out of the graveyard as fast as she can before he can come up with some smart reply.